DROWNING WITH OTHERS

ALSO BY LINDA KEIR

The Swing of Things

DROWNING WITH OTHERS

LINDA KEIR

LAKE UNION
PUBLISHING

Text copyright © 2019 by Linda Keir
All rights reserved.

Published by Lake Union Publishing, Seattle

www.apub.com

Amazon, the Amazon logo, and Lake Union Publishing are trademarks of Amazon.com, Inc., or its affiliates.

ISBN-13: 9781542041454 (hardcover)
ISBN-10: 1542041457 (hardcover)
ISBN-13: 9781503902992 (paperback)
ISBN-10: 1503902994 (paperback)

Cover design by Shasti O'Leary Soudant

Printed in the United States of America

First edition

For Brandon and Marya, again

Prologue

No one can keep a secret these days, thinks the boy as he leads them all down to the lake, its flat surface the color of nickel in the cloudy Illinois evening. He had intended to take just a few eager freshmen, but someone told someone else, and then one of them told his girlfriend, and soon they had become a party of twelve guys and five girls, all of them on their way to break the rules at his instigation.

It's his father's fault. His father, who attended Glenlake Academy and instilled in him a reverence for the school's traditions. Many of those traditions—the locked journal in which students chronicle their four years, meals with the faculty, the senior page—are alive and well, but others have lost their place, forgotten or even banned by the faculty charged with upholding Glenlake's sense of history. But his father remembered them.

For over a hundred years, on the first full moon of fall term, seniors led freshmen down to Lake Loomis to jump—fully clothed—off the lifeguard tower. Swimming tests and legal worries put an end to the ritual, but the boy grew up with his father's stories. His knowledge of Glenlake's arcane ways has given him status during the previous three years, and now he plans to cement his reputation by restoring this dangerous, forgotten rite.

Too bad they can't see the moon.

And too bad half the kids are wearing swimsuits under their clothes and carrying towels, a far cry from the chaotic dunkings his father described. But the air is charged with whispered rumors that two of the girls plan to jump naked.

They can't do it from the lifeguard tower, of course. They'll be heard, or seen, and nobody wants to start the semester with demerits, him least of all—they're rebels, but they aren't stupid. So, reaching the lake, they take the perimeter road, grouped in twos and threes, propelled by nervous anticipation, until half a mile later, progress slows to the accompaniment of *Are we there yet?*

But he isn't the crew coxswain for nothing: He marshals them, exhorts them, gets them *stoked* for the next half mile and a two-hundred-yard bushwhack down a dirt road overgrown with brush and saplings. To the top of the cliffs.

The crumbling rock wall is taller than the lifeguard tower, looming twenty-five feet over the shoreline. As they peer over the edge, a cool breeze ruffling hair and clothes, it feels even higher. Across the water, the lights of Glenlake's old, stately buildings twinkle in the humidity.

"That water looks so . . . black," says a girl, shivering.

"How do we get out?" asks a stocky boy with false bravado.

"It's deep here, but just swim to your right and there's a beach," explains the boy. "A trail leads back to the top."

"How do you know?"

"My dad told me," he says, not wanting to reveal that he has come here every year in secret, planning for this moment. Wanting to sound like he hasn't calculated the angles. Wanting to sound like he hasn't already made a practice jump.

Which, in fact, he hasn't.

"You first," someone says.

In his mind, seniors don't jump—they make others do it. But he suddenly realizes the only way to pull this off, to engrave his legend, is to go first. But hell if he's going to do it in his clothes and walk back in soggy jeans.

He takes off his shoes and socks, then his shirt, and then, with only a moment's hesitation, his pants, hoping the outline of his junk isn't visible in his boxer briefs.

"Wait a minute!" says a girl. "Let's get this on camera!"

He's seen her on campus before, always the one taking pictures, sometimes with her phone and sometimes with a small but fancy antique-looking digital camera. She works on the school paper or the yearbook, maybe both.

Before he can say anything, lighted screens are bobbing like fireflies, and the girl and one of her friends are heading down the trail to shoot his jump from below.

He's torn, imagining the likes, shares, and comments on dozens of social media feeds, but yells, "This is secret! Do you want to get me expelled?"

Slowly, grudgingly, the fireflies wink out.

He wishes he hadn't waited this long, thinking about the drop. Goose bumps prickle his skin.

"Jump already!" yells a kid who doesn't want to miss out on the return of tradition.

From his daylight scouting missions, the boy knows he needs to jump out to avoid the rocks in the water at the base of the cliff. He can't see them now. But he would rather die than turn back.

He takes three fast steps toward the cliff, feeling soil give under his right foot as he pushes off and yells, "Glenlake!"

He hits the water straight on, plunges deep, and sees a fading halo of gray light above him.

As he kicks for the surface, his foot hits something hard and sharp. It hurts like a thrown rock.

He pulls himself out onto the beach to scattered cheers, echoes of "Glenlake!" from above, and the girl with the camera shoving a blurry video under his nose.

"I couldn't resist," she says. "You can delete it if you want."

Her fragrant hair brushes his wet shoulder, and he shivers. After watching the video, which is too grainy for anyone to identify him anyway, he probes the cut on his foot matter-of-factly, a four-sport athlete used to injuries. It's deep but not dangerous. He'll ask someone to bring down his socks and shoes so it doesn't get dirty.

"Oh my god, you're bleeding," she says.

"There's something down there," he tells her. "Something metal."

"It's probably an old shopping cart or some junk. I bet the townies sneak out here to dump their trash."

"It sure didn't feel like a shopping cart. I wish I could get a closer look."

"Want to take a picture?" she asks coyly.

She pulls a waterproof bag out of her pocket, a knotted bikini bottom peeking over the waistband of her jeans. She puts her phone in the bag and seals it tight, tracing her finger across the plastic to turn the flashlight and camera on.

"I brought the bag in case I went in," she explains. "But I don't think I'm going to."

Voices carry and word travels fast to the top of the cliff that the senior has cut his foot on something in the black water. No one else wants to go in either.

Compelled as much by curiosity as by the freckled chest and peeking bikini of the girl with the camera, the boy wades back in, triangulates his landing place, and kicks into the water, the glowing camera light rippling ahead of him like some bioluminescent fish.

Reaching the spot, he porpoises and dives down, the light on the phone only making the rest of the water look darker. He needs to go deeper, so he exhales, emptying his lungs as he kicks down, down,

down, seeing nothing, until abruptly the flashlight picks up a glint of glass or chrome. He sees it through the screen first: a car, broad and dark and resting right side up.

Water pressure plugs his ears as he exhales the last of his air and makes a final kick, anchoring himself on the door handle, inadvertently opening the door as he pulls himself toward the car.

It's an old muscle car, like he's seen on cable car-auction shows or in town, driven by some aging gearhead slowly trolling for compliments.

He's light-headed with lack of oxygen and the thrill of discovery and knows he needs to push for the surface, but he wants the prize: a peek inside. A picture of the car at the bottom of the lake.

He angles the phone's screen. It shows the silt-covered car, the cracked-but-intact windows, and, through the open door, a steering wheel.

And heaped around a still-buckled seat belt: Bones. A rib cage. A cracked skull.

Chapter One

Once again, everything had changed and nothing had.

Or, more accurately, Ian thought, nothing had changed except the students and the fact that he and Andi were twenty-plus years older—and Glenlake Academy was breaking ground on a new writing center, a small but sleek building where students could read and write and meet with faculty in an environment casual enough to rival a Silicon Valley start-up.

Well, maybe not Silicon Valley but Silicon Prairie, which was what business boosters had taken to calling Chicago, forty minutes to the south.

Leaving their bags at the Old Road Inn, whose rooms and halls were small and crooked enough to be called historic, Andi and Ian left the car and walked the half mile to campus, enjoying the crisp, dry air of a perfect autumn Friday afternoon. Orange and yellow leaves fell on the sidewalk and broke under their shoes, dry, musty, and astringently fragrant.

Ian reached out for Andi's hand. As her fingers closed around his, a memory arrived unprompted, of walking the opposite direction with her on this very sidewalk, his school tie loosened, both of them smoking cigarettes and feeling very adult as they headed into town for a cup of coffee at Glenlake's only diner. Where they would see *real people*.

Though they both now looked every inch the moneyed prep school parents they were, recalling himself as a wannabe grown-up made Ian feel he was still a student playing a role—only actually wearing the clothes of an adult.

Andi looked up at him, even more beautiful than she had been then, with her dark, wild curls, and he flashed ahead to later tonight when, tipsy, they would stumble through the door of their room at the inn and—he hoped—into bed. Hotel rooms always made his wife horny. They didn't travel together often enough.

"So we're skipping the welcome talk, right?" she said.

At the last three annual parents' weekends, they had dutifully filed into the auditorium while the school's president, various department heads, and a major donor had droned on for over an hour. Andi was right—there was no need to go. They were veterans.

"Should we surprise Cassidy instead?"

Andi punched him lightly with his own fist, their fingers still interlaced. "Total dad move. Yes, she'd just love to be caught off guard while she's with her friends. No, we'll see her when we see her."

As they walked up the long, winding drive, Ian felt a familiar flutter in his chest: happiness at being back here. They passed the turnoffs for the faculty cottages and, a few hundred yards later, the freshly painted, gothic-lettered Glenlake Academy sign. Then they were crossing the oval in front of the Copeland Academic Center, built with a gift from his great-great-grandfather Augustus Copeland, a robber baron of the first order.

"Should we dust the bust?" asked Andi, their standard joke, referring to the aged bronze sculpture of old Augustus that stood atop a six-foot marble plinth just inside the entrance.

Ian shook his head. He couldn't blame his ancestor's ghost for his youthful dislike of the old redbrick building—but the legacy had weighed heavily all the same.

Cutting between the arts building (whose halls he'd seldom darkened) and the science building (where he'd been more comfortable), they passed the student union, crossed the field-hockey turf, and wandered among the places where the actual life of the school took place. They passed the freshman residence halls where they'd first stayed, then circled the grand old manors where they'd had rooms as upperclassmen, before crossing the grass to the mossy old peristyle where they'd smoked pot and, on the back of one of the columns, neatly chiseled their initials.

As time ran short, they meandered back toward McCormick Mansion, the former seat of this grand estate, now a warren of administrative offices. But first they stopped in at Holmes Library, whose interior walls were covered with framed, handwritten journal pages. They climbed the stairs to the third floor, stopping now and then to read one that caught their eyes, before locating their own class of 1997 senior pages, hung in opposite corners of the same study room.

Andi read Ian's aloud in a monotone before making the joke she always made: "Are you sure you didn't pay someone to write this for you?"

Despite Glenlake's focus on literature and creative writing, Ian had never felt particularly comfortable expressing himself on paper. Or aloud, for that matter. It still embarrassed him that his strained and dutiful passage—about hard work, growth, and the value of service—would be framed for as long as the school stood. He wished he'd had the guts to choose something honest, like the entry Andi had been bold enough to submit. While most students, like him, had produced anodyne statements calculated not to offend, she had mused about the private nature of journaling and how carefully curated everyone's senior page actually was, before concluding with a poem:

These Best Years
Bridging the gap between childhood and
    adulthood
Prepared, precisely prepped, on the path to our
    predestination
Are we about to wake up?
Or have we just fallen asleep?

Every time Ian read her senior page, he thought about one of his entries from freshman year—the day he met her, September 20, 1993.

A new girl started today. Her name's Andi Bloom. She just showed up in algebra after missing the first two weeks. It was funny, she acted like she'd been there all along and kind of rolled her eyes when Nadelman introduced her to the class. I would hate being late and new, but she just shrugged it off.

Everyone is saying her dad is some Hollywood big shot. So, of course, everybody thinks if they can be friends with her, they'll end up meeting movie stars or getting to hang around on a movie set. I haven't talked to her yet, but I will.

She looks and acts really different than the usual girls around here. In a good way, I think. She somehow makes the dress code seem cool, which is hard to do, and acts like Glenlake is no big deal. It probably isn't to her, since she's from California and everything. I don't think she's stuck-up, though.

I can't stop thinking about her.

And the locks on these stupid journals better be good.

While other parents joined their students for a gathering with boxed wine, one kind of beer, and soft drinks for the kids, the several dozen alumni gathered in a walnut-paneled reception area just outside the school president's office, where a black-vested bartender waited behind a full array of bottles. Glenlake's administrators liked to get the alumni together every chance they could. Alumni were key to the endowment and future enrollment—especially alumni whose names were set in stone above the entrances of campus buildings.

Ian and Andi had just gotten drinks—a passable sauvignon blanc for her, a glass of cabernet he'd regret—when their names were called from across the room.

"Ian and Andi," the voice said in wonder, a simple declarative that almost put a period after each name, as opposed to the way their names had been said throughout their years at Glenlake: *IanandAndi*.

Turning, Ian feigned recognition at a face he didn't recognize at all, while, out of the corner of his eye, he saw Andi brighten.

The man addressing them had aged faster than they had, his hair gray, his face wider, with bags under his eyes and a middle-aged gut.

"Tommy Harkins!" said Andi, giving the man a hug and politely ignoring his open appraisal of her still trim, admittedly eye-catching figure.

"Good to see you," said Ian, shaking hands, still trying to put a youthful face to the familiar-sounding name.

"I thought for a minute you didn't recognize me," Tommy said to Ian, his droopy eyes twinkling. "Totally understandable. Most people tell me I look younger now than I did then, even though I go by Tom now."

"*Tom*—of course," said Andi.

Then it clicked: Tom had dated Andi's best friend, Georgina, during senior year. If memory served, it hadn't ended well. Ian slipped an arm around Andi's waist, and with a warm glance up at him, she reciprocated.

"It's been years," said Andi. "Have we even seen you since graduation?"

Tom shook his head. "My daughter just started this year. It's wild to see the place again."

"I feel like we never left. Our daughter Cassidy is a senior, and our twins, Whitney and Owen, start next year," said Andi. "Assuming they get in."

"As if Glenlake would dare decline a Copeland after all the greenbacks your family has shoveled into this place," teased Tom.

Andi smiled demurely. "The Copelands are big believers in education."

She played the *we're so rich we don't talk about money* card perfectly. Given her roots as a rich Jewish girl from Beverly Hills, it hadn't come naturally. She'd been a quick study, though—grasping Waspy Midwestern understatement almost immediately when she'd arrived as a student at Glenlake and mastering it long before they settled in hidebound St. Louis.

Tom took a slug of his IPA. "So you two stayed together? Or did you divorce your first spouses and have some kind of storybook reunion?"

"There's not much to tell," said Andi, before launching into their oft-repeated thumbnail biography, telling how they got back together at the end of senior year and then stayed together while she went to Smith and he went to Amherst. Their New York experiment had ended with Cassidy's birth, when they moved to St. Louis so Ian could reboot a family wine-import business and she could dabble in publishing, mostly coffee-table books. It always struck Ian as strange how life stories were summed up with dates and places but not emotions. No one who meant it ever told a stranger, *It was love at first sight, and we are more in love now than when we first met.*

Gerald Matheson, who had been assistant head of Glenlake when they were in school, crossed the room like a tugboat navigating a crowded harbor. His bald head was flushed, and his drinker's nose, only starting to bloom when they'd known him, had gone a royal purple.

"I remember you two!" he crowed. "You were our famous couple. When you broke up senior year, even faculty talked about it."

Tom stuck out his hand and reintroduced himself. "Glad to see you're still around."

"I've been retired for a few years, actually—traveling, dithering—but I've recently been elected to the board of trustees."

Matheson had been a brooding, anxious presence behind the old headmaster, Lincoln Darrow. Retirement definitely suited him—or maybe it was full-blown alcoholism. Either way, he seemed merry and at ease now.

Across the room, Ian caught a glimpse of the new headmaster, Joshua Scanlon, and the assistant headmaster, Sharon Lysander, moving toward the front of the room to make their heartfelt fund-raising appeal to Glenlake's most established families. Suddenly, Ian wished they hadn't come. He wouldn't be able to make more than a token contribution this year.

"Any good scuttlebutt from the board?" Andi asked Matheson slyly.

"Oh, I wouldn't know. I'm just starting my term," said Matheson. "I can tell you we're all very excited about this year's writer in residence."

Andi leaned forward. "That program is the best thing about Glenlake! Who is it?"

"His name's Wayne Kelly. He's a longtime investigative reporter and former editor for the *Philadelphia Inquirer*. Apparently, he's using his fellowship to work on a book, but we're very excited to have an award-winning journalist offer a break from the usual novelists, memoirists, and occasional poet."

Though no one else would have noticed, Ian saw Andi stiffen at the word *poet*, her eyes going slightly vacant above her perfect party smile. His own smile suddenly felt similarly painted on. As a fork tapped against a glass, quieting the room so the headmaster could speak, Ian put his mouth close to her ear.

"What's wrong?" he asked as innocently as he was able. "You seem preoccupied."

"Nothing at all," she lied, kissing his cheek.

～

Following an exchange of no fewer than eleven texts, tonight's brief sighting of Cassidy had been scheduled for six forty-five, shortly before they were to walk through a truncated version of her class schedule, visiting each classroom in turn. After leaving the fund-raiser, Ian and

Andi waited for her at sprawling Copeland Hall, where Cassidy had a college-application coaching meeting and where they would be meeting this year's teachers.

She arrived in a rush, pushing through the doors, striding across the lobby to where they were waiting, and giving them firm but perfunctory hugs before collapsing onto the bench next to them.

Ian thought she had aged a year in the month since they'd dropped her off, and she looked more like a young woman than ever. His mind raced ahead to future milestones: moving her into the freshman dorms, college graduation, walking her down the aisle, and, hopefully someday, grandchildren.

"Dad's favorite place on campus," Cassidy snorted, bringing him back to the here and now. She raised her eyebrows toward Augustus on his plinth.

Their daughter had always been conflicted about the status conferred by her family name. Ian remembered with heartbreaking clarity her dismay upon learning, at six years old, that most families did not have buildings named after them.

But that's not fair, she'd said, pouting.

"I brought brass polish and clean rags," Ian shot back. "You can get to work as soon as we leave."

She pushed a lock of wavy brown hair—more like his than Andi's—behind her ear. "Most of the kids here pretend they have no idea that's my last name on the building, but you'd be surprised how many others are all about collecting friends from the 'important families.'"

"Just carry on with your usual low-key regal bearing," said Ian wryly. "Are you sure you don't want to join us for dinner later?"

As Andi gave him a *don't overparent* look, Cassidy drove home the point by adding, "Can't. First I have to learn how to get accepted to the college of my dreams, and then I'm either doing homework or sneaking off to town with the rest of the girls to meet and marry local boys."

"Far be it from us to stand in the way of progress," Andi responded with a smile. "See you tomorrow at brunch."

"Ten thirty sharp," she said.

Cassidy was already rising, everything about her—hair, backpack, school uniform—perfectly tailored to suggest careless disregard. He wondered if her effect on boys was as devastating as Andi's had been on him.

A quick hug and she was gone, accelerating up the stairs to catch up with a friend going the same way. For a moment, they watched the parents pour through the doors, scrutinizing campus maps and class schedules as if they were written in Greek.

"So," Andi said, with a lilt that boded well for later back at the inn, "want to play high school sweethearts?"

~

Ian shifted uncomfortably in the classroom desk chair, wondering how teen hormones could have raged so hard in such a sterile setting. This year's writer in residence stood facing the roomful of expectant parents.

"I know the first question on your minds," he said. "How does a Filipino kid end up named Wayne Kelly?"

There was a nervous silence, as if the assembled adults were afraid they might accidentally answer—and, worse, answer with cultural insensitivity. Wayne Kelly was a handsome guy, fortyish, with jet-black hair and a close-cropped salt-and-pepper beard. He pushed his Warby Parker glasses back, then put them all out of their misery.

"If you were my students, I would ask you to form a working hypothesis and then tell you to *check it out*. But since I only have you for seven minutes, I'll give you a one-word answer. Adoption."

There were a few chuckles, and the room relaxed ever so slightly. Ian himself had never taken the famous Glenlake writing seminar, but Andi had spent a lot of time in this room.

Kelly tugged at his new-looking tweed blazer and sat on his desk. "If you've already checked me out, you'll know I've been a working journalist and editor for seventeen years. I'm here to draft my first book and to teach investigative journalism. My students will learn how to report a story, how to write it, and how to suffer the slings and arrows of outrageous editing."

Ian glanced at Andi and saw she was studying the teacher carefully. For the first time all day, she seemed unaware of Ian's presence. He wondered if she was wishing things had turned out differently, that she'd never traded poetry for coffee-table books.

"Journalism is not an abstract concept. For us to commit an act of journalism, we need a story. I had a lesson plan for the year, but a few weeks ago, I put it aside. Because, fortunately, we have a doozy of a story right here on campus."

A few of the parents glanced at each other, suddenly uneasy with the idea of their children's expensive education being any part of a "story." Others, like Andi, waited expectantly, eager to hear what was next. When she was fully focused, as she was now, she gently chewed on the left side of her lower lip.

Kelly walked into the rows of desks, headed for the back wall. "Some of you may already know this, but earlier this week, some students made a discovery in Lake Loomis. They were swimming at night, so they were in violation of Glenlake's rules of conduct, a matter which has been addressed with some severity by the administration. I believe several of them may have been forced to take my English composition class as punishment."

Over a few chuckles he asked, "Would somebody please dim the lights?"

An obliging parent fumbled with the row of switches by the door, eventually finding the right balance. Kelly worked some other controls, and a white rectangle of light projected from above onto the whiteboard at the front of the room.

The room was completely rapt now. Like everyone, Ian was wondering how this would produce a story worth the scrutiny of a nationally known investigative reporter.

"The kids found a car at the bottom of the lake. One of them, who I recruited for this class, turned out to have excellent reporter's instincts. At night, in twenty feet of water, he managed to take a picture of that car."

On the whiteboard appeared a blurry, murky picture of a car covered in so much mud it looked like cake icing.

Ian heard Andi's sharp intake of breath. He felt his stomach tighten.

"This car wasn't some junker dumped in the lake to avoid a wrecking fee," continued Kelly. "This was a very specific car belonging to someone who went missing twenty-two years ago."

He advanced the slide, showing the car dangling from a crane on a construction barge that had been anchored next to the distinctive cliffs on the north side of Lake Loomis.

Its passage out of the water had caused some of the mud to wash off, and here and there the car's original metallic-blue paint job showed through.

He wished one of Andi's hands would find his and squeeze it tightly, but they remained palm down on her desk.

"*Inside* the car, the police found human remains. After so many years underwater, they were completely skeletonized. But license plate records revealed who owned the car, and the deceased has been identified tentatively, pending confirmation from dental records."

Uneasy murmurs rippled through the room as a name, long unheard, echoed in Ian's mind.

"So you're saying our kids will be investigating a . . . *murder?*" asked one shocked father.

"Who said this was a murder?" said Kelly. "Our job will be to gather every shred of information we can find, to shadow the police investigation, and, eventually, to tell the story of how this happened."

"This has been . . . approved? By the headmaster?"

Kelly ignored that comment, moving on to the next slide, a decades-old head shot. Suddenly, Ian was a senior again, limping along a wooded path, rage blurring his vision.

Hating his secret.

Beside him, Andi was rigid, as though the only way she could master her emotions was to not move a muscle.

"Forensic analysis has yet to confirm this," continued Kelly, "but the owner of the car was in fact a predecessor of mine—a former writer in residence here at Glenlake who went missing shortly before his year came to an end.

"His name was David Walker," he said. "But he went by the name Dallas—Dallas Walker."

Chapter Two

Andi Bloom's Glenlake Academy Journal

Monday, September 2, 1996

*After three years of journaling practically every day of the school year,
you'd think I'd have something clever or inspirational to write the night
before the first day of senior year. Honestly, though, the only thing that
comes to mind is this:*

I hate poetry.

I dread reading it.

I hate analyzing it.

I despise trying to write it.

*I get that this makes me full-on shallow, illiterate, even a fraud.
Whatever. It's not like I'll ever say I hate poetry out loud.*

*I can't. I mean, I'm Andi Bloom, the girl who left Beverly Hills to come
to Glenlake Academy in the middle of Nowheresville, Illinois, because of
the school's renowned writing program. Not to mention my supposed gift
for the sport of writing.*

At least that's what everyone around here thinks.

*Never mind the real reason I was shipped off had more to do with the
burden raising a teenager placed upon my dad, the great and important
Simon Bloom. That, and his world-class talent for convincing people he's*

fulfilling their deepest, darkest desires by giving them exactly whatever it is he wants.

He started by convincing me that none of the day schools in LA had quite enough to offer me, his oh-so-talented daughter. Then he flashed a couple of my middle school writing awards, name-dropped the movies he'd produced, added a few bucks to the deal, and voilà (!), Glenlake bent their firm rules and admitted me three weeks into fall semester.

Christening me the literary It Girl from California.

Luckily, I love it here. It's more like home than home has been for years. I was even glad to get back to the stifling Midwestern heat and humidity this fall. So much so that I could easily wax poetic about spying my first yellow-tipped leaf and the seductive crunch of impending autumn beneath my feet.

I'd best save all that imagery because I'm going to need every bit of poetry I can conjure up. After all, legit literary It Girls love poetry. It simply rolls out of their brains and onto the page.

Fuck.

For the past three years, I've petitioned and gotten into a seminar offered only to seniors. The writers in residence have been a short story writer, a novelist, and a memoirist. Now that I'm finally a senior, and can't possibly bail out of my rightful spot in the one class everyone at Glenlake expects me to take, how is it they decide to bring in a poet?

Ah, the fucking irony.

And not just any poet, but Dallas Walker, known for his macho, bad-boy elegies to love and loss, and who, according to an article in Interview *magazine, gave his class at an unnamed Ivy League a collective C because "I needed to kill some darlings."*

I bought a copy of his book, American Son, *and it's all beer and old cars and mill workers' houses and sex between people who wear Kmart underwear. (He uses the word* pussy *twice.) Some of the imagery is kind of amazing, I have to admit, but I don't get what he's trying to do. At all.*

Fuck. Fuck. Fuck.

Tuesday, September 3, 1996

Not even Ian's take ("Dallas Walker sounds like a fake name. Besides, poets are wimps and douchebags, so who cares?") made me feel any less anxious about entering Copeland Hall today.

I expected to step into my own twisted Dead Poets Society *hell—the rows of desks, the 1920s bookshelves, the blackboard, the hissing radiator in the corner, and Dallas Walker, his back to us as we, his unsuspecting students, entered the room. He'd be writing out some super-famous line from a poem no one really ever got, including him, but that we were expected to parse and somehow write a three-to-five-page essay on, due tomorrow.*

That, or we'd file in, take our seats, and wait for the bell to ring. Once we started to give each other the what-the-hell face, but before anyone actually wondered aloud if the poet knew he had a class right now, ominous footsteps would reverberate down the hall. Dallas Walker, a short, bald, older man with combed-over wisps of gray hair and a stained cardigan that barely contained his bulging belly, would saunter into the room. Naturally, he would be quoting the aforementioned inscrutable poem in his deep bass voice.

(Note to older self: if this year's journal entries sound more like a scene or exercises in dialogue than my earlier diary entries, it's because I've decided that if I am going be a writer someday, I have to practice. Anyway, back to the story.)

Either way, we'd be given the same heartless assignment, on which I would inevitably get my heart broken with the first F I've ever received.

Ever.

I felt like puking. So much so, I waited until the class started to fill before I took a deep breath and willed my legs to move.

I forced myself into the room just as the bell rang.

Dallas Walker was not only present but leaning casually against the front of his desk—looking nothing, of course, like I imagined. He was younger, but not young, taller, but not tall, graying, but not gray, and anything but paunchy. Instead, he was wiry and muscular, like a boxer or a distance runner. If he weren't wearing a pair of those hideous suede slip-on

Merrells, I might even have described him as handsome—in a rugged, cigarette-smoking, seen-a-few-things, older-guy kind of way.

Our eyes met briefly before I turned toward an open seat a few rows back from my usual spot in the front.

When I got settled and looked back up, he flashed a smile.

The nervous feeling in my stomach engulfed my whole freaking being.

"Poetry is about laying bare the collective secrets of our souls," he said. "To that end, I want you to pull out a piece of paper and write down something that truly terrifies you."

"Is this for a grade?" Philip Martin asked.

"Not unless you're stupid enough to put your name on it," Mr. Walker said.

"Mr. Walker?" Kate Hill asked.

"Mr. Walker is my father. I'm Dallas."

"D-Dallas," Kate stammered. "What if you have more than one thing that truly terrifies you?"

"Let's just start with one per person. Cool?"

With the word cool, *Georgina (who is currently sitting on the bed across from me, writing in her journal and chewing on a hank of hair) and a few of the other girls giggled.*

Dallas Walker definitely has an edge none of the other Glenlake teachers have, but I wasn't about to fawn over him or his supposed "vibe." Taking advantage of the guaranteed anonymity, I went ahead and did exactly what he'd told us to do.

It didn't take long before we'd all jotted down one of our deepest fears and passed identical college-ruled sheets of paper up to the front of the room.

We sat in silence as he scanned each of the fifteen answers we'd handed forward and set the pile on the desk beside him—all except for a single sheet of paper.

He smiled again. This time more broadly.

"Poetry should *scare you," he said in his raspy voice, and, I swear, he looked directly at me. "It scares the shit out of me."*

Wednesday, September 4, 1996

I wish Dallas (why is it so difficult to even think of a teacher by his first name?) had assigned us a three-to-five-page paper comparing and contrasting William Carlos Williams with William Butler Yeats or something miserable like that. Instead, he let us out of class a full forty-five minutes early with a "simple" assignment:

"I want you to write a poem about whatever it was that you said terrifies you, without stating your fear by name or putting your names on your papers."

"How will you grade them if our names aren't on them?" Philip (of course) asked.

"If you turn something in, you get a passing grade."

Given what I'd read about him, I didn't have the stomach to ask his definition of a passing grade.

"Can we use synonyms?" Georgina asked.

"I don't know," Dallas said. "Can you?"

She giggled, this time flirtatiously.

Georgina doesn't realize how pretty she is, despite the fact that I tell her all the time. I think it's because she hates that she's a redhead. Luckily, she's as handy with the whole flirtation thing as she is at knowing everything about everyone. In the midst of a move-in-day fiasco when we were somehow matched with people OTHER than each other after three years as roommates and besties, she masterfully batted her eyes until creepy Mr. Landry agreed to switch Lola McGeorge out of my room and into what would have been Georgina's room with Jules Norton.

I don't feel bad about the swap, because they are as neurotic and alike as Georgina and I are opposites, but I digress.

"How long should the poem be?" Meg Archer asked.

"However long it needs to be," Dallas said. "Oh, and avoid the words fear, terror, scared, *or any of their derivations."*

A snap, right?

Needless to say, I finished my Latin, physics, and AP History in the time it took me to come up with something that wasn't too frightening to pass for a poem about, but not mentioning the word, poetry.

Class today was a blur as Dallas spoke about "ingrained tendencies to be literal in communication" and how that didn't work with poetry.

"You have to learn to tamp down your desire for literal certainty and let the words of a poem roll around in your head. Otherwise, you screw yourself out of a major opportunity to understand the poet's take on the human condition."

Jules Norton, who writes down every word every teacher ever says, had just finished jotting "poetry equals higher truth expressed in a nonliteral, nonlinear way" when Dallas asked us to pass our homework forward.

He shuffled the papers, passed them back out randomly, and had us take turns reading whatever had landed on our desk.

Starting with Tommy Harkins, who read:

Ashes to ashes or so they say.
No way that's going to happen
To me.

"Oh, but it is," Dallas said in response to the author. "Since we're all going to die someday, you might want to think about keeping the cliché down to a dull roar. For the sake of your legacy."

Georgina read:

My stomach flops.
My life force drops.
And then it stops.

"Who knows what this one was about?" Dallas asked.

"Roller coasters," three different people said in unison.

"I actually wrote the one I read," Georgina purred.

"Rhyming poetry generally belongs in the nursery," Dallas responded.
Georgina looked crestfallen.
"Although in this case, given the subject matter, it kind of works.
Emphasis on the 'kind of.'"
And then Connor Cotton stood.
He cleared his perennially phlegmy throat and began to recite the words
that I'd stayed up half the night trying to compose:

> My thoughts emerge
> Full-fleshed
> Free of the ache
> Of the great unsaid.

The class was silent.
"What do you guys think this one's about?" Dallas asked.
Thank god the bell rang.

Thursday, September 5, 1996

Georgina thinks poetry class is going to be way cooler than any other
English class she's taken and that Dallas Walker is "kind of a fox, in, like,
an older-Kurt-Cobain-mixed-with-Eddie-Vedder kind of way."

Kate Hill already dropped the class. She says it's because Dallas doesn't
teach like a normal poetry teacher, but I'm sure it's because she has to get an
A, or she's screwed for getting into any of the Ivies.

Ian isn't taking the class, of course, but Dallas has apparently
embraced the tradition of the writer in residence serving as the ceremo-
nial head of one of the sports teams. He's not into any of the actual sports
offered at Glenlake, so he's started "coaching" the first ever billiards club
at the school.

I think it's pretty cool in a weird, antisports kind of way.

Seeing as Ian has a billiards room in his basement at home and has been playing with his dad since he could hold a cue, he wasn't about to miss the first meeting tonight.

"The guy is definitely a pompous douchebag, just like I predicted," he said afterward. "But he's really good at pool."

Friday, September 6, 1996

Today we spent the entire period comparing our interpretation of popular song lyrics with the songwriters' actual meanings.

Fun Facts, as relayed by Dallas Walker, poet in residence:

Bob Marley's "I Shot the Sheriff" wasn't a protest song but was inspired by his fights with his girlfriend over birth control. The sheriff being the doctor who prescribed her the Pill.

In the "Summer of '69," Bryan Adams was ten years old. His nostalgia wasn't inspired by the year but by his fondness for a certain sexual position!

And Dallas only had to say "Lucy in the Sky" before half the class yelled out, "LSD!"

But the song's inspiration was actually a drawing by John Lennon's son Julian.

Just before the bell rang, he assigned us to choose a song, explain what it means to us, and then research the actual meaning.

"This one ought to be a snap," Dallas said as we stuffed our things into our book bags. "Even for our resident reluctant poet, Ms. Bloom."

"Andi," I heard myself say. "Ms. Bloom is my . . ."

I couldn't finish that particular sentence. The subject of Mom is totally off-limits. I waited for the last few students to dribble out.

When I was the only one left in the room, I asked, "Why do you think I'm the one who wrote about poetry?"

"I don't think. I know."

"How's that?"

"The same way I know Crystal Thomas wrote the poem about—"

"The fear of standing out in a crowd?" I asked. "That's not exactly psychic. I mean, she is one of a few African Americans at the school."

"Fair enough," Dallas said. "But Kate Hill definitely wrote the poem about snakes."

"Because . . . ?"

"It was so shitty, she and I both knew she'd never make it through the class."

"She dropped because she needs an A on her transcripts for college," I said. "And rumor is, that's a near impossibility with you."

"For her, anyway," he said.

"Who wrote that great poem about ghosts?"

"Originally? Sylvia Plath, mostly."

"It was plagiarized?"

"There's one in every class," he said. "But only until I figure out who she is."

"How do you know it's a she?"

"Plagiarizers pick material they can relate to. If they're smart."

I've come to expect a certain something extra from the writer in residence, but Dallas seems to blow the rest of them away.

"You still haven't said why you think I'm the one who's scared of poetry."

"Logically, you're the one person who couldn't have written it."

"Because?"

"Because you're the darling of the English Department."

I felt my ears burn.

"Which is why I had every intention of putting you through the paces."

"But you've changed your mind?"

"I'm cool with a healthy rebellious streak," he said. "Especially when you back it up with talented work."

Talented work . . .

I couldn't help but notice his eyes were emerald, the perfect shade of cliché green. "Poetry terrifies me."

"We're all terrified of something," he said.

"What about you?" I found myself asking.

"The future," he said with a smile.

Chapter Three

Dad's hungover and Mom's salty but trying not to show it, thought Cassidy as she sat down opposite them at a dining-hall table. *Actually, maybe Mom's hungover, too.*

They had worked their way through the buffet line, all three of them hitting the omelet station as if it were a delaying tactic, before staking out a marginally quieter corner of the large, echoing room. The first wave of brunchers—eager freshmen and their parents—was already clearing out, so it wasn't elbow to elbow.

Just as she'd planned.

"So how's—" began Mom.

"Don't say *school*," Cassidy interrupted, only half playfully.

"I was going to say *cross-country*," finished Mom, definitely fully hungover.

That was unusual. Typically, the only times she got shit-faced enough to show it the next day were New Year's Eve, weddings, and the occasional book club that got out of hand. Your average-mom social drinker, although she'd heard both Mom and Dad make reference to partying hard in college. If her four years at Glenlake were any indication, their high school years also had included a drunken moment or three.

"Humor us, Cassidy," said Dad. "We only get to do this four more times, starting next year with the twins."

Cassidy sighed and played along, even though she was starving and dying to dig in to her swiss cheese–and–mushroom omelet. "Lighten up, Pops. I'm just kidding. But you were always the one who said that general questions lead to generally boring answers."

"Cross-country is specific enough."

"Fine. Briana Sanderson is going to be varsity captain, but Coach said I'm the alternate or whatever."

"You have enough on your plate with college applications and everything else," said Mom, taking a tiny sip of coffee.

"Did you meet Mr. Kelly?"

"We didn't meet him, but we did hear him speak." Mom's tone was noncommittal, like she wasn't super impressed.

Cassidy started forking food into her mouth. Dad practically laughed at her. Whatever. Five-day-a-week training runs had her constantly craving protein. Protein, carbs, sugar—and sometimes even a fresh salad.

"I'm super excited about it," she said, trying to swallow most of the food before spitting out the words.

"I guess I don't know why you're taking the class," said Dad as Mom sliced a cantaloupe into dainty pieces and ignored her own egg white–and–spinach omelet.

True, she wasn't into writing as much as Mom was, but she'd always preferred creative nonfiction to fiction when given the choice—and journalism was like the ultimate nonfiction, right? Cassidy didn't know what she wanted to study in college or be as an adult. All she wanted was to feel excited about something. Maybe she'd found it?

"It's not like I get to choose the writer in residence," she said. "I figured you'd want me to take advantage of the famous senior seminar."

"Of course we do," said Mom unconvincingly.

"And I'm interested in how journalistic techniques can be used in creative nonfiction," she added, because it sounded like something they would like to hear.

Dad lifted his coffee mug and swabbed the ring underneath it with his napkin. "I presume he won't be teaching the 'creative' part."

That was true. Mr. Kelly was all about the facts and nothing but the facts. *But that doesn't mean you can't write about factual material using creative-writing techniques,* thought Cassidy. Although first they had to gather as much information as possible. He had already told the class to start digging: *Some of you are legacies, meaning your parents attended Glenlake. Given the time period, it's possible that some of your parents even knew the deceased.*

"So was Dallas Walker here when you were?" *Dig.*

Her parents glanced at each other before answering. It lasted about a second, but still—weird.

They both nodded, but Mom answered first. "Yes. I was taking his poetry seminar when he disappeared."

"I managed to avoid his writing classes, but I did join his pool club," said Dad.

"Pool? As in . . . ?"

"Pocket billiards. Eight-ball, nine-ball, and rotation. Walker wasn't interested in coaching any of the traditional sports, so he started what he called the Cue Sports Society."

"Your dad didn't like him much," said Mom, looking off into the distance.

Dad turned toward her. "I thought he was a blowhard, but I think that's how most teenagers feel about most of their teachers."

He almost looked mad at Mom, which was as weird as her hangover. They never fought—at least not in front of anybody. Sometimes they aired their differences to her or the twins directly, saying, *Your mother and I have a difference of opinion,* or, *Your father and I disagree,* but it was always over small stuff, like spending or a curfew. From a sociological perspective, it was fascinating, but Cassidy found herself wanting to defuse the tension. So she said, "Not me. I find them all worthy of my utmost admiration and respect."

That got chuckles from both of them.

"Did you guys know he was dead?" *Dig deeper.*

This time they didn't look at each other. Neither of them shook their heads. Mom stared at the table, seemingly having lost all interest in food.

"I hadn't heard a thing until last night," she said.

A freshman who was FaceTiming someone—total violation of the rules, but she'd learn—cruised by their table, narrating her journey across the dining hall, putting them in her background for a moment, and making it worse by adding, "And here's a family enjoying their meal!" Mom and Dad waved politely at the tiny face on the girl's phone, and Cassidy scowled until the frosh moved on.

"Do you have any big projects in your other classes?" asked Dad.

Now *he* was changing the subject. "Yeah, in math class we're trying to prove Einstein wrong. Dad! This is huge. Your heads must be spinning if you haven't heard about this."

"It's definitely a shock," said Mom, the look on her face confirming it, and probably explaining why they were both acting so weird. "I haven't thought about Dallas—he told all of us to call him by his first name—in years. I remember at the time feeling kind of betrayed that he'd left, because I'd always hated poetry, and I was starting to get it, and then he was just . . . gone."

"That must have been crazy."

"Well, it was and it wasn't," said Dad. "I mean, if there was a teacher you'd nominate to just disappear in the middle of the school year—"

"It was near the end," interrupted Mom.

"—it was him. He had a reputation as a wild man. A scandal, yes, but it wasn't as if some mild-mannered civics teacher suddenly walked away from a long career. He was only here for the year—he drove around in this muscle car, windows down, even in winter, and then one day he and his car were just gone. I always thought he just got a wild hair up his ass and went to Mexico to write poems or something."

Dad clearly hadn't liked the guy very much. That was as many sentences as he'd ever strung together to describe someone.

"He was different from the other teachers," agreed Mom. Not much of a dissertation.

"He liked to come across as a tough guy," Dad added. "He used to swear like a sailor while he taught us pool. But in the back of my mind, I was always like, *Come on, you're a poet, not a mill worker.*"

Cassidy tried to think back to Mr. Kelly's principles of investigative journalism: *Ask hard questions. Repeat the questions with slight variations. Look for inconsistencies. Think of yourself as a cop investigating a suspect—even innocent people hide details that could be helpful.*

Inconsistencies: Mom liked Dallas Walker. Dad didn't. Dad was doing most of the talking.

"Mom, what did you think happened to him? What did the kids in the poetry seminar think?" *Dig deepest.*

Mom gave her a penetrating look. Cassidy knew she was a little disappointed that her daughter wasn't a total Literary Person like she was. Cassidy enjoyed the writing program but didn't live for it or anything. In a way, she was a balanced mix of her parents, because she wanted to be outside doing sports—lately running, mostly—just as much as she wanted to be inside learning.

"To be honest? I don't know about the other kids, but I thought he just got bored with us and left," said Mom. "Now, I hope we're allowed to ask *you* a few questions. Seeing any cute boys this year?"

"Mom," she said, in what they called her Teenager Tone, before she could stop herself.

"I'll take that as a yes," said Mom, smiling and ready to launch her own interrogation.

Cassidy stood up. "I need more coffee."

Truth was, after four years of barely dating (because her parents seemed to eye *every guy* as a potential life partner), she had a real crush on Tate Holland. Mr. Kelly had asked him to join their class, even though he'd been suspended for a week and was on probation for the semester, because he was the one who'd found the car. It wasn't like he was destined to be some crack investigative journalist, either, but he was funny, self-deprecating, and cool enough to nearly get himself kicked out of school trying to revive the Freshman Plunge. Besides, he'd gotten hot over the summer. After making sure that his rumored relationship with a freshman yearbook photographer was only a rumor, she'd started sitting in the desk next to his so she could flirt a little. It took him a while to realize what she was doing, but when she saw him kick Noah out of the desk one day while she was entering the room, she realized she was on the right track.

They were now, in other words, an item. Not that she was ready to subject him to parental interrogation.

When she got back from refilling her cup, her diversionary tactic had worked: her parents were talking to each other, and Mom had decided not to hound her for details.

"We can tell you're excited about this journalism project," said Dad, breaking off abruptly. "Just remember you have five other classes, plus your college applications, that all need your attention, too."

"Duh, Dad," she said, thinking that Tate was in only one of those classes. Between him, the teacher, and the class project, it was bound to be the most interesting.

Mom piled her silverware onto her uneaten food and pushed the plate aside. "Still, we'll be curious to know what Mr. Kelly's class finds out. We're just as curious as you are."

"Oh, I'll keep you in the loop, all right," she promised. "And if you remember anything that would help our investigation, you'll let me know. Right?"

Chapter Four

Andi left brunch feeling more rattled than she'd felt in, well, twenty-two years. While Cassidy bounced off to cross-country practice and Ian headed back to the hotel for a hangover-curing nap before the annual all-Glenlake stickball game, she walked aimlessly toward the forested edge of campus.

From the moment Cassidy's journalism teacher projected the first photo on the whiteboard (installed over the very chalkboard where Dallas once left new stanzas of his poems), her thoughts had been all over the place.

And not anyplace she wanted to go.

What would Dallas have said about ending up entombed in his beloved Dodge Charger at the bottom of Lake Loomis?

More than a little clichéd, don't you think? It's like Bruce Springsteen meets Virginia Woolf.

She thought about a line from one of her favorite poems he'd written: *Would you rather be drowning with others, or swimming alone?*

With the revelation of his whereabouts, Andi felt like a little mole she'd had forever had suddenly risen and turned black.

In the distance, the dark water of the lake glittered.

She and Ian had both expressed how shocking it was that Dallas had been found after all this time. They'd briefly discussed texting Georgina, but she decided to wait since Georgina was picking her up from the airport on Sunday anyway. During some evening bar chatter with Tom Harkins and a few other parents, Tom had reminisced about how disruptive the disappearance had been, even though everyone had seemed to adjust to the long-term substitute teacher and move on as graduation approached.

Seemed being the key word.

For her, Dallas's disappearance had been the same as his appearance on campus.

Fraught with possibility.

When a set of new parents joined the conversation and wondered aloud if they should be worried about foul play, Ian assuaged them by spouting the most popular theory—Dallas had gotten drunk and committed suicide.

Ian then proceeded to drink too much himself.

One too many cocktails and her husband was generally snoring the moment his head hit the pillow. Last night, however, the mixture of alcohol, the unsettling nudge of mortality, and the anticipation of hotel sex had made Ian not only alert and horny but insistent in a way he hadn't been for years.

Andi liked that he was all over her as they'd walked home from the Limelight Lounge, the only bar in town. As he nuzzled her neck, working his way down into her cleavage, it reminded her of freshman year, when they'd steal away to make out in the wooded area behind her dorm or the Halcott Field bleachers—really anywhere they could get a few minutes alone.

Their lovemaking last night had had a frantic energy that harkened back to when they'd first started doing *it* in mid-tenth grade. Were she not feeling so unsettled, she'd have been excited by his drunken vigor. Instead, she found herself wondering what Ian could possibly be thinking but not saying. She could always read his reactions, especially when they were out socially and he was least likely to express his true thoughts: the tilt of his shoulders when he was engaged in a conversation, the slight raise of an eyebrow that meant he thought someone was full of shit, the way he unconsciously jingled the change in the pocket of his chinos when he was bored. Other than twisting his watch around his wrist once (and not multiple times, which he did when he was worried), he didn't seem to be thinking much of anything. It had been more than two decades, and he'd really known Dallas only in the context of that faux-macho pool club that became such a thing among the twelfth-grade boys.

Right?

He'd never known her secret, and he couldn't know. Even the strongest marriages hid tiny cracks that, if widened, could cause the whole foundation to crumble.

In the morning, Andi woke up planning to tell Ian how much she'd enjoyed last night. To begin again the process of plastering over the crack. She'd changed her mind after watching him wake up grumpy and hungover, fumbling through his shower and shave before they were due at brunch.

Brunch with their cub-reporter daughter, who was now investigating how and why Dallas Walker had met his end.

Andi's stomach roiled and her head throbbed at the thought of Cassidy unearthing even the smallest scrap of information about Dallas's presence at Glenlake.

The reason for his sudden absence.

At the empty shoreline, the floating dock bobbed gently in the tiny swells, leading the way to the lifeguard tower, which was actually built on the lake's bottom. Nearby was a bike rack with several of the bright-red Glenlake Academy cruisers that dotted the campus. It took a moment to adjust to the weight and balance of the clunky one-size-fits-all dimensions, but she was soon rolling along on Lake Loomis Road.

Ironically, it was the most poetic day she could possibly imagine. The sky was a deep azure dotted with impossibly puffy clouds. The warm air held the cool warning of winter's encroachment. The dead leaves crunched under her tires, while those still clinging to the shady canopy of trees above shouted their impending demise in a riot of color.

Anthropomorphize nature, Dallas once said. *It brings human understanding to that which is beyond our comprehension.*

Dallas, who'd been hiding right here in the landscape all along.

At the time, most of the rumors had sounded believable, although violent death at the hands of a modern-day outlaw was clearly a stretch. The rest of the theories centered around Dallas taking off and living under an assumed name somewhere: Mexico, Central America, even the Australian outback. Of course, there was a woman involved—and not just any woman, mind you, but someone so alluring he had no choice but to follow her siren song.

Andi had googled his name over the years. But she'd never found anything beyond the short story collection that had put him on the literary map, the book of poems that had won him a Los Angeles Times Book Prize and solidified his reputation, and a few poems he'd published in literary journals before coming to Glenlake.

As Andi made her way around the lake road, she spotted a grouping of white oak trees. Taller now, they stood together in their familiar ascending order like papa, mama, and baby. She veered off the road, located the large flat rock that served as a trail marker, and set down her bike in the brush so a passerby wouldn't assume it was up for grabs and ride it back to campus. She plucked one of the sweet, edible green acorns from a low-hanging bough of a white oak and nibbled it as she made her way along the abandoned road overgrown with familiar memories.

~

Saturday, September 28, 1996

Today, instead of going on the weekend outing to the Field Museum in Chicago or hanging out and watching a movie with Ian, I went on a nature walk. A fucking nature walk. It wasn't like I had a lot of choice. Dallas assigned us to go outside, walk around, and then write a "kick-ass" poem.

Due on Monday.

Georgina invited me to walk with her tomorrow, but Ian's parents are in town for a trustees' meeting, and I'm invited to join the family for lunch before they head back home. In other words, today was the day.

I've been in the class long enough to know that "kick-ass" means Dallas wants a poem that somehow encompasses everything about Robert Frost we've been studying all week: reality, clarity, simplicity, metaphysical elements, etc., etc.

If that's possible. I mean, there's only one Robert Frost for a reason.

I started by walking around campus, looking at the trees and the birds and the grass, blah, blah, blah. Instead of feeling inspired, I felt like marching into Holmes Library, locating the oldest, dustiest poetry book I could find, and exhuming a ripe verse or two. Too bad there was no risking Dallas's encyclopedic knowledge of every poem ever written. I don't think Tori Miller (or anyone else in the class) will ever plagiarize anything ever again, not after having to write fifty original poems on honesty and integrity. That or get reported and (per Glenlake's strict code of ethics) expelled.

Instead, I headed down toward Lake Loomis, drinking plasticky-tasting water from my Nalgene bottle and begging nature to sing to me.

All I heard was the sound of a muffler.

I turned and saw a squat, squared-off blue muscle car with a grille that looked like an open mouth.

As the car slowed and pulled up beside me, I spotted the devil himself behind the wheel.

"As Mr. Frost reputedly said, 'The middle of the road is where the white line is—and that's the worst place to drive,'" I quoted.

Dallas laughed. "I wonder how far down the road he's got. He's watching from the woods as like as not."

"Maybe because he, meaning me, isn't quite feeling dramatic or lyrical on my nature walk yet."

"Perhaps it's time for office hours in the great outdoors." Dallas reached across the passenger seat and opened the door. "Hop in."

The next thing I knew, we'd spun halfway around the lake and were parking by a stand of white oak trees.

As we got out of the car, Dallas plucked an acorn from a low-hanging bough.

"Taste it," he said.

"I'm not a squirrel."

"Pretend you are," he said. "They're only truly in season once every four years."

"Aren't they poisonous?"

He shook his head, took a bite, and looked off into the trees.

I took a tiny taste. The acorn meat was oddly sweet.

"Now, follow me," he said.

"Where?"

"To a place I just found but that I've been looking for forever."

We started out on a deeply rutted dirt road that Dallas said he wouldn't risk driving with his "cherry '69 Charger." I probably should have felt a little weird to be hiking alone with a teacher, but somehow I just didn't. I mean, he was basically giving a lecture while we walked about the native trees and plants of Illinois and nature symbolism in poetry.

"See this?" he asked, pointing out a big gray mushroom that looked like an elephant ear and had to be poisonous. "It makes me think of the primary theme of 'Two Tramps in Mud Time.'"

"The bright and dark aspects of nature," I said, remembering yesterday's lecture.

"Bravo to the brilliant Ms. Bloom," he said. Did I imagine a slight emphasis on the word brilliant?

Meaning he actually thought that about me?

"I definitely feel the danger and the beauty with my feet in the sand, looking out at waves crashing onto shore," I said. "But nature here feels sort of . . . bland."

"You can take the girl out of California . . ." He shook his head but chuckled softly. "How did you end up at the very best boarding school that isn't on the West or East Coast, anyway?"

"It's kind of a long story."

"We've still got a bit of a walk," he said. "And you can skip the whole business about coming here for the school's esteemed writing program. I know you came in as some kind of literary prodigy and still managed to wow everyone with your talent and winning personality."

I felt flattered beyond belief but completely exposed at the same time.

"That's pretty much it," I managed to say.

"Bullshit," he said. "Which seems to work on everyone else around here . . ."

"But not on you?"

"You and me," he said, stopping and turning so quickly I almost bumped into him. "We're different from everyone else, aren't we?"

"I suppose we are," I said, noting that up close he smelled not only of cigarettes but something warm and fragrant. Like a man, or at least someone who wasn't wearing his blue button-down shirt one time too many to avoid doing his laundry.

We walked in silence that wasn't silent at all. Leaves rustled in the breeze, and the air was alive with the buzz of cicadas, birds practicing for their upcoming journey south, and even a plane crossing overhead.

"My dad created a myth for me that I've spent the last three years trying to live up to," I finally admitted.

For the first time. To anyone. Even Ian.

"By all accounts you've succeeded," Dallas said.

"I mean, I love Glenlake and the writing program," I said, hoping he wouldn't see how plum red my cheeks had to be. "But coming here wasn't really a choice."

"Shipped off to boarding school in the prime of your young Beverly Hills life?"

"More like the prime of my dad's busy career and new life playing ador-ing husband and doting father to my stepmom and the bouncing baby half sisters they keep popping out, saying they're for me."

"Yikes," Dallas said.

"Honestly, I spent this whole summer listening to Sesame Street blare on the TV and missing Glenlake."

"What about your mom?" he asked.

"Dead," I said with a finality I'd learned would end the conversation.

"I'm sorry," Dallas said, taking the hint.

I tried not to think about Mom, mostly because it always hurt when I did. But sometimes I avoided thinking about her because I was half con-vinced she was now everywhere and all-seeing.

Stupid, I know.

We walked in silence again until the trees began to thin and the rut-ted road came to an abrupt end. Suddenly, we were in a grassy clearing overlooking the lake.

Dallas took my hand and led me to the rocky ledge.

I told myself the butterflies in my stomach were from looking over the sheer cliff and down to the shimmering water below. But that didn't explain why my fingers suddenly seemed so sensitive. It was hard to think about any-thing except the fact that my teacher was touching me and I was touching him. It felt almost intimate. I hoped my palm wasn't sweaty.

I stepped back quickly. "I don't like heights."

"You're safe," he whispered, gently leading me back toward the edge. "I promise."

I willed myself to relax the trembling in my legs.

"Beneath the beautiful calm, turmoil and storms lurk," he said. He let go of my hand and gently but firmly grasped my shoulders instead. "Now close your eyes."

I did.

"When you open them, I want you to tell me everything you see. And feel."

I stood there, eyes squeezed shut, for a long time before I did.

"The sharp, rocky edge of the earth falling away to . . ."

"To?"

"Chilled, wind-dappled quicksilver."

"Not bad. You can do better."

"The certainty of what fall and winter will bring—the cold embrace. Everything unknowable that lies below the surface."

"Beautiful," he said, pulling me back from the edge. He looked into my eyes. "Truly."

~

Andi looked over the edge of the cliff with an entirely different sense of trepidation from the first time she'd been to this spot, so long ago.

Instead of unspoiled nature, as in *the sharp, rocky edge of the earth falling away to chilled, wind-dappled quicksilver*, there was churned-up shoreline cordoned off with tattered lengths of yellow evidence tape.

Just as she knew there would be.

She tried to imagine the hood of the now-rusty Charger breaking the surface of the lake, water draining out of its cracked windows. How, once the car was resting on the barge, someone had been first to open the door, to see slimy, once-dark-blue-and-white custom leather seats, the black steering wheel that had shone like onyx, and a skeleton.

After all these years, Dallas had been found. Plucked from beneath the sun-dappled water.

She closed her eyes and opened them again, just as she had on her nature walk with him so many years ago.

Only one word came to her: *murky.*

And something she hadn't thought about until that very moment— Dallas was the same age on the day he died as she was now.

And Cassidy was exactly the same age now as Andi was then.

Chapter Five

Ian woke from his nap disoriented, his phone alarm an alien trill, his mind lost in a vivid dream in which he and Andi were dorm parents, living in the apartment on Cassidy's hall and hosting a weekend social for the students in their charge. At the end of the dream, there had been a *Twilight Zone* moment of panic when he'd had a chilling revelation: *wait a minute; we're the same age as Cassidy!*

And then the alarm had gone off.

He got up slowly, reorienting himself, feeling a sore spot on his back where he'd slept on top of the lumped-up covers. The maid hadn't come while they were at brunch, and the sheets smelled of sex, sweat, and the alcohol he was still burning off. After slipping off his pants, he moved slowly toward the bathroom, ready for his second shower of the day.

Did not need drinks three, four, and five, he thought as the hot water scalded his back. *Or six.*

The evening had taken a left turn with Wayne Kelly's ambush revelation. After three years of visiting as a parent and two decades of sporadic returns for fund-raisers and class reunions, Ian had finally stopped holding his breath, thinking the subject of Dallas Walker had truly been laid to rest. And now, like a revenant from one of the poet's own verses, he had come howling back to tranquil Glenlake to disturb the peace. If it were a Dallas Walker poem, the corpse would have pointed a smug finger at the dumb townsfolk and imparted a lesson about how they were all living their lives in fear.

But Dallas Walker had not authored this particular composition.

What the hell was Kelly thinking, assigning a death investigation to a class of juniors and seniors? It might seem like a game to teenagers, but bodies had consequences. His own daughter's questioning at brunch this morning had been earnest, but Kelly had armed the students with rakes and shovels and sent them into a minefield.

Or, more accurately, over a cliff.

That cliff.

At least it looked like suicide. And he couldn't have driven off accidentally. With luck, the police would agree, and the kids wouldn't find anything to contradict that supposition. Or learn which students had seen Dallas outside class during his final days.

Maybe it was better not to leave things to chance. He couldn't lose Andi again. He'd always assumed Dallas had left of his own accord because of what happened. Was his death also in some way connected? Had she ever had a sense this day might come?

Head somewhat cleared, he dressed casually—chinos, polo shirt, trainers, and windbreaker—and got in the car to head back to campus. Before he left, he made sure to hang the tag on the door handle, asking the maid to make up the room.

Some of the parents and teachers would be wearing sweats and athletic clothes to the parents' weekend stickball tournament, but Ian didn't bother. Most years this was due to his disdain for the phenomenon of flabby middle-aged people in tracksuits, as well as not wanting to look like he was trying too hard. It was more fun to be the guy who shows up dressed for the barbecue and surprises everyone with a grand slam.

But this year he just didn't give a damn.

As he neared the fields, his phone vibrated with a text from Andi.

Are you up yet?

On campus, he wrote back, mildly annoyed but unable to defend his need for a midday nap. Where are you?

Student union. Coffee with Mrs. Henry.

Tell her I said hi, he wrote. See you at the game.

I'll be there, she texted back.

He pocketed his phone and was scanning the early arrivals at the playing fields when he saw a ghost.

No, not a ghost, but a face that gave him a chill. He'd never expected to see the man after leaving Glenlake, much less to see him wearing a groundskeeper's uniform. Now grizzled and stoop shouldered, the man pulled a wagon down the third-base line toward home plate. Age had not been kind: once upon a time, he had been tall and tough and terrifying to Ian's seventeen-year-old self.

What was his name? *R* something. Ray? No, Roy.

Roy.

~

Friday, October 11, 1996

Today the pool club took a field trip. Dallas told us that since none of the schools we compete against in "soccer, lacrosse, and field hockey" (as if boys play field hockey) have "cue sports teams," we would have to "seek out competition in its appropriate environment." Which turned out to be a bar.

"I hope you all brought quarters," he said as we pulled up in front of a sleazy-looking dive called Kyle's Kabin. The other guys were practically peeing themselves when they saw real live Harley-Davidsons out front, but there were only two of those. It was afternoon, so it wasn't like a scene from Road House *or anything.*

It was practically empty inside, which seemed to bum Dallas out, but there was a scary-looking guy named Roy who was obviously expecting us. He was HUGE and had homemade-looking tattoos on both arms and one on his neck. Dallas gave him a bro hug and told us he drank beer and played pool with Roy all the time. Possibly true, but Roy didn't seem as into it as Dallas.

We formed three teams and had a little tournament. Roy, Dallas, and I were the strongest players, so we were all on different teams. Mike ended up on Roy's, and Jacob had to play with Dallas. Patrick was with me. Roy's and Dallas's teams played first, and even though Roy's technique looked terrible, he almost never missed. I think Mike was crapping his pants, but he only got one turn, and it didn't matter. Roy made shots one-handed and left-handed and kind of smirked about it. They won, naturally.

Then it was our turn to play Dallas and Jacob. Patrick is better than Jacob, and I'm almost as good as Dallas, so it was a close game . . . and we won! I could tell Dallas was pissed, especially when Roy said, "Loser gets the beers."

Then when Dallas came back with two beers, Roy said, "What about these guys?" Obviously meaning us.

Dallas said, "But they're minors," and Roy mimicked him: "But they're minors."

When Dallas seemed like he was going to get us beers after all, Roy stopped him and said, "You trying to get us both arrested?"

I almost felt sorry for Dallas, but it was kind of funny.

After it was over we were cramming ourselves back into his Charger (I got shotgun) and Dallas muttered something about "a life made vain by three spheres of insidious ivory," which he told us is from a poem by Edwin Arlington Robinson.

Jacob asked him what the poem was about, and Dallas said, "Look it up. Ever heard of the library?" or something like that. I guess he was still mad about losing twice.

Dallas may be cooler than most teachers, but he can be kind of a dick, too.

~

Roy wasn't scary now. His big frame looked like it was caving in on itself, and his neck tattoo was faded and wrinkled above the threadbare collar of his uniform shirt. Ian watched as he took bases out of the wagon and put them in place on the infield diamond, then set a bucket of balls against the backstop and a selection of sticks in each dugout.

Then, with a focus that seemed borne of bone-deep fatigue, he chalked a clean first-base line while students, teachers, and parents milled about forming teams and generally ignoring Roy.

Roy had to be in his sixties now, and it looked as though he had lived every one of the intervening years hard and fast. Ian wondered how long he'd been working for Glenlake. Back when Ian was a student, he hadn't even thought about what Roy did for a living—he probably would have guessed that Roy rode around on his motorcycle, sold drugs, and hustled pool. Maybe committed a little burglary on the side.

Fortunately, even Dallas had had the good sense to announce right off the bat that they weren't playing for money.

Ian and the other students had fed off the adrenaline of that trip for days. The two boys who hadn't made it were miserable with envy, thinking they'd missed a massive rite of passage, and Ian, Mike, Jacob, and Patrick reinforced that perception as much as possible. Only later had Ian come to realize that Dallas's seeming act of antiestablishment rebellion should have been a warning sign.

There was a loud whistle, and Glenlake's athletic director began moving through the crowd with a huge canvas sack and a rainbow assortment of pinnies. The annual parents' weekend stickball tournament had been a tradition since the early part of the twentieth century, the common street game chosen on the assumption that none of Glenlake's privileged attendees would be familiar with it, and all would be equally disadvantaged. To foster camaraderie, teams were chosen at random from students, parents, and faculty, with an effort to break up families and groups of friends by handing them each a different color to wear.

Once formed, teams played a short tournament on the two adjacent softball fields, with scorekeeping and play-by-play performed by alums who no longer trusted themselves to run the base paths. Players on the winning team would sign and date one of the batting sticks, which would be duly installed—if not exactly given pride of place—in the school's trophy case.

Ian caught Tom Harkins's eye just as the athletic director handed him a red pinny. Tom raised his own: blue. They both shrugged wryly as the bullhorn-voiced coach directed red teams and blue teams to separate diamonds. Then, spotting an unaffiliated Wayne Kelly just a little way off, Ian tugged a second red pinny out of the sack as the unaware director moved on.

He pushed through the crowd and handed the pinny to Kelly.

"He said you're on my team," Ian told him, inclining his head toward the athletic director.

Kelly raised an eyebrow but pulled the pinny on.

"You ever play stickball?" Ian asked Kelly as they headed for their assigned diamond to play the green team.

Kelly grinned. "I lived in North Philly until I was twelve."

"So you're a ringer?"

"I thought that was why you wanted me on your team."

"You're going down, old man!" heckled Cassidy from the diamond where she was playing, blue against yellow.

Ian grinned at her.

"From the way you two are trash-talking, you must be Cassidy's dad," said the teacher.

"Guilty," said Ian, thankful his daughter had unwittingly provided the conversational opener he needed. "I hope she's not too much of a handful in class. She can be pretty headstrong."

"Are you kidding?" said Wayne. "That's exactly the trait a journalist needs. Curiosity. The refusal to take no for an answer. Even being a bit of a pest."

Ian filled a paper cup with water from a cooler on the end of the bench. The water was lukewarm, but he took a deep drink anyway. "Well, I'm not sure she's planning on being a journalist, but she's certainly excited about the class. The way she was questioning my wife and me, I should probably have asked if she was wearing a wire."

Wayne laughed. "That's exactly what I'm talking about! She and Tate really seem to be on fire for this."

"Tate who?"

"Tate Holland," said Wayne. "The boy who found the car. They're always hanging out together."

"Interesting," said Ian, picturing a kid named Tate Holland. What were the chances he didn't have gelled blond hair, a freckled snub nose, and a closet full of J.Crew clothing? He was a bit surprised his free-wheeling daughter would go for a preppy kid—but then wasn't that exactly what her mother had done? "She's reached the age where relationships are as closely guarded as state secrets."

"Huh. But she was questioning you? So that means you were here when Dallas Walker was, too."

"My wife and I were seniors," said Ian, wishing he hadn't brought Andi into it, knowing it didn't matter. Cassidy would tell him anyway.

"Wow," said Wayne, and again Ian wasn't sure what he was responding to. "So if you were here when he disappeared, that must have been huge. The talk of the campus and the town. You had to have a theory."

He's not just a teacher; he's a professional journalist, Ian reminded himself as he thought about how to answer. He'd hoped to be the one extracting information, but Wayne had effortlessly reversed their roles.

"Dallas Walker saw himself as a bad boy," he finally said. "I think he was compensating for being, you know, a poet. He wanted to be a red meat–eating, beer-drinking regular guy, and he prided himself on breaking the rules and being unpredictable. Some people thought he disappeared to Mexico. Others thought he'd picked up a hitchhiker and been murdered."

Far off across the fields, he saw the slumped figure of Roy pulling his wagon.

"I guess I was always suspicious of the townies he hung out with," he added. "He was rumored to run with a rough crowd—bikers and actual criminals."

Wayne frowned. "Was there any proof of that?"

"I don't know, but I was in his pool club, what he called the Cue Sports Society. He took me and some other students to some pretty sketchy poolrooms to play. One of them was a biker bar."

Wayne whistled.

"I have to admit, I'm a bit surprised the administration is supporting your project," said Ian.

"Oh, they're not," Wayne said casually. "But they hired an investigative journalist this year, not a poet."

Ian wondered how much Wayne Kelly would make of his remarks. He supposed reporters were trained to make a meal out of the tiniest crumbs. But if Ian tossed the right crumbs, that might not be such a bad thing.

"If I were you," he said, "I'd start with the lowlifes Dallas Walker ran with. I'm sure you won't have to look farther than that."

Chapter Six

"Your dad definitely seemed to be getting along with Mr. Kelly," observed Tate, finding Cassidy in the crowd as the games broke up and the players and spectators straggled toward the table where the awards awaited presentation. Naturally, Dad's team had won. Even though the ceremony wasn't serious at all—by tradition, the winners were dunked with a "bucket of water" that was actually confetti, a gag that fooled only the first-year students and their parents—Cassidy found herself hanging back, not wanting to be in the front row as Team Captain Ian Copeland hoisted the cheap trophy.

"He was probably just excited to find out that Mr. Kelly's as good at sports as *he* is," she said. She wasn't sure why it bothered her to see the two of them being so buddy-buddy. Maybe it was just because her parents usually made a point of not inserting themselves into her life at school.

"My parents already talked his ear off about how great I am. You know, used their first spare second with him to try and game the system," said Tate.

At least her parents didn't do that. The Copeland Way would have been to make a casual comment to someone who knew someone and knew how to respond, without the real subject ever being discussed. It was a big advantage in life, but it was also maddening, because they rarely talked about the thing that was on their minds.

Still, in all her parents' stories about Glenlake, why hadn't there ever been so much as a mention of Dallas Walker and his sudden disappearance during senior year?

"What did your parents say about this whole Walker business?" she asked Tate.

"My mom said I'm just lucky I didn't get my ass kicked out over my 'stunt,' because life as I know it would have been over."

Cassidy felt an unexpected sense of loss just thinking about the investigation, and the school year itself, continuing without Tate. "And your dad?"

"He was here a long time before Walker and didn't really seem all that interested. He was super proud of me for having the balls to try and bring back the Loomis Leap, though."

"My hero," she said, just to watch him blush.

The back of his hand brushed against the back of her hand. Her skin prickled.

"Sorry," he said quickly.

Sometimes he was such a dipshit.

She looked around to see if anyone was watching. The only thing wrong with Tate, really, was that her parents would love him because he was prep-school perfect and—moonlight dives aside—perfectly safe.

But why should she hold that against him? She didn't love him, but she liked him a lot. And it's not like they had to know about him anytime soon.

In fact, if there were things they weren't telling her, she definitely didn't have to share this development with them.

Feeling a grin form on her face, she tilted her head back and kissed him on the lips.

Chapter Seven

ANDI BLOOM'S GLENLAKE JOURNAL

Sunday, September 29, 1996

"I'll never get you out of my system," Ian said one night last year. I was super touched until he followed it up with, *"My dad says I will, but I won't. Not ever."*

I tell myself it isn't a big deal, because we were a little drunk and a lot high, but I can't stop thinking about it every time the Copelands come into town, which is regularly because Mr. Copeland is president of the board of trustees.

They are super polite because they don't like me.

Mr. Copeland, "Cope," greeted me at lunch today by shaking my hand way too firmly, like he always does. Mrs. Copeland, "Biz," gave me an air-kiss. She's always friendly enough, but she's only invited me to St. Louis once in three years—last November, when she knew I was already meeting Dad and the brood for a "special New York Thanksgiving" that I would have just as soon skipped. Ian says I'm going to be invited to their cabin in Michigan this summer, but I'm not holding my breath.

"They're weird about having you at the cabin because of the boy-girl thing," Ian used to say when we were first together.

Never mind half the kids here seem to have a place on the same lake, and Ian's house is ground zero for all get-togethers, coed and otherwise.

"They're super traditional when it comes to our relationship," Ian says now.

We both know it's code for You're Jewish.

We both know they're worried that he'll marry me, one of Glenlake's glorious tokens of diversity. Good thing he didn't fall for Crystal Thomas, who is (gasp) African American. I mean, how bad would it look at the country club that I'm not technically eligible to join, due to my dark curls, discernible curves, telltale nose, and otherwise obvious non-Episcopalian heritage? When his parents mention the place, which they somehow always manage to do ("Oh, this pasta salad is just like the one the club added to their menu"), I want to make the entirely bourgeois statement that my dad could buy the place outright.

But I don't.

Instead, I smile, nod with feigned interest, use my forks correctly, and act altogether like I went to cotillion in Beverly Hills. Never mind that I hadn't even heard of cotillion until I reached the Midwest.

"How are the college applications going?" Mr. Copeland asked.

"Well, thank you," I said.

"I assume you're applying to schools in California?" Mrs. Copeland asked a little too hopefully.

"A few," I said.

"Great," the Copelands said in unison.

"But I'm looking all over."

"Have you settled on a number-one choice?" Mr. Copeland asked.

"I'm waiting until I see where I get in."

"Smart," both of them said, again in unison.

"I'm hoping she gets into Smith," Ian proclaimed.

"Right down the street from Amherst," Biz said and took a dainty bite of salad that somehow required an inordinate amount of chewing. "Wouldn't that be nice."

"Can't wait until you're wearing purple and white, son," Mr. Copeland said, patting Ian on the back.

"I'm sure Andi will have lots of schools to choose from," Mrs. Copeland said.

~

Monday, September 30, 1996

We had a sub in poetry class today. Dallas was sick or had a meeting or was in the middle of a poem he had to finish.

I'd be lying if I said I wasn't a little disappointed. I worked super hard on the nature poem and was looking forward to his reaction.

Georgina seemed even more bummed than I was. She has a full-on crush on him. She says she doesn't, but she talks about him all the time. She claims it's because we're both in the same class and he's such a demanding teacher. Maybe so, but she's usually saying something about the "cute for an older guy" plaid shirt he's wearing, wondering if there's a Mrs. Dallas Walker, declaring him "probably hot" as a teenager, or mentioning that she saw him driving a cool old car.

I didn't dare tell her that I had a ride in said car, or that he was wearing the plaid shirt in question on the nature walk we took together. I definitely didn't mention to Georgina that his hands had been on my shoulders. When the sub, Mrs. Cates, asked me how I'd gotten my inspiration for the "delightfully evocative 'Eating Acorns,'" I said, "A walk around Lake Loomis," and left it at that.

~

Tuesday, October 8, 1996

The great thing about Ian and me is that we never annoy each other.

Almost never, anyway.

Except for tonight.

For one thing, he kept smacking his gum while we were working on essay prompts for our college applications. For another, he kept trying to kiss me and/or feel me up whenever he thought no one in the study lounge was looking.

He can be really handsy sometimes.

I might not have minded the groping, but his constant need for my input on practically every sentence he wrote was making me nuts. I totally get that I'm "the writer" of the two of us, but we were only doing rough drafts we'll be developing tomorrow in college prep class and rewriting a million more times before they're ready to send off.

Either way, I really couldn't get traction on the prompt I was working on: Write a haiku, limerick, or short poem that best represents you.

Ian and Andi
Together forever more
But not right now, 'kay?

~

Thursday, October 10, 1996

"The applications committee must be hard up for cheap laughs," Dallas said, looking over the essay prompt. "I mean a college-admission limerick, for god's sake? How might that go?

"There once was a boy named Dallas / Who wanted to live in a palace. / He went to college, / Seeking money and knowledge, / But learned mostly what to do with his phallus."

"Ha," I said, willing my cheeks not to turn crimson.

"I'm glad you're amused." Dallas put his hands behind his head and leaned back in his chair. "Let's hear what you've got."

Even a month ago, there was no way I'd have considered answering a college prompt in verse, much less tried to come up with a limerick on the spot.

"There once was a girl from Glenlake Academy . . ."

The words weren't even out of my mouth before I was trying to figure out what, if anything, actually rhymed with academy. Agony? Strategy? Vanity? Extended family?

"She wanted to go to college so madly."

I had no idea where I was going, but committed anyway.

"That she asked for some tips / From a teacher so hip / And he taught her to rhyme dirty, but badly."

"Ha, indeed." Dallas smiled and shook his head. "But as said hip teacher, I feel obliged to advise you that submitting a limerick is a risky gambit. The better it is, the more people on the admissions board it's likely to offend."

"What about haiku?" I asked.

"Haiku is for Japanese seventeenth-century masters and twentieth century poseurs."

"Which is why I've been working on this," I said. I handed him a poem I'd finally started during my study session in the library with Ian and then reworked with the college counselor.

"Where are you applying, anyway?" he asked, scanning the poem.

"My reach schools are Stanford, Columbia, and Brown."

"But of course."

"I'm also applying to NYU, Berkeley, Northwestern, Bowdoin . . ."

"And, let me guess, Tufts, as a backup?"

"I was thinking more along the lines of University of Iowa—for the writers' program."

"I'd save that one for grad school," he said. "That is, if you think you'll grow in that little hothouse of overfertilized verse and prose."

"Isn't that a little harsh?" I asked.

"I like the first line of your poem," he said, changing the subject. "Who is this prompt for, anyway?"

"Smith."

"Great school for writers."

"So you approve?"

"Sure," he said. "I wouldn't necessarily have pegged you as a Smithie, though."

"Ian's going to Amherst if he gets in," I said, his name both escaping my lips and somehow sticking slightly to my tongue. "So we were thinking—"

"We were thinking?" Dallas asked. "Or he was thinking?"

I couldn't answer that question, so I didn't.

"Promise me you won't automatically buy into what they tell you, especially about how you have to take the overpriced, overrated, bullshit Ivy trip," he said, looking into my eyes. "Not unless it's where you really want to go."

I was thrown off but also oddly relieved. Since arriving at Glenlake, I've felt nothing but pressure about where I'll get into college. I wasn't entirely surprised, though. After all, hadn't Dallas arrived at the school accompanied by the legend that he'd given average grades to the supposedly best and brightest? "So you're telling me not to do what everyone else tells me to do but what you think I should do?"

"You'd be way better off," he said with a grin. "Speaking of which, this poem you've given me definitely represents what you can do."

"But . . . ?"

"It doesn't represent you."

I exhaled with frustration. "So it's back to the drawing board?"

"Hardly," he said, and began to recite a poem from memory: "Eating Acorns."

My poem.

> What is a nut but a seed
> A germ of a thing that will grow?
> An idea of an oak in a smooth brown hull
> A vessel for its journey into the dirt
>
> What is a girl but a seedling
> Stretching toward the sky?

Seeking air, seeking sun, seeking water
Alone yet part of the forest

Seed, taproot, shoot, seedling
My teeth break the skin
The acorn's meat
Is strange and sweet

"That," he said. "That's you."

~

Saturday, October 12, 1996

Tonight is my fourth and final Fall Fling. Georgina thinks I need to wear the bright-pink linen dress I wore to the first dance freshman year and then request that the DJ play "Love Shack" by the B-52s, the first song Ian and I ever danced to. Sylvie, being Georgina's ultimate hanger-on and yes-woman, of course agrees. (If I thought we'd see less of Sylvie after she got placed in a different house than us, I was wrong.) I was planning to wear the silver metallic Calvin Klein dress I bought while I was home. I kind of feel like people expect me to bring the "girl from California" style, especially to events like this, but we still have the Winter Formal coming up. To be honest, that's probably a more suitable occasion to bust out something slinky and backless. Besides, I'll match better with Ian, who will be wearing the charcoal suit and white shirt he always wears. Not that I'm complaining. He looks cute and preppy in it—just like he does in everything. I swear, he could make leather pants look like they came from Brooks Brothers.

No matter what, I'm looking forward to slow-dancing with Ian, who (despite how antiquated and Midwestern it still sounds) definitely picked up a move or two at cotillion.

~

Sunday, October 13, 1996

Top Ten Reasons Why It Was the Worst. Night. Ever.

1. Ian got caught up prepartying with the guys on his floor and told me he'd meet me at the dance.

2. They all showed up together half an hour late, calling each other "broham."

3. He gave me a contraband Jell-O shot from his jacket pocket "as an early anniversary gift."

4. It tasted like orange cough syrup.

5. I looked and felt like a ninth grader in the dress, which was a little too middle school and a lot too neon.

6. Ian didn't even remember that I'd worn it before, anyway.

7. He was in the bathroom when the DJ played "Love Shack."

8. While we were slow-dancing to "Nothing Compares 2U," Patrick Morris decided it would be hilarious and unquestionably super mature to give Ian a wedgie.

9. Dallas was one of the faculty chaperones.

10. When he wasn't looking bored or bemused by Ian and the idiots known as his "Cue Sports Society," he was totally flirting it up in the corner with Miranda Darrow, the headmaster's big-haired, bigger-boobed trophy wife.

Somehow, watching Dallas flirt with Mrs. Darrow bothered me more than almost anything else.

~

Monday, October 14, 1996

To add insult to injury, Daaa-lisss (as Georgina drawls, like she's ever spent more than a weekend anywhere in Texas) was our faculty dinner table host tonight. I might have been pleased that he chose to sit at one of the long "community" tables in the seniors' section of the dining hall if she hadn't spent the whole meal preening, flirting, and trying to get his attention.

"Daaa-lisss"—hair flip—"please pass the butter . . ."

"Daaa-lisss—giggle—"while you're pouring dressing, do you mind putting a little on my salad?"

"Daaa-lisss, are we going to do a unit on Pablo Neruda?"

As if all that wasn't obvious enough, she even had the balls to ask if he had "a wife or a girlfriend or anyone you're, you know, serious about?"

He told her he didn't, which is a mistake with Georgina, but she was actually the least of it. Sylvie and Patrick, who apparently made out at some point during the dance (when he wasn't giving people wedgies), were alternately ignoring each other, stealing furtive glances, and making everyone else feel uncomfortable. Despite, or because of, the palpable sexual tension, Michael and Jacob spent dinner trying to crack each other up by calling the other "gay" using increasingly obnoxious slang.

"Do you two need some alone time to work this out?" Dallas asked at the tail end of "sausage jockey," causing Michael to blush and Jacob to spray milk out his nose.

In the awkward silence that followed, Ian tried to reestablish dinner decorum. Everything was yes sir, no sir, and please pass the potatoes, sir. Given that Dallas is faculty and we are students, I should have been proud of my boyfriend's efforts. Not to mention his flawless table manners. I usually am.

"Dallas likes to be called Dallas," I whispered in his ear.

"Dallas, sir," he said the next time.

I wanted to die a little.

Especially when Dallas said, "Hanging is the word, sir; if you be ready for that, you are well cooked."

Everyone at the table, including Ian, looked at him like he was speaking in tongues.

"Shakespeare," I said, totally guessing but apparently getting it right.

As Dallas smiled and everyone else nodded like they'd known that, too, I counted down the minutes until I could get out of there.

The second we were excused, I mumbled something about needing to do homework I'd actually completed, then did my best to get lost in the crowd heading toward the double doors.

Dallas must have exited through the faculty doors while I was stuck in a slow-moving cluster of sophomores, because he was already in the quad, leaning against the brick pillar closest to the student entrance when I made it outside.

"Andi," he said, my name seeming to echo despite the babble of voices surrounding us.

As I walked over, wondering why he'd waited for me, I noticed for the first time how uncomfortable he looked in the khakis, ill-fitting button-down shirt, and too-short tie he was required to wear for Sunday dinner. How un-Dallas he looked out of his usual jeans and faded chambray or plaid shirt.

"I volunteer to be a table host in the hopes of enjoying your scintillating dinner conversation," he said, "and you barely say a word."

"It's just that . . ." I shrugged, unable to answer.

"What?"

The courtyard was starting to clear, but it was still an awkward place to be having this conversation. I'd bolted from the table, so Ian, Georgina, and the gang would be coming out at any moment.

I glanced over my shoulder to make sure they weren't already in the doorway. "I was so embarrassed by the way my friends were acting."

"They aren't a reflection of you," he said, tucking a stray piece of hair behind my ear.

Then he recited a verse of poetry. I like it when Dallas reads or recites—he doesn't do that lofty "poet voice" everyone uses to make themselves sound more important. He just says the words like they matter.

"This town slumbers in its blanket / The mayor wears a mask / The police chief has plugged his ears / The breath of their wives is deep and dry / No one even murmurs in their sleep / But you and I are awake!"

"Who wrote that?" I asked.

"Me," he said. "It's called 'Bloom.'"

~

Tuesday, October 15, 1996

Bloom *as in a flower or* Bloom *as in my last name?*

It had to be a coincidence.

Unless it's a subconscious noncoincidence.

He's a famous poet, for fuck's sake. Everything he does is intentional. The subconscious is his conscious.

He told me he'd volunteered to be a table host in order to enjoy my dinner conversation.

And he'd tucked my hair behind my ear.

But that could be fatherly. Or teacherly. We definitely have a teacher-student bond.

Which makes perfect sense given that I'm Andi Bloom, literary It Girl at Glenlake.

Bloom *as in the poem's title . . .*

~

Friday, October 18, 1996

Ian keeps asking if everything's okay.

I keep telling him I'm just stressed out with college apps, keeping up my grades, and the normal stuff.

Which is true.

I can't tell him everything feels weirdly not okay but that I'm probably just overthinking things. Things I can't even get myself to write.

Tonight, when he asked, I said, "I'm just having really bad cramps," which was also true, even if they weren't bad enough to bail on the screening

of Ferris Bueller's Day Off, *which I really wanted to see (again). "I think
I need to hang out in my room instead."*

"I'll stay with you if you want," he offered.

"Go see the movie," I said, feeling guiltier than I already did. "It's okay."

*"Are you sure?" he asked, watching the other kids file past and disappear
into the auditorium.*

"Positive," I said.

*I meant it, too, even if I'm not positive about anything else where we're
concerned.*

~

Monday, October 21, 1996

*Dallas showed up to class late, hair and eyes wilder than usual, look-
ing like he'd been up all night. Per the syllabus, we were starting a unit on
Langston Hughes.*

"I sing the body electric," he said.

*Which I assumed meant we were going to discuss Walt Whitman
instead?*

He turned to the chalkboard and began to write.

We sat in silence as a poem emerged.

> Spit your brandy in the glass
> Unsmoke your cigarette
> Lift your crumpled napkin from the plate
> And smooth it in your lap
>
> Unspeak all you've spoken
> Save that and your laughs for me
> Groom your plate with knife and fork
> And return it to your host

Drive backward down the highway
Watching the road ahead
Miss your turn deliberately
And find my driveway instead

Turn around and face me
I'll be waiting on the step

Then, looking in my direction, if not exactly making direct eye contact, he asked, "What am I trying to say here?"

I felt like every response was half-garbled and in slow motion.

"That brandy tastes terrible?" Tommy Harkins said.

"It's an acquired taste." Dallas smiled. "Get back to me about that in twenty years."

"It's kind of about being done with a meal," Lola McGeorge said.

"Metaphorically," Crystal Thomas added. "I think it's more that you're asking someone to do just the opposite of what they've been doing."

"Exactly." Dallas nodded. "Any other thoughts?"

Everyone and everything in the room felt like it had fallen away as I summoned up my courage. My voice cracked as I said, "You're asking someone to do something with you."

~

Tuesday, October 22, 1996

I really thought Ian was everything I ever wanted.

I love the way his hair flops into his face and the way he brushes it away just as quickly. I love watching him play soccer and basketball. I love that we both love Bit-O-Honey, which most everyone thinks is totally weird. I love that he's kind, considerate, dependable, and that he loves me. I love him. I really do. The thing is, I can't remember him ever making me feel as fluttery as I do now. 24-7. (If I put "fluttery" in a poem, I think Dallas's grading pen would push through the paper.)

I'm not sure I'm in love with him anymore.

Maybe I've just grown out of him. Grown up.

I don't want to lose him, but it isn't fair to leave him hanging, wondering why I'm not there for him, for us, the way I used to be. Why I'm so distracted.

I can barely sleep or eat.

It isn't fair to keep avoiding Ian, to keep reassuring him, when I can't tell him where my mind really is.

I have no other choice.

It's the right thing to do.

But what if I'm wrong?

What if I'm making up everything I think is happening?

~

Wednesday, October 23, 1996

In the early-evening darkness, I might not have recognized Dallas, leaning against a bench outside Copeland, except for the light of the bright-orange cherry and the narrow plume of smoke.

"Unsmoking your cigarette?" I asked, stopping in front of him.

Instead of answering, he took the cigarette out of his mouth, exhaled, and put it in mine.

Miss your turn deliberately.
And find my driveway instead.

~

Friday, October 25, 1996

I don't know if I'll ever get over the look of pure pain on Ian's face, how it clouded his eyes when I told him I thought we needed to take a break.

66

I've had to accept that fact, and as bad as it makes me feel, Ian does, too.
Still, I feel like I have actual rocks in my stomach.
"Why?" was all he said. "Why . . . ?"
There was no way I could tell him the truth.
I can't honestly believe it myself.
And yet it's all I've been able to think about, can think about all day long.
"It's not you," I actually said. "It's me. I need some time to be me."
How's that for the worst of all clichés?
He turned and walked away without another word.
I deserve everything he's thinking. Feeling.
And yet I have butterflies like I've never felt before.
All I can think about is Dallas.

Chapter Eight

On Sunday, after a texted goodbye to his unsentimental daughter, Ian checked himself and Andi out of the Old Road Inn and got behind the wheel to drive Andi to O'Hare. She would board a plane for the short hop to St. Louis, where his parents had been looking after the twins, and Ian would drive back on Tuesday after attending a convention in Chicago. He felt a strange sense of relief to be off campus; once they'd left Glenlake, the world beyond it seemed to be going on as usual, with no sign of the revelation that threatened to turn their world upside down.

"So should we expect further questioning from Scoop Copeland?" he asked as they flowed past Des Plaines on I-294, breaking the silence with the only thing on his mind.

Andi was watching a large flock of starlings wheel above the billboards. "When I reminded her that she promised to keep us in the loop, she told me how the phrase 'in the loop' originated years ago in Chicago."

"By the end of the semester, she'll be wearing a porkpie hat with a press card tucked in the band."

"Bantering rapid-fire, like she's in a 1930s screwball comedy."

Their own banter felt forced, and neither of them laughed. Ian wished he knew what Andi was really thinking. For his part, he kept seeing the digital photo from Wayne Kelly's class, imagining the creak of chains as the ruined Charger hung suspended from the crane on the barge, water sheeting out of its ruined floorboards and rotted door gaskets.

"And how, exactly, will she be updating us?" Ian asked as he merged onto I-190 for the final approach to O'Hare. "We know she hates calling. And Skype allows us to see where she is and what she's doing."

"I told her even texts are fine. We're just curious about that class . . . along with everything else that's going on this semester."

Along with everything else, thought Ian. It would be hard to remember to ask about cross-country or science class or the student Amnesty International organization.

After pulling up at the departures terminal, he put the car in park and hopped out to get Andi's bag from the back. As he put it next to her on the sidewalk, he straightened and met her eye. Unbidden, he remembered part of a lecture from the crusty old professor who'd taught his English composition class at Amherst.

Jealous *is one of the most misused words in the English language today, mistakenly used in place of the word* envy. *To be jealous is to guard your treasure—whether it is literal treasure or a woman you love.*

That guy, with his bushy white hair and sprouting eyebrows, had looked like a caricature of a classical composer, with pretentious diction that had students competing for the best impression around a keg. But it was funny how many of his insistent opinions had stayed with Ian.

The look on Andi's face now was one of impatience, one he'd seen in varying degrees ever since they first started dating. She was fast; he was slow. She was the one who simply ghosted when leaving a party, while he was the one who insisted on finding and thanking the host, and shaking the hands of the people he expected to see again soon.

There it was again, that word: *ghost.*

"That guy wants you to move your car," observed Andi, as an airport traffic warden rolled up on a four-wheeler.

Ian snapped out of his reverie and gave her a hug and a quick kiss. "Give my love to the kids. See you Tuesday."

"See you then," she said, picking up her bag and disappearing into the terminal.

~

Traffic was still light on the late Sunday-morning roads, and he made it downtown in near record time, finding his hotel in River North easily. His room, however, wasn't ready. Unwilling to begin his convention in the jeans and Glenlake sweatshirt he was wearing, Ian left his bags at the bell desk, bought a coffee, and made his way to the Chicago Riverwalk.

It was a cool day, and with a blustery breeze coming in off Lake Michigan, his fingers grew cold despite the steaming-hot cup in his hand. Still, he made his way west, under traffic that thumped and whizzed overhead on the drawbridges, hoping a walk would clear his head and make him more enthusiastic about the task at hand.

Global Wine and Spirit was an annual trade show for US importers, distributors, and retailers that took place each year in New York, Chicago, and San Francisco. While his head buyer would be doing the real work of tasting and ordering, Ian had found the show useful in terms of keeping up on trends, forging relationships, and sniffing out the occasional new product line for Grape and Barley, his three-location chain of high-end stores selling wine, spirits, and beer.

When he'd decided that New York and high finance were not for him, Ian had recognized right away the need for a new line of work. Idly mulling the offbeat portfolio that made up the Copeland family empire, he had thought about the dusty old wine shop called St. Louis Wine Importers, a store that hadn't changed much since the 1960s but had a killer location in Clayton. Having noticed the trend toward wine boutiques from visits to Chicago, he'd realized St. Louis was ripe for its own version—and he'd moved at just the right time, talking his dad into letting him take over the shop and give it a complete remodel and rebranding.

With his business empire now comprising three locations and seventy employees, he was well on his way. He'd even allowed himself to look at a few property listings in Kansas City.

There was just one problem: the two new stores were new buildings, and building costs had exceeded estimates, and he wasn't profitable. He should have been—he *would* be—but this was a pinch year.

A late-season tour boat glided by on the river, a guide's amplified voice telling the dozen passengers huddled on deck to crane their necks and appreciate one of the skyscrapers towering above them. Ian complied, not sure which one he was supposed to be looking at. He had taken the tour Cassidy's freshman year and had enjoyed but forgotten most of what he'd learned. The end of his nose growing cold, he decided to walk to the next bridge and turn back.

Desperate wasn't the word for it. Copelands never felt desperate. But he was concerned. Ian didn't want to go to his dad for cash because the old man's reserves weren't what they had been, not to mention that he'd already fronted a fair amount of money for store number three. Which was why he'd swallowed hard and hit Andi's dad, Simon, up for a short-term loan of $350,000.

Without telling Andi, who'd flat out said no when he floated the idea.

She had recently made investments of her own in Blooming Books, her publishing company, moving to new offices with storefront retail near the wine shop in Clayton. Some of the money had been a small-business loan, but most had come from Simon; even though there was plenty more where that came from, Andi's pride had overruled asking for more.

"Find it somewhere else, Ian," she told him. "We owe him enough already, and there's a limit to how much I want him in our lives."

Andi's relationship with her father had always been something of a mystery to Ian, a complicated history that began with her mom's death from cancer when Andi was in second grade and peaked with her dad's decision to pack her off to Glenlake. They could go weeks without speaking, and Andi could refer to Simon with a dismissiveness that would have seemed coldhearted and unthinkable even in Ian's admittedly not warm-and-cuddly family. But when they were together, Andi acted perfectly comfortable with him. Loving even, at least when Andi's stepmom, Lorraine, wasn't in the room. Their own kids had long ago gotten used to the fact that their half aunts, Sage and Savannah, seemed more like big sisters, and everyone had learned to politely ignore Lorraine's vapidity. Everyone except Andi, to whom Lorraine's every breath must have seemed like a betrayal.

Ian had always chalked up his lack of understanding to inexperience with complicated family dynamics. His parents may not have been demonstratively affectionate toward each other, but they had always been together, always been there.

Every other difference—from the way Simon bragged about big-money deals to the way family dynamics were discussed with family members present—he attributed to California.

Ian turned around and headed back, now into the wind. He tossed his half-empty coffee into a trash can so he could jam both hands into his pockets.

Did he like Simon? He found him interesting, maybe even fascinating. In some respects, Simon lived up to every stereotype he had of a Hollywood mover and shaker, even if Simon's role didn't quite allow him to tread the red carpet. After doing different jobs on smaller movies as a young man—driver, carpenter, assistant location manager—and then going back to school to get a degree in accounting, he'd become a film accountant and eventually a line producer who'd worked on dozens of films. Only one Oscar-nominated film (the Simon Bloom oeuvre tended toward modestly budgeted action films starring just-past-their-prime

A-listers) and only one smash hit (for which he'd wangled a producer credit and profit participation), but it all amounted to a steady and highly lucrative career.

Visits to LA felt to Ian like visits to a film set of a movie about Hollywood life: late breakfasts; egg-white omelets; eighteen-dollar smoothies with chia, acai, and other ingredients that never graced the Copeland kitchen; and lots and lots of name-dropping. Despite his public reputation as a ruthless operator, Simon seemed to genuinely like kids and had doted on Cassidy, Whitney, and Owen, making it harder for Ian to square Andi's father issues with reality.

Then again, it was always easier one generation removed.

Ian was too leveraged for another bank loan, so Simon had been his only choice. He'd made the request for cash in person, telling Andi he was going to LA to see a supplier he could have simply emailed. As the day neared, Ian felt himself getting nervous. His own father would have made it a formal affair of state, with a lecture in the study, a silent and careful writing of an actual paper check, followed by a glass of Scotch and a stern admonition to *Be careful.*

If he'd still had that kind of cash. The Copeland fortune had been divested from railroads and invested in real estate at exactly the wrong moments. There was still enough money in blue-chip stocks to keep everyone comfortable and pay the dues at various clubs, but the days of six- and seven-figure endowments and investments were over.

Simon had been more casual. He'd chuckled and said, "Is that all?" when he heard the amount—stopping Ian's heart for a moment—before suggesting that "our people" could exchange data and handle the transfer electronically. He'd taken Ian to lunch for a truly horrifically sized pastrami sandwich (*Only once a week, or my doctor doubles my treadmill time*) before Ian headed back to the airport, and all in all, it had seemed a genuinely amicable affair, with only one exception.

As he dabbed his lips with a napkin, Simon casually lobbed the big question: "I presume Andi is on board with this?"

Ian answered using the words he'd carefully rehearsed: "I'd appreciate if we could keep it between the two of us."

Simon nodded thoughtfully, dropped his napkin on his plate, and added one more term to their agreement, "just to prove we're both serious men." If Ian failed to make repayment within a year, Simon would take a 20 percent ownership stake in Grape and Barley Incorporated, cementing his role in Ian and Andi's future indefinitely. Timing was everything, and Simon was a shrewd negotiator: After saying yes, how do you say no?

He tried not to think about the way Andi called Simon a "gangster" and joked about the bodies buried in his Bel Air backyard.

Reentering the hotel lobby, Ian checked in at the front desk, where the clerk assured him his room was almost ready. He found a secluded chair and checked his phone. On Facebook, Andi had shared a few pictures of parents' weekend while waiting for her plane to take off. The captions, needless to say, didn't mention anything about dead poets in submerged muscle cars.

Catching up with fave high school teacher Mrs. Henry!

Father vs daughter stickball. Which team won? I'll never tell.

Another great parents' weekend at Glenlake.

His sense of cognitive dissonance only deepened: Was he relieved by her posts' lightheartedness or disturbed that she hadn't made a single mention of the big mystery on campus?

Finally, his phone pinged with a text that his room was ready. He collected his bags from the bellman and took the elevator to the twelfth floor and a room with a sliver of a view of the river where he'd been walking. After changing quickly into slacks, a dress shirt, and a sport coat, he palmed a small stack of business cards and headed back downstairs. He hung the badge around his neck, took a deep breath, and put on his game face before entering the exhibit hall.

As a smaller, regional show, GWS didn't have the range of some, but exhibitors still hawked everything from boutique and mass-produced wines and spirits to stemware, cocktail napkins, bottle openers, wine savers, insulators, toothpicks, olives and cherries, custom T-shirts and aprons, and more. Ian ignored all of them, making a beeline for his newest supplier.

He found Preston Brandt in a small booth where a modest sign on the pipe and drape identified his eponymous company: THE BRANDT GROUP: VINTAGE AND COLLECTIBLE SPIRITS. Trying to capitalize on the next hot trend, Ian had taken a flier and laid in quite a bit of the unique stock, despite a high up-front cost. The only problem was, for some reason, his customers weren't really biting.

Preston, busy arranging a museum-worthy selection of amari, herbal liqueurs, vermouth, rum, vodka, gin, and whiskey, saw him coming.

"How are things in St. Louis?" said Preston as they shook hands.

"They could be better, which is part of the reason I'm here," said Ian. "Your stuff looks terrific in my stores, and my sales team tells me the bottles are great conversation starters, but unfortunately, it's just not moving."

Preston raised his eyebrows. "I'm surprised to hear that. We're doing real business here in Chicago, not to mention New York, San Francisco, and Seattle. Some of the craft cocktail bars are buying from us and paying top dollar—it's not like you can get a bourbon bottled sixty years ago wholesale."

"Our bar scene is still catching up, but I should have plenty of well-heeled customers who are looking for a showy bottle."

"And you've got it displayed prominently?"

"Right up front in the locked cases with high-end Scotch and cigars."

Preston pondered a moment and then said, "Close your eyes."

Puzzled, Ian did as he was told. He heard a bottle's neck tap the rim of a glass and then a single glug as something was poured.

"Open," said Preston, handing him a crystal tumbler with a pinkie finger of amber liquid. "And drink. I guarantee you've never had anything like it."

Ian lifted the glass to his lips and drank. It was bourbon, but not one of the smooth, ultra-aged single barrels that were currently so popular. It tasted familiar, but he couldn't place it. And, if he was being honest with himself, it was just okay.

"What is it?" he asked.

"Old Forester. 1953."

Ian suppressed a chuckle. "That tumbler looks like something from my grandparents' bar."

With a flourish, Preston produced the bottle and set it down on the counter so Ian could see for himself the vintage label and original price tag. "You sell these bottles one at a time, and all the details matter. They make better bourbons today, but you're not selling them the best bourbon. You're selling an experience: drinking as time machine. The buyer gets to taste it the way it tasted back then."

Sipping again, Ian had to admit that seeing the old bottle sparked his imagination in a way that the blind tasting had not.

"People are paying hundreds of dollars for a single cocktail made with all-vintage pours. This stuff is by definition *limited edition*. There's more of it around than you'd think, but the prices aren't going to get any lower."

"So, basically, you're saying it's a training issue," said Ian.

"I'd be happy to schedule a session with your team the next time I'm in St. Louis," said Preston. He grabbed a tumbler and poured himself a splash of the Old Forester. "I'll come to you and work with your staff. Selling is selling. At some point you gotta grind it out."

Ian knew the man had a point. But the clock was ticking on Simon's loan. Just how long would the grind take? And how long could he keep his financial struggles secret from Andi?

For as long as she'd kept her secret from him?

"Sounds like a plan. I'll show you my stores, and we can do dinner," said Ian.

"Perfect," said Preston as they clinked glasses. "Here's to meeting you in St. Louis!"

Chapter Nine

"I can't believe Dallas Walker's body was in his *car* at the bottom of Lake Loomis this whole time!" Georgina exclaimed, missing the exit from Lambert Field toward I-70, easy enough to do even if she were looking at the road and not incredulously at Andi.

Georgina had offered days ago to pick Andi up, saying she had a home-shopping client to see in the Central West End, anyway. Translation: she wanted the freshest gossip from Glenlake. Andi couldn't have canceled without giving her a full report over the phone *and* trying to explain why she preferred to take an Uber.

"Shocking. Isn't it?"

"Crazy."

Somehow, Andi felt shakier than she had all weekend. She wanted to think it was due to Georgina's sharp U-turn, or the entitled way she piloted her snow-white Range Rover through traffic, but recounting everything to Georgina had made the reality of Dallas's reappearance that much more, well, real.

"How weird is it that no one spotted a submerged car for so many years?" Georgina asked, checking her coiffed strawberry-blonde hair in the rearview mirror. Her bangle bracelets, straight off the display shelf at her Ladue Road boutique, jangled as she cut off a Ford Focus. "People swim there."

"He wasn't found anywhere near the swimming area," Andi said. "It was on the other side of the lake."

"So he drove his ridiculous car off that cliff?"

"That's the working theory," Andi said, unnerved that Georgina knew that much about the wooded area.

"He was always so moody and distracted. Don't you think?"

"I guess," Andi said, the low roil in her guts bubbling to a simmer. "But this year's writer in residence and his class are spending the semester looking into it."

"Say what?" Georgina asked, fumbling for something in the center console and missing the exit for the Inner Belt. "Shit!"

"It's just as well. I-70 to Kingshighway is quicker."

"I hate going that way," she said—suburban white St. Louis code for *I'm afraid to drive through the north side and most city neighborhoods in general.*

"It'll be fine," Andi said. As much as she'd grown to love St. Louis, she still struggled with the often inscrutable, yet seemingly hardwired, socioeconomic, racial, and religious stratification that kept St. Louisans from venturing out of their various bubbles, both psychologically and physically.

"Looking into it how?"

"He's a journalist, and they're investigating what happened as some kind of project. Cassidy's actually in the class."

Georgina chuckled. "How about that for history repeating itself?"

"Meaning what?" Andi asked, trying to keep the edge out of her voice.

"Just that you took all those writer-in-residence classes yourself."

"Like mother, like daughter, I guess," Andi said with as much light-heartedness as she could muster.

Georgina applied the Bobbi Brown lipstick she'd finally wrested from the console as she exited the highway. "I assume she knows you were in Dallas's class senior year?"

"Of course," Andi said.

"Including the fact that he was quite the hottie?" Georgina asked, sounding like the seventeen-year-old version of herself.

"I didn't think that little bit of information was necessary," Andi said, shifting uncomfortably in her seat. "Did you really think he was hot?"

"Didn't you?" Georgina asked.

"I wasn't the one who flirted with him all the time," Andi said, feeling the words catch in her throat.

"I flirted with everyone back then," Georgina said. "Thank goodness you played matchmaker for me when you did. If you hadn't, who knows how much wilder I would have been?"

Georgina lived the good life with her successful lawyer hubby and their passel of ginger-haired kids. Andi had set it all in motion. She'd sown the seeds for Georgina to get together with Tommy Harkins during senior year by pointing out that he was always stealing glances at her during poetry class. She'd fixed Georgina up again in college when she came down from Trinity for a weekend visit. William was a cute, smart fraternity brother of Ian's with a weakness for sassy redheads. Georgina had a weakness for cute guys.

Just as Andi expected, it was love at first sight.

"What does Cassidy think about our once-beloved Dallas?" Georgina asked.

"*Beloved?* Speak for yourself," Andi forced herself to say, giving her a playful punch on the shoulder. "You and he never . . . ?"

"For god's sake," Georgina said. "He was our teacher."

"Our *hottie* of a teacher," Andi added, copying Georgina's tone.

"So you admit you had a huge crush on him, too."

"I—"

"Don't try to tell me you didn't stare at him like a lovesick cow from the beginning of class until he . . ."

Disappeared. The unsaid word hung in the air between them.

"I'm not sure how you noticed, given how busy you were having the world's stormiest relationship with Tommy." Knowing she had to say something to divert Georgina from going *there*, she added: "And, by the way, I saw him at parents' weekend. He goes by Tom now."

"Seriously?" Georgina's voice increased by an octave. "How does he look?"

"Like he's definitely not the one who got away."

"Too bad, so sad," said Georgina breezily. "So back to your school-girl crush on Dallas—"

"Georgina, stop it. The man's dead. It's a tragedy."

"I just remember wondering if you broke up with Ian because you were hoping Dallas would notice you."

"Hardly," Andi forced herself to say. "I decided I was too mature for him and felt impatient, smothered by his high school–boy nonsense." She laughed as they turned into Portland Place. "That damn poetry class had me thinking I knew everything."

"Little did we know we knew nothing then," Georgina said with uncharacteristic poetry as they pulled up to the house. Back then, Andi would have laughed had someone told her that despite being from Beverly Hills, her adult self would be continually awed by the grandeur and sheer beauty of her 1904 World's Fair–era limestone mansion. She felt relieved to be home, away from Glenlake. Just the opposite of how she'd felt as a girl.

"Too bad Sylvie dropped off the grid," Georgina said.

"Or you'd already be on the phone with her?"

"Pretty much," Georgina said with a sly smile. "It's too interesting a story to keep to myself. With all those wacky theories about what happened to him, can you believe he was right there all along?"

As Georgina finally unlocked the car doors, Andi replayed the conversation she'd had during the stickball game with Mrs. Henry, who had been her favorite teacher and dorm mom, and the only one who'd ever come close to filling the hole where her real mom was supposed to be. She was now the grandmotherly head of the English Department.

I know this is going to sound bad, Mrs. Henry had said with a sigh. *But we wouldn't have cared about Dallas at all if he drove away and lived his life, so I don't know why we're making such a fuss now. The visiting writers are good for the school, but they've always been more trouble than they're worth.*

～

"Welcome home!" Biz said, greeting Andi in the foyer with the lukewarm hug she had long ago learned was her mother-in-law's bony equivalent of the bosomy embraces given by her Jewish relatives.

Biz and Georgina greeted each other with polite air-kisses and an even lighter embrace while Rusty, the family's middle-aged Irish setter, startled Andi by wetly licking her fingers before she could pull her hand away.

"Wonderful to see you," Biz and Georgina told each other, practically in unison, followed by the expected "You're looking well."

"You were so sweet to fetch Andi from the airport," Biz continued, smoothing her silky gray hair as if buoyed by the obligatory compliment. "I called for pizza from this charming little place off Euclid, and it was just delivered. Will you stay for lunch, Georgina?"

Andi knew her mother-in-law didn't actually mean it. She habitually ordered a bit less than enough, even without accounting for a guest, but would never be so impolite as to not extend an invitation.

"Sounds delicious, but I have a trunkful of clothing I have to bring over to a client," Georgina said, raised well enough that she'd never dream of imposing.

Possibly having smelled the pizza, the twins came bounding down the stairs, looking, however improbably, taller than when Andi had left on Friday. They were trailed by their slightly out-of-breath but still handsome grandfather, whom Owen took after. Whitney, with her straight light-brown hair and elegant posture, was already a dead ringer for a teenage Biz.

"I always forget what a trek it is from the third floor," Cope said, absentmindedly carrying a Ping-Pong paddle and waiting for Whitney and Owen to hug Andi before greeting her himself.

"Can you imagine how hot and sweaty it would have been to *dance* up there, back in the day?" Georgina asked.

Once ballrooms, the big open areas that spanned the top floor of most of the grand old homes in the neighborhood had long ago been transitioned into studies, art studios, or rec rooms—primarily due to the impracticality of throwing a big party two stories above the kitchen. That, and the inability to properly cool or heat such a large, drafty room in what was effectively the attic.

"It's always been a perfect space for the young people to be with their friends," Biz said politely but dismissively, letting Georgina know she'd uttered the definitive word on the subject.

Andi was less concerned about Georgina's opinion of the third floor than the too-grown-up side-eyes and smiles Owen and Whitney exchanged. There was little chance they wouldn't get into Glenlake, but given Owen's predilection for boyish risk-taking and Whitney's budding beauty and popularity, she shuddered at the possibility of having to play third-floor parent patrol throughout high school parties.

"Cassidy says hi to everyone," she said, trying not to get ahead of herself.

"How was the weekend?" Biz asked.

"And how's that writing center coming along?" Cope added, speaking over her. He'd finally resigned from the board of trustees just as the fundraising campaign for the newest campus building was getting underway.

"Of course it was great to spend time with Cassidy, and the writing center is nearing completion, which is just going to make the campus that much more—"

"Get to the interesting part!" Georgina interrupted.

"There's an interesting part?" Owen asked sarcastically.

Whitney raised her eyebrows. "Is it about Cassidy?"

"Not exactly," Andi said.

"They found—" Georgina blurted, before thinking better of it. "Sorry. It's your news."

"It's no one's news, exactly," Andi stated. "Do you remember Dallas Walker?"

"Familiar name," Cope said as though leafing through a mental file of everyone he'd ever known. "Wasn't he one of the writers in residence way back when?"

"They found his car in Lake Loomis early last week. With human remains inside."

"He's *dead*?" asked Biz sharply, with a quick glance at Cope.

"They think it's him, but they still have to make sure," Andi said.

"That's freaky," Whitney said.

"Even more freaky is the fact that your mom and I knew the dead guy," Georgina told her. "He was our poetry teacher when we were seniors."

"He disappeared in the middle of the year," Cope said, nodding with the memory. "That was quite the headache."

"Wait a minute," Biz said, waving her hands. "Back up. He was found . . . *in the lake*?"

"By a group of students attempting to revive the Freshman Plunge," said Andi.

"Things like this don't happen at *Glenlake*," muttered her mother-in-law.

"And all this time we thought he'd just taken off somewhere," added Georgina. "I mean, he seemed like the kind of guy who might do that."

"So cool," Owen said, visibly excited by the prospect of a body and a mystery entering their lives. "I can't wait to be at Glenlake."

"Speaking of 'cool,' I'm afraid I'm going to have to reheat the pizza," Biz said.

"And I should go," Georgina said, pulling her phone from her purse along with her keys.

As soon as they'd said their goodbyes and thank-yous, and the door was firmly closed behind Georgina, Biz rolled her eyes. "That girl is just like her mother. She's going to be on the horn with every single person who's ever gone to Glenlake by the time she gets home. Thank goodness they didn't have cell phones back then."

It was true. Fortunately, while Georgina could be trusted to broadcast any and all information that was dropped in her lap, she wasn't any more intellectually curious now than she had been back then.

Which was something Andi could use to her advantage.

Hopefully, she wouldn't have to.

Chapter Ten

"Quiet and don't move," Cassidy admonished Tate in a mock-scolding voice, worried as she did that she sounded like a schoolmarm.

"Yes, ma'am," he said, confirming her fears in that honeyed Georgia drawl that had sounded so stupid in ninth grade but was sounding sexier every day.

Cassidy flipped open her laptop and launched Skype. Mom was online, so she initiated a video call.

Tate wiggled his big toe in the hollow of her knee and nearly made her drop the laptop just as Mom's face filled the screen, eyes a little unfocused, suggesting she couldn't quite see her yet. Cassidy composed herself just before their eyes met.

"Hi, Mom!" Chipper, cheery Girl Wonder at Boarding School.

Tate rolled his eyes. Cassidy tunneled her vision. Mom was at the breakfast bar in the kitchen, her large evening glass of wine not quite out of frame. Parents' weekend had been only two weeks ago, but she looked older. More tired, anyway.

"Hi, honey. How was your day?" Then, without waiting for an answer, she lifted her head and called offscreen, "Ian! It's Cassidy!"

They made out-of-sync niceties for a few seconds until Dad showed up, standing a couple of steps behind Mom, his face shadowed in the dimly lit kitchen.

"Hi, Cassidy."

"I'm calling about the Mystery of the Waterlogged Poet," she said. "It's now officially part of my homework."

"Great," both of them said in slightly offbeat Skype unison.

Mom slugged wine. "*Is* it a mystery?"

"It's an investigation. Mr. Kelly said the Lake County Sheriff's Office is 'working the case.' He's hoping to get one of the detectives to visit our class to talk about it."

For a moment, neither of her parents moved, making Cassidy think the stream was frozen.

"I was wondering if you could tell me more about what Dallas Walker was like. I mean, if he didn't go missing until two-thirds of the way through the school year, and you guys both had stuff with him, you must have known him pretty well, right?"

Tate looked up from his own laptop to mouth, *Smoooth*.

Yes, it was an abrupt transition, but she figured they'd had some time to process and remember since she'd first questioned them at brunch. Besides, Mr. Kelly had told the class that reporters elicited the best answers when they avoided beating around the bush and got right to business before their subjects had time to prepare. Since she didn't have any real subjects, and her parents were her only sources of firsthand information, she might as well practice, right?

"So what was he really like, Mom? Dallas Walker. Did he seem depressed?"

Another drink of wine, like Mom was somehow pissed about this whole conversation, even though she'd asked for updates. Tate shifted his position slowly, totally on purpose.

She might have been imagining it, but Mom moved forward ever so slightly, as if she'd been nudged from behind.

"I'm not sure how a student would really know that about her teacher," she finally said. "I do remember something he once said in class, early in the year: the thing that scared him the most was the future. Not that he ever acted like it."

"Can you think of anyone who might know that about him?" Cassidy asked.

"No," Mom said flatly.

Dad thought about it. "No. Although it kind of seemed like he lived a double life—or at least wanted to. When he took the Cue Sports Society to a roadhouse, which was totally inappropriate, I thought he seemed disappointed there weren't more of his low-life friends around so he could introduce us."

Mom took another drink of wine while Cassidy pictured Dad as a teenager in a bar and tried to think of a follow-up question. But he saved her the trouble.

"You know, I didn't put this together until just recently, but there's actually a guy on campus, a maintenance worker, who used to run with that crowd and was there that day. He clearly knew Dallas."

"What was his name?" asked Cassidy.

"I can't remember, but he does have a distinctive tattoo on his neck—a snake or something."

Mom turned around, looked at Dad, and said something the microphone didn't pick up.

"I was as surprised as anybody to see him working there," Dad told her.

Cassidy felt a tug on her right foot and glanced up. Tate was slowly pulling her sock off. She wanted to mouth *no*, to shake her head, but could only sit helplessly as the fibers slowly dragged across her extremely ticklish sole.

"Is someone else in the room, Cassidy?" asked Mom. Of course.

"Nope," she lied quickly. "Dad, do you suspect this guy of anything?"

"I think that's a job for the sheriff's department, not me," said Dad, who had disappeared offscreen. The fridge door sucked shut as he returned with a bottle of beer that required him to then hunt for an opener.

The sock was off. *Quit it,* she willed Tate telepathically, a message that obviously didn't get through since he started slowly removing the sock from her left foot.

She wasn't going to be able to keep this up much longer.

"Actually, most of the class thinks it's murder," she blurted, watching her parents carefully as Tate melodramatically mouthed the word *MURDER!*

Dad swigged his beer, and Mom fingered the rim of her glass before saying, "That's an awfully serious conclusion to jump to, isn't it?"

"God, Mom, it's not like our opinions are legally binding or anything. Mr. Kelly's just teaching us how to report and how to think critically."

"And what does Mr. Kelly think?"

"He won't tell us, but he says if the police are looking into it, it's well worth a look by us, too."

"That sounds professional, at least," said Dad.

"He said you should never assume foul play. But he also said it's okay to have a hypothesis. And if our hypothesis is that it's murder, we should look for evidence to disprove it, not confirm it. If we *can't* disprove it, that's when we'll know we're onto something."

"Moving on from this sordid subject," said Mom. "How are you coming with recommendation letters? Have you asked Mrs. Henry?"

She really had to end the call. Tate was, ever so slowly, starting to rub her feet. It tickled *and* made her want to make out before her roommates came back and Mrs. Stout, the housemother, told him to clear out.

"Great and yes, Mom," Cassidy said. "Look, I gotta turn in. We're running six miles in the morning."

She ended the call before Tate could hear their *I love yous.* After closing the laptop, she shoved it aside and climbed on top of him, kissing him hard and wondering just how many minutes they had alone.

Being turned on didn't stop her from making a mental note to type up her parents' comments from the call. Or from looking forward to telling the class that they now had their first suspect in the case.

Chapter Eleven

ANDI BLOOM'S GLENLAKE JOURNAL

Saturday, October 26, 1996

The light on his front porch was off, but I could see him through the living room window as he sat on his couch, strumming his guitar. I could hear him singing Leonard Cohen's "Suzanne" while I stood in the cold dark, working up my courage to knock on his door.

I was utterly silent, and he couldn't possibly see me from where I stood, but he looked up and out the window.

As if he knew I was there?

Or was hoping I would be?

My pounding heart froze as he leaned the guitar against the couch and stood up.

As his footsteps approached, I raised my knuckles to the door.

He opened it before I managed to knock.

"You're here," he said.

I nodded.

He scanned the darkness I'd worn like a cloak as I rushed away from the dorm, telling Georgina I was going to the library for a physics study session so she wouldn't offer to tag along. I'd made my way across campus to Evans Circle—and the six houses that made up the faculty cottages. I knew the writer-in-residence cottage was set off from the others, so I went through the woods toward a single light. The relief I felt at spotting his Dodge Charger in the driveway was quickly replaced by a much larger, all-encompassing panic.

What the fuck was I doing?

"No one saw me," I said.

"Cool," he said, stepping aside and shutting the door behind me.

The cottage smelled musty, and the furniture was way more old-fashioned than I'd imagined. I'd pictured something Spartan but strewn with piles of manuscripts and dog-eared poetry books. But there was no evidence of his work in the living room. An afghan was draped over the checked couch, and a framed cross-stitch proclaimed, Home Is Where the Hearth Is.

"It came furnished," he said, reading my mind.

"I broke up with Ian," I blurted out.

"I'm sorry for him," he said. "But I'm afraid it was inevitable."

"I'm seventeen," I said.

"And more mature than almost anyone I know."

"Maybe so. But—"

"But I can't stop thinking about you," he said. "Haven't been able to since you first stepped into my classroom."

"We really shouldn't . . ."

"You're here."

"Yes," I said.

And then I leaned in and kissed him.

～

Andi felt dazed as she closed the laptop, drained her glass of wine, and crossed the kitchen for a refill. "A police investigation . . ."

"They pulled a body out of a lake," Ian said, reaching for his beer. "What do you expect?"

"I don't know, but does our daughter have to be part of it?"

"Wayne Kelly's journalism class has no legal standing."

"That's not the point," she said, noticing that her wine bottle, vacuum sealed to last several days, was down to the dregs. She grabbed a fresh chardonnay from the wine fridge and brought it to the sideboard. "I feel like she's playing detective, not journalist."

She started removing the foil from the bottle with the tip of the corkscrew.

"Use the foil cutter," Ian said.

"I'll be fine. I don't feel like looking for it."

"It's in the drawer next to you."

She ignored him, stabbing upward, snagging the tip before changing direction, and wiggling the curly dagger through the red seal and pushing downward, toward the hand holding the bottle.

"Andi—" he warned sharply.

Too late. She saw the corkscrew puncture the flesh between her thumb and forefinger a moment before she felt it.

"Fuck!"

She raised her left hand to her mouth before heading to the sink and running cold water over the wound. "Just don't say anything."

He didn't. Being careful to keep his expression neutral, Ian rose from his seat, wiped the tip of the corkscrew on a paper towel, located the foil cutter, and finished the job, opening the bottle with a muted pop. He gave her a careful pour and slid the glass over while she applied pressure with a paper towel.

"Why did you have to bring up that guy with the tattoo?" Andi asked.

"Is there some reason I shouldn't have?"

A reason she could never say.

"It's just that Dallas Walker is dead, and no amount of speculation is going to bring him back." After examining her cut and throwing away the towel, Andi lifted the glass. "If we start dragging other people into it, who knows where it will end?"

"How do you feel, knowing he's dead?" Ian asked, watching her carefully.

Another good question she couldn't answer. She certainly didn't feel closure. She'd achieved that as soon as Dallas was gone. There were few questions at the time, and no one out there looking for answers. Now that he'd been found, everyone seemed to want to know the whys and hows. Everyone, it seemed, but her.

"It doesn't matter whether I think Dallas was a genius or the world was better off the minute he disappeared. But we can't encourage Cassidy."

"Andi, murder doesn't happen—"

"At a place like Glenlake?"

"Well, what does happen at a place like Glenlake?" he asked.

It was as if his eyes were asking a question of their own. But he couldn't know, could he?

"Nothing happens anywhere," she said. "Until it does."

Chapter Twelve

Ian Copeland's Glenlake Journal

Monday, October 28, 1996
"I need some time to be me" isn't much of a fucking reason.

~

The trustee was panting when he picked up the phone, little gasps that reminded Ian of a terrier he'd had when he was a boy. It was weirdly intimate and made him wish he hadn't called.

"Gerald—" Pant. "Matheson."

"This is Ian Copeland. Did I catch you at a bad time?"

A chuckle, interrupted by a pause for breath. "No, I'm sorry. Damn treadmill. Apparently five miles an hour at a slight incline is enough to redline me these days."

Ian made what he hoped were appropriately sympathetic noises and waited for Matheson to catch his breath. Finally, he did.

"I think I was too tired to properly express my surprise: Ian Copeland! What a pleasure it is to hear from you."

Ian rotated slowly in his office chair, eyeing the partially open door and wondering whether he should have pushed it closed before starting the call. The last time he'd seen Andi, though, she'd been in the kitchen, eating a salad and scrolling on her phone.

How to ease into it? He had no idea, so he went for the abrupt transition: "The past suddenly seems to be very present at Glenlake."

Too oblique. The moment's silence on Matheson's end confirmed it, but the former assistant head of the school picked up the thread.

"Oh, you mean the unfortunate . . . discovery . . . of Dallas Walker."

"I'm guessing there have been some interesting conversations between the administration and the board."

Matheson barked a laugh. "You always were a sharp pupil."

"You're remembering my wife," said Ian before he could think better of it.

"I remember both of you very well."

Ian turned back to the window and watched the wind shake the bare branches of the big elm tree at the side of the house. A few withered leaves gusted up while sparse, dry-looking snowflakes whirled down.

"Our daughter Cassidy is in the writer in residence's journalism seminar."

There was another, longer pause, and when Matheson resumed, his voice had a cadence that made Ian think he'd been fiddling with the controls on his treadmill and was now striding along. Three miles per hour, no incline.

"Wayne Kelly is every bit as brilliant as advertised. The subject of his course caught the entire school by surprise. The lesson plans he shared said nothing about investigating a death."

"To be fair, he couldn't have known."

"To be fair, he didn't have to take it upon himself to involve his students. What does your daughter think of all this?"

"She loves it. Feels like she's a real-life journalist. Kelly struck me as charismatic, so I'm guessing her classmates feel similarly."

Matheson was definitely walking again. His words came almost on the downbeat. "Well, between you and me, Ian, the headmaster—with the full support of the board—asked Kelly to put an end to this ridiculous investigation. Everyone on the board believes the death was surely a suicide or some kind of freak accident, and the detective assigned to the case, Gavras, has indicated he feels the same way."

"And how did Kelly take it?"

"He *refused*. Refused!"

"Can he do that?"

"Well, the school could certainly fire him, but—"

"But then you'd have double the headlines."

Had he heard a creak in the hall? Seen movement reflected in the window? Ian turned in the chair, but the doorway was empty.

"Kelly assured us he isn't trying to stir things up and that he personally believes there was no foul play. He says he's using this incident to teach proper techniques of investigative journalism because 'it has the students' full attention.'"

"It certainly does."

"And with phones and screens and everything else, I suppose attention is harder to come by these days," said Matheson, panting between words.

Slowly, so his chair wouldn't creak, Ian stood and crossed the rug to the doorway and looked out. He didn't see Andi or anyone else. He quietly closed the door.

"You've been worried about this, too?" asked Matheson.

"I just wouldn't want Glenlake's name to be dragged through the mud," said Ian.

"With all the Copelands have given the school, financially and otherwise, I imagine that name must feel synonymous with yours."

"That's exactly right," Ian murmured, even if his motivation had little to do with his family's name. All he wanted—all he had ever wanted—was to protect Andi.

"Well, don't worry," said Matheson. "I know you realize everything I've said is in confidence, but we're keeping a close eye on the situation, believe me. I wouldn't want you or your lovely wife to worry. The last thing we need is a character like Dallas Walker coming back to haunt us."

Chapter Thirteen

Thursday, October 31, 1996

Well, Halloween was awkward.

Ian won't speak to me. Even if he would, I can't answer the only question he really wants answered. The question in his eyes: Why?

Despite the agony of pretending everything's normal when my whole world's been overturned, my only question is, When? When will Dallas and I be alone together again? It's been nearly a week. A week of watching him teach without hearing a single word he says. A week of reliving every second of kissing and touching. Not knowing what's going on between us is killing me.

I think Ian expected me to wear my half of the Winona Ryder–Johnny Depp costume we'd planned together. He showed up at dinner sporting the gelled hair and fake tattoos. He looked disappointed, at least for the split second he deigned to look at me, when he saw me dressed as Sylvia Plath instead. Not that he or anyone seemed to know who I was. Since I didn't have the time or inclination to fashion an oven out of a cardboard box and wear it over my head, I basically looked like a typical 1950s coed.

When people guessed, "Glenlake class of '52?" I just smiled and nodded.

Costume aside, I was mortified at participating in the Glenlake "tradition" of trick-or-treating our way across campus, but no one skips Halloween unless they're on their deathbed. We—as in me, Crystal Thomas, Georgina, and Tommy Harkins (they got together two weeks ago and are now not only inseparable but dressed as Tommy Lee and Pamela Anderson)—started at the headmaster's mansion, where tacky Mrs. Darrow, dressed as a sexy nurse (big surprise!), gave out Hershey's Kisses. We went on to the apartments of the various dorm parents. With every ring of a doorbell, my heart began to thump harder. By the time we reached Evans Circle and the faculty cottages, I could hardly breathe.

Luckily, the others were oblivious to the fact that my legs were shaking as we trudged down the driveway to cottage number three. Tommy rang the tinny bell before I could catch my breath, much less gird myself for feeling like an idiot girl trick-or-treating at . . .

"Happy Halloween," Crystal, Georgina, and Tommy said in unison.

I couldn't get the words out.

Dallas looked us over and smiled wryly. "Interesting juxtaposition."

"We're Tommy and Pamela," Georgina said with a wink, like she had at practically every other teacher's door.

"Accompanied by the Cowardly Lion and their best pal, the literary lioness Sylvia Plath. Tragically deceased."

"You recognized the costume," I said, my body relaxing ever so slightly.

"I bet she submitted a hell of a poem on her Smith application," he said, setting the bowl in his hand on the table by the door. "Hang on. This crap is for the regular students."

Dallas stepped away and returned with four full-size European candy bars.

"Awesome," Tommy said as Dallas dropped a Caramilk into Crystal's bag and Cadbury Flakes into both his and Georgina's.

"Only the best for Glenlake's best," he said.

"Thanks, Dallas," both Crystal and Georgina said.

"My pleasure," he said, dropping a Toblerone into my pillowcase.

"Thank you," I managed to say.

"Enjoy," he said, and I wanted him to wink or brush my hand even though I knew he was smarter than that.

"He seems smaller out of the classroom, older somehow," Crystal said as soon as the door closed and we headed back down the driveway. "I don't really get what the fuss is all about."

"Me either," I added, glad that Georgina was too absorbed in Tommy to weigh in.

Then I saw Ian coming toward us with his gang and a few girls, including a very giggly Sylvie.

He pretended to be so deep in conversation with her that he didn't notice me as they headed toward Dallas's door.

"You okay?" Crystal asked.

"Fine," I said, feeling better and worse than I ever had.

"Sylvie's having a particularly challenging Halloween," Georgina said. "I mean, now that I'm with Tommy, she's been kind of at loose ends. And then there are her eating issues and everything."

"Georgina!" I said. "You shouldn't—"

"She has eating issues?" Crystal asked.

"Bulimia," Georgina whispered. "But don't tell anyone."

I shook my head, but even though I'd like to think I'm a better person than that, I didn't totally hate that she was talking shit about Sylvie. Not that I'm worried, because Ian would never be into her, but the way she was hanging on him, it looked like she was totally going in for the kill.

When we reached the gym, the Halloween party was in full swing, complete with party games and a DJ to drown out further gossip from Georgina.

Crystal went off to the bathroom, and Georgina and Tommy decided to dance.

I had no interest in hanging around the edges of the party, fielding random questions about my breakup with Ian, but I had to stay long enough to duck out without raising any eyebrows. To pass the time, I rifled through my pillowcase, pulling out the Toblerone—the only candy that held any *particular appeal. Back home, I'd have thrown it out upon discovering that the top of the triangular cardboard box opened a little too easily. Since I knew exactly where it had come from, however, I turned it over and slid out the foil-wrapped chocolate.*

A small piece of paper slipped out with it.

Checking to make sure no one had noticed, I unfolded the note.

Saturday. 12:30. Our spot. Rain or shine.

Chapter Fourteen

"Hannah Chang? What have you got?"

Mr. Kelly was at the front of the room, ass half-parked on the corner of the desk in that way of his, ready to lunge over to the whiteboard and make more notes in his weird, backward-slanting handwriting. A tattered cardboard pumpkin had been pinned to the bulletin board in acknowledgment of Halloween, but Cassidy guessed it had been put there by someone else in the English Department.

Hannah opened her steno pad—they were all using steno pads now, like real reporters—and flipped through her notes.

"I visited Mrs. Franti in Records, who asked why a student would need a record of every Glenlake Academy employee who worked here during the 1996–97 school year."

"A good investigative reporter often gathers a hundred times more information than needed," said Mr. Kelly, "because they don't always know what they're looking for until they find it. Did she give you the records?"

"She didn't want to."

"And you said?"

Hannah shook her head, like she couldn't believe her own words. "That I would file a Freedom of Information Act request if needed."

"And did that work?"

Hannah opened a folder and took out a photocopied list of names, stapled at the corner.

"Good work. We'll make a reporter out of you yet."

Cassidy raised her hand, and he nodded at her.

"Mr. Kelly? I thought you said FOIA requests were only for government records."

Her teacher slid off the desk and unfolded his arms, pacing animatedly. "You are correct, Cassidy. Hannah made an idle threat. We could not have compelled Mrs. Franti to produce those records without legal standing in this case. But if her ignorance of the law caused her to voluntarily relinquish the information . . . I'd call that damn good reporting."

Cassidy was impressed but still wanted to score a point. "But is that ethical?"

"Excellent question. Reporters must walk a fine but sharply drawn line at all times. If Hannah had misrepresented herself as an officer of the law, an officer of the court"—there was laughter from the class—"or presented other false credentials, that would have been unethical. What she did is more like one citizen saying she'd give another citizen a parking ticket: it's an empty threat."

Cassidy had to admit it: she'd never had a class like this. She'd always liked school just fine, mostly anyway, but she honestly couldn't wait to come to the journalism seminar. The other kids in class obviously felt the same way. You never knew what was going to happen, and you couldn't wait to see what did.

Most of that had to do with Mr. Kelly—she'd never had a teacher like him, either. It wasn't just that he was willing to have his students test the rules and question authority—it was the fact that he treated everyone in the class like an adult. He could be a little bit of a hard-ass, but the fact that he held people accountable just made them want to please him that much more.

Mr. Kelly returned to his position at the desk. "Hannah, get that scanned and uploaded to Google Drive if you haven't already. Tate, what have you got?"

"Well, as you know, four of us were assigned to obtain Dallas's class roster and to research any students or faculty who might have had extracurricular relationships with the deceased involving clubs or athletics."

"The deceased," repeated Mr. Kelly approvingly. "I like it."

Cassidy felt proud of her *boyfriend.*

"We have a total of sixteen names on the class roster," continued Tate.

"Have you learned anything?"

"We haven't started calling anyone yet."

Mr. Kelly sighed, rubbed his face with both hands, then stood and started pacing. "Look, I get that you are all just high school students, and you're consumed with trick-or-treating and college applications, but this is an honors seminar. You guys are supposed to be the best of the best. Show some initiative. We've got four groups, right? Group one, led by Hannah, is school records, faculty, and extracurriculars. Group two interviews the students in Walker's class—that's you, Tate. Group three is research, with Rowan in charge. I want you guys to dig deeper on what was reported at the time. Group four is captained by Felicia and will act as librarians, keeping us organized and constructing a detailed timeline that takes into account everything we've learned. Got it?"

Liz, assigned to group two, raised her hand. "Besides the obvious background stuff, what else should we be asking in the interviews?"

"Find out who was unhappy—and with whom and why. Happy people don't commit crimes. Unhappiness leads to motives. Who among the adults didn't like Walker? Which students might have had a reason to hate him?" Mr. Kelly sat down and then sprang up again just as quickly. "You're all obsessed about grades—did he flunk someone?

Did he give someone a C minus, and they couldn't get into Harvard as a result? If we can't see transcripts, we can always ask."

Tate spoke up. "One thing we have learned is that three of Walker's former students have kids who are currently enrolled at Glenlake. One of them is in this very class: Cassidy Copeland."

Everyone looked, so she gave them a royal wave.

"An interesting coincidence," Mr. Kelly said with a nod. "But a potential red flag for objectivity."

Cassidy raised her hand, feeling confident she'd interviewed her own parents more thoroughly than any other student could. "I took the initiative to interview my parents twice. Once right after the project was announced and then again the other day."

"And you felt you were able to maintain a professional distance?" asked Mr. Kelly, his smile showing that he was kidding. Probably.

"I pretended I barely knew them. It wasn't hard."

That got a laugh.

"What did you learn?"

"My mom was the one who had him, in this same room, I guess, and she seemed to like him. She said one really interesting thing—that once, in class, he told everyone that what scared him most was the future."

Heads nodded. A couple of kids scribbled in their notebooks. For the first time, Cassidy pictured Mom in this room, writing in her own notebook, looking up toward the front of the room at Dallas Walker.

Now deceased.

"What about your dad?" prompted Mr. Kelly.

"He said Dallas Walker seemed like the kind of guy who could live a double life."

"Was he basing that on anything in particular?"

"Well, apparently, Walker took the Cue Sports Society—that's what they called the pool or billiards club or whatever—to an actual bar to play pool, which is where they met some scary people. One guy in particular."

"I heard something about that." As Mr. Kelly walked to an unused whiteboard at the side of the room, Cassidy wondered if he'd heard it from her dad, and, if so, why her dad would have gone out of his way to share that. But if Mr. Kelly knew more than he was letting on, she was grateful that he was playing dumb. Having Dad involved wasn't just puzzling—it was embarrassing.

"And what was so scary about the one guy?" he continued. "Why did your father mention him?"

"Well, I guess he was this huge, tattooed biker dude, and Mr. Walker seemed to love hanging around with guys like that," said Cassidy. "But the weird part is that he works at Glenlake now."

There was an actual, audible gasp, and it gave Cassidy a rush to be the one with news that could silence a room.

"I presume he's teaching physics?" asked Mr. Kelly.

"He works on the grounds crew," said Cassidy over rising laughter.

"Well, if your class hypothesis is that Dallas Walker was murdered, at some point we need a list of suspects, even if only for the purpose of elimination. Should we add this mystery employee?"

Nods and murmurs of assent rippled around the room while Cassidy suddenly wished she could take it back. It had all seemed like fun and games, but now, watching Mr. Kelly write *MYSTERY EMPLOYEE* on the board in block capitals, idle speculation was becoming cold, hard reality.

Mr. Kelly put the cap back on the marker and dropped it in the tray. He turned around and faced the class.

"Cassidy, since you sourced our first potential suspect, how about you take the lead on what will now be group five: persons of interest."

"Okay," she said. "How do I start?"

"First, find out this man's name. Then see if you can prove him innocent."

Chapter Fifteen

ANDI BLOOM'S GLENLAKE JOURNAL

Saturday, November 2, 1996

Dallas put down his yellow legal pad and patted the space beside him. He'd put the blanket far enough back from the cliff that I wouldn't be scared, but close enough that I could still see silvery ripples on the water's surface.

"What were you working on?" I asked, sitting down.

"Poems."

"How surprising," I said. "About?"

"Man's search for meaning, the indifference of nature—the things I usually write about on sunny days." He kissed me gently.

"It killed me not to see you all week," I said.

"We saw each other every day," he said.

"It was impossible to pretend everything was normal between us."

"Agonizing. I felt like I was living for that moment every morning when I first saw your beautiful face."

"I hated not knowing when . . . if—"

He kissed me again. "Our rules have to be different."

"I know," I said.

"Then we both already know everything we need to know about . . . what we are to each other."

We ate a crazy but somehow delicious lunch that he must have picked up at the convenience store just outside of town, consisting of beef jerky, cheese sticks, yogurt, Doritos, and some of his leftover Halloween chocolate. We drank the half bottle of wine he'd brought. When we were finished, he picked up his notepad and started writing again.

I lay down beside him, closed my eyes, soaked in the warmth of the late fall sun, and waited for him to take a break.

To touch me some more.

~

Saturday, November 9, 1996

I usually love it when Simon comes to Chicago for business. He always makes sure to schedule time for just the two of us. No Lorraine and no babies.

This time, he surprised me by showing up at school to take me to the city for the weekend. The plan: dinner at Spiaggia, a two-night stay with him in a suite at the Four Seasons, shopping on Michigan Avenue, and something cultural on Saturday night. Theoretically my dream weekend. On past visits he's taken me to plays at Steppenwolf and the Goodman and concerts at the Chicago Theatre, so I knew I'd love whatever it was he planned to surprise me with.

"How are you doing, baby?" he asked as we drove away from campus in the Viper he'd rented "for shits and grins."

"Good," I said. I was almost touched that he'd decided what I needed most was a surprise getaway from the stress of school, college apps, and my breakup with Ian.

The thing is, I already had plans.

Dallas and I had worked out all the details. On Saturday night, I'd walk to the outskirts of town, he'd pick me up, and we'd disappear to some-place in the city where no one could possibly recognize us.

The irony wasn't lost on me: in surprising me with a "dream" weekend, my father had ruined my fantasy of going on my first proper date, in public, with my secret boyfriend.

"I figured a weekend away would get your mind off everything you have on your plate," he said as I picked at the clam bucatini I usually crave. "But you seem distracted."

Understatement of the year.

When Simon showed up on campus, I nearly shit a brick. I used his cell phone to call "all" my teachers to let them know I'd be missing my Saturday morning classes, including poetry, which I didn't have on the weekend. Everyone answered their phones and wished me a good weekend.

Everyone but Dallas.

For him, I had to leave the most awkward, fumbling message I've ever recorded. I could barely get out the words Mister *and* Walker, *code for* This is important. *I had to focus to keep from sounding as shaky and upset as I felt while I added, "It's Andi Bloom from your poetry seminar. I won't be in class tomorrow, Saturday, because my father came into town and surprised me with a weekend in the city. I'm really sorry for any problems my absence may cause. Please know I'm eager to make up anything I missed when I return on Sunday. Afternoon. Again, I'm sorry. If you need to reach me, I'll be at the Four Seasons, and I'm also available on my father, Simon Bloom's car phone. The number is . . ."*

"Jesus, Andi, it's one class, not a semester," Simon said when I finally hung up.

"I was supposed to have a test tomorrow," I said lamely.

"I'll write you a note," he said. "He'll let you make it up."

"I'm sure the message I just left will be fine." The mere thought made me queasy.

As I looked across the table at my father, for the first time ever I felt weirdly self-conscious about being out with him. Dallas was younger than my dad, but how much younger could he be? Dad was forty-five and Dallas had to be at least thirty-five. Did any of the other diners at Spiaggia think we weren't father and daughter—but on a date? When and if we were ever able to go out in public together, would people think Dallas was my father?

Feeling suddenly shaky, I put my fork down and it rattled against my plate. I gulped water.

"You haven't said anything about Ian," Simon said.

"There's not much to say," I said. "We're not together."

"Is it permanent?"

I shrugged. "I don't know."

"Got someone else on the line?"

"No!" I said too quickly and too loudly.

He arched an eyebrow but thankfully let it go at that.

Saturday morning, he took me on a shopping spree that included visits to Marshall Field's and Neiman Marcus, and my choices, Guess and the Gap. We had lunch at Bandera because of the view, and headed back to the hotel to chill before the evening's cultural event, which he promised I was going to absolutely love.

I still hadn't heard from Dallas. It was bumming me out, but I started to think maybe it was for the best: What if Simon answered when he called?

"You know, honey," he said, sitting down beside me on the couch in the living room of our suite. "When your mom died . . ."

"I don't want to talk about Mom," I said.

"I understand, but you need to know that when you suffer a loss, it sometimes feels like you'll never love again."

"I broke it off with Ian," I told him. "Not the other way around."

Before he had a chance to respond, his cell phone began to vibrate on the end table beside the couch.

He picked it up, looked at the number, and handed it to me. "Local area code. I'm guessing it's for you. I'm going to stretch out on my bed for a few minutes before the show."

I said hello just as the door closed to his room.

"Can you talk?" Dallas said. No Hello, Andi.

"Yes," I said, trying to sound like I was talking to a teacher, which I was.

"What the fuck is going on?"

"Simon just showed up out of the blue," I said, crossing the room and lowering my voice to a whisper. *"I literally had to call you from the car."*

"Simon?"

"My dad."

Silence.

"I'm so sorry," I said, my voice suddenly scratchy. *"I really wanted to be with you."*

"It's cool," he finally said.

It didn't sound all that cool.

"How about next weekend or the weekend after?"

"Next weekend is the English Department's faculty retreat. Not sure about the weekend after." He sighed.

"I miss you," I said.

"You too, babe," he said. *"Catch you when you get back."*

The evening surprise ended up being tickets to Chicago Shakespeare Theater. Thankfully it was Twelfth Night *and not* Romeo and Juliet. After the show, over dessert and coffee at Gordon, Simon started in again.

"Who is he?"

"Who is who?"

"Your new boyfriend."

Simon Bloom is nothing if not perceptive.

"I don't have a new boyfriend," I said, trying to keep my expression as neutral as possible.

"There's always someone else in these situations."

"Just because you work in Hollywood doesn't mean—"

"Andi," my father said, grasping my hand. *"You don't really expect me to believe you were waiting for a call from your teacher, do you?"*

Thankfully Simon Bloom isn't quite as perceptive as he could be.

～

110

Tuesday, November 12, 1996

I had only two hours to spend with Dallas before Georgina and Tommy would return from making out in the back row at the movie theater in town and wonder why I wasn't in my dorm room. Dallas, however, was rubbing my feet with his left hand and scribbling on a legal pad with the other.

"Why are you always working when I'm around?" I asked.

"Because being around you inspires me," Dallas said.

"Be inspired after I leave," I said.

"I thought you'd be impressed watching a poet at work."

"Not when I want the poet to pay attention to me."

"Fair enough," he said with a laugh. "But try to think about it as though you're posing."

"Like for a painting?"

"I'm writing this about you."

"Your literary model has questions," I said.

"Ask away," he said, working his way up my calf.

"Why did you start going by Dallas?"

"It's my middle name. I was born there, and my parents lacked imagination. My dad was also a David, and I didn't want to be a Junior."

"How old are you?"

"I'll be forty."

"When?"

"February."

"February what?"

"Tenth."

"So you're an Aquarius?"

"Don't tell me you put any stock in that particular bullshit."

"I don't, but . . ."

"But you're beautiful," he said, unbuttoning the top two buttons of my shirt and pulling it aside to lightly lick my collarbone.

"Clever as a crow / With raven hair / And bones like a bird's / She keeps her wings out of sight / Only opening them at night."

I don't know how other people react to having famous poets write and recite poems about them, but it gave me a full-body shiver, even though he said, "It's a little rough. And I'll have to get rid of the rhyme."

I could never describe Dallas as beautiful. If I was going to write a poem about male beauty, it would have to be about Ian—the sun-bleached streaks in his hair, his cobalt-blue eyes and smooth features, like he was sculpted. Dallas was gray at the temples, had a furrow between his eyebrows, and the skin around his eyes crinkled when he smiled. Sexy, I thought, as he slid his hand under my bra and lightly circled my nipple with his finger. Fucking sexy was what he was.

"You told Georgina there's no Mrs. Dallas Walker."

"There isn't," he said. "Not currently."

He couldn't possibly mean that he was eyeing the future. It just wasn't his way. "So you were married?"

"Until it didn't work anymore."

"You don't have kids, do you?"

"Never a goal of mine."

"What was your wife's name?"

"Susan."

"Did you love her?"

"I love every woman I've ever gotten involved with."

Including me?

He made me shiver again when he stretched out and pressed the weight of his body against me.

Kissing me again.

"I want to make love to you," he whispered.

Heat traveled through me like I'd never, ever felt.

"I do—"

He put his finger to my lips. "No, you don't."

"I don't?" I said, momentarily startled, having never ever been turned down by a boy . . . which is where I stopped myself. Hadn't I abruptly left the world of boys?

"Not yet," he said.

"When?" I asked.

"When the timing is absolutely, positively right."

"Which will be?"

"You won't need to ask. We'll both just know."

~

Wednesday, November 13, 1996

"My thesis is that William Blake's poetry is fundamentally about romance," Georgina said, leaning back on her bed, with pen and paper in her lap.

"He was definitely a pioneer of romantic poetry in English literature," I said, looking up from my desktop computer. *"Which I think means he was one of the first to employ symbols and imagery, not that he necessarily wrote about romance."*

"Dallas was certainly going on about the sexual imagery in 'The Garden of Love.'"

"True," I said, even though I knew it was code to let me know he was thinking about our currently snow-covered rendezvous spot out by the lake and wishing we could meet up there. "I probably wouldn't write my whole essay on it, though."

"What are you writing about?"

"Blake's protest of the Industrial Revolution in England."

Georgina had a moony look on her face. *"I'm sure you'll get an A, like always, but I'm all about romance these days."*

"Really?" I said, tossing a pillow at her. "Hadn't noticed."

"I can't believe I ever thought it was Dallas and his passion for poetry that was getting me all worked up in class when it was really Tommy I was into."

"*Love is a mystery,*" *I said, happy that I didn't have to worry about Georgina and her relentless flirtation with Dallas anymore.*

"*Tommy wants to do IT,*" *she said.* "*Don't tell anyone.*"

"*You know I won't,*" *I said.*

"*He's a virgin,*" *she said.* "*Which is also a secret.*"

It was no secret that Georgina had done IT over the summer with a guy who worked at the boat dock in Michigan, and had hooked up with Connor Cotton on and off all of junior year.

"*I want it to be special our first time.*" *She blushed.* "*I mean, for Tommy.*"

"*That's sweet,*" *I said.*

"*How did you know when the timing was right?*"

I couldn't very well tell her the timing had felt right to me from the first time Dallas and I kissed, that he was the one insisting we wait, and that I was blown away by the intensity of my desire pretty much 24-7.

"*When it's love it just feels so different,*" *I said instead. That was definitely true with Ian, but with Dallas I felt much more me than I'd ever thought possible.*

"*Is that why you guys waited?*"

I could only nod.

"*Interesting,*" *she said.* "*I mean, Ian was so into you.*"

I felt sad that I couldn't share who I was really thinking about.

"*He's still totally into you,*" *she said, misreading the expression on my face.* "*From what I hear, girls are coming out of the woodwork to try and . . . I mean, I hear Sylvie is talking about joining Cue Sports Society. How desperate is that?*"

"*He's free to do whatever he wants to do,*" *I said.*

"*And you're okay with that?*"

"*No,*" *I said, which was really all I could say. I hate the idea of Ian being with anyone other than me, and I feel like a complete asshole for even thinking it. I also wish he didn't hate me so much, because I miss our friendship.* "*But we're not together right now, so . . .*"

I can't imagine him getting together with Sylvie anyway.

"I really don't get why you split up in the first place. I mean, come on, Andi, he's perfect!"

"We're on a break," I said, the same thing I'd been telling everybody.

"I hope you guys get over whatever it is. You belong together. Forever."

"I don't know about that."

"I know how much fun we'd have double-dating," she said.

Picturing me and Dallas on a date with Georgina and Tommy made me laugh out loud.

"What's so funny about that?" asked Georgina.

"Nothing," I told her. "Nothing at all."

Chapter Sixteen

Andi spotted Georgina's white Range Rover as her friend parallel parked across the street from Blooming Books. The ability to anticipate an unexpected visitor was one of the many advantages of having a store-front location.

Andi's publishing company produced high-end coffee-table books and several well-received general-nonfiction titles highlighting the art, architecture, and culture of St. Louis and the surrounding area. With a little luck and another year in the black, thanks in part to her Central West End office-cum-store where St. Louisans could stop in to browse and buy, she would expand her business model to more cities in flyover country. She'd even considered the idea of adding a fiction imprint focusing on Midwestern writers.

It was financially risky, but her brief career as an assistant editor at a New York publishing house during Ian's ill-suited stint on Wall Street had given her an understanding of the pitfalls and potential rewards. Getting pregnant with Cassidy had cut short what could have been a satisfying career, but starting her own publishing concern had proven to be even more fulfilling. She no longer dreamed of writing the Great American Novel, but she hadn't ruled out the idea that she might publish it.

"I couldn't wait a minute longer," Georgina said over the jangle of the door. "Did it come yet?"

Andi couldn't say her visit was a total surprise—she had told Georgina the official proof of *Lovely Ladue* was coming in today. With a gorgeous photo of Georgina's sprawling plantation-style mansion gracing the cover, Andi knew her friend would want to be the first to see it. She just thought Georgina would have waited for a text letting her know it had actually been delivered.

"UPS doesn't usually come before one," she said.

"Perfect," Georgina said, reaching into a brown paper bag. "I brought corned beef sandwiches."

"I shouldn't," Andi said as Georgina unwrapped her favorite sandwich in the city and handed it over along with a black cherry soda. "This is pure evil."

"Speaking of which," she said as Andi took a delicious first bite, "everyone is abuzz about the death of our old friend the poet."

Given that Georgina had undoubtedly pulled out the alumni roster and texted, called, or emailed everyone she could find who'd attended Glenlake with them, this conversation was inevitable. In fact, Andi was surprised Georgina hadn't led with the gossip that was the true purpose of her early arrival.

"What are they saying?" Andi asked, both needing and not wanting to know.

"Everyone seems to have a different theory of who they think killed him."

Despite the perfectly spiced and incredibly moist corned beef, Andi's throat felt so dry she had to take a sip of soda to help her swallow. "Even though all signs point to him killing himself?"

"But if it *was* a murder, the killer is undoubtedly someone we knew," she said with far too much enthusiasm. "It could be a faculty member with a secret vendetta or a student who had a serious bone to pick."

"I swear, you sound like one of the kids in Cassidy's journalism class."

"Like a certain Liz Wright, who called from Glenlake, asking if I wouldn't mind giving her a few minutes of my time to speak about a teacher I once had named David Dallas Walker?"

"What did you tell her?" Andi asked, dread tightening her throat even further.

"That I would much prefer to be contacted by my goddaughter, Cassidy Copeland."

Andi shook her head. "You didn't."

"I got a paragraph-long explanation about how their teacher insists they maintain journalistic objectivity, meaning they assigned themselves to former students with whom they have no association."

"Apparently, Cassidy didn't get the message before she grilled Ian and me," Andi told her.

"She must have gotten special permission or something," said Georgina with a chuckle. "They're interviewing everyone at Glenlake who had any association with Dallas. That teacher of theirs seems like the real deal."

"Cassidy's certainly in awe of him," Andi said, the words heavier than she expected as they emerged from her mouth. Remembering her own infatuation with Dallas. Picturing Cassidy staying late after class.

"Since I know you're wondering, I told Ms. Wright I was just kidding, and patiently endured her interrogation."

"What did she ask you?"

"Lots of open-ended and slightly repetitive questions: What was Dallas Walker like as a teacher? How would you describe his teaching style? Would you say he was close to the other faculty members? To the students?"

"Not exactly *Was it Professor Plum with the lead pipe in the library?*" Andi said dryly, wanting to make sure her friend spilled absolutely everything she'd been questioned about or told.

"No, but the purpose of her line of questioning was fairly direct: finding out if I knew anyone who had reason to hate him or want him gone."

"And what did you tell her?"

"That most of the guys thought he was kind of a douche."

"In those words?"

"When I added that all the girls thought he was sexy as hell, though, I could hear her scribbling furiously."

"'Girls' primarily meaning *you*, Georgina," Andi said. "That is, until you found true love with Tommy Harkins."

"Who I actually spoke to yesterday."

"You called him?"

"And then he friended me on Facebook," she said.

"Sounds kind of dangerous," Andi said. "He's single and probably desperate."

"You saw him," she said. "Even if I wasn't happily married, there's no way I'd give him a second thought."

"If you say so," Andi said.

"It was all business. And you have to admit, he seems to be doing well for a guy who barely made it into his safety school. He thought we should start a Facebook group for the people who were in Dallas Walker's class. We can share tidbits about the kids' little investigation."

"*Little* isn't exactly the word I'd use to describe kids who are up to their elbows in death." Andi thought for a moment. "Any sign of Sylvie on Facebook?"

"Her last post was years ago, from Taos. At the time, she was living in an apartment, working part-time at a rock shop or 'mineral gallery,' and New Age as all get-out. Where that little lost soul is now, I cannot say."

"I'm not sure we should be gossiping about the case on social media," said Andi, wishing she hadn't phrased it so primly.

"It's all in fun."

"Georgina!" Andi said. "Dallas was a person we knew, a teacher who mattered to us. How can you be so flippant about this?"

Midway through a bite, Georgina laughed, then coughed as some food went down the wrong pipe. She cleared her throat. "Dallas was an egomaniac of the highest order. He'd love knowing a whole class was looking into his death."

"You may be right about that," Andi admitted.

"I bet he'd also love the tension this whole business is creating between the administration and Wayne Kelly."

"What do you mean?"

"From what I hear, they're worried about the school attracting any more unwanted media attention than they've already had."

"I wish I knew whose bright idea it was to hire an award-winning investigative journalist to be writer in residence in the first place. Of *course* he ends up investigating the school itself."

"They had no way of knowing," Georgina said. "And, who knows, maybe those kids will come up with a logical answer about what actually happened to Dallas."

"Hopefully," Andi said weakly, grateful to see the UPS driver appear at the door with the box they'd both been waiting for.

As Georgina savored her first look at what would inevitably be her fifteen minutes of local fame, Andi couldn't help but wonder how close she herself was to an entirely unwanted form of notoriety—and how lasting it would be.

Chapter Seventeen

Thursday, November 14, 1996

Cue Sports Society was just me and Mike. Jacob and Patrick were studying for exams and bailed. Playing pool sounded more fun than studying, so I talked Mike into coming, too. Dallas almost seemed surprised to see us when we walked into the student union. He was leaning back in a chair with his feet up on the pool table and reading a book.

"Just the two of you?" he asked.

Mike said yes and Dallas said, "Keep your coats on."

We followed him outside to his car, and he drove us down to Chicago in like ten minutes. I swear we hit three g's. Mike had a boner he loved it so much.

Dallas parked on this skeezy street and led us up to a second-story pool hall called Chris's Billiards. I wondered if it was going to be a repeat of Kyle's Kabin, but it didn't seem like he knew anybody there, and they didn't even serve beer.

"No bar, no pinball machines, no bowling alleys, just pool . . . nothing else," said Dallas.

He said it like he was reciting a poem, but it sure didn't sound like a poem. I must have looked at him funny, because he said, "That's from The Hustler. *A movie with Paul Newman. It was the one before* The Color of Money.*"*

We mostly played cutthroat because it's a three-player game, but pool is really better with two or four people. I won the first game on a lucky shot, but then Dallas started winning. I guess he wanted it more. To be honest, I kind of lost interest. I started trying to make the hardest shot on the table every time, bank shots and combination shots, and then even Mike started finishing ahead of me.

Dallas wasn't very into talking to us, and I wondered if it was because he was hoping we'd meet some lowlifes for him to play. Or maybe he just wanted to soak up the atmosphere and use it as material for his poems. (Which I've hardly read any of. Andi probably has them all memorized by now, though.)

At one point some guy came over and watched us for a while and asked Dallas if he played any one-pocket, but Dallas told him no and the guy left.

After Dallas won like the seventh game in a row, he suddenly said, "Class dismissed," and we took off. Some class. Basically, he spent the whole time beating us without giving us any advice to make us better players.

It was rush hour when we headed back, so the trip took almost an hour, and Dallas seemed pissed about it. But when he dropped us off, he said, "Hold up," and went around to his trunk and took out a six-pack of Milwaukee's Best that was still ice cold.

"Consolation prize," he said, handing me the beer. "This didn't come from me."

"Damn, Dallas, thanks!" said Mike, practically ready to shotgun them then and there.

Mike headed back to Stimson, and I started to follow him, but Dallas put his hand on my arm.

"Everything going okay?" he asked.

I shrugged.

Then he said, "I heard you and Andi broke up."

Great. So even the teachers know. Did they also know Sylvie and I made out at the Halloween dance, or that Sarah Ann Janeway stuck her hand down my pants while we were watching Dazed and Confused *on video in the common area at her house? Did they know it was like an out-of-body experience each time I opened my eyes and saw someone's face besides Andi's?*

"I'm fine," I told him.

"Cheer up, Ian. This school is full of brainy, beautiful chicks. I wish they looked at me the way they look at you."

I told him thanks and took off. Sometimes I can't believe they let this guy teach prep school.

∽

"I don't touch anything less than twenty years old because it makes me feel like a pedophile," said Preston with a grin, facing the selected members of the Grape and Barley sales staff who had assembled in the Clayton store an hour before opening.

As several of them laughed—one of them, a newer team member with gelled, spiky hair, a little too hard—Ian winced. Preston was undoubtedly a good businessman and knew how to close a sale, but he could be a little crass. Andi would have used the word *oily*. Ian had several big customers who wouldn't appreciate that kind of humor.

Perhaps sensing Ian's discomfort, Preston recalibrated. "Of course, you have to know your customer. A safer opening line is *I hope you're not looking for anything new.* Because people are constantly being pitched what's latest and new. That gets their interest."

Then again, thought Ian, *maybe it takes a little oil to grease the wheels.*

Preston put both hands on the small table in front of him, bookending a half-dozen bottles of various vintages.

"This is not Budweiser," he told the group. "It's not even craft beer or craft spirits. The price points rule out ninety-nine percent of your customers, so don't waste your time upselling a guy who just wants a bottle of Irish whiskey. Identify the one percent and build relationships so you can sell to them again and again. Find your whales, harpoon them, and keep them tied to the boat."

To Ian, he added, "You should think about having an exclusive after-hours party in the store to really kick this thing off."

Ian nodded, thinking it was probably a good idea.

"Once they get a taste for it," Preston went on, "it's like a hobby, and they'll want rarer and rarer items. People get seduced by the idea of rarity, of history, of owning and then consuming something that is one of a kind and can never be replaced. But the real beauty of this product is that *no one* knows how this stuff is supposed to taste. They're buying an idea and an experience, and you're marking it up as far as the market will bear."

After lifting into view a bottle wrapped in a brown paper bag, Preston poured tasting portions into thimble-size cups and invited everyone to take one.

"Your boss made me promise to keep you sober," he joked.

Ian sipped the molasses-colored offering. It was rum, obviously. A little rough, but with imagination, it could have been sitting in a shuttered bar on some Caribbean island until Preston or one of his scouts liberated the stock.

"What are we tasting?" asked Preston.

"Demerara," said Ian's head buyer quickly, proving himself to a fellow expert.

"Nailed it. Now when was it bottled?"

Shrugs all around. No one wanted to guess and be off by a decade or two.

"2017," said Preston with a laugh. "Sells for thirty-three bucks. But if I'd told you it was 1975, you would have believed it, right? And paid as much as three hundred?"

"What's your point?" asked his buyer.

"My point," said Preston, pouring the next sample, "is that success with this product depends solely on salesmanship and perceived value."

"Well, how *do* they know it's genuine?" asked the spiky-haired newbie.

Preston's eyes twinkled. "How do they know it's not? With only a few exceptions, we always sell sealed bottles. But wines and spirits age differently. Some spoil. We sell everything as is, caveat emptor."

Ian could see his team getting interested and buying in. And he had no doubt they'd move more product after this. But could they possibly move the stock fast enough to balance the books and keep Simon Bloom out of his business? Once Simon came on board, there would be no way to hide it from Andi.

He wondered whether he was as good at keeping secrets as Andi—and if she was better at it than he knew. For years, he thought he'd known her deepest, darkest secret and assumed her recent jumpiness was simply due to the unwelcome reminder of what happened so long ago. Was it possible she had even more to hide?

Chapter Eighteen

Moments after the bell rang, Mr. Kelly came into the classroom, closed the door behind him, and leaned against the corner of his desk.

"Updates," he announced, shaking his head at Noah Jacobs as he opened the door and tried to slip in late and unnoticed. "Alumni interviews first."

Everyone was sitting with their working group, desks pushed together for what Mr. Kelly called "newsroom collaboration." Cassidy's excitement about her assignment was tempered by the fact that Noah was, so far, the only other person in her group. Tate had promised to help outside class, but in it she was forced to deal with the annoying, entitled, and lazy Noah, who slumped into his seat across from her with a look that said, *Now I'm here, the party can start.*

Liz Wright, one of the girls in Tate's group, summarized the interviews that were already in the class folder by saying that, basically, the alumni they'd talked to so far had thought Dallas Walker was pretty cool, that he'd seemed different from all the other teachers at Glenlake, and that they had no idea why he'd disappeared. They were all uniformly shocked to learn he had spent the last twenty years in his car at the bottom of Lake Loomis.

"They all seemed really interested in what happened, but they didn't have any useful information," summarized Liz. "Except that he was a hottie."

While people snickered, Mr. Kelly moved to the whiteboard and tapped the photo of Dallas Walker that had been printed out and taped to their growing collage. He grinned wryly.

"Journalism is the art of separating the subjective from the factual. Was the deceased poet, in fact, hot?"

Liz blushed and tried to defend herself with a half-hearted "Eew! He was old!"

Mr. Kelly smiled and shook his head, speaking over the laughter. "When you're talking to these people, are you using the interview techniques I went over in class? Are you asking open-ended questions, letting them talk, and avoiding agreeing with them? Are you asking the same questions in different ways? Most importantly, are you looking for motive?"

"I'm trying to," said Liz, "but it's weird to treat them like suspects, because they were teenagers back then—it's not like any of them killed him."

"We don't know that," said Kelly, making the room fall suddenly silent. "If you don't think teens are capable of murder, I suggest you start reading your parents' newspapers. That is, if your parents still subscribe to newspapers these days."

Tate spoke up. It seemed to Cassidy as though he was trying to save Liz from further mortification, and she liked him for that. "We're still waiting to hear back from eight former students," he added, "but we're making good progress."

"Just make sure your interviews don't turn into gentle strolls down memory lane," said Kelly, perching again on the corner of his desk. "Find out who was unhappy and why."

Rowan Krause pushed his glasses back on his nose and raised his hand. "We've been reading old issues of the *Glenlaker* from the '96–'97 school year. Scans of the articles specifically referencing Walker are on the shared drive. But I also found an anonymous student editorial about grade inflation in the fall poetry seminar. The author sounds like a brainiac who was pissed off that students who didn't work as hard were also getting As. Hang on a minute . . ."

With a few clicks on his laptop, Rowan brought up the work in question so he could find the line he wanted to share.

"Maybe Dallas Walker was right to give his whole poetry class Cs, as he notoriously did several years ago at another school. Maybe we at Glenlake need to wake up and realize success is earned, not bestowed."

Mr. Kelly whistled. "Nice work, Rowan!"

"We couldn't find the author's name," said Rowan apologetically. "All those files were destroyed."

"It's possible the author wasn't even in Walker's class," said Mr. Kelly. "But it's still an important clue. Did he give his whole class at Glenlake Cs? Were the grades later inflated? Has anyone mentioned that?"

Everyone in Tate's group shook their heads.

"Well, ask! Call 'em back if you have to!" He paused, remembering something, and turned his attention to Cassidy. "Your mom was in his class. Did she ever say anything about this?"

She shook her head. "Mom's famous in the family for having a perfect 4.0 GPA at Glenlake and at Smith."

"Confirm that with the registrar," said Mr. Kelly, getting another laugh.

Cassidy played along. "I won't have to. She probably still has her old report cards."

"Since I've got you on the hook, does your group have a report on the mysterious employee?"

Noah gestured toward Cassidy, like he was going to generously let her make the presentation, when in reality he hadn't done anything more than look at her notes and nod and grunt.

She opened her laptop and scanned what she'd written. "We don't know too much yet. My dad mentioned that he had a neck tattoo, so I just asked the first groundskeeper I saw, and he said the guy's name was Roy. The school website lists a Curtis Royal under *Building and*

Grounds Maintenance Crew. There's no picture, but the name was too similar for it to be a coincidence. I went to Mrs. Franti in Records, and all she would do was confirm he's employed here."

"Did you threaten to FOIA them?" asked Hannah.

"I didn't have to," Cassidy told her. "She said she'd looked it up and personnel records are private. She also said to tell you you're busted. But we know from what you got last time that Roy didn't work here when Dallas did."

"Oops," said Hannah, her earlier embarrassment at having conned Mrs. Franti having become pride that she'd pulled it off.

"I googled him, but he's not on any social media, and I hardly came up with anything. It looks like he's gotten arrested a few times for stuff like pot and failing to pay his speeding tickets."

"A jailbird?" said Noah, forgetting he was supposed to know this already. "He totally did it."

"It can't be anything serious or they wouldn't let him work at Glenlake," said Cassidy, feeling strangely defensive.

"Maybe they have different standards for the groundskeepers," said Felicia primly.

Mr. Kelly clapped his hands. "All right, let's hold off on the other reports until our next class. Before we break into groups, does anybody have anything else?"

Liz swiveled around in her chair and gave Cassidy a look that was hard to read. "Did your parents say anything about how they broke up senior year?"

Caught completely off guard, Cassidy felt like someone had just pulled her pants down in front of the class. Her parents' Glenlake story was one of unbroken bliss—nobody had ever mentioned a breakup.

"W-why would they?" she stammered.

"Your mom's friend Georgina is super talkative. I just remembered that she said your parents had a 'spectacular' breakup senior year."

"Aunt Georgina has a tendency toward hyperbole," said Cassidy defensively. "Besides, I don't see how that's relevant to this project."

"Well, your mom was in Dallas Walker's class," said Liz weakly. "Like Mr. Kelly said, we're supposed to learn everything—"

"I'm afraid I side with Cassidy here," interrupted Mr. Kelly, to Cassidy's grateful relief. "I appreciate your questioning instinct, but I'm afraid this seems unrelated. Let's spare your classmate the mortification of thinking about her parents as creatures with romantic and sexual desires."

Which somehow made it worse. But then, thank god, the bell rang.

As Cassidy stuffed her things in her backpack, out of the corner of her eye she saw Tate hurrying over so they could walk out together. As glad as she was to see that, she wished she could be alone with her thoughts.

Her parents had broken up in *spectacular* fashion but had obviously gotten back together. Why? Maybe their storybook romance had some secret chapters?

All she knew for sure was that she needed to find out.

Chapter Nineteen

"Isn't it just easier to fly Cassidy home for Thanksgiving?" Ian asked through a mouthful of toothpaste. He spit into the basin on his side of the marble vanity they'd decided to restore instead of replace when they'd renovated the house. One of the infinite number of household decisions on which they always seemed to agree.

"I heard a rumor that Chi Town Publishing is struggling," Andi said. "I should really get up there and meet with them."

"You can't just call and find out what's going on?"

She could have. But ever since she'd heard the journalism class was looking into old files and records, she'd been thinking about loose threads she had to snip so no one could start pulling. To do so, she needed a legitimate reason to get to Glenlake.

"If Chi Town is seeking an investor or, better yet, looking to sell, I need to make sure I put in the first and best offer," Andi said. "I've been wanting to expand into a bigger market, and this is the ideal opportunity."

"What about Thanksgiving prep?" Ian asked. "There's a ton to do with both of our families coming this year."

"It may be at our house, but it's still Biz's holiday. You know she'll be here at daybreak, reorganizing the kitchen before we get started."

"I'm not going to be able to help out as much as I usually do ahead of time, though. I have to be at the store for the 'whales' that are starting to come in now that it's the holiday season. I've made nearly seven grand on a dozen bottles already this week. Someone paid eight hundred bucks for a bottle of 1957 J.T.S. Brown."

"Whatever that is. I'll only be gone from Monday morning until midday Tuesday."

"What about weather?" Ian said, the weakness of his argument masked by an unexpected intensity in his voice. "It's supposed to get bad."

"Which could leave Cassidy stranded at O'Hare," she said, wondering why he was being so stubborn.

"I just don't want to worry about the two of you getting stuck in a ditch along the interstate," he said.

"Honey, I promise I'll be extra cautious," she said. After all, wasn't her entire motivation for going an abundance of caution?

He pursed his lips, always a sign he wasn't going to repeat what was on his mind.

Had she already brushed her teeth, she'd have given him a comforting kiss. Instead, she patted him on the bottom to let him know he had an IOU to cash in as soon as it was convenient.

And that there was absolutely nothing to worry about.

Chapter Twenty

Monday, November 18, 1996

So Andi and I finally talked. If that's what you'd call it. I guess we said words to each other and we both heard what the other one was saying, but the words didn't seem to matter.

It was her idea, actually. I was coming around the corner of Leggett, and all of a sudden she was right there. It was too late to change direction. She was like, "Hi," and I was like, "Hi," and then she just asked if I wanted to get coffee, and I said okay. I figured she meant at the student union, but then she said, "Three o'clock at the diner."

I had to skip practice and sneak off campus to do it, but the fact that she chose "our" place made me wonder if she had something big to tell me. The whole way there I was thinking about if I'd take her back (answer: obviously) and how I'd tell Mike and Sarah Ann and if it would make me look like I was pussy-whipped or not. By the time I got to the diner I was more or less expecting to be back together with Andi and . . . I was practically fucking skipping.

But then I got there and she was in a booth in the smoking section, playing with her lighter and letting her cigarette burn in the ashtray. (She's always liked the idea of smoking a lot more than actually smoking.)

And she didn't look at all like someone who wanted to admit she made a mistake.

"So what's up?" I asked.

"I just wanted to see how you're doing," she said. "We can still talk, right?"

Here's how stupid I am: it took me five more minutes to realize we weren't getting back together. She said a lot of stuff about how we were practically adults, so we could be grown-up about things, but really I think she wanted to see if she'd broken me too badly to put back together. Maybe so she didn't have to feel guilty.

"Why?" I asked, interrupting something she was saying about how she was concerned about me.

"Why do I still care about you?" she asked.

"Why don't you want to be with me?"

"You have to admit, we've been 'Ian and Andi' for a long time," she said. "Three years—don't you want to try just being Ian?"

"Looks like I don't have a choice."

For the first time, she looked like she might actually be a little bit sorry.

"Are you seeing someone else?" I asked.

She took way too long to answer, and when she did, she looked over my shoulder and said, "There's no one else who could make me feel the way you did"—which isn't exactly NO, now is it?

I almost told her about Sylvie and Sarah Ann, and that there's three other girls who would have sex with me in a minute if I asked. But then she might think those other girls mattered, so I didn't.

When the waitress finally came over to take my order, I told her I wasn't staying.

"Whoever he is, I hope you're happy," I told Andi. I didn't recognize my voice. I might have been crying a little bit.

Andi definitely was.

Good.

Chapter Twenty-One

A week later, as they kissed goodbye, Ian still seemed perturbed, if not pissed.

Maybe it was the sex they'd never gotten around to.

Maybe he was picking up on her jangled nerves and sensing there was more to Dallas Walker's resurfacing than he could possibly know. Maybe recent events had made him suspicious.

Or maybe it really was the weather.

Ian was right about the bad conditions, a combination of blowing snow and black ice that put her Volvo's famed Swedish stability to the test. She didn't dare admit to him that she nearly slid off the shoulder as she merged onto the highway after getting gas. Worse, she'd come within inches of rear-ending the car in front of her on Lake Street as she scanned for a parking spot near the offices of Chi Town Publishing.

The meeting with the husband and wife copublishers turned out to be even more cursory than she'd anticipated, consisting of a quick coffee, a guarded discussion of their financial woes, and a vague agreement to consider a purchase offer or partnership proposal in the new year.

As a result, Andi reached Glenlake well ahead of the 4:00 p.m. Thanksgiving Feast—a tradition for kids and any parents who happened to be on campus to fetch their offspring. After rounding the woods by Copeland Hall, she pulled into the visitor parking lot in front of McCormick Mansion. Grabbing her hat, gloves, scarf, and coat from the passenger seat for later, she then quick-walked into the building, shoes crunching on the heavily salted sidewalk.

She traded hellos with Mrs. Hodges in reception, inhaling the pleasant smell of a fresh mug of herbal tea on the desk.

"I got here too early to check in at the inn," Andi told her. "So I thought I might try to catch Cassidy for a quick hello, if possible, before the feast."

"Let's have a look," said Mrs. Hodges, consulting a computerized program that enabled her to locate the schedule of anyone on campus, student or faculty.

Along with attending to loose ends, Andi had been planning to pop into Cassidy's journalism class, which she knew was at the end of the day. While she really wanted to stay as far away as possible, she needed to have a friendly word with Wayne Kelly to remind him that parents were watching and real people were involved.

"Her physics class just started," Mrs. Hodges said, eyeing Andi over her readers. "You might try to catch her during the passing period before she heads to her journalism seminar at three o'clock."

"Perfect," Andi said. "In the meantime, I think I'll head to the student union and warm up with a cup of something hot."

After accepting a visitor's pass, Andi bundled up before going back outside and walking in the general direction of the union. Instead of stopping there, however, she veered off toward her actual destination, a small freestanding house in which she hadn't set foot since early March of her senior year.

Back then, the infirmary had been manned by a certain Nurse Ratched (the not-so-clever nickname given to the short-tempered RN with the steel-gray hair and matching stare), whose treatment for all but the most serious medical concerns consisted of a grunt, a thermometer, and two aspirin.

Over her four years, Andi experienced more than a few of those mundane visits. There was also one appointment that she'd never chronicled in her journal and had done her best to block from memory.

It was early spring of senior year. The ground had started to thaw. Students were instructed to stay on the paved pathways to protect the newly sprouting grass and avoid tracking mud throughout the school. Birds were chirping again, and daffodils had popped up in the flower beds around campus. Mostly, the smell of spring filled the air, fresher and more fecund than Andi could remember, making her feel oddly emotional and, strangely, a little nauseated.

After a week of Andi's feeling alternately okay and downright ill, Mrs. Henry insisted she go to the infirmary.

Flu, Andi had written on the sign-in sheet.

"No fever," Nurse Ratched pronounced, brandishing her trusty thermometer.

"I think it's a stomach flu," Andi said. "And it's kind of weird because one minute I'm hungry and the next I'm trying not to throw up."

The nurse made a note on Andi's chart and proceeded to press on her lower abdomen.

"Any pain?" the nurse asked.

"Just a little crampy when you push."

"Have you been having diarrhea?"

Andi shook her head.

"When are you due for your period?"

"Anytime now."

Nurse Ratched narrowed her eyes. "Meaning you're late?"

Andi's heart began to pound in her chest. "I . . . don't get it on exactly the same day every month."

"So you could be overdue?"

"No," Andi said quickly, as much to convince herself that what Nurse Ratched was implying was wrong . . . there was no way. "It has to be either PMS or a stomach bug."

"We can do a test," the nurse said pointedly.

"No, it's fine," Andi replied, trying to remember the date of her last period. Thinking about the night they'd done it in Dallas's car.

He'd pulled out, so everything was okay.

Right?

There was no admitting that she'd been sexually active, even to the nurse. Given the way rumors traveled in the cloistered confines of Glenlake, privacy was never guaranteed. She couldn't risk it with the secret she'd been keeping.

"Very well," intoned Nurse Ratched before rolling her chair over to the glass medicine cabinet.

Andi had to stop herself from sighing with relief when the nurse handed her a bottle of Pepto-Bismol and began to recite the dosing instructions. Her solace morphed into a fresh bout of nausea when Nurse Ratched reached into a nearby drawer, pulled out a pamphlet, and thrust it toward her.

"If you don't get your period in a day or two, you'll want to give these folks a call," the nurse said. "They're the ones to help you from here on out."

The memory was still fresh as she breathed into her scarf to shield her face against the frigid wind. Andi reached the infirmary, now known as the Roth Wellness Center. Even though the waiting area had been updated and was painted a muted pastel blue instead of a bright, clinical white, Andi swore she could still hear the scratch of Nurse Ratched's pen as she scrawled in Andi's file on that day a lifetime ago.

Andi needed to find out if there was a record of what she'd written.

If so, she needed to eliminate the evidence.

"Sorry! I didn't realize anyone was here," said a young, pleasingly plump nurse who appeared from the exam rooms. She had a welcoming smile and bore no resemblance whatsoever to Nurse Ratched.

"No problem," Andi said. "I'm Andi Copeland."

"Cassidy's mom! Of course! I totally see the resemblance."

"I'm hoping you can answer a question for me."

"Sure," the nurse said. "But Cassidy hasn't been in for quite a while."

"Good to know, but I'm wondering how long you keep health records on students?"

"They're computerized, so indefinitely. At least theoretically."

Indefinitely.

"If you want to see Cassidy's records, I need you to fill out a parent/ guardian request form," she continued.

"Actually, I'm not looking for Cassidy's health history," Andi said in a warm tone she hoped would put at ease the nurse, who'd clearly dealt with an overprotective parent or two. "I'm trying to see if I can get ahold of my own."

"Yours?"

"I was a student here," Andi said, moving on to her excuse. "I've been dealing with some digestive issues that started during my senior year, and my doctor thinks that if we can trace them back to their start it may be helpful."

"Got it," the nurse said, looking relieved that she wasn't about to embark on an awkward struggle between a nosy parent and her reluctant daughter in the last hours before Thanksgiving break. "But I wouldn't have anything in my computer older than ten years."

"But you do keep them?"

"I'm not sure," she said. "Check with Mrs. Franti in Records."

───

"What can I do you for, dear?" asked Mrs. Franti, a mole-like woman Andi had never seen before, but who may well have been at Glenlake for as long as Mrs. Hodges had been working the front desk.

"I'm told you're the person to talk to about archived files," Andi said as casually as she could.

"So it would seem," she said.

"I'm wondering if you still have my health records from when I was a student here."

Mrs. Franti looked at her like she was crazy.

"I'm trying to diagnose a digestive issue that's been troubling me since my teens, and I'm hoping the records could give my doctor some insight." Like any decent white lie, the story rolled off her tongue more easily the second time. "I'm here a little early to get my daughter for Thanksgiving, so I thought I'd come check."

"Did you graduate before or after the year 2000?"

"Before." Andi hesitated to add 1997, the exact year in question.

"We started computerizing files right after that Y2K hoax," Mrs. Franti told her. "So there'd be nothing in the computer archives."

"What about paper files?" Andi asked, hoping the question had masked any outward expression of relief.

"We keep employee records forever, but all the handwritten health records from before 2000 were purged at that time."

Andi pretended to look disappointed. "I see."

"I'm sorry I can't be of more help," Mrs. Franti said.

"At least it's one less thing for you to do right before break," Andi added.

"I'm counting the hours," said Mrs. Franti with a shake of her head. "It's been like Grand Central Station around here since they found that car in the lake."

"What do you mean?"

"It's bad enough I'm running around, digging up class rosters, club memberships, and staff lists for the students in that journalism class. I make a set for one of the kids, put the file away, and the next thing I know I have to go right back and pull the same files—and a heck of a lot more, too—for the detectives in the Lake County Sheriff's Office."

Hearing those words, Andi's momentary sense of relief evaporated, only to be replaced by something even worse than what she'd felt before.

❧

Andi waited for the passing period to end before she entered Copeland Hall and started up the stairs. She paused on the landing leading to the all-too-familiar third-floor classroom and took a deep breath, trying to stave off a sense of dread that brought to mind how she'd felt before she'd entered that very room on the first day of senior year.

How different might everything have turned out had she listened to her gut and simply not taken that poetry class in the first place?

Willing her legs to move, she turned the corner at the top of the stairs and spotted a note written in big black letters and taped to the closed classroom door.

RADIATORS NOT WORKING. CLASS CANCELED!
HAVE A GREAT HOLIDAY BREAK!

An overwhelming sense of déjà vu was tempered by muffled voices coming from inside the room.

Laughter.

She stepped closer and peered through the wavy glass pane in the door. The room appeared to be empty, but craning her neck to the right, she spotted the back of Wayne Kelly's head. Putting her ear to the door, Andi heard the squeal of marker as someone wrote on the whiteboard just out of her view.

"Attagirl!" said Kelly, before stepping in closer to the student and reaching around her to add to whatever it was she had written.

They both disappeared from view.

"I love the way you think," he said.

The response was achingly familiar. "You and me both."

A rush of ice-cold adrenaline coursed through Andi with the distinctive giggle that followed. She pulled the door open before she knew what she was doing.

"Mom?" Cassidy asked as she stepped into the room.

141

Wayne Kelly moved away from Cassidy a bit too quickly for Andi's taste. Then again, he was crossing the room to greet her.

"Mrs. Copeland, I presume?" he asked.

"Call me Andi," she said, extending her hand and looking him directly in the eye. "I got here earlier than I expected, so I thought I'd stop by and sit in on the class."

"Of all the days to cancel class," Kelly said. It was cold in the room, as evidenced by Cassidy's sweater and scarf and her teacher's thick tweed sport coat. "I wish I'd known you were coming."

I'll bet you did, she couldn't help but think. Andi scanned the side whiteboard, a jumble of notes and details about the investigation, organized in crooked columns and connected by arrows, displaying varying penmanship and hues of dry-erase marker.

School Records, Faculty, and Extracurriculars / Hannah, Davis, Fletcher, Avi

Interview Students in Walker's Class / Tate, Liz, Ryan, Quinn

First-semester grades vs. colleges attended?

Employment records?

Group Four: Librarians / Felicia, Aidan, Nicole, Finn

"Double Life" & Non-Glenlake Friends:

Curtis Royal (Roy)

Others?

"There's an impressive amount of work here," Andi said, trying to ignore the heartburn she felt upon reading the word *others.*

"Not too bad for a three-day-a-week class," Wayne said, with pride in his voice. "Actually, this is just a running recap of some of the latest developments. We keep everything on Google Drive so the class can access it at any time."

"And it doesn't accidentally get erased," Cassidy added.

"We lost a bit of info yesterday when someone, probably a janitor, rubbed against the board while cleaning."

"Innocently, I'm sure," added Cassidy, à la Nancy Drew.

"Luckily, your daughter was able to fill in the missing information," Wayne said. "By the way, her interviewing skills are first-rate. She's our go-to investigator when it comes to the tough questions. I'm giving her nothing but the highest praise in my recommendation letter."

Cassidy smiled a little too broadly. Or maybe that was just Andi's perception, given what she said next.

"Speaking of which," Cassidy said, "did you and Dad really have a 'spectacular' breakup during senior year?"

"Wow," Andi said, feeling suddenly unsteady but resisting the urge to sink into a nearby desk. "You guys really are leaving no stone unturned. Sounds like someone's been talking to my hyperbolic friend Georgina."

Whom, right now, she wanted to kill.

Cassidy, her beautiful but right now annoyingly smug daughter, waited for the answer with arms folded across her chest.

"I'd use a different adjective: *predictable*," Andi heard herself say. "We were both stressed out about college and leaving Glenlake, so we took a break for a little while."

"It's weird that it never came up in all your Glenlake stories," said Cassidy.

Andi forced a laugh. "It all seems so silly now. I honestly think the fear of being apart drove a wedge between us." She'd never actually thought of it that way, but as she said it, she couldn't help but feel it rang true. "Luckily, we came to our senses."

"First-semester senior psychosis," Wayne said with a smile. "We haven't seen any of that around here lately. Have we, Cassidy?"

Cassidy responded with a conspiratorial giggle that bothered Andi almost as much as the jarring question she'd posed.

"If memory serves, we need to get in line early, before the Thanksgiving feast gets underway," Andi said, eager to escape further questioning. Her eyes drifted back to the whiteboard as she wondered what else they'd uncovered. "It's a shame I didn't get to hear your discussion."

"Agreed. Hopefully, you'll stop in next time you're on campus."

"It's a plan," Andi said.

Andi was relieved to say goodbye. She would have been even more relieved if either Cassidy or Wayne made a move to follow her.

"Cassidy," Andi said. "Ready to stuff your face with me?"

"We aren't quite finished here," Cassidy said, with more exasperation than was strictly necessary.

"They'll run out of dark meat if we don't get seated early."

Dark meat being the only turkey Cassidy ate.

"It doesn't matter," Cassidy said. "I'll eat whatever."

"We'll finish up on Monday," Mr. Kelly said, taking the hint. "Go enjoy your time with your mom."

"Are you sure?" Cassidy asked.

"You're good, Cass," he said, with a smile that left Andi feeling anything but.

Despite bitter cold, the sun was out and the roads were clear as they headed back to St. Louis. While Andi was well rested after a good night's sleep thanks to Ambien, Cassidy was conked out in the passenger seat after a traditionally sleepless night of merrymaking in the dorm before everyone scattered to go home.

At least she hoped that's where her daughter had been in the wee hours of the night.

Cassidy's phone, very much awake, pinged with a stream of texts.

Unlike some parents she knew, specifically Georgina, Andi maintained a firm policy of not snooping on her children's emails or texts. With necessary exceptions, of course: Owen had been cc'd in a minor middle school kerfuffle in which a girl had sent out an inappropriate photo that needed deleting. Andi had checked Whitney's emails after the school principal had asked everyone to watch out for online bullying. But she had never checked Cassidy's communications.

The phone pinged yet again.

Andi found herself thinking about the reaction of the nurse at the infirmary, when she thought Andi was there to view Cassidy's files. What if she was hiding something on Cassidy's behalf? Andi knew she was spiraling into paranoia, but she couldn't quite stop herself from pulling on the power cord attached to the phone, which had slid between the seat and the console. Or looking when the phone emerged with the screen facing her.

The sender was labeled not with a name but a heart emoji.

The message: How am I supposed to make it five days without u? was too compelling to not scroll down and see what else he'd written.

Are you going to get your dad's side of the breakup?

Do your parents know? About us?

She looked up, spotted a chunk of tire in the middle of the road, and swerved.

Cassidy's eyes opened. "What the . . . is that my phone?"

"I was checking IDOT for road conditions," Andi said, fumbling for the internet browser button. "It was a mess around here yesterday, so I was checking to see if there are any problems ahead."

"Why do you have to do that on my phone?"

"It was right there," Andi said, pointing to the spot she'd lifted it from while Cassidy slept.

"And yours is right there," Cassidy said, pointing to the console.

"It was the first one I saw. I was trying to be safe."

"Way to go with that."

Having told Cassidy a million times not to check her phone while driving, Andi couldn't defend herself.

"I think you were reading my texts."

"I don't appreciate your tone or your implication."

"And I don't appreciate being spied on."

"I wasn't spying on you."

"Yeah, *right*."

"Although, if I were, I wonder what I'd find out. I didn't think you allowed anyone to call you Cass, for example."

"I don't."

"Mr. Kelly did."

"I must not have noticed," she said quickly.

"Well, I certainly did," Andi said.

"Why are you acting so weird, Mom?" asked Cassidy, tossing her phone into her bag and zipping it up.

Andi paused. "Maybe I'm just concerned about the amount of time the two of you are spending together."

"Investigating the biggest mystery in the history of Glenlake?"

"Working on something that closely, that intensely, sometimes leads to a familiarity that can be—"

"Inappropriate?"

"Yes," Andi said.

"What's inappropriate is a mother spying on her daughter. Trust goes both ways."

Chapter Twenty-Two

IAN COPELAND'S GLENLAKE JOURNAL

Wednesday, November 27, 1996

When Dad picked me up to take me home for Thanksgiving break, I noticed right away that he didn't mention Andi. No How's Andi doing? *or* Where is Andi spending Thanksgiving this year? *Instead, he wanted to talk about sports. And only sports.*

He drove up Tuesday night and got in so late I didn't even see him. He stayed at the Old Road Inn like always. And at 8:00 a.m. sharp he was on campus with the car running. He didn't even come up to my room.

We talked about football and basketball until we were past Joliet, and then for the rest of the drive we listened to the radio when Dad wasn't reading stuff off billboards. He thinks bad grammar on small-town signs is hilarious.

Mom didn't say anything about Andi, either, which was weird, but I wasn't going to be the one to bring her up. She was already busy making Thanksgiving dinner, so Dad and I went to the video store and rented The Natural *(Dad's choice) and* Say Anything *and then got a pizza to go.*

Mom and Dad went to bed after The Natural, *and I stayed up to watch* Say Anything *and immediately regretted it. Andi liked making fun* of that movie, but we both kind of loved it, and it made me think about her way too much.

The next day, Mom waited until about half an hour before everyone started to show up before she finally told me what was on her mind.

"You've been moping around like someone, I don't know, killed your dog," she said, cutting me off as I headed to the fridge for a can of soda.

"I'm just tired from school," I said.

"Your adviser tells me she's worried about your grades. She also said you and Andi split up."

I don't know why I thought there might have been anyone left in the world who didn't know. It weirded me out to suddenly realize that she and Dad must have been talking about it all along. "My grades will be fine."

"Fall grades still count on your college apps, so you need to keep it together, Ian. Right now you may be feeling like it's the end of the world, but when you get older, you'll look back and realize this was only a hiccup."

A "hiccup"? I didn't say anything. I mean, how was I supposed to respond to that?

Dinner was the usual giant thing with all the leaves in the table and all the aunts and uncles and cousins and Grandma and Grandpa Copeland. Mom and Dad seemed so cheerful they could barely contain themselves, and I couldn't help but think it was because they were happy Andi and I are over and done with. When Dad made his usual toast where he said something about everyone at the table, he said I had a bright future ahead of me, like he and Mom wanted to make sure to reinforce the message or something.

Later, all the kids at the kids' table started cracking up because Chrissie had the hiccups and couldn't stop. She tried to drink milk and hiccuped, and milk came out of her nose. Everybody was dying of laughter even though Grandma Copeland clearly thought the End Times were upon us.

I couldn't laugh. I just kept thinking: hiccup.

Hiccup.

ANDI BLOOM'S GLENLAKE JOURNAL

Thursday, November 28, 1996

The whole way to the airport, everyone in the van went on about how jealous they were that I'm going to have a warm, sunny Thanksgiving. I swear, some of them think we eat our turkey dinner on the actual beach. Midwesterners don't seem to understand that mashed potatoes and gravy don't mix well with wind and sand. I don't ruin their fantasies by explaining that Californians do dine indoors, particularly on Thanksgiving. Given that my house is just off Mulholland Drive and miles from the actual ocean, it's unlikely that I will even feel sand between my toes this trip. And while Simon has been known to rent a beach house when the mood strikes him, he's not all that jazzed about chasing toddlers up and down Malibu, trying to keep them from becoming shark bait. Or, I should say, watching the nanny do it while Lorraine arranges Thanksgiving dinner in bowls and platters as though she actually cooked it herself and didn't order everything from Gelson's.

I'm not complaining exactly. The food is way better than anything she could possibly whip up.

Mostly, I'm just missing Dallas, who headed off to Ohio to be with family.

He didn't even say where in Ohio. Or which members of his family.

I think he tried to call the home phone once, but Simon answered, said hello, and then hung up, irritated no one was there.

"How are things at school?" Lorraine asked, putting on kitchen mitts to remove the precooked turkey from the oven.

"Good," I said, taking rolls out of the bag, putting them into a basket, and hoping one-word answers would keep Lorraine from any in-depth questioning.

In-depth questioning not being Lorraine's strength anyway.

"Still on a break from Ian?"

"Yep," I said.

"Are you interested in anyone else?" she continued, undoubtedly asking for Simon.

My pulse quickened just a little. He couldn't know . . . could he?

"I'm just doing my own thing right now," I said, casually.

~

Saturday, November 30, 1996

I had planned to kill two birds with one stone (bad cliché but, hey, it's my journal) by spending the next two days working and taking suntan breaks by the pool.

I had my supplemental essay topics organized by school and spread out on the dining room table. I had a towel, sunscreen, and a cooler full of cold drinks on the patio. I was headed outside to start my half hour of soaking in vitamin D and deciding how I would answer Tell us about a person who has influenced you in a significant way *when the phone rang.*

"Got it!" I yelled before Simon or Lorraine could pick up an extension.

I said hello and heard a familiar and welcome voice. "Congratulations, you've won the Publishers Clearing House Sweepstakes."

"I just knew I would," I said, smiling.

"You'll receive your prize tomorrow night."

"What?" I said, thoroughly confused.

"I'm headed back."

"To Glenlake?"

"Chicago," he said. "I'll be there tomorrow. Come back early and meet me."

Simon wasn't happy, but how could he argue against an opportunity for me to go back a day early to consult with a college counselor in Chicago?

I hated lying to him, although I rationalized it by telling myself that Dallas was a college counselor, in a way. I said I was staying with a friend, which was also kind of true, too.

Simon questioned me all the way down the 405 to the airport.

Why the last-minute notice?

Counselors really meet with students over Thanksgiving break?

There's really no way they could fit you into the schedule if you go back when we planned?

I just kept on lying, knowing I would be with Dallas in a few short hours.

When I finally landed, Dallas was waiting for me at the gate, but there was no kiss.

"Welcome back," he said, sounding more like my teacher than my lover. I was disappointed, but I guess kissing in public probably wasn't the best idea.

It wasn't until we got to his car and double-checked that we couldn't be seen that we finally kissed.

Needless to say, our reunion was well worth his caution.

So was the momentous evening that followed, even if it took place at a chain hotel near the airport.

I'm not going to cheapen the moment by trying to describe it. Amazing? Life altering? Passionate? (See, it's impossible without making it sound like a line out of a cheesy romance novel.) It was far too overwhelming to try and capture on paper. The intensity of making love to a man as opposed to a boy is thrilling, if a little scary. If I'm being entirely honest, I did think about Ian. Mainly because he always hugged me afterward, no matter how many times we did it.

It wasn't like that at all with Dallas.

Part of that comfortable, safe feeling comes with time, I'm sure.

Chapter Twenty-Three

Cassidy had the house to herself, and she knew it wouldn't last. The calm before the shitstorm of Thanksgiving guests. Mom was out shopping for the big dinner at Schnucks with the twins, and Dad was picking up a case of wine from one of his stores. She had weaseled out of helping by saying she'd been up late the night before working on college apps.

As she went into the kitchen in her socks, Rusty snuffling at her feet, anticipating the rattle of fresh food in his bowl, she actually had a moment of what she might have called *prenostalgia*: she was going to miss this place, and it wouldn't be all that long before she did.

But she hadn't stayed home alone to mope, even though she was still annoyed at Mom after that weird lecture on the ride home from Glenlake. Maybe she shouldn't have been so sarcastic with the *What happens at Glenlake stays at Glenlake* line she'd said under her breath, but what the hell.

Ever since Liz Wright's little buzzer-beating revelation that her parents had broken up during senior year, Cassidy hadn't been able to get it out of her mind. According to Georgina, as related by Liz, it had been the talk of campus: They'd tried to do it quietly, but as the It Couple, their news all but made the headlines of the campus paper. They were both seen with other people, but neither of them seemed to settle into a real relationship. Then, a few months later, they were suddenly back together, acting like nothing happened.

And Mom was still pretending it was no big deal.

None of this had anything to do with the Dallas Walker investigation, obviously, but it raised one big question for Cassidy: Why hadn't her parents said a single word, ever? Their relationship wasn't just Glenlake legend; it was family legend, all but carved into the walls of the Copeland family manor.

Her mom had always decorated the place to within an inch of its life, and the walls were lined with not only generations of family photos but framed letters, sketches by artist friends, and fragments of prose and poetry, some of them handwritten. Like the Glenlake tradition of framed senior pages, she'd curated key artifacts from everyone's lives—and Ian and Andi's Glenlake romance was given a particularly prominent spot with a timeline that proceeded as you ascended the stairs.

With a diet soda in hand, no longer trailed by Rusty, who was now noisily crunching food in his bowl, Cassidy headed for those very stairs. Snapshots of Glenlake, covers of the campus literary journal where Mom had published several short stories, team and individual photos of Dad on a seemingly endless number of sports ball teams were all arrayed around four frames containing pages from Mom's journal, written in her impossibly neat, tiny hand.

For freshman year, there were two pages framed side by side, next to a picture of Mom and Dad looking impossibly young and super dorky, even though they must have been totally cool at the time. Those haircuts!

"So you're the new girl. From California."

Those are the first words Ian Copeland said to me. That is, after he asked me to dance.

I danced with other guys, too—a Colin, a Tanner, and a boy whose parents seriously named him Steele Hammer, but dancing with Ian Copeland is major, or so says my new roommate, Georgina, who grew up with him in St. Louis, where he is like everything or something.

We danced to three songs in a row, which supposedly practically killed Georgina's friend Sylvie, who has loved him forever.

Because Georgina and Sylvie (who actually said, "If Ian is going to fall for someone other than me, at least it's someone who totally breaks the mold") think Ian asking me to dance is the most important thing that's ever happened since the beginning of time, I figured I should mention it in tonight's journal entry.

My thoughts about Ian Copeland, in no particular order:

His hair is brown with highlights like he spent the summer outside, but not surfer-blond highlights like the boys back home.

It (his hair) is the type that always looks tousled.

So do his clothes (in a cute way).

He's into the Beastie Boys. I know this because he said, "I love this band," while we were dancing to "Sabotage." I'm not all that into the Beastie Boys, but I'd put that in the style-points-plus category.

He is tall, but a little on the skinny side.

His eyes are blue and his nose is super straight.

He smells like cinnamon (gum) and cedar, like the sweater he was wearing came from one of those old-timey closets they have here to keep the moths from eating everything.

He told me he thought I was pretty . . .

The sophomore-year entry was a single page and was paired with a picture of Mom and Dad at the fall mixer. They were obviously a real item by then, given the way they side-hugged for the camera without leaving a single micron of space between them.

Today is our one-year anniversary!

Georgina insists we're off by a week because it was love at first sight and that our relationship started at the fall mixer.

Then again, Georgina is a hopeless romantic.

I'd be lying if I said Ian wasn't on my radar after that night, or that I didn't notice him every day when I came out of math class, and at the field house after his soccer practice and my one and only nightmarish season on the field hockey team. Still, it wasn't until he sat next to me in the dining hall at Wednesday-night dinner and asked if I was going on the weekend off-campus activity that I knew, for sure, he wanted to go out with me.

And it wasn't until Saturday, when he kissed me by the indoor fountain at the Glenlake Valley Mall, that I pressed GO on our relationship timer.

I swear, whenever I hear trickling water and smell chlorine, I will always think of that kiss!

Unfortunately, the chemistry lab smells the same way.

Ian made that work for me, too, by tutoring me for like a million hours about ionic-covalent bonds AND making me flash cards in his (adorably) perfect handwriting. Not only did I get a miracle A– on the test, but he was waiting outside the science building with anniversary and congratulations kisses, Hershey's and real!!

Ian + Andi 4ever!!!!!!

Junior year was two lines alongside a black-and-white photo that must have been taken by one of Mom's friends on the yearbook—*Lacrustine*—staff. It was at the peristyle, and they actually looked a lot more grown-up despite their school clothes. Although the reason they were at the peristyle was undoubtedly to sneak cigarettes.

The whole school assumes we're going to get married.

I don't know about that, but I can't really imagine life without him . . .

Senior year offered only a single line. Paired with photos of them in their caps and gowns for graduation, it offered a literal picture of excitement about the future, but Cassidy couldn't help noticing that her mom revealed less and less with every passing year.

I'm going to Smith, and Ian just got his acceptance letter to Amherst!!!!

Even from the attic she heard them coming home: first Rusty barking, then slamming doors and Mom yelling at Whitney and Owen to carry in the rest of the groceries. Cassidy was opening boxes and thinking about how much her family's attic resembled a stereotypical attic in a stereotypical movie: vast, with piles of boxes mingled with outgrown toys and antique furniture. Why didn't her parents get rid of this stuff?

Maybe—she shuddered—they were saving it all for *her*.

There was a lot of stuff, but at least it was well organized: even the papers had been filed in storage boxes and labeled in Mom's handwriting. And when Cassidy found two full boxes marked GLENLAKE: IAN and GLENLAKE: ANDI, she thought she'd hit pay dirt.

She'd started with Dad's just because it was on top, but so far hadn't found much except report cards, yearbooks, multiple clippings from student newspapers where Dad had scored the game-winning point, and a stiff, neatly folded letterman jacket. She was just lifting the lid off a shoebox full of what Mrs. Demarest, the Glenlake librarian, would have called *ephemera* when she heard the twins thumping up the attic stairs.

"What's up, Cass?" said Whitney, Owen right behind her.

"Nothing, Whit," said Cassidy irritably. Mom was right: She didn't like to be called that. But she hadn't thought twice when Mr. Kelly had done it. From him it seemed . . . nice. Respectful, in a weird way. Like they were equals.

"I hate it when you call me that," her thirteen-year-old sister said, pouting.

"Then remember this: It's Cass-i-dy. Three syllables."

"All right, all right," grumbled Whitney.

"I'm going to shorten both names from the front," said Owen brightly. "Dee and Nee."

They ignored him. That was really all you could do with a thirteen-year-old boy.

"What are you doing with Mom and Dad's old school stuff?" asked Whitney, all ready to pal up with her big sister.

"Does this have anything to do with the mystery your class is investigating?" asked Owen, stepping on an ancient wooden skateboard and rattling across the floor.

"Not directly. I'm just trying to get a better idea of what Glenlake was like back then," Cassidy said over the racket. Not saying, *I'm looking for evidence of our parents' big breakup back when they were seventeen.* It didn't seem like something they needed to know.

Whitney had made her way over and found the GLENLAKE: ANDI box. "Can I look in this one?"

"Be my guest," Cassidy told her, lifting a handful of photos, notes, and ticket stubs out of the shoebox as the petrified rubber band holding them together fell off in pieces.

She flipped through the first few pictures and set them aside. What she really wanted was something more personal. She'd found a few letters and postcards written from Mom to Dad during summer vacation, spring break, and other separations. The letters were much juicier than the postcards, for obvious reasons. One included a soft-porn description about how Mom would feel when *our bodies are again as one* that made Cassidy shudder and stop reading.

She preferred not to think about her parents having sex, thank you very much, and would definitely guide her siblings away from those. But wouldn't any breakup have been reflected in writing? Maybe in Mom's journal?

Dad's journal wasn't in his box. And a quick search of Mom's box alongside Whitney revealed hers wasn't there, either. Not that Cassidy was sure she could bring herself to pick the locks, anyway.

Cassidy's own journal, after a few dutiful freshman attempts, was a wasteland of white space, as were the journals of most of her classmates: she planned to write her senior page much as she would write a college essay and wondered when Glenlake would finally get with the times and curate students' Instagram posts.

Owen, bored by the mementos, left to take the skateboard outside, where he would undoubtedly try to jump over a trash can. Whitney stayed with Cassidy, both of them delighted by report cards (aside from Dad having a bad patch in senior year, both of them had nearly straight

As, so Cassidy could confirm *that* for Mr. Kelly), yearbook entries (they cackled over one where Mike wrote to Dad: *Dude, I love you, but that doesn't make me gay*), and pictures revealing their hilarious mid-1990s taste in hair and clothes.

"I guess their friends all looked like that, too," said Whitney, marveling at their parents' inexplicable popularity.

Still, after twenty minutes, she lost interest. Cassidy had been at it for a lot longer than Whitney and was getting ready to give up herself.

Then Whitney, rooting aimlessly, withdrew a metal bracelet that looked handmade. "This is actually kind of cool," she said. "Do you think Mom would care if I wear it?"

Cassidy shrugged and put the lid back on the box. "I can't see why she would."

~

Usually, Grandma Biz and Grandpa Cope hosted everyone at their house, but after some not-so-subtle hints that decades of hosting had taken their toll, Mom had volunteered to take over and received Grandma's relieved blessing.

Not that Biz had been able to keep herself from acting as executive chef. She'd arrived before Cassidy even woke up, to "help," but really to oversee the operation in her daughter-in-law's kitchen. Dad and Grandpa had only two jobs, turkey and drinks, so they spent most of the day watching football.

Simon, who insisted that he and Lorraine were to be known by their first names—*no granny or gramps shit*—arrived just after noon along with Lorraine, Aunt Savannah (who wasn't all that much older than Cassidy), and Savannah's boyfriend, Tyson. Aunt Sage had gotten married last year and was with her new husband's family in Arizona. In typical Simon fashion, he announced that he was taking Lorraine, Savannah, and Tyson to the Bahamas and staying in St. Louis only overnight. Cassidy had always thought her SoCal aunts were airheads, but she couldn't help liking Simon. He had a teasing familiarity that was a lot more fun than the cutting observations that passed for jokes among the Copelands.

Even better, he brought presents. Cassidy didn't think she was materialistic, but Simon's gifts, extravagant and casually presented, were an irresistible reminder of his Hollywood lifestyle.

When Rusty went nuts, signaling their arrival, the twins tore downstairs, yelling at Cassidy to hurry up.

She closed her laptop, where she had just found a bibliography of Dallas Walker on the website of the Poetry Foundation. It was brief, just like his life span, and included a collection of short stories, his debut book of poems, and selected publications that included the *New Yorker* and *Harper's* among a handful of magazines she hadn't heard of.

In the front hall, Rusty was squirming between legs and barking joyfully as everyone came to greet the family. Cassidy arrived just as Simon bear-hugged her slim Grandma Biz, who would really have preferred the kind of hug where both hands briefly touch the shoulders so a dry kiss could be brushed across the cheek.

Seeing Cassidy, Simon beamed. "How's Glenlake, kiddo?"

"Great!" she told him, descending the stairs and accepting his crushing hug. He even smelled different, like warm weather and an expensive cologne that probably took Lorraine a whole afternoon to pick out.

Never one to stand on ceremony, Simon fished in his coat pocket and brought out a small wrapped gift.

"For you! Open it!"

She fumbled with the paper while everyone watched. Inside was a top-of-the-line Garmin running watch.

"I know cross-country's over for the year, but I presume you'll be running in college," he said.

"Thank you," she told him, pleased.

"Drinks!" said Grandpa Cope, his favorite topic, and the whole troop moved farther into the house, Mom taking coats and bags and giving them to the twins, Dad and Simon doing an awkward side hug that Dad used to ward off Simon's embrace.

"What's your pleasure?" asked Dad.

"Vodka rocks with a splash of soda," said Simon. Lorraine shot him a look over her shoulder just before she disappeared into the kitchen. "Actually, make that the other way round."

"Coming right up," Dad told him, heading into the den, where a wet bar took up one corner of the room.

Cassidy spotted her opportunity.

She hurried into the study just as Dad was screwing the cap back on the soda bottle. Football players grappled and collided on the TV in the corner.

"I put the vodka in last and hardly stirred, so he'll think it's a stiff drink," he told her with a smile. "I think we have to work with Lorraine on this one."

Simon's drink fizzed on the small bar, a perfect curlicue of lemon peel floating dead center.

"Dad?"

"Yes, Cassidy?" he asked, reaching for another cocktail glass.

"Why haven't you and Mom ever said anything about breaking up in high school?"

He froze, just for a moment, before plucking the glass off the shelf and turning around. His expression seemed guarded.

"Who told you that?"

"Georgina told someone in my class," she said, not wanting to reveal that she'd mentioned anything to Mom and wondering if she'd get a different answer. "They were asking about Dallas, and I guess she mentioned that it was something that happened that year. It sounded like a big deal, because you and Mom were like *the* couple or something."

He worked on the drink, obviously thinking about what to say, but before he could answer, Simon came into the room, propelled by a cheerful Grandpa Cope.

"We've paid our respects to the kitchen, and now it's time for the traditional rites of masculinity," said Grandpa. Addressing Ian at the bar, he added, "I recommend making your mother's a double. It might make things easier for your wife."

Cassidy hoped for a look from Dad, something that told her *We'll talk later.* But instead he nodded at Cope, said, "I'm on it," and busied himself with the drinks.

~

At dinner, the bowls and platters were starting to go around the table, everyone passing to the left as directed by Grandma Biz, when Mom saw Whitney's wrist trembling slightly under the weight of the mashed potatoes. Or, more precisely, she saw what was on her wrist. Only Cassidy seemed to notice her sharp intake of breath.

"Where did you get that?" Mom demanded.

"It was in an old box in the attic," said Whitney with a guilty look.

"What were you doing, digging around up there?"

"We were helping Cassidy—she was looking for something," said the little rat.

The bowls and platters continued to go around, and serving spoons clinked quietly on rims as everyone else listened curiously. Cassidy tried to think objectively, the way Mr. Kelly had taught them to, wondering how this reaction squared with her mom's usual lack of concern for her personal property. She didn't particularly mind sharing shoes and lipstick, for example—sometimes she even encouraged it.

"I was just looking at your old Glenlake stuff," Cassidy defended herself. "I wasn't looking for anything in particular. I was just curious about what it was like for you back then."

"It was harder, wasn't it?" kidded Grandpa Cope, chuckling. "The teachers were twice as mean, and the walk to class was uphill both ways."

"You should have asked first, Cassidy," Mom said.

Cassidy looked around the table for help, but her father was frowning at his plate, and the other adults seemed oblivious to her mother's suddenly dark mood. "God, Mom, it's all just lying around up there. It's not like I broke into some family vault."

"The Great Copeland Caper," chimed in Simon. "Speaking of mysteries, what's going on at that criminally expensive school of yours—you know, with the laddie in the lake?"

Cassidy's ears perked up. In trying to change the subject, he'd inadvertently made a crucial connection. Maybe that bracelet had been a gift to her mother from another boy. Maybe *he* was the real reason her parents had split up.

"Hardly talk for the dinner table," said Mom, practically gritting her teeth.

"It made the Associated Press," continued Simon as things threatened to spiral out of control, "but was a notable omission from that monthly newsletter they keep sending, still hoping for more donations."

"I hope you're still giving," cracked Cope.

"If they can't keep their faculty alive, I don't know if I should," answered Simon.

"That's enough, everybody," said her dad with an intensity that thankfully shut everyone up for a hot minute. He nudged her mom to take the cranberries he'd been holding aloft. She accepted the bowl and spooned a tiny amount onto her plate.

"Is there something about that bracelet in particular?" asked Cassidy. *Digging.*

"Well, it's my property, for one," her mom said, her voice catching. "And I made it in a metalworking class, so it's special to me. I really don't want it broken."

There went her theory about it being a gift.

"I'll be careful," said Whitney, dropping both hands into her lap, obviously wishing she'd never worn the thing in the first place.

~

Wanting to avoid hours of car time with Mom, Cassidy spent Saturday afternoon texting friends, and by Sunday morning had arranged a ride to school with Jane Berg from Spanish class, lying to Mom that another cross-country teammate was going, too.

"That's fine," said Mom distractedly. "I'm looking for that bracelet Whitney was wearing, and it's not in her room. Do you know where it is?"

She did. Whitney had given it to her, tears of embarrassment in her eyes, right after Thanksgiving dinner. Cassidy had tucked it in her own suitcase without quite being sure why.

"She gave it to me. Mom, you embarrassed the shit out of her."

"Language, Cassidy."

Cassidy rolled her eyes, knowing it would wind her up even more.

"Your sister needs to learn not to make assumptions about other people's property."

"Now you sound like Grandma Biz," said Cassidy.

"I do not!"

She did. And she'd had a stick up her butt ever since she came into Mr. Kelly's classroom last week at Glenlake. How could her mom ever possibly think she'd be a geezer squeezer?

"Go get it. I want it."

Pissed, Cassidy stomped upstairs to her room. After digging the bracelet out of a side pocket in her suitcase, she held it in the palm of her hand for a moment, then set it down on the bedspread, angled the lamp for better light, and took two pictures of it with her phone before she gave it back.

Just in case it *was* a clue to why her parents had broken up.

Chapter Twenty-Four

Saturday, December 21, 1996

Dallas kissed me on the snowy front porch, forgetting even to look to see if anyone was watching. Seeing as everyone was still at the Winter Formal, there wasn't much reason for concern.

"I have a gift for you," I said, handing him the box.

"I have something special for you, but it's not going to be ready until after break." He kissed me. "But I promise it will be worth the wait."

I watched while he tore off the paper and opened the box. Inside was a copper bracelet I'd made in metalworking class.

The bracelets are a total thing on campus. Some people in the class are practically mass-producing simple hammered versions and selling them to underclassmen. I had used the whole semester to make two extremely detailed matching braided bracelets.

"You made this," he said.

"I did," I said, showing him the other one, which was more delicate but otherwise identical. I'd just slipped it on for the first time.

"I love it," he said, smiling as he put the bracelet on his right wrist. "I'll never take it off."

"You promise?"

"Only if you promise to slip out of that slinky silver dress. I've been dying to get you out of it all night."

~

Wayne Kelly may have considered Cassidy a crack sleuth and the go-to investigator in his class, but she was still very much a teenager, a fact evidenced by the way she'd left for school with her bedroom in total disarray.

The irrational part of Andi wished she could rub Kelly's nose in the incontrovertible evidence of her daughter's not yet fully developed frontal lobe—the dirty clothes on the floor, the unmade bed—before giving him a furious earful for encouraging Cassidy's investigative audacity. She couldn't believe her daughter hadn't even thought to ask before digging through her things and then giving one of her most prized keepsakes—*that* bracelet—to Whitney.

After her outburst, she had done her best to keep cool while waiting patiently for Cassidy to return to Glenlake. As soon as she was safely out the door, Andi made a beeline for the bedroom "to pick up after her"—that, and jiggle the mouse on her desktop computer. As she expected, it had been abandoned in sleep mode, not powered off like it was supposed to be.

Unlike the guilt she'd felt snooping on Cassidy's text messages— and paid for all weekend long with her daughter's icy demeanor—Andi felt well within her rights as she located and opened the Google Drive folder labeled *Dallas Walker Investigation*. After all, she and Ian paid the bills that allowed their daughter to own the computer, attend Glenlake, and take an investigative journalism class in the first place. More importantly, she had to find out what the class already knew.

Before doing anything else, she keyword-searched *bracelet*.

No results.

Moving on, she started scanning, eyes peeled for even the vaguest hint that Cassidy held too special a place in her teacher's heart. An investigative journalist's equivalent of the verse Dallas had composed solely for Andi and yet chalked on the board for all to see.

At the time, Andi had been so flattered by the attention. And while her feelings now were complicated—recognizing that their passion had been real, even if it was wrong—it made her sick to think she'd been naive enough to be taken in by a man who was the same age as she was now. A seventeen-year-old was not a woman.

She couldn't let Cassidy be seduced like she had.

So far, she hadn't found anything in any of the documents that was unusual beyond seeing her daughter's name more often than she might have liked. While Cassidy was officially assigned as leader of *Group Five: Persons of Interest*, she also seemed to have contributed information to groups one through four. Andi's and Ian's names cropped up with troubling frequency, too.

In the file named *School Records, Faculty, and Extracurriculars*, Andi, Ian, or both were listed as 1996–1997 members of the student body, members of the class (Andi), members of the Cue Sports Society (Ian), and organizers of the spring poetry slam (Andi again). Andi's name also appeared in a list compiled by Cassidy of the college alma maters of the poetry class.

She had to give grudging credit to Kelly for the impressive amount of information the kids had collected on both faculty and students. Especially as she scanned their collective *Still Needed to Be Done or Determined* file:

—*Police reports from the time of Dallas Walker's disappearance (public record?)*

—*Fall grades in Dallas Walker's class: original marks vs postsemester corrected grades.*

—*Exclude random motives, e.g., robbery gone wrong*

—College applications vs acceptances for class members. Did anyone get rejected from first-choice schools as a result of poetry class grade?

—Persons of Interest Interviews: Curtis Royal (Roy)

Andi was relieved to see *Irregular schedule, not interviewed yet* written beside his name.

Less comforting were the former student interviews in which Cassidy had reported every word Andi and Ian had said about Dallas Walker, from Ian's description of Dallas as a *blowhard* to Andi's comment about his prescient fear of *the future.*

Along with their comments were a number of inconsequential interviews with classmates and members of the Cue Sports Society.

He was cool, but kind of scary. (Clair Sommerfeld Cramer)

He had the best car of all time. Probably worth six figures at Mecum Auctions now. I can't believe they found him inside it. (Michael Reynolds)

I learned a lot from him. Until he disappeared, that is. Do you really think he was murdered? (Crystal Thomas Ronello)

After everyone and their parents complained about our fall grades, Dallas raised them to what they should have been, I got into Princeton, and everything turned out fine. For me, that is. (Philip Martin)

One comment triggered a surprisingly familiar stab of jealousy.

He was flirtatious with the headmaster's wife, said Roland James, their chemistry teacher. *I mean, we all were, but I wouldn't have been entirely surprised to hear there was some hanky-panky going on there.*

Andi did another keyword search for *Miranda Darrow* and *headmaster's wife* to see if anyone had looked into that particular angle. Finding nothing, she made a note of her own.

The longest alumni interview by far was that of Georgina Holt Fordham.

Naturally.

And just as Georgina had reported, she actually had told Liz Wright, her student interviewer, that *most of the guys thought he was kind of a douche, but all the girls thought he was sexy as hell.*

Andi shook her head, growing even more bothered, just like the day she'd found a fiery red hair on Dallas's dark peacoat.

"Georgina hugged me because I gave her an A on a paper," Dallas had said.

Georgina, who had told Liz in a second interview about her then boyfriend Tommy Harkins and the poetry grade that *doomed him to a state school, not that he was all that smart anyway.*

There was more, most of it noise and random gossip and Georgina's explanations that none of her classmates had anything to do with Dallas's death because she *just knew.*

Georgina had also let slip the one sentence there was no reason at all to blab.

Other than Dallas's disappearance, it was a completely uneventful year. Besides Andi Bloom and Ian Copeland's spectacular breakup and makeup, that is.

Chapter Twenty-Five

Detective Deno Gavras looked like an insurance salesman, thought Cassidy. He wore pleated chinos, a V-neck sweater over a not-too-crisp button-down shirt, and a shapeless sport coat. On his feet were the kind of rubber overshoes she associated with grandparents—not *her* grandparents, of course, but the kind of grandparents who shoveled their own snow and brought their groceries home in two-wheeled carts via city sidewalks.

Although, come to think of it, as he and Mr. Kelly conferred while the students slowly straggled in, it looked more like Mr. Kelly was the salesman and Detective Gavras was the reluctant customer, his nods and body language noncommittal in the extreme.

When the bell rang, Mr. Kelly called the class to attention.

"Settle down, journos. As promised, we have a real live detective here, and he's agreed to give us half an hour of his extremely valuable time. So let's make the most of it. I hope you are as prepared as I asked you to be."

It didn't look to Cassidy like Gavras was busy or in any particular hurry. In fact, he projected a kind of blankness that almost looked like stupidity. But her first impression of a not-too-bright insurance sales-man disappeared as soon as he opened his mouth.

"Can you tell us a little bit about your role with the sheriff's department, Mr. Gavras?" asked Mr. Kelly quickly, seeming anxious to get the preamble over with.

"I've been on the force sixteen years, detective for five," said Gavras, in a voice that sounded like he smoked, drank, and yelled enough to have fried his vocal cords. "We investigate any crimes that take place outside municipal jurisdiction and also have agreements with a number of the towns that aren't big enough to handle their own criminal investigations."

"And you're the lead detective on the Dallas Walker case?"

"Yes," said Gavras flatly, folding his arms. He had parked his ass on Mr. Kelly's favorite desk corner, leaving her teacher to pace in no-man's-land.

"Can you think of a case similar to this one, in your experience?"

"Not in my experience, no."

"Is there anything about the evidence that suggests Walker's death was suspicious in nature—that is, anything other than suicide?"

Gavras gave Mr. Kelly a look that was so hostile Cassidy would have yelped if it had been fixed on her. But Mr. Kelly didn't even seem to notice. *He must have talked to hundreds of cops and other people who didn't want to answer his questions,* she thought. He would have very thick skin.

"I told you I wouldn't talk about any details of the case," said Gavras.

"I wouldn't ask you to reveal anything that's not public knowledge," conceded Mr. Kelly.

"Well, until we conclude our investigation, I can't tell you what we think."

Mr. Kelly took a deep breath and walked around the perimeter of the room, winding up at the back, so he was talking to Gavras across the rows of students. It made Cassidy feel like he was one of them, that they were all facing Gavras, all thinking the same questions.

She flashed back to Mom all but asking her if she had the hots for Mr. Kelly. God, no. He was awesome, but who looked at their teacher and thought, *yeah, I want to get my mouth all over that middle-aged face?*

"Detective Gavras, is the fact that you're still investigating after two and a half months unusual?"

Which was a good question. Were they just not taking this seriously?

"You tell me," said Gavras.

"I'll tell you what we do know," said Mr. Kelly. "And it's not a lot. We know that Dallas Walker was a popular if controversial figure during his time at Glenlake. He was an iconoclast who was known to have let his guard down around the students: He swore in class, asked his students to call him by his first name, and could be capricious in his grading. He also coached, if you can call it that, a pool team or club called the 'Cue Sports Society.' One of its former members confirmed that on at least one occasion, he provided them with beer."

"Wayne, I told you I would talk about general police procedure, how we solve crimes," said Gavras, annoyed, the faintest trace of complaint in his voice.

"Kids don't learn from generalities, Detective Gavras," said Mr. Kelly. "Which is why we are investigating the same case as you. We don't flatter ourselves that we'll actually be able to solve it, but by following the investigation in the same way a professional journalist would, my students will learn the necessary skills."

"In other words, fake news," said Gavras dryly.

"We've done a lot of research into the background and character of Walker," continued Mr. Kelly. "We know what he was like. We know when he arrived on campus, when he was reported missing, and when his body was discovered in the lake by Tate Holland."

Tate slouched down in his chair as Gavras spotted him and gave him a nod. Cassidy was glad Mr. Kelly didn't remind everyone that Tate was still on academic probation for the rest of the semester, even if Mr. Kelly had talked him into taking his class.

"How do you go about identifying suspects, Detective Gavras?" asked Mr. Kelly.

Gavras took his hands out of his pockets and looked, for the moment, ready to play along. "Well, obviously we analyze the crime scene for physical evidence and look for anything that would point to someone else being present at the time of death. In this case, there wasn't much to go on. We found a few things in the car we're looking at. Then, we canvass. If it's something that happened recently, we knock on doors. If it's something that happened in the past, we create a timeline and then try to locate the last people who saw him, and so forth."

Who was the last person to see Dallas Walker? It could even have been Mom or Dad. Some purely random moment as Walker drove off campus, no one realizing it was the last time the poet would be seen alive.

Of course, if Walker was murdered, then they wouldn't have been the last people to see him alive.

"Do you also try to identify who had motive, means, and opportunity?" asked Mr. Kelly.

"That's right, Columbo," said Gavras with a smirk.

Once again, Mr. Kelly let that one roll off him. He didn't try to one-up Gavras—he didn't even act as if he'd noticed.

"And you won't tell us who's on your list," confirmed Mr. Kelly.

Gavras didn't say anything.

"Well, as a purely hypothetical activity, these students have assembled a list of suspects," said Mr. Kelly, walking over to the whiteboard at the side of the room where they'd gradually built their list.

Noticing it for the first time, Gavras squinted with interest. Cassidy thought he probably had a pair of glasses in an inside pocket and was too vain to put them on.

"You're really doing this?" asked Gavras.

"It's not much of a list," said Mr. Kelly, confirming the obvious. Most of the entries consisted of things like *Students who got bad grades?*

Robbery gone wrong? Students in his class? Students in his club? But there were several names.

Racing through Cassidy's mind was *Students in his class?* She had thought nothing of it at the time—just another scribble on the white-board during a brainstorming session—but *students* included Andi Copeland, formerly Bloom. And then Dad, under *Students in his club?* Suddenly, with actual law enforcement scrutinizing it, Cassidy felt uneasy about the implication that her parents might have been involved.

She now regretted riding back to school with Jane. Dad, not Mom, probably would have driven her, and she could have asked him again why they broke up during their senior year. Maybe whatever had happened would give them both alibis.

"Who told you about Roy?" demanded Gavras, perusing the list.

"We can't reveal our sources, either," said Mr. Kelly, eliciting a laugh from the kids even though his tone was completely neutral.

"Roy totally did it!" said Noah, prompting a bigger laugh.

Something had been building while the class watched Kelly and Gavras spar, and now, even though Mr. Kelly tried to quiet them with a classic *quiet down* gesture, it seemed to Cassidy like it might be too late.

She surprised herself by speaking up. "Despite my classmate's unfortunate way of phrasing his suggestion, it does seem like Curtis Royal would be a person of interest in any investigation. He has a crimi-nal record and was a known associate of Dallas Walker."

Gavras looked like he was ready to walk out the door. "Do you real-ize how irresponsible this is, Wayne?" he snarled. "Getting these . . . kids to speculate about who might have murdered somebody? We haven't even determined it *was* a murder."

"These young men and women are getting ahead of themselves, and I apologize," said Mr. Kelly pointedly to the room and not their guest speaker. "But if you'd be willing to answer any questions that don't leap to conclusions, I would truly appreciate a few more minutes of your time. If we're off base, tell us how."

Hannah's hand shot up, and she blurted out her question without waiting to be called on. "Could a teenager get away with a murder?"

"If they got away with it, it means we didn't catch them, so we don't know the crime was committed by a teenager," said Gavras curtly.

The class laughed and Hannah blushed, her hand falling to her desk with a lightly audible slap.

"Do you think bad grades could be a motive?" asked Rowan.

Cassidy wished the class would move on from the idea that a student could be guilty.

"Literally anything can be a motive," said Gavras.

"What about Roy?" asked Cassidy, trying again. "Have you questioned him? He works at Glenlake now."

"No comment," said Gavras, looking for his overcoat.

Cassidy felt embarrassed by the detective's disdain for her classmates and angry he wasn't taking them seriously. At the same time, she couldn't totally blame him.

Noah, who still seemed to think the class project was some kind of hilarious joke, raised his hand, and Mr. Kelly called on him.

"What if someone was going to kill him but he killed himself right before it could happen? Would you still go after the first guy for attempted murder?"

Detective Gavras pursed his lips and, finding his coat on a chair, put it on. "I think we're done here."

Mr. Kelly thanked him and followed him out into the hall but opened the door again almost as soon as it had closed behind them, returning in time to quell the *holy shit!* hubbub in the classroom.

"Well," he said, once they were listening, "that didn't go exactly as planned. Did we learn anything?"

"Gavras shops at Marshalls?" volunteered someone in the back of the room.

An annoyed look crossed Mr. Kelly's face. "You want adults to treat you with respect? Then treat your *work* with respect," he snapped.

Much to Cassidy's relief, the giggling stopped.

"Break up into your teams and use the rest of your class time wisely," said Mr. Kelly, sitting down behind his desk and opening his laptop.

Without too much more jackassery, the kids moved their desks into their working groups and opened their laptops, too. Cassidy watched Tate concentrating on his screen. He was *her* big secret. How long could she keep him from her parents?

~

Cassidy's job was to track down Roy, but so far, she hadn't had much luck at it. She'd called the facilities department number repeatedly, only to be told that he wasn't working or wasn't available. She'd located a home phone using 411, but it rang and rang without an answer or even a voice mail prompt. And she hadn't seen him on campus. According to her dad, he had been there during parents' weekend, but at that time, Cassidy hadn't even known he existed.

If she was honest with herself, she hadn't given much thought to the existence of any of the groundskeepers, but that was a liberal-white-guilt matter for another day.

The class researchers had been unable to locate a photo of the elusive Roy, but she had little doubt she'd recognize him when the time came: neck tattoos weren't exactly common around Glenlake.

Eyes watering from the wind, she pulled her scarf up over her nose to make it easier to breathe. Passing the field-hockey fields, where the frozen snow looked like whitecaps on a lake, she went by Fairleigh House, where her mom and Georgina had once been roommates. A narrow lane led to the facilities compound, which consisted of a tiny house that served as the office, a large wooden shed, and a big brick building with four garage doors.

Cassidy walked right past the office, where her phone calls had been so unhelpfully answered, and headed for the door at the side of the big brick building.

After letting herself in, she saw a large, open space filled with various vehicles painted Glenlake green. It was warmer than outside, but still cold enough that she could see her breath. In the near corner, a smaller room—really, a building within the building, with a roof and windows and a door—looked occupied.

And what if he actually was there today? Her fantasies of cracking the case and catapulting to fame as a seventeen-year-old journalist ready for the big time started to fall apart with the realization that she didn't know how to start the interview. Did she really think she was going to get a murderer to confess?

Her feet were getting literally cold, too.

Before she could turn around and leave, the door to the room opened, and a man wearing coveralls, mittens, and a thick cap came out. He looked surprised to see her. With his coveralls zipped up to his throat, there was no way she could see if his neck was tattooed, but at any rate he looked too young to be Roy.

"Is Mr. Royal here?" she asked.

He looked baffled for a moment, then laughed. "Oh, *Roy*." He pointed behind himself with a thumb. "He's in there."

Leaving the door open, he moved past her to a stack of sidewalk salt, hefted a bag, and carried it over to a small four-wheeler that had been rigged with a salt spreader.

"Shut the damn door," said someone inside.

Stepping inside, she did just that.

The room was equipped with tables, chairs, a worn-out couch, and a kitchen area that consisted of a fridge, a microwave, and a coffee maker. An industrial gas-powered heater made it almost too hot. A man slumped at the table, his back to her, playing solitaire on a small tablet with a cracked screen that badly needed wiping.

Crawling up over the collar of his long-sleeved uniform shirt was a faded blue snake tattoo.

"Trying to let all the heat out?" said Roy over his shoulder as he swiped the electronic cards with dizzying speed.

"Are you Curtis Royal?" she stammered.

Roy whirled around. He was old and his skin drooped, but his eyes were hard. Cassidy's heart thumped, and she suddenly wished they weren't alone.

"What's your name?" he asked.

"Cassidy," she told him.

"Cassidy what?"

"Copeland."

She didn't move while he dragged his chair into position, allowing him to stare at her without contorting his body.

"Copeland Hall," he muttered.

She wasn't sure if it was a question, so she just nodded.

When he asked, "What do you want?" she realized that he was interviewing her, which was the wrong way around.

Get to the point, she told herself, hearing Mr. Kelly's voice as she did.

"Did you know Dallas Walker?" she asked, the words feeling thin and fragile in the overheated air.

"What's your interest?" he asked, again avoiding an answer.

Be truthful when confronted.

"My class, the journalism seminar, is investigating the circumstances surrounding Mr. Walker's death. We're talking to everyone who knew or interacted with him at Glenlake to see if they have helpful information."

Roy chuckled. "Oh, I didn't know him at Glenlake."

"But you did know him?"

Roy's eyes made her uncomfortable. She didn't like standing while he sat, feeling like he was inspecting her.

"Does your teacher know you're here?" he asked.

"Of course," she lied, wishing she'd told him. Or Tate. Or anybody.

Roy glanced at his tablet, seemingly anxious to get back to his game. He reached for it, slid it over, and moved a couple of cards.

"How long have you worked at Glenlake?" she asked, changing tactics.

"Long time," he said.

"Is it a full-time position?"

"Usually."

"How did you know Dallas Walker?"

"I didn't say I did."

"But someone told us you were friends."

His attention had been drifting toward the game, but now he looked up again, sharply. "Who?"

My dad.

"Students," she told him. "Who were here at the time."

Roy looked up, and Cassidy had the uncomfortable sensation that he was scanning faces in his memory and lingering on her teenage dad.

"They might have made a mistake."

"It's always possible," said Cassidy, wanting to sit down, wanting to leave. "Which is why it would be helpful to have your version of events."

"I have no 'version of events,'" said Roy dismissively. "Now get back to class and don't bother me again."

Chapter Twenty-Six

Tuesday, December 17, 1996

I am not "going out" with Sarah Ann Janeway, even if a) she did French-kiss me the first time we ever kissed, and b) she basically took my hand and put it up her shirt right before she put her hand down my pants.

I have never given Sarah Ann any indication that we are boyfriend and girlfriend, but I did agree to go to the Winter Formal with her. There's no way I'm going stag, especially after Mike told me Georgina said Andi was going with James "Whip It Out" Whitmer. I can't fucking believe it. James is famous for two things: one, a date he went on last year with a freshman girl in which he supposedly took his dick out of his pants while they were watching a movie and then moved the popcorn when she reached for it so she touched his dick instead. He doesn't deny it, so even if it isn't true, he wishes it was.

And two, he thinks it's hilarious to piss on people in the shower room. He wouldn't dare try it with me, but I saw him sneak up behind Grady Sylbert after football practice and start whizzing. Pee's warm, water's warm, and Grady had no clue until we all started yelling. James wasn't even embarrassed, just told us his dad used to do it when he was in high school, and his big brothers did it, too.

So Andi, who I've managed to mostly avoid since Thanksgiving break, is going to the Winter Formal with this asshole. Are they going out? Did she actually BREAK UP WITH ME so she could be with him??? No one will tell me. Maybe everyone is afraid to tell me.

Sylvie keeps sending me notes. She told me she wishes we could go to Winter Formal, but she understands that I can't ask her because of her "close" connection to Andi through Georgina.

～

"Can I introduce you to our owner?"

The sales associate with the gelled, spiky hair, whose name Ian had momentarily forgotten even though he remembered the hair as a reason he almost hadn't made the hire, touched the customer's elbow to turn him toward Ian.

The locked-door VIP event the team had been jokingly calling "WhaleFest" was well underway, even though Ian had just arrived. Ten minutes ago, he had been signing invoices on a pallet of imported beer when he discovered a crucial shipment of holiday champagne had been billed but not delivered. Five minutes after that, he'd taken a call from the Webster Groves store and learned that a seasonal hire had gotten a full-time job and would not be coming to work that evening. And just now he'd realized he'd forgotten to tighten the knot on his tie.

"Ian Copeland," he said, offering his hand to the customer, trying to hide his disappointment at how few guests had arrived.

"Vinay Patel," said the customer, helpfully adding, "Jared was just telling me a little bit about your new offerings."

"He means *old*," added Jared, laughing a little too hard at the lame joke.

As much as Ian wished his staff felt more confident after Preston's training, he appreciated Jared's caution in not wanting to put a foot wrong. The inventory sent down from Chicago was so varied that by the time they learned the pitch on a 1963 Bénédictine, it was replaced by something different and equally hard to describe.

Ian would rather have been on his way to Glenlake to pick up Cassidy and get some pictures of her and her date (whom she'd refused to reveal) at her last Winter Formal, but Cassidy wanted to fly home on her own, and he had reluctantly conceded he was needed more urgently in St. Louis. This December was make-or-break if he planned to pay off Simon's loan on time. The five-week period from Thanksgiving to New Year's could account for as much as one-third of his annual sales, and if he had any hope of joining Andi and the kids for their annual skiing trip in Colorado over winter break, he had to put in the work now.

And Patel, dressed in Banana Republic casual but with shiny $300 shoes and a massive Rolex, looked like exactly the kind of customer they needed to cultivate.

"So what's the deal with this stuff?" asked Patel. "Looks like a museum case in here."

"It does," said Ian. "Except in museums you can't touch, and the treasures aren't for sale. Here you can touch, taste, and take home whatever you want. Want to know what a martini tasted like to a Madison Avenue advertising man in 1960? Mix it with this gin and this vermouth, both of which were bottled that year."

Ian saw Patel light up at the *Mad Men* reference. "Just like Don Draper, huh?"

"You'll have to supply your own secretaries," Ian told him. "And I recommend fresh olives."

The chitchat went on for another ten minutes while Ian watched the front door, willing more invitees to arrive. Several did, but it wasn't going to be enough to create the boozy buying atmosphere he'd hoped for. He probably should have invited Andi and asked her to bring some guests as ringers—Georgina could probably outsell half the people on his team—but by instinct he hadn't even told her about the party. The last thing he needed was to bring her to ground zero of his source of stress, or to have her make any connection between his new investment and the reason he needed it to be successful.

Patel pondered almost $1,500 worth of purchases but, in the end, dropped just under $300 on 1970s manhattan mixings.

"I like that *Mad Men* line," said Jared after they'd all shaken hands and Patel had gone off to pay. "I'm going to use that."

"I think we're going to have to work some 1970s sitcoms into the mix, too," said Ian, trying to keep it light.

But not feeling it at all, especially after Ross Woodston, trust fund barfly and alcohol overenthusiast, popped into the store like he always did when there was a free tasting.

"What are we drinking tonight?" he asked far too loudly.

"A 1957 J.T.S. Brown," Jared said, as per Ian's pre-event instructions. "Just like 'Fast Eddie' Felson drank in *The Hustler*."

As Woodston downed the sample and handed his glass back for more, Ian managed to shoot Jared the *go easy with this one* look.

"Gotta spread it out so everyone gets a taste of yesteryear, my good man," Jared said, getting Ian's drift.

"I hear you," Woodston said. "But I swear this tastes identical to a brand-new bottle I opened yesterday." He swished and swallowed. "Definitely the same."

"Crazy how consistent some of the brands can be. Even over time," Ian said, stepping in.

He took a sip, mainly to dull the stress of having one of his intended targets overhear Woodston's loud pronouncement. To Ian's consternation, he couldn't completely deny that Woodston had a point. The vintage J.T.S. Brown did taste brand-new.

Was it possible?

Saturday, December 21, 1996

I don't know any other way to tell this except by starting at the beginning.

I feel like killing myself. Or somebody.

Sarah Ann wanted to preparty with her friends, so I told Mike I'd meet him later and went to Rosen House, mainly because there was zero chance I'd run into Andi. Sarah Ann kept going on about a big "surprise" that turned out to be a bag of dried-up weed and a box of warm white wine. It started snowing again while we walked to the old ballroom in McCormick for the dance, and Sarah Ann wouldn't stop complaining about how wet her feet were getting.

"Do you want me to carry you?" I finally asked, but I guess I didn't sound nice enough because she started to pout.

Once we got to the dance, she got over it and started acting like nothing was wrong. I told her I didn't feel like dancing yet, so she went out on the floor with her girlfriends and did that thing where they all dance together in a circle. Mike and the guys weren't there yet, and I'm guessing they were having a better preparty than I did.

The faculty chaperones were Mr. Matheson, Mrs. Henry, and Dallas Walker, who I figured warmed up on a cold night with straight bourbon or some other manly drink. I actually thought about asking him if he had a flask or something—I mean, he gave us beer, right?

I kept watching for Andi and Whip It Out, and sure enough, they came in, just the two of them, making me wonder if they'd had a long, romantic walk in the snow.

All of a sudden, Sylvie was next to me, looking all serious and sad.

"Ian, are you all right?" she asked, and I was so sick of being asked and so disgusted at seeing Andi with Whitmer that I said, "I need to talk," even though I didn't want to.

We went upstairs into a dark hall, and I didn't say anything, just started kissing her, and she was really into it.

Then I realized she was crying. I stopped kissing her.

"This is so nice, and I like you so much, Ian," she said, "but I know you're really thinking about Andi."

"You have no idea what I'm thinking," I said, and left.

I went through the balcony doors and sat there for a little while. I saw Sarah Ann looking for me. I saw Mike and the boys show up with their dates, and it looked like they were having a lot of fun. I saw Andi slow-dancing with Whitmer, and the thought of him grinding his crotch against her made me want to bash his face in.

After a while, Mike found me. I guess Sylvie told him where I was.

"Have one of these," he said, handing me a little airplane bottle of Jack Daniel's. "Louis Johnstone's aunt is a stewardess."

I opened it and drank it right down. My stomach felt warm.

"Dude, Sarah Ann looks smokin' tonight," said Mike. "And she's totally into you."

Down on the dance floor, Andi was laughing with Georgina.

"Come back down and at least pretend to have a good time, dipshit," said Mike. "Stop acting like your life is over. You're Ian Fucking Copeland."

I followed him downstairs. I danced with Sarah Ann and told her Sylvie was just an old friend. I saw Andi dancing with Georgina and rolling their eyes at the guys who were mouthing, Dykes. *She never gave a shit about anyone, that's one of the things that was so great about her.*

Except now she didn't give a shit about me.

Mike and I split another airplane bottle of Jack in the bathroom. I felt good, which means I wasn't feeling much of anything.

And when Andi and Whip It Out left, I did, too. I didn't say goodbye to anyone. I just slipped out the nearest exit and ran around to the other side of the building, where I saw them disappearing under a footpath light, the snow swirling around them like a snow globe.

My coat was still in the gym, but it was too late. I followed them, just far enough behind that they had no idea I was there. Maybe I was hoping for a reason to kick Whitmer's ass. If he whipped it out, I'd do it.

But he just walked her to the door of her house, and that was it. I could tell he wanted to kiss her, but I could also tell, even from a hundred yards away, that she didn't want to. She just gave him a little wave from the step and went inside.

Whitmer looked pissed, but what could he do? He kicked the snow and turned around, probably headed back to the dance to see if there was someone else who wanted to look at his dick.

Andi's light went on, and I walked toward it, stopping under the shadow of a big tree. I pictured her getting ready for bed, writing in her journal, maybe opening a book to read. I was getting wet and cold and starting to feel a little creepy for spying on her when suddenly her light went out. Maybe she's really tired, *I thought.*

Then I saw movement on the back porch.

Andi came out, wearing a parka over her dress and snow boots.

What the fuck, *I thought.*

I followed her again. She went across the soccer field, between Leggett and the Science Center, almost like she was heading for the main driveway, before she suddenly turned off Campus Drive and cut through the woods. I couldn't figure it out. It was like she told herself, Screw this place, I'm out of here.

If it wasn't for the snow on the ground, it would have been impossible to follow her, but the whiteness made everything glow, so I could see her footprints along the path she took and, every now and then, her figure up ahead.

I almost yelled at her. Something like, Andi, where the fuck are you going?

But I was afraid she'd lie to me. And I wanted to know the truth.

At least, I thought I did.

After a couple hundred yards, we came out of the woods onto the street with the faculty cottages. I was starting to think she was just taking a short-cut to town or something.

Then she turned left.

I had to let her get really far ahead so she wouldn't see me, but at least there were a couple of streetlights so I didn't lose track of her. Not that it really mattered, because as she reached the last house, the one set apart from all the others, I suddenly realized exactly where she was going.

I want to write something like, Then it all made sense *or* I saw it coming, *but nothing about it made any sense at all. It was like one of those movies where someone rips off a mask, and you realize they aren't who you think at all. That the person you love, and who you thought loved you, has betrayed you in a way you couldn't ever have imagined in a million years.*

But it wasn't her I wanted to kill.

When Dallas Fucking Walker opened his door, kissed Andi, and let her inside, I wanted to stop that smug bastard from ever smiling again.

Chapter Twenty-Seven

♥: How's Colorado?

CC: Cold. How's Florida?

♥: hot

CC: Been nice talking to you

♥: haha

She was only teasing Tate, but it was true that she found texting a less than satisfactory way of communicating with her boyfriend, even if she still stumbled on the *b*-word. Still, she supposed it was true that if you stayed in daily contact over winter break, it was more than a casual thing: you were going out.

Unlike most of her friends, Cassidy actually preferred talking on the phone to texting, Snapchat, and Instagram. But talking on the phone wasn't exactly going to work at this moment while she waited for her dad to come out the door of the ski shop with his loose binding tightened.

She considered taking her own skis off and ducking back into the shop—the hand from which she'd removed a mitten so she could text was getting cold, and she could already see the chill starting to drain her battery—but decided against it. With perfect Ian Copeland timing, Dad would be finished the moment she unzipped her jacket indoors.

♥: how's the fam?

CC: OK. Mom's still frosty. I think she still thinks I have the hots for Kelly. GROSS.

♥: I'm offended

♥: they should be worried about me

♥: I'm a bad influence

CC: I'll say. :)

♥: can't believe they never said they broke up

♥: did you get your dad's side of the story?

CC: Not yet.

Just then, her dad came out the door carrying his skis. As always, he looked like a middle-aged model for the latest and greatest skiwear with everything new and perfectly zipped and tucked. Seeing her, he put down his skis and stepped into the bindings.

CC: Speak of the devil. Gotta go.

♥: miss you. can't wait to see you again

CC: Feast your eyes on this then!

She texted him a picture from the Winter Formal, one where she had posed with her chest out and slutty eyes while an unaware Tate grinned normally. Sasha, her friend from cross-country who'd taken the pic with Cassidy's phone, had totally cracked up. In the edited version, captioned *Bae and Boo*, Tate had hearts for eyes and a lolling tongue.

♥: omfg

CC: XOXO

♥: stay warm, snow bunny

CC: Don't get sand in your butt crack ;-p

She locked her phone and zipped it into a warm interior pocket, sliding her frozen hand back into the mitten just as her dad glided across the packed, crusty snow outside the main lodge.

"Ready?"

"I was, but now I'm thinking about going back in for hot chocolate."

He grinned and lowered his orange goggles. "We'll warm up by skiing."

Unfortunately, Dad's idea of warming up consisted of a quick run down a blue groomer, which he insisted was to loosen his muscles before any truly strenuous skiing, followed by a blue mogul run that was barely more interesting. They had to go down carefully to avoid contact with a mob of second graders and their moms.

Groan. She started thinking it would have been more fun skiing with Mom and Whitney, even though she was mad at Mom, and Whitney didn't do anything tougher than a blue groomer. Owen was hopeless: he spent his time at the snowboard park watching the boarders do stunts and occasionally attempting a 180 or a grab.

Which made Cassidy wonder. "Dad, you're not doing this for me, are you?"

"I don't want to blow out a knee. Not that it hurts you to ease into things, either."

They reached the bottom of the run, barely even breathing hard. "Well, okay. We're warmed up now. Can I pick where we go next?"

"Be my guest," he said, his smile a little tight.

She chose a black run that wasn't too far away; on the lift up, he gave her some pointers on her technique that she pretended to politely listen to. It wasn't that he was wrong—her dad had been skiing his whole life and knew what he was doing—it was that every year, he seemed to forget that she had been skiing *her* whole life and knew what *she* was doing, too.

"I don't understand why you're so cautious sometimes," Cassidy said. "Is it because you broke your leg when you were in high school?"

She'd seen a picture of him in a family album, leg in a cast, looking miserable next to Biz and Cope, who were dressed to go skiing.

He nodded and said, "Let's just say it wasn't my best sport."

"I thought your best sport was all of them."

He snorted, warming up a little. "Apology accepted. Is there something you want?"

She watched the end of her skis dangling in space, colorful helmets and ski jackets dotting the slope below them. She wished Tate would be waiting for her back at the lodge. It was a long time to be without him.

"An answer," she said finally. She needed to get this out before they reached the top.

"I'd need a question first."

"Why did you and Mom break up during senior year at Glenlake? I asked you at Thanksgiving, but we got interrupted."

He looked at her intently. He had lifted his goggles up to his helmet, and his blue eyes seemed clear but chilly.

"I mean, it's just so weird that no one ever said anything. The way you guys got together is this family legend—if you broke up and got back together, doesn't that make it even better?"

For a moment they both listened to the creaking cables as they bounced ever so gently up the mountain. He seemed to decide something.

"You can't tell your mom we talked about this," he said.

"Why not? Did she dump you for somebody else or something?"

"It was complicated."

"Oh my god, Dad," said Cassidy, genuinely shocked. Despite her mom's strange reaction to the bracelet, she still hadn't thought it could be true. "Who?"

Staring up the slope, he shook his head. "No one important, obviously."

"That sucks," she said, knowing there was no sense pressing him for a name. Not right then, anyway.

"It's funny, after twenty years, it's hard to believe it happened. Like it was a dream," he said. "Back then, she told me she needed time to be herself. And I think that's true, even if she was seeing someone else. We had been together for three years, and that's a long time when you're that young. I always knew she was the one for me, and once she figured out that was true for her, too, she came back for good."

There was something about his tone that almost made her catch her breath. He was trying to say it almost offhand, but there was a deep sorrow just below the surface that threatened to strangle his voice.

They were very nearly at the top.

"It's all very . . . romantic." Cassidy didn't know what else to say.

Her dad raised the bar and got ready to glide off the lift. "As romantic as it gets."

As they lowered their goggles into place, she felt a sudden urge to share something, too. She had never seen him this vulnerable before.

"Dad? I have a boyfriend. At Glenlake."

His head turned suddenly, like he had been jerked out of his memories. Then he grinned. "What's his name?"

"Tate Holland."

"I've heard of him. Did you go to Winter Formal together?"

She nodded, then pulled out her phone and showed him a picture—*not* the one she'd texted Tate.

"Good-looking kid," said Dad. "Does he do any sports?"

"Soccer and lacrosse."

"Is it serious?"

Cassidy laughed, cringing because it sounded more like a giggle. "God, who knows? It's just . . . nice."

"Nice works," he said.

"Dad," she added, "can we please keep this between us for now? I don't think I'm ready to make this an official part of the Copeland family history."

Her dad gave her a side hug. "I'm happy for you. However it turns out."

Chapter Twenty-Eight

Ian Copeland's Glenlake Journal

Wednesday, January 1, 1997

Happy fucking New Year. Is Andi in New York City with Simon, like every year, or is she off somewhere with Dallas Fucking Walker? Fucking Dallas Walker. I should write a letter to the headmaster. Better yet, I should make this my goddamn senior page: How a Teacher Came to Glenlake and Stole My Girlfriend. *He should be fired. He should go to jail. She's only seventeen. I could use my journal from the Winter Formal, not even wait until graduation, just make copies and put them on every bulletin board on campus. Slip them under everyone's door. Mail one to the police.*

Mom and Dad, Mom especially, are dying to know who it is. They totally know she's seeing someone else. I mean, I'd be hurting if Andi just broke up with me—I was hurting already when I didn't know why. But that was NOTHING compared to knowing it was someone else and knowing WHO.

Last night, when she was trying to get me to come down for the champagne toast, Mom asked, all innocent, "Do you know who she's seeing?"

And I said, "Someone she shouldn't," before I realized I shouldn't even have told her that much.

Not until I can figure out what to do.

~

Thursday, January 2, 1997

Life is great.

Just fucking great.

So, yesterday, we were skiing, and I was thinking about different ways to get revenge on Dallas Fucking Walker when I realized something huge, and it put me in a shitty mood. Then I was stuck on the lift with Dad, and he said something about how I was skiing "recklessly." We got in a huge argument, which sucked because you can't exactly escape when you're dangling thirty feet in the air.

When we got to the top, I skied away and went to look for my friends, who told me they'd be in the back bowls. I didn't see them at the top of the lift, so I decided to see how fast I could get to the bottom. Just go as straight as humanly possible like an Olympic downhill. It was a huge rush. I think it took like sixty seconds, and I totally caused a yard sale, but I was going so fast I'll bet they won't remember what I look like.

I waited by the lift for a while, but my friends didn't come down, so I went up again and decided to hike up to the north bowl and take a run there. No way I could have done that one in a straight line, so I pretended I was going for the slalom world record. No breaks, just as fast as I could get down. I was about halfway down and flying when I caught an edge and lost it. Right away I knew something was wrong with my leg. One of my skis had slid away from me, but it hurt too much to even stand up and go get it. I just kind of lay there swearing until some guy came up and asked if I needed help.

Taken off the mountain on a sled—check that one off my bucket list— and ended up having an X-ray in the emergency room at the base of the mountain.

My leg is broken. Well, no shit.

~

Friday, January 3, 2017

Well, the good news is we go back home tomorrow, so I only have one day where I have to sit in the condo while everyone else goes skiing. Mom offered to stay with me, and I was like, god no. Just me, the TV, my journal, and the book I'm supposed to read for English class. I'll read it on the plane. Or maybe I'll read it during basketball practice, because I'll be lucky if I get back before the end of the season.

I don't even know why I'm writing in my journal—it's winter break and it's not like I have to—but it sucks not being able to talk to anybody. And I really can't. The thing I figured out before I broke my leg was that, as much as I want to ruin Dallas Walker's career by telling everybody about him and Andi, I won't do it.

Because I still love Andi. I mean, when I picture them together, I want to fucking puke. And she definitely deserves part of the blame because even if he is a famous poet (it's not exactly like being really famous, except to someone like Andi), she went along with it. He hit on her and she said yes. How can I compete with that?

But I can't tell the world, or anybody, because it will hurt her as much as it hurts him. And it will hurt me because I'll look like a fucking jackass. The girls who want to hook up with me now won't just feel sorry for me— they'll think it's kind of funny that my girlfriend dumped me for a guy who's going to start losing his hair in a couple of years.

I have to keep it secret. But there has to be something else I can do. Kill him for real?

⌒

Ian slid the door closed, holding the champagne glasses and bottle in his right hand, then walked carefully across the icy deck to the hot tub, where Andi was already immersed up to her chin. After setting the precious cargo down, he stepped out of his shower sandals and shrugged off his robe, feeling the bitterly cold mountain air wash his chest and legs.

"No other takers?" asked Andi as he eased into the frothing, steaming hot water, the smell of chlorine more powerful than he would have liked.

"I may have mumbled my invite," said Ian.

"I can't imagine why you don't want the twins playing water tag on top of us."

"I think I'm also ready for a break from Cope's stories. But they won't miss us. Cassidy's texting her friends, and Whitney and Owen are going to watch a movie with Cope and Biz. Biz is going to make her famous popcorn—with butter *and* salt."

He poured glasses for each of them, trying to remember when he'd started calling his dad by his nickname—it certainly hadn't been in high school. Sometime after Cassidy had been born, maybe. It was strange to think how many years they'd been coming to this very place on this very mountain. As a young man, Cope had purchased an old chalet that had served as home base while Ian learned to ski, and the chalet had been modernized and retrofitted several times throughout the years.

Once Andi had officially joined the family, and she and Ian had started having skiers of their own, they'd needed more space, so they'd torn down the chalet—not without some boozy toasts from Cope before the demolition began—and built a modern house with multiple balconies offering stunning views the chalet's little windows had only hinted at.

"Happy New Year," said Ian, clinking glasses with Andi.

"It better be," she said flatly.

They both drank quickly and then put the glasses down so they could dunk their hands back in the warm water.

"What's that supposed to mean?" he asked.

"I'm just glad the saga of Cassidy's college apps has finally come to its conclusion," said Andi peevishly. "If she didn't spend so much time on that phone, she might have gotten them done before the very last minute."

Ian knew the real reason for Andi's irritation had something to do with the fact that Cassidy had decided early on not to apply to her mother's alma mater, Smith. Even worse, she *was* applying to Amherst. Ian didn't understand their daughter's reasoning any better than Andi but thought they shouldn't take it personally.

"She got them done on time," said Ian. "You've been awfully hard on her lately."

"Imagine if I hadn't been."

"Then the college counseling office at school would have made sure she got them done. That's part of the reason we sent her to Glenlake."

"Maybe we shouldn't have."

"Sent her to Glenlake?"

Andi reached a hand out of the foam for another drink. "I'm worried there may be something inappropriate going on with her teacher. With Wayne Kelly."

Ian suddenly felt cold to his core, his mind reeling with the possibility. *"What?"*

"When I saw them together before Thanksgiving, I had a strange feeling about it. And then there were some texts on her phone."

"From Kelly?"

"They had to have come from him—but they sounded like a boyfriend."

"And what did they say?"

"Do your parents know? About us?" she quoted. "And one of them said, *Are you going to get your dad's side of the breakup?"*

"Anyone could have written that." Ian wanted to tell Andi she was jumping to the wrong conclusion because of her own experience, not her daughter's. But what good would it do her to learn he'd known about it all along, ever since he saw her embrace her poetry teacher on the doorstep of his cottage? They'd never discussed it.

The chill gave way to hot anger, anger that after all these years he was still dealing with Dallas Fucking Walker.

"You've heard how she talks about Kelly, Ian, how much she idol-izes him," she was saying. "And it's apparently mutual. She's the star of his class, and he wrote her a recommendation letter that sounds like he wants her as his personal assis—"

"Cassidy has a boyfriend, Andi, and it's not her teacher," he said, unable to keep the anger out of his voice. Cassidy's request that he keep her secret was less important than strangling Andi's suspicions. "His name is Tate."

Andi stared at him. "How would you know? Why would she tell you?"

"Because you've been riding her too hard, and your mistrust is the very thing that made it impossible for her to confide in you. They went to the Winter Formal together."

"That doesn't—" she started to say, and then stopped.

He could have finished the sentence for her, but didn't. *That doesn't mean she can't also be seeing her teacher.*

"Our daughter isn't hiding some dark secret," he said. "She seems happy. I think this new relationship may be part of the reason she's been asking about us and what happened back at Glenlake."

Andi seemed startled. "Goddamn Georgina and her big mouth. It's none of her business."

Now it was Ian's turn to stare at Andi. He reached for his cham-pagne glass, downing half of it before plunging his hand back into the roiling hot tub.

A hot surge of emotions caught him off guard. It suddenly felt like months since they'd really talked, like they'd been navigating around each other. Clearly, she'd been as preoccupied with the ghost of Dallas Walker as he had.

As on the night when Walker had resurfaced in their lives, jealousy and anger fused with longing and lust, and he felt an urgent need to make her forget about Walker and remind her that he, her high school sweetheart and now husband, had been there for her all along—and would always be there for her.

Remind himself that he'd won, and not Dallas Fucking Walker.

Ian slid in close and kissed Andi. Deeply. Hard.

"What are you doing?" she asked as they came up for air.

He put his hand on her breast, over the sexy red bikini she always wore in Vail, but only in their hot tub.

"I want you," he whispered.

"Not here, Ian. Not now."

No one could see them. The great room was downstairs and looked out onto the valley. The hot tub, which led off from the upstairs master suite, was around the corner and off the side of the house, almost built into the slope of the mountain.

"We're as good as alone," he said, trailing his hand between her thighs.

She moved his hand away gently but firmly.

"I'm cold," she said.

With that, she rose dripping from the tub, wrapped herself in her robe, and went indoors. Apparently, she preferred to spend time alone with her memories.

"Not every girl wants to fuck her teacher," he called after her, craning his neck to watch her go.

She didn't respond. He had no way to know if she'd even actually heard him.

He filled his glass again.

Happy fucking New Year.

Chapter Twenty-Nine

"Did everybody have a good winter break?" asked Mr. Kelly as the bell rang and Noah slipped through the door, running late as usual.

Several people actually started answering his question, talking over each other about snow, sun, and sand before he abruptly silenced them with a cleared throat and raised hands.

"I hope it doesn't hurt your feelings, but I'm not actually interested," he said, and Cassidy couldn't stifle a snicker. "I was just saying that as a social convention. Now that we're all settled"—he looked significantly at Noah, who was for some reason still standing—"I have news."

Cassidy leaned forward, realizing that half the class had just done the same thing.

Mr. Kelly settled onto his desk corner, waiting until the room fell silent.

"Yesterday, while most of you were undoubtedly winging your way back to O'Hare, the Lake County Sheriff's Office took Curtis Royal into custody."

The room erupted.

"I knew it!" said Noah, with an idiotic fist pump.

Two other students actually high-fived.

Cassidy couldn't help feeling a rush of pride. After all, her dad had been the first one to mention Roy in relation to Dallas Walker's death, and she had been brave enough to interview Roy herself—even if she hadn't exactly cracked the case.

Across the room, Tate was giving her a discreet thumbs-up, the look on his face reminding her that it had been three weeks since they'd even managed to kiss.

"Everybody quiet down!" shouted Mr. Kelly, looking almost angry.

"Whether you want to grow up to be a real live investigative journalist or you just want to get an A in my class, you have to learn to avoid assumptions. To avoid rushing to judgment. First of all, I never said he was arrested in relation to this case. Remember, he has a record for other crimes. And just because someone has been arrested for a crime, it doesn't mean they've done it. If you've paid the slightest attention to the stream of death-row exonerees in this state, you know that to be true. And it's not just big cities like Chicago, either. Our very own Lake County Sheriff's Office has a sordid history of extracting confessions through questionable means."

Cassidy raised her hand, puzzled. "So are you saying he *didn't* do it?"

Mr. Kelly sighed, stood up, and started pacing. "Here's what we know: Roy was taken into custody yesterday. Within twenty-four hours, they'll have to charge him or release him, so we should know more soon. I've got a call in to a source I've been cultivating, and I'm waiting to hear back. That's it."

"Do they have the death penalty in Illinois?" asked Noah.

Rolling his eyes, Mr. Kelly ignored him. "Clearly, Roy is a person of interest. They will be interviewing him—just as our own Cassidy Copeland did last month, though I'm guessing they will have their supervisor's permission before doing so."

Cassidy blushed, but she could tell Mr. Kelly wasn't really mad. He was never mad if someone showed initiative. She stared straight ahead but could feel everyone's eyes on her.

"They'll be checking his answers carefully," continued Mr. Kelly, "and while we should follow their investigation closely, I want you to continue to investigate all possible leads. Dig deeper. Where are we on the grades angle? You've all spent the last few months in the hell of college applications—now that they're in, I want you to think about the pressure you've been under. Could that have been a motive? Where are we with that investigation?"

Hannah raised her hand. "I went through all the interviews of Walker's poetry students and compiled a list of the colleges they applied to."

"Excellent," Mr. Kelly said. "Have you posted it on Google Drive?"

"Earlier this morning," she said, nodding. "I compared it to the list of the schools the students actually attended, and two names stood out: Connor Cotton applied to only Ivies, but ended up taking a gap year."

"Meaning he got wait-listed," Rowan said as heads nodded around him.

"He eventually got into Cornell," Hannah said.

Mr. Kelly tapped his chin. "Someone needs to look into what he did during that gap year and how he felt about it."

"I will," Liz volunteered. "I've talked to him before."

"And then there was Tommy Harkins," continued Hannah.

"What about him?" Mr. Kelly asked.

"He ended up at University of Illinois. His safety school."

More than one person gasped.

Mr. Kelly shook his head. "I know it may sound shocking, but some successful people actually went to state schools. I survived four years at Penn State and went on to become a productive member of society."

Cassidy had applied all over—ten schools in total. She wasn't exactly dying to go to Mizzou, but if that was the only place she got in, she planned to make the best of it. Given her family name, their legacy at various colleges, and their long history of writing healthy checks to various alma maters, she suspected she'd have more than a few options. The Copeland name could be a burden, but it was also a blessing.

"Do we have any other leads or possible suspects?" Mr. Kelly asked.

"I don't know if it's a lead," Liz said. "But, apparently, Sylvie Montgomery started going to Cue Sports Society because she had a crush on a guy in the club."

"Who was it?"

"As rumor has it, Cassidy's dad," Liz said.

Noah catcalled and everyone laughed.

"That's enough," Mr. Kelly said.

"What's her connection to Walker?" asked Cassidy, mortified and anxious to change the subject.

Liz shrugged. "Other than going to his club, none that I know of."

"Where did you come up with this information?" Mr. Kelly asked Liz.

"Georgina Holt Fordham emailed me," she said. "She also mentioned that we should look into faculty if we haven't already. According to her, Dallas Walker didn't totally fit in with the other teachers."

"I think we know that much already," said Mr. Kelly thoughtfully. "This Sylvie seems like a stretch, but it can't hurt to look into her and see what she has to say. As for the faculty angle, I assume your group is already on it, Hannah?"

"We are," she confirmed.

"Sounds like this Georgina chick was keeping pretty close tabs on Walker herself, if you ask me," said Noah out of the blue.

"An interesting observation, Noah," said Mr. Kelly, seeming surprised. "Does anyone else find it interesting that she's always right there with helpful, timely information?"

Chapter Thirty

Ian didn't feel like going to Georgina's fund-raiser any more than Andi seemed to, but it wasn't as though either of them had a choice. He was attending because Georgina was Andi's best friend, at least usually, and he'd donated the bar stock because he knew the event would be swimming with whales. He hadn't been wrong. Three attendees had already made appointments to come down to the store for personal tours and tastings of Grape and Barley's vintage spirits showcase.

As for Andi, she was doing a good job of concealing her lackluster enthusiasm for all things Georgina with a businesslike smile. While he mingled in the crowd, she oversaw the brisk sales of *Lovely Ladue*, featuring Georgina and William Fordham's sprawling, overdecorated plantation-style mansion, with 20 percent of the profits benefiting the Missouri Botanical Garden.

Ian kept an eye on his wife, or more accurately the level of wine in her glass, noting how often she went back to the bar for a refill. Andi was always a picture of social grace, particularly when one of her publications was featured at an event, but he worried about the potentially combustible combination of her growing distress and anger with an extra glass of wine.

Georgina was simply being herself, acting like she always had. Ian didn't know if she was capable of behaving any other way. But Andi hadn't been herself for months, ever since the ghost of Dallas Walker had come howling out of the past to shatter two decades of tranquility.

Fortunately, the two of them had been kept apart most of the evening, with Andi hovering near the sales table, making sure every guest saw the part of the book featuring Georgina's house while their hostess with the mostest mingled with the crowd of well-heeled St. Louisans. Ian figured if things stayed that way, they could get home at the end of the night without any tipsy friction between the two longtime friends.

The evening proceeded more smoothly than he'd anticipated—until he happened to overhear Georgina in conversation with two random guests.

"It's just so fascinating to have an inside view of a cold-case investigation, even if it is being done by high school students," she said, pausing to sip some of the Mumm he'd told her to pour for the most promising donors. "I've got a lot of helpful information, so I'm in regular contact with one of them."

Ian turned around. "Not Cassidy, I hope," he said before he could stop himself.

"This is Ian Copeland," Georgina said, introducing him to the others. "His wife was in the dead poet's class, and now his daughter is investigating the murder. Isn't that *amazing*?"

Suddenly furious, Ian nodded hello but ignored the guests, angling his body to cut them out of the conversation.

"No, Ian," Georgina said, with cheerful exasperation, "I'm not working with Cassidy, much as I'd like to. The student they assigned to me is named Liz Wright."

The two guests moved on, and Georgina gave them an apologetic wave.

"Has it occurred to you that it might be in bad taste to treat the investigation like it's some kind of reality show?" asked Ian sharply.

"Sorry," said Georgina, wounded. "I didn't think—"

"Obviously, you haven't been thinking. This is real. It touches real people."

Ian saw a flash of anger in Georgina's eyes, but she apparently possessed more self-control than he did.

"No, you're right. I guess I've . . . forgotten . . . how real it is. It seems like such a long time ago. And sometimes I forget how closely the Copelands are identified with Glenlake."

Ian let her think it was about that. "Just please consider what you're saying, and to whom."

Georgina nodded, giving her glass to a passing server and telling him she wanted a refill of the Mumm.

"Anyway, it's all academic—pardon my pun," she said brightly. "Now that they have a person in custody."

"What? Who?"

"Some townie Dallas used to play pool with. Curtis Royal."

Ian took a sip of his melting ice cubes just so he'd have a moment to think. Roy. He wished he'd heard it first from Cassidy. He'd tell Andi in the car.

"I'll keep it quiet for you, Ian, but it's only a matter of time before the story gets out. A groundskeeper kills a teacher and gets caught twenty years later? That's national news!"

∾

On the ride home, Ian was glad he'd limited himself to one drink and another he'd abandoned halfway. Andi wasn't drunk, but he wouldn't have bet money on her reflexes, either. After his encounter with Georgina, the hostess had avoided both of them, and Andi had ended the evening pleased by healthy book sales and somewhat less irritated with her friend. But she hadn't, apparently, been oblivious to Ian's encounter with Georgina.

"What were you and Georgina talking about just before she stomped off?" she asked, once they were on the street.

"Apparently, Curtis Royal, the maintenance guy, has been picked up by the Lake County Sheriff's Office," he told her, keeping his eyes on the road.

He heard her sharp intake of breath. "For?"

"The students don't know yet, so she doesn't know. It could be completely unrelated."

"Could be."

Ian signaled a turn, stopped carefully at a stop sign, and looked both ways before pulling out.

"And she's spreading it around?"

"I told her not to," said Ian, omitting Georgina's remark about *national news*. Which was in all probability correct.

"I wish Dallas Walker had never fucking come to Glenlake," said Andi quietly.

It was twenty years too late, but he was glad to hear her say it.

Chapter Thirty-One

ANDI BLOOM'S GLENLAKE JOURNAL

Monday, January 6, 1997

I had to stop myself from rushing straight to Dallas's cottage the second I got back to school last night. I mean, it's been three freaking weeks. Other than the postcard he sent thanking me for my Christmas gift, signed Mr. Walker, it's like the two of us never existed.

For all I know he sent the same three lines to everyone, whether they gave him a coffee mug filled with candy, a plant, or a braided metal bracelet they'd spent an entire semester trying to get just right. Lovesick dummy that I am, I kept rereading the generic poem for a secret message.

My poem is just to say
I'm glad you did not overlook
This festive holiday.

"Overlook," as in our secret spot overlooking the lake?

I missed talking to Ian, too. He came back to school in a cast and on crutches. A skiing accident on a double-black run, according to Georgina, who of course knew the whole story. I saw him on my way to French class.

All I got was thanks when I said I was really sorry, and yeah when I said I knew it had to be awful for him to miss his senior basketball season, but hoped he'd be okay in time for baseball.

It's killing me that he hates me so much.

The welcome-back dinner was an excruciating exercise in repeating that I'd spent part of break at home and the other half in Mexico, and pretending to be interested in where everyone else spent their vacations. Mostly, I scanned the dining hall for a certain salt-and-pepper head of hair.

Dallas was nowhere to be seen.

By bedtime I felt like an idiot for wearing my new jeans and sweater so I'd look sophisticated yet casual for him. Even though I knew there was no way we'd be able to say anything more than hi when we ran into each other, I'd still sprayed perfume behind my ears, hoping we'd find ourselves alone long enough for a kiss.

Instead, I threw the jeans, which smelled like airplane, into my laundry basket and spent the night tossing and turning. By morning I had no choice but to hope my winter tan contrasted with my dress-code drab and the dark circles under my eyes.

I wanted to sprint over to Copeland early, run up the stairs, and rush into Dallas's arms before anyone else arrived in class. Instead, I spent an extra minute checking my hair and makeup, then timed my entrance with the bell so I was the last person to walk into the room.

The last student, anyway.

"No sign of Dallas yet," Georgina said, reading my puzzled expression as I entered the classroom.

"He must be on Texas time," Tommy said to laughter that was mostly from Georgina.

"Not that I care if he ever comes back," Connor said.

"Did you get a shitty first-semester grade, too?" Philip asked.

"So shitty."

"I literally cried thinking about the schools I'm not getting into now," Jules added.

"My parents called to complain," Lola said. "I've never, ever gotten a B minus."

I didn't say anything. Neither did Crystal. I couldn't tell whether it was because she also had an A or she didn't want anyone to know how bad her grade really was.

Ten minutes later, Dallas still hadn't shown up.

"Maybe someone should tell Mrs. Kucinich or someone that he isn't here," Crystal finally said.

No one volunteered.

Another ten minutes passed, all of us watching the clock or the door.

"I don't know about you guys," Philip said, picking up his backpack, "but I'm out of here."

"Me too," Tommy said. Georgina shrugged and went with him.

The rest of the class filed out in twos and threes.

I waited another ten minutes before I finally gave up, too.

∽

Wednesday, January 8, 1997

There was a note taped to the classroom door, and it wasn't in Dallas's precise, compact handwriting:

Poetry class has been canceled today. Please use your free period wisely and read three poems by Langston Hughes in preparation for Friday.

Like I could focus on Langston Hughes, or any poet, not knowing where Dallas is and why he hasn't contacted me.

I decided to use the time to do something nice for Ian. It's been awful seeing him hobble around campus. Worse, the Sunday outing is a trip to an indoor water park. There's no way he'll go just to hang out, and I can't stand the idea of him moping around his dorm room. I know he doesn't want sympathy or anything else from me, but I walked to the town drugstore and made him a care package of M&M'S, Bugles, Bubblicious gum, a Sports Illustrated, and the movie Rookie of the Year—to get him looking forward to baseball season. I put it all in a gift bag and left it at his dorm with a card that read, "Heal fast! XO."

If we were still together, I would have also included a Bit-O-Honey since we both love them and we always shared one when we watched movies. I know he's going to think the get-well gifts are from Sarah Ann, who Georgina says he's kind of "with" now, or some secret admirer in the sophomore or junior class. What can I do, though?

～

Friday, January 10, 1997

I walked into class and there he was—jeans, chambray shirt, scruffy beard, and crooked grin. FINALLY!

"I presume you all enjoyed the unexpected extra days of break?" Dallas said to everyone but me.

He had to know I'd been dying—not just to see him but to know where he'd been for the past four days.

He explained that he'd been delayed first by a "family situation," and then his flight back to Chicago had been canceled due to weather. He'd been stuck until the airlines could rebook him on a flight last night. Given the grades situation, no one but me seemed to care. The second he finished talking, they all started shouting their questions at once.

Dallas quieted the room with a deafening whistle.

"I gave everyone exactly the grade they deserved based on effort, enthusiasm, and test scores," he said after everyone was quiet. "And you all know it."

"But . . . ," about half the class objected simultaneously.

"But being the key word," Dallas said. "The English Department, surely at the behest of your parents, who seem to believe their children are incapable of attaining less than an A in a class that shouldn't be about grades at all, is itself terrified about the effects of said grade on your college acceptances and the acceptance statistics for Glenlake. *Therefore, they begged me to revisit each of your marks for the semester.*"

No one breathed while he paused.

"*To say I'm disgusted doesn't begin to describe my feelings about the lying and hypocrisy this involves.*"

I prayed for invisibility. The thought of Dallas, my secret lover, destroying my friends' futures was more than I could take.

"*That said,*" he continued, "*I also get the pressure you guys are under to get into the bullshit schools you've been talked into.*"

Everyone was basically staring at their desks by this point.

"*So I've agreed to increase everyone's grade by a full letter. Unless, of course, you already had an A, in which case, there's nothing I can do to inflate what you've actually earned.*"

As audible relief rippled through the class, he added, "*I won't be agreeing to anything like this ever again, so don't expect another free spin this semester.*"

I tried not to smile as Dallas confirmed he was, in fact, every bit the man I knew him to be.

After he launched into an uncharacteristically emotionless lecture on Langston Hughes, it took forever for the bell to finally ring. Another eternity passed while everyone crowded around to thank him for upping their grades.

"*Such complete bullshit,*" he said the second everyone was out of the room and out of earshot. "*I should have told the administration to shove it.*"

Then he kissed me.

"*I might not have come back if it weren't for you,*" he said, and kissed me again. "*I didn't think I'd make it through class with you sitting there, not being able to touch you. Don't you have a free period right now?*"

"*Right after AP Calc.*"

"*I'm headed back to my cottage,*" he said with a smile that melted me. "*I'll be there waiting for you when math class is over.*"

I could barely focus on Mr. Lyle's explanation of inverse functions while I listened for the bell to ring.

Dallas didn't ask how I'd gotten there (by circumnavigating the campus and sneaking through the woods to his back door), so he didn't hear about how I brushed off Georgina (who wanted to talk about how the change of grades was going to save everyone's bacon, especially Tommy's, who'd practically failed first semester). He just pulled me into the house and led me directly to the bedroom.

"You're all I've thought about for weeks," he said, unbuttoning my coat and pushing it off my shoulders.

"It killed me when I got back and you weren't here," I said, looking around for the gift he'd promised as he started on my blouse. "Why didn't you let me know?"

"Our 'Mr. Walker' code doesn't exactly work when I want to get you a message on campus."

"But if you got home last night—"

"If it hadn't been so late, I swear I would have tossed pebbles at your window."

"Really?"

"I almost did anyway," he said with a wicked grin.

A car with a very sick muffler rumbled loudly outside.

Instead of leading me toward the bed, Dallas pulled me away from the open doorway.

"Shit," he said. "Someone's here."

My blood froze in my veins as the engine noise grew closer and then stopped. Whoever it was had parked in the driveway.

Dallas kicked my coat and blouse out of sight and pointed me toward the small attached bathroom. "Wait in there."

While he went into the living room and answered the front door, I stood in the tiny bathroom, calves pressed against the cold edge of the tub, too nervous to even tremble.

Nightmare scenarios flashed through my mind as I fast-forwarded from my inevitable suspension to a future that included a GED and a fast-food job or, if I was lucky, community college and a dead-end career.

"How long do you think this will take?" Dallas said, loud enough for me to hear.

"Not long," a male voice said.

Was it a maintenance worker needing to do an urgent repair? The thought of cowering in the bathroom while he worked made me feel trapped and panicky.

"Let me just grab my coat," Dallas said, entering the bedroom.

Putting his head into the bathroom, he mouthed, "Don't go anywhere. I'll be right back."

The driver, whoever he was, fired up the vehicle, and Dallas was gone.

I waited. I waited a little longer. I waited until "I'll be right back" meant that if I waited any longer I was going to miss my next class. Then I grabbed my coat and sneaked into the kitchen. Obviously, my present, if there was one, wouldn't be coming today.

I was peering through the window above the sink, checking to make sure the coast was clear, when Dallas's phone rang.

Frozen, I heard four rings, the click of his answering machine, and his reassuring rasp as the outgoing message carried into the kitchen:

"You've reached Dallas Walker. I'll get back to you."

I was much less calmed by the incoming message:

"Hi, Dal," a woman said, with a too-sweet lilt that made my skin crawl. "Miss you already! Tulsa isn't the same without you. Come back soon. 'Kay?"

Chapter Thirty-Two

Ian Copeland's Glenlake Journal

Saturday, January 11, 1997

We played Forest Heights last night, but I didn't go. Coach keeps telling me that even though I can't play, I'm still part of the team, but I'm sick of wearing my stupid jacket and tie and sitting next to him on the bench. He pretends like I'm part of the coaching team since I'm team captain, but basically that means he shows me the play he wants after he's drawn it up and before he calls time-out. We're losing anyway. Griff can't guard anyone to save his life, and we look like shit on the floor.

So I told Coach I was getting a cold and didn't want to give it to anyone on the team. When I mentioned to Sylvie that I wasn't traveling with the team, she asked, "But Mike is going, right?" Yeah, Mike was going. He's been getting more minutes with me out, too. "What time does the team get back?" she asked.

She had this look in her eye, and right away I totally knew what she was getting at. Sylvie is kind of this weird combination of a little bit mousy and smart, but definitely cute, and when she gets this look, it makes me think she might have a wild side.

After she sneaked in and up to my room, I found out I was right.

I wasn't right about the gift bag someone left in front of my door. I figured it was from either her or Sarah Ann (who wants to tell everyone we're together even though I told her I'm not making it official). They were both pissed when I asked them about it.

My bad, I guess.

Chapter Thirty-Three

ANDI BLOOM'S GLENLAKE JOURNAL

Sunday, January 12, 1997

I've been avoiding Dallas since I left his place on Friday.

I don't want to see or talk to him, maybe ever again. I have too many questions, and I'm afraid of the answers.

I'm also not a fan of water parks and couldn't care less about slides, lazy rivers, and wave pools, but since Georgina, Tommy, Crystal, and a bunch of other actual seniors were all going on the Sunday outing, I agreed to tag along.

I wish I hadn't for the following reasons:

1. The main reason I went was to get away from thoughts about how pissed I am at Dallas. (It didn't work.)

2. Georgina and Tommy got into a big fight because she thought he was flirting with Tara "Tits" Tomlinson. (He was.)

3. I got my period and didn't have a tampon. Even the machine in the bathroom was jammed. The only thing I could scrounge up was a pad, so I couldn't even swim.

4. Sylvie asked Georgina if I was "still with" James Whitmer. (Like I didn't totally see that one coming.) When Georgina said we were never together, Sylvie went in for the kill. (Not that I care.)

5. I did care that Ian came on the outing after all. "With" Sarah Ann.

~

Monday, January 13, 1997

I told Georgina I had cramps and blew off poetry class today. I even waited until I knew Dallas was having office hours before I went out to get something to eat at the union.

He was standing outside my dorm, waiting for me.

"Long time, no see," he said.

"Sorry," I said, avoiding looking at him. "I haven't been feeling well."

"I didn't have a good way to get ahold of you."

I wanted to say duh, *so I didn't say anything.*

"While I was standing here, I realized that we can leave each other messages and things." He pointed to a hollow knot in the tree beside us. "Right here. We'll both check every day."

"Like Scout and Boo Radley?"

"Only neither of us has to be a shut-in," he said. "Obviously, we don't sign any notes."

"Obviously."

"You're still mad about the other day," he said. "Aren't you?"

"I'm fine."

"I really didn't mean to leave you at my place for so long."

Before I could think of what I wanted to really say, Georgina and Sylvie came up the footpath.

"Hi, Andi, hi, Dallas," both of them said as they passed.

"That Sylvie is an interesting one," Dallas said as they disappeared into the dorm. "She signed up for cue sports."

"Oh great," I said. "She goes after any guy that's ever shown any interest in me."

Dallas wrinkled his nose. "She's so skinny."

"Maybe you can get her to eat while she's not playing pool and coming on to you," I said.

"That's way above my pay grade," he said.

"*Just watch out for her,*" I said. "*She's got problems.*"

"*Will do,*" he said, literally watching her. "*But only if you tell me what's going on with you.*"

"*I thought you were with family over the holidays and then your flight got delayed,*" I finally told him.

"*I was.*"

"*But you were really in Tulsa?*"

"*So that's what this is all about?*"

"*It's not like I was snooping,*" I said, feeling defensive even though I'd done nothing wrong. "*I was just standing there when the message started to play.*"

"*That was Tracy.*" He paused. "*An old friend. You have nothing to worry about.*"

"*But you flew to Oklahoma to visit her?*"

"*I admit the 'family situation' was BS for my Glenlake masters. If I lose this job, I lose you. Tracy has a very comfortable guest room in a home that's incredibly conducive to creative inspiration,*" he said.

"*Oh,*" I said.

"*You're really cute when you're jealous.*" He smiled. "*But don't be.*"

~

Friday, January 17, 1997

It's hard to stay mad at someone when they leave you a handwritten message on fancy paper in a secret hiding place. Even though the envelope says Merry Christmas *and is three weeks too late, when what's inside is the most beautiful love poem you've ever read, it's all but impossible.*

When every damn thing reminds me of you
The curve of the road
your hips
The fire on the hearth
your hair

Even the can of beer I crack at the end of the day
Is a bittersweet reminder of
your kiss
I toss and turn in these motel-room sheets
Thinking I need a dog so it can run away
Because if I lose my job, I'll lose you, too
As every country-song cliché comes true

He told me he made my hair red in the poem because he submitted it to a poetry journal. I asked him why it had to be red (was he thinking about Georgina?), and he said blondes make for boring poetry.

And that I am his muse.

~

Saturday, January 25, 1997

There are definite downsides to having a secret relationship.

Dallas and I were planning to sneak off campus together at some point today or tomorrow, but Glenlake is completely snowed in. The off-campus activity became an on-campus movie and hot chocolate night, and I had to watch him ladle hot chocolate into mugs and fake flirt with Mrs. Darrow, who he calls "Dimwit Barbie."

On the other hand, maybe it's for the best, because it turned into drama night for all the out-in-the-open couples:

Sylvie and James, who got together at the water park, broke up by the end of the movie.

Georgina started a fight with Tommy over him hanging out too much with his friends and ignoring her.

Worst of all, I watched a just-dumped Sylvie corner Ian outside the bathroom and pull him to an out-of-the-way spot by the maintenance room. I wasn't totally surprised when she basically threw herself at him.

I guess I was surprised that he let her.

Chapter Thirty-Four

Ian Copeland's Glenlake Journal

Sunday, February 2, 1997

I'm going to take a break from journaling. I don't really feel like writing anything else. What's the point?

Maybe I'll make THIS my senior page.

Chapter Thirty-Five

Every morning, after hustling the twins off to school and sitting down for a quick cup of coffee with Ian before he left for work, Andi detoured into Cassidy's room before getting ready for her own workday. Sitting down at her daughter's desk, she checked the Google Drive folder for recent developments.

Andi was both relieved and troubled there'd been no updated information about Roy's arrest since Georgina had blabbed the news to Ian.

Primary Suspect: Curtis Royal

Age: 63

Currently in police custody, charged with possession of a controlled substance.

Criminal record includes one charge of aggravated assault and multiple misdemeanor drug charges.

There were, however, additions, updates, and changes to the *Persons of Interest* list the class had apparently been investigating simultaneously, despite the arrest of Roy. Under the heading *Glenlake Staff,* nothing had changed in regard to two of the three names:

Lincoln Darrow (headmaster). Dallas Walker flirtatious with his wife, Miranda?

Scott Stover (facilities manager). Dallas Walker reportedly irritable about issues regarding the heating and cooling in his classroom.

The third name, Lucy Kucinich, then the chair of the English Department, had been crossed off. She'd made the list for *Repeated verbal altercations with Dallas Walker over rule violations, grading policy, and unorthodox teaching style.* The latest note, contributed by Audrey T., read, *Contacted Mrs. Kucinich at nursing home in southern Illinois. She recalled Dallas Walker as "a fine man who cared deeply about educating his students. We clashed on methods, but I respected his work and his commitment to the craft of poetry enormously."*

Also crossed off the list were two students: Tommy Harkins, whose attendance at the University of Illinois, as opposed to one of the more prestigious private schools to which he'd applied, turned out to be his choice due to a superior engineering program at U of I. Connor Cotton was removed from the list because his decision to take a gap year had come after he'd already been accepted to Cornell—he'd spent six months learning Spanish in a Mexican orphanage and another three months touring South America. All in all, a fatal blow to the class's imagined motive of murderous anger over a bad first-semester grade in poetry.

She was pleased there had never been any changes of note to either her name on the list of poetry students or Ian's name as a member of the Cue Sports Society.

Still very much on the list, however, were:

Sylvie Montgomery (student). Member of Cue Sports Society.

Georgina Holt Fordham (student). Suspiciously frequent alumni source of information?

They had certainly been on her list back in the day, not for their murderous intentions toward Dallas but their amorous ones.

Even though she'd warned Dallas that Sylvie was troubled and went after anyone even vaguely associated with her, he had not only welcomed her to Cue Sports Society but given her private catch-up lessons.

"In public," he'd said. "The rec room was full of people."

None of whom missed Sylvie's flirtatious giggling.

Andi hadn't worried too much about Georgina, given that Tommy had kept her distracted during most of senior year.

Distracted enough to stay away from Dallas?

Andi had never been entirely sure of the answer. Maybe it was time to find out.

Chapter Thirty-Six

For once, Mr. Kelly didn't have to tell everyone to shut up and sit down. People could tell by his face as soon as they came in the door: something had happened. When the bell rang, he didn't even have to raise his voice.

"Last night while all of you were using Snapchat to distract yourselves from homework, I took a local photographer out for a beer," he said. "She's a stringer who covers the North Shore for various outlets and was working for the *Chicago Tribune* on the day Dallas Walker's hot rod got winched out of the lake."

Cassidy glanced at her classmates. Not what she or anyone had been expecting.

"I was working a different angle, but she had news I wasn't expecting. This is an important lesson in working your sources: Get to know everybody, because sometimes the least important person will have the most important information. Often, the most important person won't want to talk to you."

Now he was losing them.

"Get to the point already," said Noah under his breath.

Mr. Kelly cleared his throat and stood up, looking deadly serious. "Curtis Royal, our Roy, an employee of Glenlake Academy, has been charged with the murder of Dallas Walker. They'll be making a formal announcement this afternoon."

Cassidy felt her scalp prickle. It was only a confirmation of what they'd been expecting, but somehow it felt weird now that it was real.

There were a few whoops and cheers as Noah said he would have bet money on it, before Mr. Kelly calmed them down again.

"Apparently, my source is quite friendly with one of the junior detectives, who shared a lot of information without thinking where it would end up. Roy was initially detained on what you might call a fishing expedition. Stopped for a traffic violation—the arresting officer claimed to smell marijuana and searched the vehicle, finding a misdemeanor amount. An interrogation uncovered nothing significant, but the detectives had an ace up their sleeve: a jailhouse snitch. Apparently, someone who'd been arrested for armed robbery downstate tried to plea-bargain by claiming knowledge of a long-ago murder. He'd heard that the car had been found and claimed to be present at a party where Roy had threatened to kill Dallas Walker. The police likely have other evidence we don't know about."

Cassidy raised her hand. "Does this mean we're done?"

"We have two choices," he said, pacing at the front of the room. "One, we can simply report the trial. That's what most news organizations do. It's the job of law enforcement, after all, to put forth the suspect, and the job of the judicial system to try him. In most cases, the Fourth Estate simply reports on the proceedings and the outcome. Investigative journalists get involved when there's a miscarriage of justice. But the trial likely won't get underway until you've already graduated Glenlake."

"So what's the second option?" asked Tate.

"We finish our work," said Mr. Kelly. "We've already cleared several suspects to our satisfaction. We continue to examine the available evidence until we can end the year convinced in our minds that the Lake County Sheriff's Office got the right guy for the crime."

"If option one is off the table," said Noah, "and we don't like number two, is there a third option?"

Mr. Kelly grinned. "We can always go back to my planned curriculum, which included a spring unit on the law as it relates to journalism."

"Option two, please!" said Hannah.

Just about everyone chimed in, except for Felicia, who wanted to be a lawyer anyway.

"The ayes have it," said Mr. Kelly. "Let's continue our work. Break into groups and review your to-do lists. I'll check in with you one at a time."

Cassidy was still turning her desk around when he came over and handed her a flash drive.

"This was my original objective. To support the next generation of journalistic excellence, the photographer agreed to let us look at her outtakes. She was shooting from a distance, so there's probably nothing new here, but let me know if you spot anything."

As he moved on, Cassidy plugged the flash drive into her laptop and opened the folder while Noah stood behind her, his eyes fixed on the screen. Tate wandered over, having overheard.

"I want to see," said Tate, leaning in just close enough that she could feel the warmth of his skin. "After all, I was the one who found the damn thing."

"A hundred and seventy-two pictures," said Noah. "Damn."

"Open them!" urged Tate.

Cassidy opened the first file and expanded it to full screen. A series of photos showed the operation required to lift the car out of the lake and the surprising number of vehicles that had bushwhacked their way up the old overgrown road and parked in a line leading to the cliff. She spotted a pickup truck from the town of Glenlake, a van from Glenlake Academy, two sheriff's department SUVs, a couple of vehicles she couldn't identify, and, strangely, even an ambulance.

Down below on the shoreline, yellow caution tape fluttered, and a small crowd stood watching a crew operate the crane on the barge. She recognized the headmaster, the assistant headmaster, and the operations manager of Glenlake. The photographer had gotten there before the car came up and seemed to be killing time, snapping picture after repetitive picture.

"I think we found the smoking gun," joked Noah, already bored.

"Hold on," said Tate.

Divers' heads poked above the water like seals, one of them giving a thumbs-up. Chains had been rigged to the sunken car.

A burst of a dozen photos captured the car rising, from the first glimpse of its hood to the moment it dangled above the rippling lake's surface, murky water streaming out of it. It all looked very much like the few photos they'd already seen published in the newspaper.

Then, finally, the car was down on the deck of the big barge. Sheriff's investigators in orange vests peered into the windows. The photographer zoomed in with an amazingly powerful telephoto lens, and Cassidy recognized Detective Gavras from his visit to her class. He was the first to open the door.

The next shots were from a different angle, as if the photographer had run along the cliff top to get a better view. Suddenly, there were startlingly clear images of the front seat, framed by the open door and the arms and bodies of the investigators.

"There he is," said Cassidy softly.

A heap of bones on the seat mingled with mud and algae and some kind of green underwater plant. Walker's clothes had long since rotted away.

A sheriff's department photographer on the barge obscured the next several photos, but when the stringer got another clear shot, it was of Gavras lifting a watch out of the car on a long metal probe. The watch went into a plastic evidence bag.

But something else sparkled on the seat.

"What's that?" asked Noah, touching the screen of Cassidy's laptop.

Cassidy zoomed in, but the image blurred. She zoomed out and moved to the next image. And the next.

Gavras lifted something else out of the car. In the first photo, the shape was enough to make Cassidy's stomach feel hollow.

The next photo, perfectly focused in a gleaming ray of sun, confirmed it.

"It's a bracelet," said Noah.

It was a bracelet. Exactly like her mother's.

Chapter Thirty-Seven

Andi Bloom's Glenlake Journal

Monday, February 10, 1997

Today is Dallas's fortieth birthday. We all sang happy birthday to him in class, but after the (weird, surreal, I'm just not sure how to describe it) Saturday night celebration we had together, I can't say I felt as enthusiastic as I could have. For the first time, I wished he'd stop wearing the bracelet I gave him every day. Or at least to class.

For his birthday, he told me the only gift he would accept was the pleasure of my company, so I lied to Georgina and Mrs. Henry and said my dad was in town for just one night and wanted me to stay in his hotel downtown. I had even forged a note, but Mrs. Henry didn't ask to see it, so I just wandered off with my backpack, waited until I was sure no one was watching, and then cut through the woods to the back door of Dallas's cottage, just like we'd planned.

All the curtains were drawn and only a couple of lights were on, so my hopes immediately went to a romantic dinner, followed by a long, lingering evening of being together.

Funny how fast your imagination always seems to take you places you never get to go.

"I hope you're ready for something different," he said as he kissed me in the kitchen, just long and deep enough that I felt my body starting to melt.

"Yes," I whispered, and the next thing I knew we were going into the tiny attached garage where he'd parked his car, and he told me to crouch down on the passenger floor until we were totally out of Glenlake.

When I could finally sit up, I saw that we were on Highway 41 headed north.

"Where are we going?" I asked.

Dallas just smiled and turned up the radio. The song was "You Shook Me All Night Long." He loves classic rock and just laughs when I try to get him to listen to Ani DiFranco or Fiona Apple.

A little while later we got to a bar called Kyle's Kabin. Instantly I thought of Ian, because he'd been there with the Cue Sports Society and told me about it. There were pickups, motorcycles, and some really shitty cars parked out front. It looked crowded, and I was worried about being carded.

"Don't worry, they know me here," he said, reading my mind.

He leaned across the seat and kissed me. I won't say the kiss changed everything, but it definitely made me feel better about going in.

There was a bouncer at the door, but he just nodded at Dallas and gave me kind of a gross look without asking to see any ID.

And then we were in. I've been to bars with Simon, but this was definitely the first roadhouse I've ever been in. If that's the right word. There wasn't live music or anything, but everybody seemed to be smoking and drinking beer, and there were a couple of pool tables under green-shaded lights.

Most of the patrons looked like townies except for one guy in chinos and a sweater who came in right after us and made me afraid that he worked at Glenlake or something until I realized I'd never seen him before.

Dallas went right up to a massive man who had tattoos—even one on his neck—and bumped fists.

"Roy," he said, *"this is Andi."*

Roy looked at me in a way that made me shiver, and not in a good way. I felt slimy, but for a moment I felt proud because this was the first time Dallas had ever introduced me to anyone.

Even if we were in a gross bar in the middle of nowhere.

"How's your supply?" Roy asked Dallas.

"Good, good," said Dallas, like he didn't want to talk about it.

Then Roy said, "Let me get you some beers," and Dallas said, "Hell yeah. Thanks, bro."

Since when did Dallas call anyone "bro"?

***

I'm finishing this up later because Georgina came home and wanted to ask me all about my night in Chicago with Simon, forcing me to invent a small off-Loop play that somehow involved some of the details of what actually happened with Dallas. And then I had to listen to her tell me about how she and Tommy are having issues again but it's no big deal really and blah blah blah. Everything was going great for them, which is why Georgina feels obligated to invent a little drama. She asked me if I was really done with James Whitmer, because Sylvie had been seen with him (again), and I CAN'T STAND ALL THIS CHILDISH BULLSHIT.

So, anyway, we drank beer, and I watched Dallas and Roy play pool for what seemed like hours. Dallas is good and Roy is obviously a lot better, but I liked the way Dallas kept trying again, and in the end he finally did win a game.

Roy threw his cue stick on the table and laughed and bought us all shots of whiskey. I took the tiniest sip of mine because I hate the taste. Dallas threw his back in one gulp.

Then Dallas and Roy were having a conversation with several other men and women there, and all of a sudden we were piling out the door and into our cars.

"Are we going home now?" I asked, thinking it was an abrupt end to the evening but grateful to be calling it a night.

"Party at Roy's," Dallas told me, getting ready to follow Roy's beat-up old Jeep. When Roy gunned his engine, it was so loud that I knew he was the one who'd come to Dallas's cottage that day in January when Dallas never came back.

"I'm tired, Dallas," I said.

"We don't have to stay long," he said, kissing me again. This kiss didn't work quite as well as the first one, but I didn't say anything.

I wish I had.

Roy's was an old farmhouse with a rotting porch and dirty floors, half-hidden by trees and reached by a long, rutted driveway. In the yard there were junked cars and motorcycles under mounds of snow. The house was lit by bare lightbulbs, with unmatched couches and chairs and coffee tables plunked down wherever.

There were already people there, and heavy metal was pumping out of some big speakers. It smelled like pot, dirty ashtrays, and cat pee. I wasn't the only woman there, but I was definitely the only girl, and as Dallas guided me through to the kitchen, people were looking at me, and at him, and grinning.

Dallas didn't seem to notice, but I was starting to feel panicky, like a dream where you're in school and realize you're not wearing pants.

"Too many people are seeing us!" I practically yelled in his ear, so he could hear me over the music.

"And they have zero connection to Glenlake," he said into my ear.

He got us some beers from the fridge, and I took one, just so I'd have something to hold on to. I'm not sure if I even opened it. Dallas bummed a couple of cigarettes, lit both of them, and passed me one. I thought of all the cigarettes I'd smoked with Ian at the peristyle and wondered if he still went there to smoke. With Sarah Ann? Sylvie?

A skinny guy with pasty skin and a fake-looking leather jacket came over to talk to us. He was talking really fast and not making any sense, so we *went back into the living room, and he followed us. He was talking about computers and chess players and how someday we'd all have chips in our necks so the government could track us. Then he looked at us suspiciously and asked if we already had our chips and could he trust us.*

Dallas told him to get lost.

Then Roy appeared from nowhere, said, "Is this asshole bothering you?" and hit the guy really hard in the side of the head. When the guy in the leather jacket stumbled, Roy grabbed him and literally threw him out into the yard.

"Nobody bothers the professor!" bellowed Roy.

Dallas smiled, but it looked like he was starting to feel as sick as I was. But he still wouldn't leave.

And when Roy asked him if he wanted to get geared up, he nodded. He didn't ask me if I wanted to come, thank god, but they both disappeared for ten minutes, leaving me utterly alone.

A tough-looking woman with acne scars came up and started asking me questions, obviously trying to figure out who I was. I told her my name was Angie and I went to Glenlake College. Lame lies, but they were the best I could think of.

When Dallas and Roy came back, they were totally amped up and having a crazy conversation. Then they began playing darts.

I thought the party would go on forever, but gradually the house started emptying out, even though the skinny guy from before had come back in and was shivering in the doorway to the kitchen. I wasn't really watching Dallas and Roy, but all of a sudden I heard Roy yell. When I looked, he was moving toward Dallas and holding a dart in his hand.

No—he wasn't holding it. It was sticking out of the back of his hand.

"Fucking prick!" he yelled at Dallas.

"Sorry, Roy," said Dallas, but his voice sounded weird, like he had just stopped laughing.

"Sorry, Roy," Roy mimicked. "You fucking pussy poet. You can't handle your fucking drugs. Get out of here and take your jailbait student with you."

I had been frozen until then, but when he said that, I scrambled off the couch and toward the door.

"Shit, man," said Dallas, backing up.

"You're lucky she's here or you'd be fucking dead!" said Roy.

I turned and ran out of the house. Dallas was behind me.

"Fucking dead!" we heard again.

Dallas slipped on the ice by the car and fell down. He shook me off when I tried to help him.

"Get off me," he said.

"Are you okay to drive?"

Instead of answering, he got in the car and started the engine. I got in fast, not sure he wouldn't leave me.

I almost couldn't bear to watch the road on the way back to Glenlake. Dallas seemed jumpy and kept looking at the rearview mirror like he expected someone to be following us.

"You went with Roy that day, didn't you?" I finally asked him.

He grunted. "He needed help with something."

Does he really think I don't know he was buying drugs?

"Duck down," he said when we turned onto Campus Drive, even though it was the middle of the night and no one was around.

"Take me home, please," I told him. "I want to sleep in my bed tonight."

He shook his head. "Can't. It would raise too many questions after what you told Georgina."

He drove us back to his cottage and parked in his garage. I started to get out of the car, but he reached across me and pulled the door closed.

"I want you," he said.

His breath smelled weird, and his eyes were glassy. The Charger's heater didn't work very well, and it started to get cold as soon as he turned off the engine.

"Right here. Now."

I didn't want him, not then. But he didn't seem to notice. Or maybe he just didn't care.

Chapter Thirty-Eight

While her roommate attended debate club practice, Cassidy compared the photo on her phone to the photo they'd found on the flash drive, now uploaded onto the Google Drive folder *Primary Sources and Evidence.*

As far as she could tell, Mom's bracelet at home was identical to the one in Dallas Walker's car. The one encircling the *bones of his arm.*

She shuddered.

She had to know.

Cassidy couldn't remember the last time she'd called Georgina, but she did have her number—her "honorary aunt," as Georgina called herself, was always sure to text on her birthday or other special occasions.

She answered on the first ring.

"Cassidy! Well, this is a surprise. Boy trouble?" she asked hopefully.

Cassidy suddenly wished she'd thought of a reason why she couldn't ask her mother about the bracelet. She certainly couldn't tell her mom's best friend, *I don't trust my mom.*

"Not a boy problem, George," she said. "I just had a quick question for the class project. Liz has told everybody how helpful you are."

There was an uncharacteristic silence on the other end.

"I hope you don't mind?" said Cassidy tentatively.

"Well, I've always been happy to answer the class's questions," said Georgina after the briefest pause.

Despite the circumstances, Cassidy couldn't help smiling to herself.

"Someone, I forget who, said the metalworking class was really popular during the '96–'97 school year, and everybody was making bracelets."

"Well, not everybody. Just the girls in that class. And it wasn't a craze or anything, but I do remember seeing some of those bracelets around."

"Were they all alike, or were they different?"

"They were definitely different. Everybody was trying to put personality into them and outdo each other. You know, your mom was in that class."

Cassidy tried to sound surprised. "She was?"

"You should ask her. Her bracelet might have been the best. I remember she worked on it for so long she could have made multiple bracelets in that amount of time."

Whatever involuntary words Cassidy might have said stuck in her throat. The noise she made was halfway between coughing and gagging.

More than two—one for herself and one for Dallas Walker?

"Are you okay, honey?" asked Georgina.

"Fine," Cassidy managed to say. "I shouldn't eat while I'm talking on the phone, but I'm starving."

Cassidy bristled at the thought of who in her actual family was keeping secrets.

Luckily, Georgina had to get off the phone to give instructions to a member of her household staff before she thought to ask why Cassidy wanted to know about the bracelets. Cassidy didn't have an answer she could share with anyone.

"Make sure you take care of yourself, Cassidy."

"I will."

"And make sure you ask your mom if she still has her bracelet."

"Definitely," she promised, hoping Georgina wouldn't do it first.

When she got off the phone, she stared at the newspaper photographer's picture of the bracelet for a full minute before deleting the file from Google Drive and emptying the trash. When she refreshed her browser, there was no sign it had ever been there.

Chapter Thirty-Nine

ANDI BLOOM'S GLENLAKE JOURNAL

Friday, February 14, 1997

Things have been weird with Dallas ever since last weekend. I guess I should say I've been feeling weird, and it was bugging me that Dallas didn't seem to notice or care.

At least I thought he didn't. Then today he left me this valentine in our tree:

> The little castle and the treasure chest
> Always looked fake to you
> You were fascinated by your glass walls
> And how easily they cracked
>
> You love the air, I'm glad you're here
> So cool in an unfamiliar world
> Baby, let's get lost, we'll keep breaking out
> I love you—do you love me?

He loves me.

He.

Loves.
Me.

~

Monday, February 17, 1997
   Dallas is no fan of organized events, but he took the writer-in-residence job knowing that a performance or presentation was an "expectation, not an option." Needless to say, he's been procrastinating because he's cranky about the whole thing.
   Today, Mrs. Kucinich told him the English Department thought it would be cool to do a poetry slam. He was going to tell her it was a no (he hates poetry slams) until she suggested that he "tap a student from his class" to do some of the legwork.
   We both laughed out loud about that one.
   Not only do we have a legitimate excuse to spend extra time together, but as of today, I am the "coproducer" of the first-ever Glenlake Poetry Slam!

~

Wednesday, February 19, 1997
   The official date for the poetry slam is Friday, March 7. Apparently, we have to rush so it falls on a trustee meeting weekend and all the bigwigs can attend. No pressure.
   I talked Mr. Stover, the facilities manager, into letting us have it in the student union lounge. We're going to set up a stage and a coffee bar so the whole vibe is as authentic as possible.
   Dallas says his only regret is that he didn't add "gifted event planner" to all the (socially acceptable) superlatives on my college recommendation letters.
   Then he whispered a few of the ones that weren't.

~

Thursday, February 20, 1997

I want to expand the event so that anyone in the school can perform their poems. Dallas says all the extra "crap" will crowd out the superior work produced by his students.

"Plus," he added, "it's just that much more work for us."

It's kind of funny, but I'm not sure what he's really done beyond agreeing to the event and "hiring" me as coproducer. He seems a lot more interested in making "good use" of the extra time we get to spend together.

Which is not to say I mind.

Well, maybe a little.

~

Friday, February 28, 1997

The poetry slam is now a school-wide event!

This is huge, because it means we'll have a lot of people attending instead of just faculty who have to show up, the trustees and whoever, and the handful of seniors who are either dating or friends with someone in the class.

Dallas signed off after I told him I'd form a committee from our class to screen the submissions, pick the best ones, and give them to him for final approval. His picks will get "selective guest reading slots." That was Georgina's idea.

Georgina (with help from Tommy, depending on the daily status of their relationship) is off and running with marketing and promotion. Wes, who is in jazz band, says he'll handle the music and solo performers. Crystal is talking to the painting teacher about hanging student artwork in the lounge. Everyone else in the class has signed up to work as a barista, seat people, or set up and tear down.

We even have an official name for the event:

Give Me Poetry or Give Me Death.

≈

Friday, March 7, 1997

I'm okay with Dallas putting his arm around someone and helping her off the stage—as long as it's not Georgina, who, still tongue-tied for the first time in her entire life, sobbed in Dallas's arms while he stroked her fire-on-the-hearth hair.

I avoided both of them for the rest of the night. It was easy enough to do with Dallas, because he was busy accepting praise for the poetry slam I organized. Avoiding Georgina was harder.

"I'm so embarrassed I feel like I could just die," she said, collapsing on her bed the moment we got back to our dorm room.

She smelled like Dallas's aftershave.

"Everyone gets stage fright," I said.

"Tommy picked a fight right before I went onstage," she groaned.

"What a bastard," I said, even though he was the person I was third maddest at.

She plumped her pillow and wedged it under her head, getting comfortable. "This is all his fault. I hate him so much."

"There are other fish in the sea."

"That's what Dallas said," Georgina said.

"I'm not surprised," I told her.

Georgina looked at me. "Why do you say that?"

"He seemed pretty into comforting you."

Instead of denying it or playing it down, she giggled.

She fucking giggled.

Chapter Forty

Friday, March 7, 1997

I am journaling again because I need to vent.

Mom and Dad are here for another board of trustees meeting or whatever. Tonight was the "poetry slam" hosted by Dallas Fucking Walker and his senior poetry seminar, featuring Andi as "coproducer."

That's rich.

I wasn't going to go, but Dad made me. He said it would "look bad" for him as chairman of the board if I wasn't there. He and Mom thought Andi was the reason I didn't want to go. If only. I probably shouldn't have told them she was the teacher's pet, though.

It was pure torture, and not only because it was almost two hours of poetry, ha ha. DFW started things off by stepping up to the mic and reciting some poem from memory, and everybody clapped their hands off. He didn't give a big speech, thank god. Just said, "Ladies and gentlemen, please welcome the poets of Glenlake Academy."

What made it extra torturous is that it wasn't just the kids in his class—it was every kid at school who thinks they have a poetic bone in their body. The students in his seminar kind of helped out and read their own poems here and there. Although some of the poetry students were lame, too. Georgina tried to do hers from memory but got stage fright, something you'd never expect from her. After some long, awkward pauses, Dallas put his arm around her and helped her off the stage.

I kept waiting for Andi and wondering what her poem would be about, but she went last—the last of the students, anyway. I could barely move or breathe because I was sure I was going to lose my shit, right there, sitting in between Mom and Dad.

The only lines I remember went something like:

My heart beats as fast as a bee beats its wings
I'm lost in the clover, I'm seeking my lover

She didn't say anything about getting stung.

～

Saturday, March 8, 1997

Today, while I was gimping my way to the student union with Mom and Dad to get some lunch, the sun was shining on the doors, so I couldn't see who was coming out. And guess who was suddenly right in front of us?

Dallas Fucking Walker.

I just kept my head down like I didn't see him, but he stopped so I couldn't get around and said, "Hi, Ian! Are you going to introduce me to your parents?"

He was totally fucking with me. I didn't move or say anything. It was like this red mist came down in front of my eyes, and I wanted to push him down and just whale on him with my crutches until his face was a bloody pulp.

"Ian!" Mom said, all shocked at my manners.

"Cope Copeland," Dad said, sticking out his hand. "I'm the father of this somewhat uncommunicative boy."

Count on adults to stick together.

"And I'm Biz," said Mom.

"*I haven't seen Ian at Cue Sports Society recently,*" *said DFW, patting me on the shoulder while I clenched my teeth.*

"*I'm sure it's not as comfortable to play with his broken leg,*" *said Mom.*

"*Is that the problem?*" *DFW asked me.*

I nodded, still not looking at him.

"*Too bad,*" *he said.* "*I was hoping that, without being able to play basketball, you might have more time on your hands.*"

"*I have a lot of homework,*" *I said.*

There was an awkward silence, which I kind of enjoyed, to be honest. Then finally Dad said, "*Well, we'd better get to lunch.*"

Dallas stepped to one side, opened the door, and held it for us. When I went past him, I shouldered into him intentionally.

"*Whoops,*" *he said, staring at me.*

If he didn't know I knew, he'd better know now.

"*Ian,*" *said Mom once we got inside.* "*What is going on with you? You treated that teacher like he was . . . like you were* enemies.*"

"*Well, maybe I don't like him,*" *I said.*

Dad put his hand on my back. "*I don't care if you don't like him. You are a Copeland and will behave as such. He's temporary, but our family will always be a part of this school.*"

I wondered what he'd say if he knew the truth about Dallas Walker.

Chapter Forty-One

The deputy behind the bulletproof glass at the front desk of the Lake County Adult Corrections Facility assumed Cassidy and Tate were brother and sister, and that they were there to see their father. After they'd given their real names and admitted they were not related to the inmate, Cassidy was sure the visit would be over before it began. But the deputy picked up his phone, pointed them into chairs, and said, "I'll see if he wants to see you."

They sat down in the molded plastic bucket seats and looked at each other nervously, Cassidy wondering if Tate felt the same way—half hoping the answer would be no. Her brain was so full, and her thoughts were so slippery, she had no idea how detectives ever solved a case or journalists ever wrote a story. Roy had seemed like the perfect suspect: a sketchy local with a criminal record who inexplicably hung out with the rebel poetry teacher, who had been overheard threatening his life, who even had a nasty neck tattoo, for crying out loud.

But now things weren't making much sense. In all likelihood, her mom had made the bracelet Dallas Walker was wearing when he died. Cassidy assumed that the person her mom had been seeing when she broke up with Dad senior year was another student—but what if it was *her teacher*?

There could be a reason Mom was so weird about her and Mr. Kelly.

Maybe I'm just concerned about the amount of time the two of you are spending together. . . Working on something that closely, that intensely, sometimes leads to a familiarity . . .

What was the timeline? If she and Dad got back together after Dallas Walker disappeared, *died*, wouldn't that make them . . . suspects? Stronger suspects than any of the other people who hadn't been cleared by the class?

Of course, she hadn't said a word about these new suspicions to Tate. All she'd told him was that she hoped Detective Gavras wasn't rushing to judgment on Roy, and that it would be an amazing scoop if she got an interview with the suspect even before real reporters did. If his lawyer was letting him talk.

Tate insisted on coming along for her protection. She liked the gesture, even though she was just now realizing he couldn't accompany her into the interview—not if she was going to ask the questions she needed answered.

"We don't have permission for this, Tate," she said. "What if you get in trouble again?"

"I'm off probation, and I don't think they would have suspended me, anyway. My family's not as big a deal as yours, but I am a legacy."

She was saved by Roy, of all people.

"The inmate says he is willing to speak with Cassidy Copeland only," said the deputy.

Cassidy was standing before she knew it, nerves tingling, hearing Tate's voice as if from far away.

"We can tell him no, it's both of us or neither of us," he said stoically.

"It's probably for the best," she told him. "Just in case you get in trouble again."

"Cassidy—"

"It's not like he'll be able to hurt me," she said as a guard opened a nearby door and motioned her through. "Right?"

Tate didn't have an answer, just looked at her despairingly.

And maybe the tiniest bit relieved.

She went through the door, filled out a visitor's form, turned over her backpack and her jacket, and then submitted to a metal detector and a pat down from a female guard. They let her keep her phone but that was it.

Roy was waiting for her. She'd thought they would talk on a phone, separated by bulletproof glass, like she'd seen on TV, but he was just sitting on the other side of a table in a room with eight other tables. An inmate and his visitor stopped talking and watched as she walked slowly over to Roy's table.

"Cassidy *Copeland*," he drawled as she sat down, drawing out her last name. "Here for the follow-up interview?"

Trying to compose herself, she held up her phone. "Do you mind if I record this?"

Roy shrugged.

She opened the voice memo app and pressed "Record." Should she ask him to say yes for the record? Under the table, her knees bumped a solid divider. She guessed it was so visitors couldn't pass things to the prisoners.

"Can you tell me why you're here?"

He snorted. "The reason I'm here is the reason you're here."

"I want your version of events. I'm not assuming you're guilty."

He looked at her with a glint in his eye. "That's good, because I'm not."

"Someone thinks you are."

"I'm here because some jailhouse snitch heard me giving some shit to my buddy Dallas two decades ago. Fucker's trying to plead down on an armed robbery and thought he'd trade me for three to seven years."

"Do you have an alibi?"

"They don't even know for sure what day Dallas disappeared."

Cassidy watched the time counter on her phone's screen, hoping his voice was audible. She became suddenly aware of how close he was to her, just an arm's length away.

As if reading her thoughts, he lifted his hands out of his lap and set them on the stainless-steel table, the chain of his handcuffs rattling loudly.

"Were you friends?" she said.

"We were friend-ly. I sold him some dope, but the statute of limitations is way over on that."

"Did you kill him?" she asked, wanting to sound tough and no-nonsense, but quavering, barely able to get the words out.

He looked at her for a second, then shook his head. "Everyone in here is innocent. Even the guilty ones. Nobody believes a word we say." He leaned forward. "But don't worry. I'll get out of here."

"How do you know?"

Leaning back, he raised his cuffed hands and scratched the loose skin at his neck, making his serpent tattoo wiggle. "I have faith in what you might call higher powers."

The breathtaking naivete of his statement startled her. How did a guy like him, in a place like this, hold on to such illusions? If Roy was innocent, he was going to need more than belief in God to set him free.

"Listen—"

"I know why you're here." His eyes bored into her.

She felt cold chills all over her body. She wanted to look away but felt hypnotized by his watery blue eyes. "Why?"

"Ask your mom. You know, you look a lot like her."

Cassidy pushed back from the table and stood up, shaking, barely remembering to grab her phone before she stumbled away. A deputy moved toward her.

Roy called after her. "Are you a wild child, like she was?"

Chapter Forty-Two

Andi Bloom's Glenlake Journal

Wednesday, March 12, 1997

I already felt light-headed and nauseated, like I was coming down with the flu. Then, a student messenger came to physics class with a note. For me. And definitely not from Dallas.

> Andi,
> Please come to my office for a short meeting. I'll make
> sure you're excused from any class time you miss.
> Mr. Matheson

I collected my book bag and barely made it to the bathroom before I threw up. Could it be any coincidence that he'd asked to see me on a Wednesday, a few minutes before I always sneak away to Dallas's cottage?

I couldn't possibly let Dallas know something major was happening, much less find out what he wanted me to say, or not say. All I could do was rinse my mouth, splash some water on my face, and hope I made it to McCormick Mansion.

Or maybe that I crumpled on the sidewalk and died on the spot.

I almost threw up again on my way there. I hadn't told anyone. Dallas hadn't, either, obviously. And we'd never been caught together. Did someone from the roadhouse or that weird guy at Roy's party know someone at school?

As crazy as it seems, that had to be it. That was the only place we'd been together in public.

I entered the building, planning how I'd say goodbye to everyone at Glenlake and thinking about what Simon was going to say when he heard I'd been expelled. "You were schtupping who?*"*

He'd lose his mind when I answered.

And how did Glenlake deal with teachers who had relationships with students? Would Dallas be fired . . . or arrested?

I forced myself into Mr. Matheson's office, sure I was about to find out.

"Andi," Mr. Matheson said. "Welcome."

Mrs. Kucinich, the head of the English Department, was there, too.

"Thanks for meeting with us on such short notice," she said, like I had a choice.

"No problem," I told her.

"Are you all right?" Mrs. Kucinich asked. "You look pale."

"Just feeling under the weather."

The understatement of the decade.

"We'll try and get through our questions as quickly as possible," Mrs. Kucinich said as I took the open chair beside her.

"We wanted to speak with you today because we routinely conduct interviews of student leaders to get feedback about the effectiveness of our visiting teachers," Mr. Matheson said.

"Mr. W-Walker?" I stammered.

"Dallas," Mrs. Kucinich said with a smile. "We're well aware that you call him by his first name."

"The whole class does," I said, sounding a lot more defensive than I wanted to.

They nodded in unison. It wasn't reassuring.

"You're a top performer in the English Department and in Dallas's class, not to mention all the previous writer-in-residence classes during your time here—"

"And the brains behind that wonderful poetry event," Mr. Matheson said, throwing me even more off-balance. *"Everyone loved it so much."*

"Thank you," I said.

"In any case, we have a series of questions we'd like to ask you about Dallas and the poetry seminar."

I had to ask. "Is he in some kind of trouble?"

"That's not what this is about," Mr. Matheson said.

The next thing I knew they were firing questions at me. On a scale of one to ten:

How would you rate the quality of his assignments?

How would you rate the content of his lectures?

Does he have an engaging demeanor in class? Is he a good teacher?

How would you rate your overall enjoyment of his class?

There were a lot more. None of them were:

Does he have inappropriate relationships with students?

Are you having a secret affair with him?

How would you rate his sexual prowess?

"Do you think he grades fairly?" Mr. Matheson asked.

And there it was. I wanted to feel more relieved than I did.

"I know a lot of kids were unhappy about their first-semester grades until he made adjustments," I said.

"But you weren't?" Mrs. Kucinich said.

"No," I said. *"I worked really hard in the class and got the grade I felt I deserved."*

Mr. Matheson jotted a note.

I willed myself not to throw up again.

"And what about his poetry?" Mrs. Kucinich asked.

"What about it?"

"Does he read his work to the class?"

"Sometimes," I said.

"And what is it about?"

"Nature, philosophy, love, loss," I said, sandwiching the word love as inconspicuously as possible in the middle of the list. "You know, the usual poetry stuff."

"We understand he's working on a book of poems about Glenlake," Mr. Matheson said.

"I didn't know that," I said, annoyed they knew something I didn't. "But I can't say I'm totally surprised, because there's a chalkboard where he writes out his works in progress sometimes."

"And what do you think of these poems?"

There once was a boy named Dallas . . .

"That he's a really talented poet."

Mr. Matheson's and Mrs. Kucinich's eyes met.

Somehow, I knew I'd said either exactly the right thing or exactly the wrong thing. I just didn't know which. They thanked me and sent me on my way.

I left utterly confused. There'd been no suggestion that they knew anything. On the surface, it seemed like they had really, truly called me in because I was Andi Bloom, literary It Girl of Glenlake, taker of all visiting-writer seminars, the girl most likely to . . . give an honest, well-informed student evaluation of Dallas Walker.

But there was definitely something else. Was it what they didn't say, or was it something I hadn't answered correctly? Would I be called in a second time and sentenced to public execution at the peristyle because of some question where I'd given Dallas a 10 instead of the 5 or 6 they felt he deserved? Maybe they already knew about our relationship, and the meeting had been my chance to confess.

I wanted to put a note in the tree for Dallas to let him know what happened. But what if they were watching, waiting for me to give them the definitive proof they were looking for?

He had to be wondering where I was and why I hadn't shown up at his cottage. I wanted to run over there, but I had no choice except to wait until I bumped into him or saw him in class on Friday, just like the regular student I wasn't at all anymore.

Thursday, March 13, 1997

I woke up today feeling even more exhausted and sick than yesterday. I never saw Dallas, even though I looked for him all over campus.

I got even more paranoid when I thought I saw Mr. Sweater-and-Chinos from the roadhouse parked in the visitor lot by McCormick. With the reflections on the car window, I couldn't be sure it was him, but whoever it was caught me staring just before he drove away.

Desperate to get a minute with Dallas today, I knocked on his office door before class.

He was clearly pissed about being stood up because he didn't even look at me when I came in. "Can I help you with something, Andi?" he asked.

"I got called into Matheson's office yesterday. At exactly the time I was going to see you. Mrs. Kucinich was there, too."

"Shit," he said, finally looking at me. "Why didn't you leave me a note?"

"I was afraid I was being watched. Afterward I saw a guy I'm sure was at the roadhouse the night we were there."

"I doubt it. What did they say?"

"That they'd called me in to do an evaluation."

"Of me?"

I nodded.

Appearing to relax, he actually smiled. "And how did you rank my performance?"

"This isn't funny, Dallas. I'm sure they know something."

"If they didn't come right out and accuse us of being together, they don't know," he said, way too confident.

"How do you know they weren't trying to catch us in some kind of trap?"

"You've been reading too many trashy suspense novels, my dear," he said. "They may suspect I'm having an affair with Darrow's wife, but not you."

All of a sudden I felt stupid, and his offhand comment about Mrs. Darrow made me mad.

"Why didn't you tell me you were writing a book about Glenlake?"

"You've already read almost every poem in it," he said. "I hope you told them it's going to be a modern classic. I'm hoping you're going to give me a blurb."

"Stop it," I said, irritated that he wasn't taking this seriously. Especially after my spending the last day and a half in a tailspin.

"That's what they're really worried about, Andi."

"How do you know?"

"Because they already dragged me in for a meeting, too."

"Why didn't you tell me?"

"What was I going to say? That Mrs. Kucinich and her band of barely literate, brownnosing wannabes brought me here to produce a work of great literature, and now they're crawling up my ass trying to make sure the poems will be PG-rated, 'as befits the prominence and standing of Glenlake?'"

"What did you tell them?"

"That the poems in the book are about natural beauty, educational excellence, and smokin'-hot boarding school girls."

"You didn't."

"Like that hasn't been the theme of everything ever written about a teacher's life at a boarding school? Fucking students is a time-honored tradition here and everywhere else."

Now I was angry and scared. I felt dizzy. "Students? As in me and who else? Georgina?"

"Jesus, Andi, I'm just joking," he said, hugging me and pulling me close even though the door to his office was open.

"Well, don't. I don't like this."

"Don't worry," he said. "All I have to do is change the title of one poem from 'Bloom' to 'Flowering.' That's the beauty of art. It's subjective and open to broad interpretation. Just like love."

And then he kissed me. Still with the door wide open.

"Although, if they don't stop harassing me and trying to micromanage my work, I may just have to name the collection Glenlake Girl. *"*

Monday, March 17, 1997

The Pepto-Bismol Nurse Ratched gave me seemed to do the trick.

Until today.

It wasn't like I woke up nauseated or anything. It felt more like a nervous stomach that didn't kick in until the mail was delivered and there were three letters, one from University of Iowa, one from Berkeley, and one from Northwestern.

I got into all three!

I was really happy.

So happy, I threw up.

I kept telling myself it was nerves. I mean, how often do you get your first three letters from colleges and they're all acceptances? I went with that until I got back to my room, opened my desk drawer to put the letters away, and saw a corner of the pamphlet Nurse Ratched had given me, just in case.

Then I cried.

Tuesday, March 18, 1997

I literally couldn't stomach French class. I didn't want to think about le petit-déjeuner, much less talk about food, the subject of this week's unit. Luckily, Georgina—and, I assumed, everyone else in the dorm—was already long gone to class when I dragged myself out of bed, grabbed the wrapped testing stick I got at the town drugstore, and rushed down the hallway into the bathroom. I barely made it to the stall before I threw up.

I didn't even notice I wasn't alone until someone in the next stall did the same thing.

I stood there, shaky, mortified, and needing to puke again. Which I did.

"You okay?" asked the person, who sounded a lot like Sylvie.

"I've got the flu," I said.

"Yeah, me too." Definitely Sylvie.

Sharing my misery with Sylvie was punishment enough, and then the bathroom door opened.

"Is someone getting sick in here?" called Mrs. Henry, who I had assumed was long gone teaching her first-period class.

"I've got the stomach flu," I said.

"Sylvie?" she asked.

"It's Andi," I said.

"And . . . ?"

The stall door clicked open and Sylvie shuffled out.

"I accidentally overslept," Sylvie said.

I didn't have the energy to bust her, even though she kind of deserves it for trying to hook up with every guy I've ever been interested in.

"Get to class, Sylvie," Mrs. Henry said, obviously irritated.

"I'm going," Sylvie said.

"Andi?" Mrs. Henry asked, as soon as she was gone.

"Sorry I'm missing first period, but I really don't feel well," I said.

"Anything I can do, honey?" she asked.

"I'll be all right," I said, looking at the pregnancy test and wondering if anything would ever be all right again.

"If you're not, just let me know."

"Thanks," I said.

As soon as she was gone, I unwrapped the test, stuffed the wrapper in the white bin on the floor between the stalls, and peed on the stick.

Chapter Forty-Three

Ian checked the numbers one more time. Sales had slowed as they always did in January and February, but December, goosed by Christmas and New Year's, had been good. Actually, great. With the new store open, gross revenue was up 34 percent over the same month in the previous year, and net revenue—not taking into account certain emergency loans—was up 13 percent. With St. Patrick's Day only days away, things were starting to pick up again.

As his head of sales became more familiar with the category and his biggest customers developed a taste for the stuff, the "vintage and collectible" spirits category had the potential to do real business in its first full year. A local mixologist known for his lumberjack beard and leather apron had even inquired about stock, with the idea of offering an ultra-high-end line of cocktails at his bar.

It was all good news, good enough to wash away the awkward moment during WhaleFest with that drunk Ross Woodston, and afterward when Ian had taken what was left of the bottle of 1957 J.T.S. Brown into his office and done a blind taste test with a brand-new bottle.

The difference was imperceptible enough that he'd called Preston, who assured him that J.T.S. Brown was well known for its consistency from bottle to bottle, year after year.

He would need a lot more than consistency to make a dent in the $350,000 he'd borrowed from Simon. With just over six months left for repayment, it was going to be a challenge to pay it back on time. If he didn't have an excellent summer, and if he couldn't get another loan, he'd be going into business with Andi's father. Which would be awfully awkward to explain.

Wrinkling his nose at the smell of his half-eaten dinner—a delivered order of shrimp pad thai—he closed the Styrofoam clamshell and moved it to one side, using a napkin to wipe the area where he'd been leaning over to eat. He and Andi had ordered and eaten separately, although their delivery drivers had arrived nearly simultaneously. When he'd last seen her, she was downstairs on the couch, reading book proposals.

Apparently, she was done. Coming through his door, she stepped over Rusty, who was sleeping at his feet, handed him her tablet, and sank into a chair.

"What is it?" he asked, even as his eyes found the headline: PREP SCHOOL MURDER RESURFACES.

"Just read it," she said quietly.

The art: photos of Dallas and Copeland Hall. It should have been McCormick Mansion, but Copeland was the first big building that came into view as visitors came up Campus Drive.

It was even labeled in the photo description. Seeing his family's name next to the picture of Dallas made his hands start shaking, forcing him to set the tablet down on his desk.

He read the introductory paragraphs without fully comprehending them. It was only when Andi spoke that it started to sink in.

"They've charged Roy," she said, almost moaning.

Farther down was his booking photo. With his chin up, there was a hint of his old swagger and defiance.

Curtis Royal gained employment at Glenlake Academy after the murder.

Ian's head snapped up.

"Andi?"

"What?" she said flatly.

"Since when do you call him Roy?"

Chapter Forty-Four

Andi Bloom's Glenlake Journal

Wednesday, March 19, 1997

I left a note in the tree, telling Dallas to meet me at our special spot instead of his cottage. It's such a beautiful day he assumed I wanted to have a romantic picnic and planned accordingly.

I had no appetite, and he lost his as soon as I told him there might have been a very faint pink line.

He said to go get a real test.

That he'd arrange for things to be taken care of.

Things.

It's not like there's any other solution, but did he have to be so . . . accusatory? So cold and dead eyed?

So angry.

Where was the Dallas so madly in love he writes me poems and leaves them for me in a tree?

His words today weren't poetic at all. They keep echoing in my head:

This is a fucking nightmare.

What was I thinking?

And the worst one, straight out of a bad movie of the week:

Did you do this on purpose?

"Did you sleep with Georgina?"

He sneered but didn't answer. "You did do this on purpose."

I slapped a glass of wine out of his hand, and he slapped me back.

My face stung as I looked over the cliff and thought about how good it would feel to push him off.

Chapter Forty-Five

Ian Copeland's Glenlake Journal

Wednesday, March 19, 1997

It was fifty degrees today—after the last two months, it felt like July. Basketball season was a waste, but there's no way I'm going to miss soccer, so I decided to go for a run. Now that the cast is off and I finally got the cheese scrubbed off, my leg still looks white and skinny, and to be honest, it doesn't feel that great. But I only have a few weeks to get in shape, so I figured I'd better start right away. Just two miles, I told myself. Slow.

I was headed down toward the lake when I saw Andi pick up one of the school bikes and head north on Lake Loomis Road. I had been planning on going south, but when I saw her, I changed my mind. No idea why—maybe I figured that when she turned around and came back and went past me, she'd see me running instead of gimping along in the cast. I'm sick of her having two reasons to feel sorry for me.

By the time I got to the road, she was a couple hundred yards ahead. She wasn't moving too fast, and so I sped up to keep her in sight. I didn't necessarily want her to hear or see me, but . . . I don't know. I just followed her. I'm not a stalker, OK??? I've had plenty of opportunities to spy on her, but I've never taken them until now.

After about half a mile, I was already breathing hard and starting to worry about my leg, but ahead of me Andi was just rolling along and enjoying the scenery. I don't think I was slowing down, but she was starting to pull away and leave me behind.

I guess that's what they'd call a poetic metaphor in some classes.

I kicked it up a notch and kept her in sight, barely, for the next half mile, sweating like a pig. Then she went around a curve, and I lost her, and when I came around the curve, she was gone. I should have been able to see her because the road straightened out.

I slowed down. Both my legs felt rubbery, even my good one. I almost felt like I could puke. In a little while I saw her bike, lying in the weeds by this overgrown road. I guess it was a road because it was too wide to be a path.

At first I thought something was wrong, like someone had attacked her and pulled her off her bike. Then I thought maybe she had to pee and was just squatting behind a tree or something. But then I remembered it was California Girl Andi—she'd be afraid of getting an ant up her ass or something.

I went up the old road. My legs were getting all scratched up, and it was kind of cold in the shade—my sweat felt all clammy now—but no sign of Andi. I tried to go as quietly as I could so she wouldn't hear me coming. I definitely didn't want her to think I was a stalker, but now I wanted to make sure she was okay.

The road went up for maybe a quarter mile. Then the trees stopped, and I did, too.

Andi was sitting on a rock. Next to her was Dallas Fucking Walker.

It was so sweet. He even had a picnic basket and a bottle of wine, which isn't exactly legal. Well, no more legal than doing it with your seventeen-year-old student. Andi's birthday is coming up, so I guess they won't have to worry about the sex part then?

I had never really pictured them being anywhere but DFW's cottage—I guess I figured they'd be so scared of being seen that they wouldn't get together anywhere else. But here they were in broad daylight. Even if they hadn't arrived together. It looked like DFW had a mountain bike he'd ridden all the way to the top.

He leaned in and kissed her, and put his arm around her and pulled her close. Now I really felt like I had to puke. I was about to turn around and go, but Andi pushed him away, so I waited. She started talking to him, looking really serious. She was getting upset, and DFW was trying to calm her down. Then she wiped tears off her cheeks, and I felt my eyes get watery, too.

He shrugged and poured himself a glass of wine. She fucking SLAPPED IT OUT OF HIS HAND. It was awesome—until he slapped her face. They started arguing. My head spun, and I wanted to rush down there and throw him off the cliff.

But I didn't.

I just watched.

I told myself it was because of my fucking leg, and I wasn't even sure if I could run over there without falling down. I told myself it was because Andi had dumped me, so whatever happened was her own fault. I told myself I wasn't afraid of losing a fight with Dallas.

I told myself everything except to go help Andi.

They really argued. Dallas said something, and Andi started crying hard, her shoulders shaking. He poured himself the other glass of wine and sat there sipping it, looking out at the lake.

I was so cold I was shaking, too. My leg felt like shit as I went back down the road. I could barely jog back to school, but I kept going as fast as I could because I didn't want Andi to come up on her bike and catch me.

I think my leg is fucked up again.

How is someone like him still walking the earth?

Why am I letting him?

Chapter Forty-Six

Ian had just come home from work and was standing in the front hall, separating junk mail from the two or three envelopes of interest, when a car he didn't recognize pulled up out front. A pink mustache glowed on the dashboard. Lyft.

Then Cassidy got out of the back seat, dragging a duffel bag behind her.

He met her on the porch, his heart thumping, still clutching a stack of envelopes.

"Cassidy, what's wrong?" he asked, brain spinning through different scenarios. It was a weeknight, and she should have been at Glenlake until spring break.

Ignoring his attempt to take her bag, she brushed past him and dumped it on the floor of the hallway.

"Is Mom home?"

"She's still at work. What's going on?"

His daughter looked at him and then took her coat off, deliberately, as if she was buying time.

"Tell me you're okay," he pleaded, his worry now shot through with adrenaline.

Her voice was tight, almost strangled. "Who was Mom seeing?"

Worrying about the present day, about her now, Ian stupidly didn't understand her question for a moment.

"I don't know what you're talking about," he told her, panic welling up.

"When we were in Colorado and I asked about your breakup with Mom, you basically admitted she was seeing someone else."

"I did," he said.

"Do you know who it was?"

No, he wanted to lie. *I never found out.*

Instead, he said, "She never told me."

Which was true.

She paused again, as if deciding what to say next—or deciding whether she believed him.

"That bracelet Whitney found at Thanksgiving. There was one just like it in Dallas Walker's car. I saw a picture—it looks identical."

There it was.

"Cassidy, everybody had those," he told her, his voice sounding weak and unconvincing even to him. "It was a thing. Kids were making those in metalworking class."

"I talked to Georgina, and she said they were all different," said Cassidy flatly. "That Mom's was unique. But that she'd spent so long working on it she could have made another one just like it."

He didn't answer, not trusting himself in another lie.

"Dad, was Mom seeing Dallas Walker?"

"That's ridiculous, Cassidy."

"How can you be so sure? You just said she didn't tell you who she was seeing. Isn't it possible that it was a teacher? It happens, Dad!"

"I'm well aware. That's why your mother was worried about your closeness with Mr. Kelly."

"Or maybe just feeling guilty about her own bad behavior."

While Ian thought about what to say next, Andi's car slipped past the dining room window toward the carriage house–turned–garage.

Ian finally put the mail down on the narrow marble-topped table.

Neither spoke until Andi found them. Instinctively glad to see her daughter, she reached out to hug Cassidy but, seeing their expressions, let her arms drop.

"What's going on?" she asked warily.

Cassidy took a deep breath. "You gave Dallas Walker a bracelet just like yours as a gift, didn't you?"

"Cassidy," said Ian, not knowing how to finish that sentence. Wanting to warn her. Wanting her to stop before they all went over the cliff.

Knowing it was too late.

He watched a range of emotions flit across his wife's face. Tight-lipped, Andi finally nodded.

"I don't know what's going on." Their daughter's eyes welled with tears. "I'm worried you know way more than you've been saying. For all I know, you could even be involved in this whole Dallas Walker mess."

"That's crazy," Ian said. "I don't know what's been happening in that class of yours, but your mother has nothing to do with any of it."

Knowing it wasn't entirely impossible.

Cassidy turned to him. "But how would you know, Dad? Unless . . ."

"Your father isn't involved."

Cassidy turned back to her mother, the same question in her eyes.

"We know each other," Andi said with finality, looking to Ian for agreement.

"We know each other," he echoed.

Thinking the only time he'd been 100 percent sure they knew each other was in school. Before Dallas Walker arrived on campus.

Chapter Forty-Seven

ANDI BLOOM'S GLENLAKE JOURNAL

Tuesday, March 25, 1997

> Dallas is nowhere
> His cottage is locked
> The poem tree bears no fruit
> I am alone
> With my relief
> And free

IAN COPELAND'S GLENLAKE JOURNAL

Wednesday, March 26, 1997

So the great Dallas Fucking Walker has disappeared from campus. I heard the kids in the poetry seminar are practically in mourning over that scumbag.

What can I say but good riddance?

Chapter Forty-Eight

Andi had insisted that the only reason she knew Roy's nickname was because Ian himself had used it during their Skype call with Cassidy.

He hadn't, but he'd seemed convinced. For the time being, anyway. But Ian was the one who'd alerted Cassidy and Kelly to Roy's existence in the first place. Why had he done that?

Thinking about Roy brought back bad memories of the party at his decrepit house. Having Cassidy show up at home to interrogate her and Ian about Dallas, insinuating they knew something about his death, was both surreal and agonizing.

Andi had never been more grateful for Whitney and Owen and their raucous energy. Dropped off from the after-school carpool, they'd materialized just in time, joyous to see their sister and loudly wondering why no one had told them Cassidy was coming home for the weekend.

"I was homesick," Cassidy said, saving Andi or Ian from sharing a truer, if far less believable, excuse.

Your sister came home to confront us about a huge secret that was supposed to go with me to my grave.

Or:

Your sister rushed back from school so we could reassure her we're not murderers.

With their synchronized, knee-jerk reactions, they'd hopefully done just that.

We know each other.

Starved as always, the twins insisted that Cassidy's condition could be cured only by comfort food, with an all-you-can-eat mostaccioli and meatball dinner at Rigazzi's. Cassidy seemed to perk up at the very idea, and Andi welcomed the distraction as they all piled into the car and made their way to the Hill, an area dotted with fifty-year-old Italian family restaurants. As natives, Ian and the kids were devotees, but Andi's only interest was in the wholly incongruous fishbowl margaritas.

Tonight more than ever.

Ian clearly felt the same way: he didn't even ask to see the wine list before following her lead and ordering one of his own. She flagged the waiter for a second round as the kids dunked their toasted ravioli in marinara sauce.

Despite the strain around Ian's eyes and the ramrod-straight posture she hadn't seen since their boarding-school days, he seemed to relish dinner, joking around with the kids, until she believed the threat between them had diminished. Soothed by a pleasant buzz, Andi allowed herself to pretend their inevitable summit would be softened by the lovely evening they'd shared with their three spectacular children.

After dinner they went to Ted Drewes for dessert, drove home, played a game of Scrabble, and called it a night. The kids were in bed when Ian closed the bedroom door.

"I know about you and Dallas," he said.

Sitting on the bench at the end of their bed, one shoe on and one in her hand, Andi took his words like a blow. She looked around the room at the furnishings they'd chosen together, trying to ground herself in the familiar present but finding everything strange. Until this moment she'd managed to insulate herself with her countless blessings—more than anyone deserved—always believing she'd gotten away with it all and that Ian would never know the details of what she'd come to think of as the *forgotten five months*.

"How?" she asked simply.

"I saw you two together." His voice cracked. "More than once."

But where had he seen them? What exactly had he seen? She couldn't bring herself to ask.

"How could you do that?" Ian demanded, suddenly sounding seventeen.

"I don't know," she said, starting to cry. "I don't know how it happened. It just did."

"Did you love him?"

"I've only ever loved you," she said.

He nodded, his eyes wet, one lone tear escaping down his cheek. "I thought I'd made my peace with it. But then they found Dallas Fucking Walker in the lake."

Moving in slow motion, she took her second shoe off, stood, and hugged him, but he didn't relax into her arms.

"Why didn't you ever tell me?" she asked.

"Maybe I was waiting for you to tell me."

"I thought about it. Many times."

"But you didn't say anything." The angry, wounded edge was creeping back into his voice.

As every emotion she'd ever suppressed flooded through her—fear, doubt, guilt, shame—she felt a glimmer of relief that she no longer had to hide one of the secrets she'd assumed was hers to bear alone. And that he didn't know the worst of it.

"The more time passed, the harder it seemed. And we were happy. Other than one brief interruption, we've been happy together since we were fourteen years old, Ian. I didn't want to ruin it."

He hugged her back, briefly, then let go and turned away. "That spring, after my cast came off, I went running down by the lake. I saw you ahead of me, riding one of the red school bikes."

The knot in Andi's stomach tightened.

"I wasn't following you," he continued, "but when I found the bike lying in the weeds, I got worried." He inhaled deeply, held it, and let go. "I saw you together. Drinking wine. Kissing."

"I'm so sorry," she said, tears coming harder.

"I saw you fight. I watched you break up."

Andi stopped herself from correcting him. There was nothing to be gained by telling him they'd never actually broken up.

Finally, he turned around. "How did you feel when he disappeared?" he asked.

After all these years, she could still feel the sting of Dallas's hand on her face. "Honestly?"

"Don't you think it's twenty years past time for honesty?"

"You can't possibly think we've had a dishonest marriage."

"The foundation was certainly built on a lie," he said coldly.

"You lied, too," she snapped back. "By not admitting you knew."

"You didn't answer my question," Ian said.

"My feelings were complicated," she finally said. "I got in deeper than I'd ever meant to. He wasn't who I thought he was."

"You mean, instead of being a sensitive poet to whom age was meaningless, he was just a teacher who wanted to fuck his students?"

"Something like that."

"I fucking hated that guy from the start," Ian said smugly, once again sounding just like his teenage self.

"You would have hated him even if nothing had happened between us," she said. "Sometimes you used to be closed-minded back then."

She knew the moment she shut her mouth it had been the wrong thing to say.

"So what does that mean?" he demanded. "You're defending him now?"

"What he did was wrong, but that doesn't mean he wasn't a brilliant poet," she said, stepping back ever so slightly in the face of Ian's anger. "It didn't mean he deserved to die."

A strange look passed over Ian's face. "Well, it's not like either one of us had a say in that, is it?"

She didn't know how to answer that.

When he left the room, she felt relieved. If they talked any more, she was afraid she'd blurt out all the bottled-up thoughts and fears that had been simmering since the moment Wayne Kelly projected the photo of Dallas's waterlogged car on the screen.

Things certainly looked different now that she knew Ian was aware of why she'd broken up with him. Had he been spying on them during some of their other intimate moments, too?

The thought horrified her as much as the fact that he'd kept his knowledge secret all these years.

I fucking hated that guy from the start.

Chapter Forty-Nine

Cassidy couldn't sleep. She'd been lying in bed texting Tate—all innocu-ous, nothing about her parents—until he finally ended it with a **don't you SLEEP??**, followed by a ¯_(ツ)_/¯ to let her know it was okay. Lying there, she'd heard her parents arguing, then water running, then noth-ing at all.

She wondered who was mad at whom and why. Also, how they could have been so weirdly relaxed at dinner, although that could have had something to do with the fishbowl margaritas they'd both slurped down. Mom always ordered one, but it was out of character for Dad, who usually interrogated the waiter about the skimpy wine list.

They obviously weren't telling her everything. If Mom did have a relationship with her teacher, it made sense that she would have kept it secret, even from Dad, but that didn't explain why Roy seemed to know Mom so well. And why did Roy seem so sure he was going to get out of jail? Was it really faith in a higher power? If she were unjustly accused, she'd put her faith in lawyers, not God.

And if she was right about her mom's relationship with Dallas Walker: *eew*. She'd seen pictures of him, and he wasn't bad looking, although his hair had been going gray and was obviously getting thin on top. Mr. Kelly was better looking, when she thought about it. Double EEW. Granted, there were times when even Tate could act super immature, but he didn't have beard stubble, a beer gut, or any of the middle-aged problems she heard Dad's friends moaning about, like having to get up and pee a bunch of times at night.

The worst thing about all of this was that, if the basic story of her parents' relationship was a lie, how could she trust anything else she'd taken for granted? She'd been keeping Tate at arm's length because she didn't want to be judged against her parents' perfect relationship, when in all likelihood, she had something that was more real and more honest than they did.

With her thoughts spiraling, she wasn't going to drift off anytime soon.

Sighing, Cassidy turned on her bedside light and got up, thinking leftover toasted ravioli and late-night TV sounded perfect. She could even pour herself a half glass of Mom's wine.

On the stairs, her eyes trailed across Mom's wall o' nostalgia, settling on a tiny, handwritten scrap in a three-by-five frame. Four lines of verse, unsigned.

> *"Careful you don't drown in that."*
> *She drinks, laughs, turns on her heel*
> *Her voice a bell that can't be unrung*
> *"Would you rather be drowning with others, or*
>   *swimming alone?"*

One of Mom's poet friends, she'd always thought.

Could it be the poet boyfriend? Hiding in plain sight all these years?

She continued on to the kitchen, raided the fridge and Mom's wine, and had just turned on the TV in Dad's den—muted and tuned to ESPN—when it hit her. She'd stared at pictures of Dallas Walker, interviewed his former students and colleagues, and read every trace of biographical information about him she could find, but she'd never read a single line of his poetry.

There were books in practically every room of the house. The bookcases in the den were filled with titles that reflected her father's tastes:

mysteries, history, and sports biographies. She left her snack on the ottoman and scanned the spines, then went into the living room, where neatly arranged hardbacks filled the built-in shelves. Literary fiction, biographies, memoirs, coffee-table books.

Her mom had curated carefully, shelving like with like. Contemporary cookbooks in the kitchen. Vintage cookbooks and bartender's guides in the butler's pantry. Travel books in the downstairs hall. A small hutch on the back porch had gardening books.

Heading back upstairs, she found an odd selection of worn paperbacks in the reading nook off the landing, mostly by foreign authors. There was also a shallow bookcase haphazardly packed with paperbacks dating to her parents' college days and, possibly, their parents' college days. Then she remembered a half-height bookcase on the third floor where she'd seen shelves of extremely slender volumes.

She went up quietly, careful not to wake Whitney and Owen or Mom and Dad. After turning on the light, she sat cross-legged on the floor, walking her fingers along the spines of plays and poetry until she found it: *American Son* by Dallas Walker. She opened the book to the back flap and looked at the author photo, which was an image she hadn't seen before, his sandy hair thicker and not yet graying, his face smooth and unlined.

He stared at the camera with real intensity. Poet Face.

Opening the book, she found an inscription on the title page.

To Andi, my sharpest pupil,
"Who would believe us?"
Dallas Walker

Heart pounding, she hurried downstairs and held it up to the scrap on the wall, comparing the curls of the question marks, the slashed dots above the *i*'s, the diagonal strokes of the capital *W*'s.

The handwriting was a perfect match.

Chapter Fifty

Ian was usually up before Andi on weekends, but they'd left the land of *usual* with last night's revelations, and it was somehow fitting that Andi had slipped out of bed and headed downstairs first. Even more unexpected was the sound of Cassidy's voice rising up into the back stairway as Ian made his way down into the kitchen. Her words stopped him from taking another step, although they weren't actually her words at all.

"The water is nickel gray / Lowering clouds and the gift of a new day / Who should we tell? / Who would believe us?"

"Another very nice reading," Andi said curtly, "although you're exaggerating the 'poet voice.' He certainly never sounded like that."

"Well, obviously, I never heard him," said Cassidy. "And I hadn't even read him until now."

Ian, having stopped midstride, quietly put his feet on the same riser, leaning against the wall and listening.

"Why the sudden interest?" Andi asked.

"I guess I wanted to see the big picture, and it suddenly occurred to me you might have a copy. Did he give this to you?"

"I bought it, and he signed it for me when I was a student in his class," Andi said. "Nothing out of the ordinary."

"The inscription seems a little personal."

What was the inscription? Ian wondered. He'd never even seen the book in the house.

Andi sighed, clearly struggling to remain patient with their determined daughter.

"That was Dallas. He always signed with lines from his poems, and he often chose things that were cheeky. Suggestive. He always pushed against the boundaries of acceptable behavior."

Ian hated the slight tone of admiration in his wife's voice.

They were silent for a moment, and he wondered whether the conversation had run out of steam. He waited for a covering noise so he could thump down the stairs and breeze into the room as if he hadn't heard anything.

Then Cassidy spoke again, and he remained frozen.

"I went to see Roy."

"In *prison*?" Andi sounded as alarmed as he felt.

"Jail. He's been accused, not convicted," Cassidy said tartly.

"If Mr. Kelly sent you to interview an *accused* criminal in jail, that is far outside the bounds of—"

"Appropriate behavior? That's rich, Mom."

"Don't be a smart-ass, Cassidy."

"Mr. Kelly didn't ask us to do it."

"Us?"

"Tate went with me," Cassidy mumbled. "But I did the interview alone. And, for the record, Mr. Kelly will be almost as freaked out as you are right now when I tell him."

"I am not freaked out," Andi said unconvincingly. "I assume he claimed he was innocent?"

"He said nobody would believe him, but he has faith in higher powers," Cassidy told them.

Ian pictured his daughter being searched by guards, escorted to a visiting room, and sitting across from the hulking Roy.

"It's a good thing he found religion," Andi said. "He'll need it. And if ever anyone needed to—"

"So you did know him?" Cassidy interrupted excitedly.

Ian felt light-headed and realized he'd hardly been breathing. As much as he wanted Cassidy to keep going so he could learn more, Andi needed to put a stop to the interrogation.

"I met him once," she said instead.

"For long enough to form an opinion."

"It only took a second to see what that guy was all about."

"Apparently, he felt the same way about you," Cassidy said. "He asked me if I was a wild child. Like you were."

Ian took the last of the stairs in a rush, his decision to intervene made involuntarily. He'd wanted to listen for whatever it was he couldn't put his finger on—the thing he could feel she was hiding—but couldn't listen a second longer while Cassidy picked Andi apart.

"I can't believe you're confronting your mother using the words of a criminal," he said as he burst into the room to see Cassidy sitting on one side of the island and Andi standing on the other.

"Morning, Dad," said Cassidy sarcastically.

"How much have you heard?" asked Andi, her eyes showing more relief than fear.

"Enough," he said. "Cassidy, your mother was not a 'wild child.'"

"But she was involved with Dallas Walker, wasn't she?" Cassidy said.

"Did Roy tell you that?"

"He told me to ask you about it," Cassidy said. "So now I am."

He looked at Andi, whose pleading expression told him she wasn't sure how or even whether to answer. Now that he'd arrived, she seemed more than willing to defer all questions to him. "Your mother doesn't have to answer personal questions about her past if she doesn't want to."

"So you're okay if an innocent man is framed for a crime he didn't commit?"

"I seriously doubt Roy is an innocent man," Andi said. "He was definitely a drug dealer."

"That doesn't make him a murderer."

Ian was flabbergasted. "How are you even making this leap in his defense, Cassidy?" he demanded.

"It seems like there's a case for reasonable doubt when a bracelet my mother made was on the wrist of her dead teacher," Cassidy said with an intensity Ian found chilling. "She's trying to keep her involvement secret, but she was right in the middle of this!"

In the silence that followed, Ian felt he could hear every creak, every subtle sound their old house made. How many more minutes until Whitney and Owen thundered down the stairs?

An intimate inscription, a gifted bracelet—Ian remembered well the one Andi wore, and had no idea Dallas had had one himself. Traces of Dallas Walker seemed as ubiquitous as blood spatter at a crime scene.

Andi sighed deeply. "This isn't a conversation I wanted to have with anyone, much less my daughter, the investigative reporter."

"Were you seeing Dallas Walker?"

Caught, unable to lie to their daughter's face, Andi gave the tiniest nod.

"The bracelet was a Christmas present," she said, her voice cracking. "I'm horrified that he was actually wearing it when he died."

"Were you cheating on Dad?"

At seventeen, Ian had agonized over this very question and the timing of her *I need some time to be me* speech. As an adult, he'd resigned himself to not knowing—and now Cassidy had simply asked.

"Never! I broke up with your dad before anything happened."

"But you did have a secret affair with your teacher."

"It was wrong," Andi said. "But it was complicated, too."

"It's not like I don't know this happens."

"At Glenlake?"

Cassidy shrugged. "Glenlake, here in St. Louis, wherever. Everybody knows someone who knows someone. But it's usually not their mother. And I don't know of anyone else who felt they had to help cover it up, like the way I deleted the photo of the bracelet from the server so no one else would see it and ask questions."

"Jesus Christ," said Ian. "You erased evidence?"

"Protect the family and the Copeland name at all costs, right?" said Cassidy jadedly. "Besides, it was taken by a photojournalist for the local paper, so it wasn't like I was tampering with evidence or anything. And it's not like the police don't know about it."

Numb and not sure how to answer, Ian opened a cabinet, took out a mug, and poured himself a cup of the coffee Cassidy or Andi had made.

"Thank you, Cassidy," Andi said in a small voice. "I never ever wanted anyone to know I was involved with . . . him."

"How did it happen?" asked Cassidy.

"It seems pathetic now," Andi said, meeting Ian's eyes beseechingly. "I really was happy dating your father. But Dallas was a famous poet, and he told me again and again how special and talented I was. I believed him, and somehow it made sense that we should be together."

"He was grooming you," said Ian, for his own benefit as much as theirs.

"How long did it last?"

"Until he disappeared."

"You mean *died*."

"When I heard they'd found his body, suicide or an accident involving drugs and alcohol seemed like the logical possibilities," Andi said. "And I couldn't help but wonder if I was partly responsible."

"Because you were having a relationship with him?"

"We'd been having . . . difficulties," she said, nodding.

"That's not on you," Ian heard himself say. "He was a grown-ass man."

Andi sighed. "In a lot of ways, he was younger than we were."

"So one moment you were seeing each other, and the next he was gone?" Cassidy asked.

"Pretty much," Andi said. "Until his body was found, I truly thought he'd just taken off without saying a word. Now that Roy has been arrested, of course it suggests other possibilities."

Ian sipped his coffee, which tasted bitter and burned. Cassidy must have been up much earlier than either of them and brewed the pot. With a sour feeling in his stomach, he wondered why Andi didn't tell Cassidy she and Dallas had broken up before he disappeared. That would be a small but mitigating fact.

"How did you feel when that happened, Mom?"

"I was mad at Dallas," Andi said, her voice cracking as she looked at Ian. "But I was more embarrassed and upset with myself for falling for him in the first place."

～

Andi spent the day floating above herself, not really there at all as she crisscrossed the city. She dropped Whitney off at a lacrosse clinic, then headed out to Chesterfield to catch part of Owen's soccer game before grabbing Whitney again and heading back home to fetch Cassidy, who wanted to spend the afternoon with her sister at the mall. Andi made it to an afternoon yoga class while Ian dropped Owen at a laser tag birthday party and sleepover, but she couldn't focus inward, steady her breath, or do anything more than arrange her limbs in the various poses.

When Andi got home, Ian was out on a run. She had just enough time to shower and get dressed before they were due at a cocktail party down the street.

And then, just as Andi stepped into the shower, Ian appeared in the bathroom.

"I'll hurry," she said.

"No need," he said, pulling his T-shirt over his head and tossing it in the laundry hamper. "I just got off the phone with Biz and Cope. They're taking the kids for dinner and a movie."

"Wonderful," Andi said, feeling a disproportional sense of relief as the hot water streamed down her breasts and stomach. "How did you make that happen?"

"Biz called. I mentioned that Cassidy was wiped out from all the work she's been doing in the journalism seminar and after Roy's arrest just wanted to come home to take a break. Biz was on speaker, and Cope said it sounds like everything is squared away."

Squared away.

Andi turned around and let the water spray her neck and shoulders. The *gall* of Roy, intimating that he knew anything about her—to her own daughter, no less. Thank god Ian had come to her defense. How had she not realized, as he apparently did, how much Dallas had manipulated and *groomed* her?

Unexpectedly, Ian opened the shower door. Cool air flowed in around him.

"Ian, I should have told you more. Sooner. I wouldn't have talked to Cassidy about anything at all if she hadn't been down there waiting for me. I—"

"It's okay," he said, putting his finger to her lips. "You told Cassidy what she needed to know. And me, too."

"I did break up with you before anything happened. I swear."

"It's all ancient history," he said, slipping off his running shorts and stepping inside. He kissed her insistently, convincing her that the revelations of the last twenty-four hours had done nothing to diminish his desire for her.

Afterward, they lay together, his arms encircling her.

"I've always loved you," he said. "We were meant to be together."

"I've always loved you, too," she whispered.

"That's all that matters, right?"

"Right," she told him.

Chapter Fifty-One

If Cassidy had learned one thing from Mr. Kelly's seminar, it was to use the element of surprise to her advantage. She'd totally done that yesterday. Reading Dallas's poems aloud was a brilliant touch, if she said so herself. She'd been hoping to get each of her parents alone, but when Dad literally ambushed them, the moment got downright raw.

Fortunately, instead of putting her on a plane, train, or, god forbid, back on the bus, Dad had decided to drive her back to school himself. Which meant she had a chance to learn even more.

They were somewhere between Springfield and Bloomington when she finally decided to break the silence.

"I'm sorry you had to make this drive, Dad," she told him.

"I have some business up there, anyway," he said, checking the rearview mirror as he changed lanes.

She watched a line of bare trees whiz by and thought idly about how spring seemed to arrive weeks later at Glenlake than in St. Louis.

"I'm also sorry . . ." How to say it?

He glanced over at her, an eyebrow raised.

"That I accused you guys," she said lamely. "Of being involved."

"We are involved, however inadvertently."

"I feel bad about making Mom go through all that. Making her say her big secret in front of you."

"It was a bad time that neither of us wanted to relive."

She was hungry, and she had to pee, and the next exit was twelve miles away. But she felt as though the moment the car doors opened, the pressure would be released, and the conversation would be over. She took her chance.

"What do you think happened?" she pressed.

"To Walker?"

"If Roy didn't do it."

That got her another glance, no raised eyebrow.

"Maybe he was high and drove off the cliff or something. The guy liked to party."

"Seems like a long shot, Dad."

He thought for a while as billboards appeared on the outskirts of Bloomington-Normal.

"I still think it's Roy. Occam's razor: the simplest explanation is usually the correct one."

"Except when it isn't," she said, spying an exit with a gas station, a Starbucks, and a Panera. "I really have to pee, and I'm hungry."

He smiled and put on his turn signal. "Cassidy, I'm so impressed with you. I'm not happy we have to relive this episode, and I'm obviously hoping we can keep your mom out of it, but she and I will help as much as we can. Do you think I should meet with Mr. Kelly and offer to talk to him? Maybe we could keep it off the record."

Cassidy pondered the offer. On the one hand, it felt like a scoop. On the other, since Dad had already told her everything he knew, it seemed kind of redundant. She had no way of knowing if Mr. Kelly would agree to keep it "off the record," and it was possible it might leak out anyway. And what if, once they started talking, Dad gave Mr. Kelly shit about letting her go see Roy in jail, even though he hadn't known anything about it? And if Tate got involved . . .

Rolling up the off-ramp, they coasted to a stop and considered the options.

"Starbucks," she said. "And please don't talk to Mr. Kelly. Tate was with me, and he can't get in trouble again."

"Tate was with you?" he asked sharply. "Why are you just telling me now?"

"It doesn't matter, Dad. He wasn't in the interview, so he didn't hear everything."

Rolling through a stop sign, he accelerated too quickly. "I know he's your boyfriend, but do not tell him. The last thing we need is to get more people involved."

~

Andi had kissed and hugged Cassidy goodbye and watched them drive off, confident in the knowledge that Ian would answer any of their daughter's lingering questions while reassuring her that her parents wouldn't stand by while an innocent man was convicted for a crime he didn't commit.

Last night, after they'd made love like their very existence depended on it, gotten ready like nothing out of the ordinary had happened between them, and spent the evening mingling at a perfectly pleasant cocktail party, she and Ian had agreed to support whatever efforts Cassidy felt she needed to make on behalf of Roy, if only to restore their daughter's confidence in them. Even if it meant coming forward about Andi's affair with Dallas.

Of course, since Roy had to be guilty, they both agreed—without saying so—there was no reason to worry it would ever come to that.

The second Ian's Audi left the driveway, Andi ran up to Cassidy's room to open the class Google Drive she hadn't checked since Roy was officially charged.

Cassidy's bedroom looked just as she expected, with the bed unmade, a wet towel tossed over the upholstered chair, and two pairs of shoes on the floor in front of the open closet. Unfortunately, her computer, the only thing Andi really cared about at the moment, had been powered down.

With plan A as a nonstarter, she moved on to plan B. It was even less on the up-and-up, but she'd been thinking about it all weekend. More accurately, talking herself into it.

She needed to know what was going on in Ian's head. Not the adult Ian, who she thought she knew as well as she knew herself, but the seventeen-year-old Ian, during the five months she hadn't known him at all.

Creeping past the family room, she checked to make sure the twins were happily hypnotized by the Xbox or PSwhatever. Then she ducked into Ian's study and silently closed the door. Once inside, she began an inch-by-inch search of every bookshelf, cabinet, and drawer. Certain she hadn't missed anything in plain sight, she reached into a pewter mug on the fireplace mantel and extracted the key to his locked desk drawer. Inside, there was plenty to look at, including a copy of a $1,000 receipt for a Prohibition-era bottle of bourbon, but not what she was hoping to find. She moved on to the wall safe in his closet and entered the combination. No surprises there: birth certificates, passports, a few prized photos of the kids from before everything went entirely digital, and some heirloom jewelry that had belonged to her mother.

Before moving on to another room, Andi looked around one last time—and then it hit her. At Glenlake, she'd once watched Ian hide airline-size bottles of liquor on a wooden lip underneath his dorm room desk.

She rolled the chair out of the way, then crouched down under his cherry desk, a far cry from the particle board–and–melamine dorm standard, and looked underneath the center drawer and both sides of the desk.

Nothing.

Just because she felt like it, she turned and ran her hand underneath the decorative arch at the base of the nearby credenza. Her fingers stopped on a protrusion, what felt like the spine of a book. She grabbed her iPhone from her pocket, swiped on the light, and shined it underneath.

The Glenlake crest and Ian Copeland were embossed on the cover in silver lettering.

Just as shiny was the matching silver lock.

Chapter Fifty-Two

She'd been gone only a few days, but when her dad dropped her off, Cassidy felt like she was returning after a long break. She felt older somehow, and wondered if she'd ever be able to look at Glenlake without thinking of her parents' secret history there. As she fell in with the crowd of kids, she thought, *We have no idea what really happens around us.*

Rounding the corner of the writing center, she saw Tate walking with Hannah Chang and a couple of other girls. As she hurried up and opened her mouth to yell hello, the warmth flooding her chest turned suddenly cold. Tate and Hannah were too close, their sides brushing while Tate leaned in to hear what she was saying.

"Tate," she called, her voice sounding icy even to her. Her legs frozen.

He turned and, seeing her, lit up in a way that should have removed all doubt. Without even a word to Hannah, he jogged right over and wrapped her up in a hug.

"Longest weekend of my life," he told her, kissing her square on the lips.

Cassidy hugged him back, closing her eyes so she wouldn't see the eye rolls from the other girls.

"Missed you," she whispered.

Maybe her parents' story *was* screwing with her memories. But she couldn't let it mess with her feelings.

~

After considering options that included dining alone at the Old Road Inn and watching a movie alone in his room at the Old Road Inn, Ian impulsively plugged an address into his phone and watched as the map zeroed in on a spot near Fulton Market. Putting the car in gear, he headed back down to Chicago.

After getting off the expressway, Ian pulled up across the street from the Brandt Group storefront in a former industrial space where the sidewalk ran at loading-dock height. A CLOSED sign was hanging on the front door, but there was a light on in the back.

He lifted his phone, opened his contacts, found Preston's number, and called, hoping to once again broach the 1957 J.T.S. Brown, in light of a vintage bottle of Four Roses a customer had just tried to return for a similar reason.

Preston answered on the fourth ring. "Hey, Ian, what's up?"

"I'm in Chicago unexpectedly. I know it's a long shot, but I thought I'd see if you wanted to grab dinner."

Preston didn't answer right away. There was a sound of something moving.

"Did I catch you at a bad time?"

"No, I'm actually at the store, just getting some work done."

I'm right outside, Ian almost told him, stopping because it would have sounded weird showing up before making the invitation. Instead he said, "I've never seen your space. Would you mind if I came over and checked it out?"

"Let's do that another time," said Preston. "I'm doing inventory, the place is an unholy mess, and I'm up to my eyeballs right now."

"I understand," said Ian, trying not to sound disappointed.

After they hung up, Ian watched the storefront. They were both in the business, and Ian wasn't going to be put off by seeing back-room clutter. Why didn't Preston want him to come in? Before he could start the car, the light in the store went out. Ian waited, not wanting to be spotted driving away.

A couple of minutes later, Preston came out the front door with three liquor boxes on a hand truck. He wheeled them over to the nearest dumpster, lifted the lid, and tossed them inside. Returning the hand truck to the store, he locked up before waiting for the Uber that rolled up at the curb to take him away.

Ian got out of his car, crossed the quiet street, and lifted the dumpster lid. Fortunately, it was half-full, and he didn't have to lean in to reach the boxes Preston had tossed. He opened the flaps on the first one and found empty bottles of a little-known but inexpensive bourbon. Odd, but not unexplainable. Maybe they'd had an in-store tasting.

He opened another box. This one contained label blanks in a variety of colors, shapes, and sizes—only they weren't entirely blank. They looked like misprints, but they also looked antique. For good measure, there was a glue pot with a brush applicator that didn't look like any commercial brand Ian had ever seen.

Breathing hard, Ian opened the final box. New bottles of exotic liqueurs, cordials, and aperitifs. All empty.

Andi couldn't commit the ultimate sin and break open Ian's journal.

That's what she kept telling herself.

In truth, she tried a couple of times to pick the lock without obvious tampering but didn't get anywhere. When Owen needed a ride to a friend's house, ostensibly to work on a science project, and Whitney suggested they *girl it up* and go get pedicures, Andi resisted the urge to smash the thing open with a paperweight and reluctantly put it back where she'd found it.

That evening, she was distracted from trying yet again by a call from Cassidy, who apologized for *getting into your personal shit.* In the brief conversation that followed, and without scolding her for the profanity, she told Cassidy the weekend's conversations had been a shock, but that she appreciated her candor and was thankful to have a daughter high-minded enough to care whether justice was truly being served. Andi thought she might have laid it on a little thick, but Cassidy, already bolstered by Ian, responded positively to the praise.

Andi then "leveled" with her daughter, admitting that knowing the bracelet she'd given Dallas encircled his skeletal wrist had rattled her badly. And though she was glad she hadn't actually seen it, she felt she needed to look through the photos of the scene to make sure there wasn't anything else that had been missed. Something only she would notice.

Thankfully, Cassidy agreed that was a good idea.

While she was at it, Andi suggested she examine everything that had been collected about Roy's involvement, in case she could shed any light on something that might prove him innocent. Cassidy shared her computer log-in information enthusiastically.

Andi had already made a habit of checking Google Drive, so she knew there wasn't anything in it that would change the outcome of Roy's case. Her real focus was on the new photos, even though looking at them was the last thing she wanted to do.

With every photo of the rusted Dodge Charger's watery exhumation, she thought about how much Dallas had adored his car. How he fretted over the dangers of narrow parking spaces and rogue shopping carts, even errant scratches from the rivets on a leaning student's jeans. How out of character it would have been to risk the brush and rocks on the narrow road to the cliff.

She thought about the poetic justice of him spending eternity with his *baby*. Maybe his only true love.

In the end, she flagged only one photo that showed the slightest hint of a bracelet among the bones of a man she'd mistakenly believed she loved.

And then she erased it.

She'd cried when Dallas slapped her. She'd cried multiple times over the following weeks before she moved on, back to where she'd started, and where she would end, with Ian at her side.

At least she hoped that was where all this would end.

Chapter Fifty-Three

Still shaken by his discovery the night before, Ian went for a run in the morning. While the loop around Lake Loomis was in many ways the best choice, he didn't think he was up for it. The weather was eerily close to what it had been on the long-ago day he'd followed Andi to her meeting with Dallas Fucking Walker, and that was one memory lane he didn't want to jog down. Instead, he started from the Old Road Inn and jogged several blocks before reaching the bike path that paralleled the commuter train tracks.

His mind had raced all night. Should he diplomatically end his business relationship with Preston? Report him to the police for fraud? Or simply do nothing and carry on as usual?

Forgoing the extra income would make it hard, if not impossible, to pay Simon Bloom back on time. Obviously, it was risky to continue selling the counterfeit bottles of "vintage" liquors, but even if he stopped, he couldn't count on anyone believing that he himself had been duped. He'd lose all credibility in town regardless.

After four miles in the crisp spring air, he still didn't know what to do.

He showered, changed, checked out of his room, and headed to the Glenlake campus, parking in the small visitors' lot in front of McCormick Mansion, to deal with the primary reason for his trip, one he hadn't told Cassidy. With Copeland Hall looming behind him, he had a sudden memory of his first year at Glenlake, when every time he'd passed the building bearing his family's name he'd felt spotlighted, as if people were looking at him. Or worse, talking about him. A year later, he'd learned to laugh off the connection and even make fun of it. Once he'd gone so far as to stick a fake mustache on the bust of old Augustus, just to show his friends he didn't think the hereditary connection made him better than the rest of them.

But later, when no one was around, he'd returned to make sure the fake mustache's adhesive hadn't gummed up the bronze.

Ian was acutely conscious of the status conferred upon him by his family name and, more importantly, the titanic sum of money the family had bequeathed to the school over the past century. Where some parents would be stopped at the first desk, he was recognized, known by first name, and waved through every door.

He planned to use every ounce of that privilege to his advantage today.

Smiling and greeting Mrs. Hodges in reception, he kept moving, striding up the stairs to the main offices on the second floor. Beyond the heavy oak doors of the headmaster's sanctum, he checked in with the executive secretary, who'd been there as long as anyone could remember.

"That's a nice scarf, Doris," he told her. "Is Josh in?"

"Thank you," she said, touching the floral print draped loosely over her shoulders. "He's between calls for the next forty minutes. I'll let him know you're here."

He touched her handset gently before she could pick it up. "Let me surprise him."

She smiled helplessly as he crossed the room to the headmaster's office. As he did, he caught a glimpse through a half-open door of Sharon Lysander, the assistant headmaster, with a phone to her ear. She'd taken it stoically when the board told her they were filling the headmaster's position with an external hire.

She's a good soldier, Cope had said about her then.

Ian knocked twice and opened, catching Joshua Scanlon in the act of squinting at a spreadsheet on one of his two screens.

As Scanlon looked up, Ian spotted a side table covered with newspaper and magazine clippings featuring headlines like DEAD POET SOCIETY?, a mere fraction of what had appeared online.

"How are you holding up?" he asked, as Scanlon rose to greet him.

"Not too bad," Scanlon said, shaking hands. "It's weird, though. You go through the days and weeks thinking nobody notices or cares what's going on in your little backwater—that sure changed in a hurry."

"Well, they don't care, until something goes wrong," said Ian.

Scanlon guided him over to the couch by the coffee table and settled into a comfortable chair. "I just got a call from one of those cold-case investigation shows, if you can believe it."

"I assume you said no?"

Scanlon shook his head. "We've said no to just about everything, but the board decided we should cooperate. They'd run their piece anyway, so we don't want to look like we have anything to hide. I'll just stick to the script and try to talk about all the positive things happening at Glenlake."

"And hope they don't edit it out."

"Damn right," Scanlon said with a chuckle. "Coffee?"

"That would be wonderful," Ian told him.

Scanlon jumped to his feet.

Lincoln Darrow would have shouted at Doris to fetch the coffee, thought Ian, *but Scanlon looks ready to make the coffee run himself.*

"Student union?" said Ian, rising. "We can walk and talk."

Because McCormick Mansion had been connected to two newer buildings, they were able to walk most of the way indoors, popping outside just briefly before crossing into the student union. Ian caught a glimpse of the new writing center, now fully constructed but with stickers still plastered across the newly installed windows. It certainly looked on schedule to open the following fall.

"I expect you're here about Dallas Walker, too," Scanlon said.

Ian nodded. He'd thought a lot about how to play it, and the words came easily.

"My wife and I feel a connection to this case beyond our obvious strong feelings about the school's reputation. As you may or may not know, we were both seniors during Walker's time here, and Andi was even a student in his poetry seminar. He encouraged her a lot, and they worked together on the first-ever poetry slam."

"I'm sure his disappearance must have been a terrible shock," Scanlon offered sympathetically as they arrived at the union and got in line to order coffee.

"I think it was traumatic for everyone," said Ian, remembering instead the almost giddy excitement that had percolated on campus in the following weeks. Nobody knew Walker was dead, so nobody grieved. Guessing what had happened became a fun game that everybody played.

He didn't resume until they had their coffees and had found a quiet table where they couldn't be overheard by staff or students.

"And now our daughter Cassidy—"

"—is in Wayne Kelly's journalism seminar," Scanlon interrupted, finishing with a sympathetic sigh.

"I know there's been some tension between Kelly and the administration. I have two concerns. One is that I don't understand how someone like Curtis Royal could have become an employee of Glenlake. Aren't there background checks? And two, Cassidy and the other students seem to think Curtis Royal could be innocent."

"Even if he is found innocent, he'll never work a day here again," Scanlon assured him. "But aside from that, I'm not sure what I can do for you. The prosecution will play out, and I imagine he'll be found guilty."

"I don't want to meddle," said Ian—words that always signaled the exact opposite, no matter who spoke them, and certainly Scanlon knew the same thing. "But I promised Cassidy I would do whatever I could to ensure the wrong man wasn't convicted. If I could see your records on Royal so I could ease her mind, you'd be doing me a huge favor."

The relief on Scanlon's face was visible. "Well, obviously the police and the prosecutor already have all of that, but I think we can arrange it."

"And if you could tell Kelly to stop the innocence crusade, that'd be great, too."

Ian had chosen the moment perfectly. Scanlon looked like he'd bitten into a lemon.

"The board feels the same way," he said. "And I've spoken to Wayne about it. He says his only allegiance is to the truth."

"But you're his employer."

"The . . . ah . . . *problem* is that he only owes us his allegiance for a few more months. And as a journalist, he has a platform."

Scanlon gave a pained smile, as if he were picturing the pile of headlines in his office.

Ian didn't want to betray Cassidy's confidence but felt he had no choice. "Do you think it would help matters if you knew one of his students made an unsupervised visit to the county jail?"

It was gratifying to see Scanlon pale ever so slightly.

"Two students, actually," added Ian. "And one of them was my daughter."

~

Andi was already at work and had managed to distract herself with page proofs for a book on the historic homes of Kansas City when Ian texted.

Just met with Scanlon. He's collecting a few things for me. Heading home soon. All is well. XO

The words *All is well* warmed her, almost as though she'd heard Ian speak them aloud. She set aside the proofs and opened Google Drive to take a last look at the photos. Just to be sure there was nothing else.

A new file, titled *Miranda Darrow Interview*, had been added since last night.

She opened the interview.

It had been conducted by the ubiquitous Liz Wright, whose investigative zeal paled only slightly in comparison to Cassidy's.

Subject: Miranda Darrow

Connection: Widow of former headmaster Lincoln Darrow

Tools used to locate Mrs. Darrow: Glenlake records, internet search, conversation with staff who knew her.

The following is my typed transcript of our phone conversation, which took place two days before Curtis Royal was formally charged. (Note: Sorry for the delay in uploading, but I had an exam in AP Physics and a massive Shakespeare paper I had to get done first! Liz)

LW: Hello, Mrs. Darrow.

MD: Call me Miranda. I haven't been Mrs. Darrow since I remarried nine years ago.

LW: Oops. My bad.

MM: No need to apologize. I loved being Mrs. Darrow, but now I'm Miranda Malone.

LW: I know from school records that Mr. Darrow passed away in 2009.

MM: He had a heart attack. We kissed good night, and by morning our too-brief time together was over.

LW: I'm sorry.

MM: I was, too. He was a great guy, but he was almost twenty-five years older when I married him, so what are you going to do?

Andi hadn't thought about it at the time, but the age gap between young, sexy Miranda Darrow and Headmaster Darrow was nearly the same as between her and Dallas.

MM: The hardest part was that he died in the headmaster's house, so I ended up husbandless and homeless in short order.

LW: Glenlake kicked you out?

MM: They needed it for the next headmaster, which is understandable. And all's well that ends well. I met and married my current husband and even managed to have a baby girl before I was too old to be a mom. Thom's a successful rancher, and I was blessed to be able to trade the safe boarding school world for the thrill of life out west. I guess safe is a relative term, given what happened to Dallas Walker.

LW: Did you know him at Glenlake?

MM: There was no missing that guy.

LW: Why is that?

MM: His swagger. His smile. He really thought he was all that.

LW: In some of the interviews we've conducted, people have told us he had a tendency to be flirtatious.

MM: [Laughs] It was a lot more than a tendency.

LW: Was he flirtatious with you?

MM: Are you asking if Dallas Walker put the moves on me?

LW: Umm . . . I guess so?

MM: Let me put it this way, I used to call him Wanton Walker because he was so obvious about his ulterior motives.

Dimwit Barbie clearly wasn't as dull as Dallas had claimed.

LW: Was your husband—I mean your late husband, Mr. Darrow, jealous of the attention you got from Dallas Walker?

MM: [Laughs again, loudly] Linc knew Dallas wasn't my type. He was amused by it.

LW: So you didn't reciprocate any of the feelings Dallas Walker may have had for you?

MM: That guy had nothing to offer but sweet talk and a short shelf life. That's what I thought happened: He loved Glenlake until he got bored with the scenery. [Pause] Or, maybe I should say, he discovered it was too rugged for him, if you know what I mean.

LW: I don't think so?

Andi knew only too well.

MM: He was nice looking, rakish, and not teacher-like at all. That can be a treacherous combination—especially for someone young and impressionable.

LW: Like a student?

MM: There was definitely talk about the distracting effect he was having on some of the girls. The staff was worried about one of them in particular.

The room started to spin.

LW: Worried how?

MM: That she was unstable, and interaction with Dallas, positive or negative, could make her worse.

LW: Do you remember who the girl was?

MM: It's been a lot of years, and it was just passing talk. [Pause] I'm not great with names, but I might recognize it if I heard it.

LW: Georgina?

MM: Her, I remember. Fiery with the hair to match, and definitely one of the ones we were watching, but not the girl I'm thinking of.

LW: Crystal? Lola? Kate?

MM: I feel like it ended in a vowel sound. Like Candy, or Kelly, or Emily . . .

Andi felt like she might pass out.

LW: Sylvie?

MM: Hmm. Sylvie . . . That definitely might be it.

Sylvie?

And possibly Georgina?

Georgina's flirtation with Dallas had always been a point of contention, but Andi wasn't about to broach that topic until she'd rooted through all the contact information on the class Google Drive and googled *Sylvie Montgomery* first.

Unfortunately, the search offered the same stale results: Sylvie had a Facebook page that had last been updated five years ago, when she'd been living in Taos and working part-time at a "mineral gallery." Short of paying for one of those online searches that guaranteed she'd be *shocked* by what she found—probably the same white-pages search she'd already done—there was nothing else Andi could think of to try.

Much like Dallas, Sylvie had all but vanished.

Sylvie had been a troubled girl plagued by insecurity and eating disorders, and given that she'd gone after every guy Andi had ever smiled at, it was no surprise that she might also have made a play for Dallas. She'd joined the Cue Sports Society after Ian had stopped going. Did that mean she'd known about Andi and Dallas?

And if she knew, did that mean other people besides Ian knew, too?

Or had Miranda Whatever-her-new-last-name-was confused Andi with Sylvie? If so, that meant there'd been rumors about Andi and Dallas among the staff.

Which also led her back to Georgina, if only for Sylvie's contact info.

Andi's fingers trembled as she opened the contacts on her phone.

"I was starting to think Ian had chopped you into bits and buried you in the backyard," Georgina said by way of hello.

"I've been swamped with work on a book I have coming out in the fall."

"You can make it up to me by meeting for lunch. I'm so craving a cheeseburger."

"I can't get away today," she lied. "But soon."

"I hate consuming that many calories alone. But be that way if you must."

"Hey, I have a question," Andi said. "Did you ever track down Sylvie Montgomery?"

"Funny you should ask," Georgina told her. "Tommy said someone named S. M. Katz sent him a Facebook friend request a while back. The profile photo was a waterfall, so he assumed it was some kind of a scam, but I told him he should have looked into it. I mean, S. M. Katz could be Sylvie Montgomery Katz. If she got married, maybe she set up a new profile. It would be just like her to do that instead of updating her info."

"And did he?"

"Not sure. We started talking about the place he has in Sanibel, and I told him we go to Captiva all the time and—"

"Let me guess. You made a plan to meet up there over spring break?"

Georgina giggled. "With kids and spouses, of course."

"Of course," Andi repeated. "Be careful."

"It's not like that," Georgina said, not at all convincingly. "But I'll text Tommy. If he didn't delete the friend request, maybe we can find out if S. M. Katz is really Sylvie."

"Thanks," Andi said, feeling dubious about giving her an excuse to communicate with her long-lost beau.

"My pleasure," Georgina said happily. "Why the interest in Sylvie?"

Andi knew her friend too well to feed her a *No reason, I just thought about her the other day*, so she'd called with a diversionary tactic at the ready.

"The other night, Ian admitted that he and Sylvie hooked up during senior year," she lied. "While we were on that break."

Georgina paused for half a second and said, "Then I guess it doesn't matter if I told you I totally caught them in the act. Doing *it*."

"Why would it matter?" she said, feeling wounded and unable to keep the sarcasm out of her voice. That Georgina had been able to keep such a big secret for so many years bothered her almost as much as the secret itself.

"Sorry, girlfriend. But you were both getting things out of your systems, right?"

"Speaking of which," Andi said, taking a breath in advance of the question she had avoided asking for all these years. "Cassidy told me a bit of gossip."

"Do tell," Georgina said, because *of course.*

"You remember Miranda Darrow, right?"

"Who could forget Headmaster Darrow's bombshell trophy wife?"

"I guess the journalism class interviewed her. She said she used to call Dallas *Wanton Walker* because he was always coming on to her. Other women, too."

"Like who?" Georgina asked, her voice rising in pitch.

"She didn't say." Andi forced the next words out. "But I always wondered whether he'd made a pass at you after the poetry slam."

Georgina was uncharacteristically silent.

"Georgina?"

"I . . . I never told anyone about that."

"What?" Andi asked, her face burning.

"When he walked me back to my dorm that night, he tried to kiss me. I think."

"You think?"

"It definitely seemed like he was leaning in to do it, but I dodged him."

"Oh my god," Andi heard herself say.

"I know, right?" Georgina said. "What a perv."

"Why didn't you ever tell me, or—"

"One of the kids investigating?" Georgina asked. "Because I wanted to believe I was imagining it all these years. I mean, he might have been cute, but how gross would that have been?"

"Very," Andi managed.

"Speaking of which, I never could believe that Ian actually went for Sylvie," Georgina went on. "She was such a total bone wreck back then."

"That she was," Andi said, trying not to think of the bone wreck that was once Dallas Walker and the circumstances leading up to it. "And she basically threw herself at him, and any other guy I ever looked at sideways."

Had she gone after Dallas, or had she, like Georgina, been smart enough to see him for what he truly was?

"So you wanted to look up Sylvie and satisfy yourself that she's still a sad little mouse, someone to pity and not fear."

"Something like that."

"I'll let you know what Tommy says."

As soon as they hung up, Andi tried, with no success, to lose herself in some copyediting.

Georgina texted her back within minutes.

S. M. Katz IS Sylvie! She married the owner of that weird store she was working at in Taos and they moved to some rich hippie enclave outside Santa Cruz. Apparently, Katz has cash. Then again, maybe it's hers.

Did she tell Tommy all this in a chat? Andi texted back.

He just accepted her friend request and saw her updated information. I sent her a DM.

"Shit," Andi said aloud, wishing she'd thought through Georgina's involvement to its inevitable conclusion. What did you say?

Georgina responded by sending a copy of the message:

Hi Sylvie!

Your ears must have been burning when you sent Tommy Harkins that Facebook request . . . Andi Bloom Copeland (she and Ian have been married for TWO DECADES!) and I were just talking about you! How are you? What have you been doing since we graduated? I'm sure you've heard by now that Dallas Walker's body was found in Lake Loomis! Can you believe it? The theories about what happened have stopped now that one of the locals has been charged with his murder, but boy were they creative! Even more so than the ones we made up way back when about where he'd gone. Anyhoo, I hope you'll accept my friend request. It'll be great to catch up!

XO,

Georgina

P.S. You should call Andi. I know she'd love to catch up with you, too!

She'd included Andi's cell phone number at the bottom.

~

Scanlon had told Ian the records request would take an hour, maybe more, so he drove back into town, had an early lunch at an overpriced and underwhelming Chinese restaurant, the decor unchanged since his student days, using the weak Wi-Fi signal to check his work emails on his laptop.

He considered writing one to Simon Bloom: *WELCOME ABOARD, BUSINESS PARTNER.* Or to Preston: *FRAUD IS A BREACH OF CONTRACT.* Or maybe, he thought, he should introduce them. They'd probably get along, and they both had a stake in his business.

After seventy-five minutes, he went back to campus. In the distance, knots of students moved between buildings, practically vibrating with cheerful energy. For a long moment, he felt like a mournful ghost, remembering exactly how carefree those few short years had been.

He entered the building and saw Sharon Lysander coming toward him, coat on as if she were headed to lunch.

"I thought I saw you earlier," she said, stopping to shake hands.

"You were on the phone, and I didn't want to interrupt," he told her.

"Well, I'm glad I caught you. Acceptance letters are in the mail, and it is my distinct honor to tell you the envelopes for Whitney and Owen Copeland contain very good news."

Ian smiled, not sure how to react. He'd never been much for fist pumping, whooping, or public displays of emotion. Andi called it the *Copeland chill.* Depending on her tone, it could sound like a compliment or a cancer.

"Thank you," he said. "That's wonderful to hear."

Lysander tucked a strand of chestnut hair behind her ear, and he couldn't help but notice a quarter inch of gray at the roots. Did she hope to outlast Scanlon, make one last bid for his seat?

"I'm sure it was a foregone conclusion," she told him.

"They are wonderful children and excellent students, but we took nothing for granted."

"I hope we'll see you again soon, Mr. Copeland," she said, heading toward the doors.

In the basement, Mrs. Franti greeted him at the counter, if greeted was the way to describe the calm, subterranean regard with which she beheld him. It struck him as odd that the Records Department was the only place in Glenlake where staffers stood behind a counter. It was as if they were service workers. Or guards keeping watch over a short, stout wall.

"Headmaster Scanlon said you'd have a packet for me?" said Ian, pleasantly but firmly, putting weight on the title.

"Ready and waiting," she said, barely glancing down as she lifted it from under the counter.

Was it just his imagination, or did she leave her hand on the buff-colored envelope a moment longer than necessary? An involuntary proprietary gesture.

"Thank you," he said, breaking eye contact and turning to leave.

What she said next stopped him in his tracks.

"You're very welcome. How is your wife feeling?"

"Excuse me?"

"The poor dear must really be suffering with that stomach issue of hers."

Ian forced a nod.

"I felt bad I couldn't help her more with the old records she was looking for when she was here late last fall. I hope she was able to get the information she needed to figure out what's been going on."

"It's truly been something of a mystery," he said, his words chasing him all the way to his car.

Chapter Fifty-Four

"Please tell me the meeting I just had with Headmaster Scanlon was a bad dream," Mr. Kelly demanded. "Tell me you and Tate didn't actually go down to the county jail and interview Curtis Royal."

Cassidy inhaled sharply. When she'd asked Dad to steer clear of Mr. Kelly, why didn't she tell him to stay off campus completely? He must have run into Scanlon or something.

"I was the only one who actually interviewed Roy," she said. "I told Tate to wait for me outside."

"What the f—" He caught himself. "What on *earth* were you thinking?"

Cassidy was disappointed he'd caught himself before dropping the f-bomb. "I'm sorry, I wasn't trying to get you in trouble."

"Too late for that," Mr. Kelly told her, breaking eye contact for the first time and settling unhappily into his office chair. "If I wasn't already leaving at the end of the semester, I'm sure I'd be cleaning out my desk."

Cassidy's stomach felt suddenly hollow. "But it's not your fault."

Mr. Kelly sighed and interlocked his fingers behind his head. "I'm ultimately responsible. My class, my students, my project."

Her legs feeling a little weak, Cassidy slumped into the visitor's chair and scanned the empty shelves, messy desktop, and smudged window of the narrow little office. She pictured Mom here with Dallas Walker and then stopped herself before she could imagine what they might have been doing. For the first time since making the discovery, she felt sorry for the girl her mother had been when her pervy teacher seduced her.

"This is my fault," Cassidy said. "I'll make things right."

Mr. Kelly looked skeptical.

"I interviewed Roy," she continued. "I went home and told my parents about it, and I worried them enough that my dad talked to Scanlon. I'll make sure you aren't held accountable for my actions."

She couldn't quite bring herself to say *I'm a Copeland, it will all work out*, but she hoped he got the message.

"My dad and mom may be upset, but they support what I did."

Mr. Kelly leaned forward. "Cassidy, it's important to be fearless, not careless. Assuming I don't get fired, you don't get expelled, and the school doesn't cancel the class entirely, the police can't be thrilled you went in there and grilled that guy."

"He has the right to receive visitors."

He put his head in his hands. "Jesus."

"He swears the police informant made up the accusation to try to get out of a three-strikes charge. If that's true, we have to help him, and my parents agree."

"Cassidy," he said with a sigh. "Under normal circumstances—"

"Normal circumstances don't apply if he's telling the truth."

"You're not going to give up," he said. "Are you?"

"If you want to grow up to be a real live investigative journalist, you have to learn to avoid assumptions. To avoid rushing to judgment. Just because someone has been arrested for a crime, it doesn't mean they've done it."

"Is that an exact quote?" he asked.

"I'd have to consult my notes before I published it," Cassidy said.

He grinned wryly. "I've created an investigative-journalism monster."

Cassidy smiled back. "On a quest to uphold innocence."

"All right. Assuming I keep my job, what do you propose we should do?"

"Look into the snitch and see what his deal is."

"What else?"

"Look again at the remaining suspects."

"I really don't think there are any."

"How about Scott Stover, the facilities manager, who got chewed out by Dallas Walker on a regular basis about the heating and cooling issues in the classroom?"

"Having been in that room all year, I'd say the man had a point," Mr. Kelly said. "Stover tore his ACL and was on workers' comp at the time of the disappearance. Group three just turned in a report."

"What about Aunt—I mean, Georgina Fordham?"

"Despite her curious need to insert herself into everything, she has no real motive."

"Not one we've found yet, anyway."

"Next," Mr. Kelly said.

"What about the new interview, where Miranda Darrow said Sylvie Montgomery was unstable?"

"That's not a bad lead, but nobody's located Sylvie."

Cassidy raised an eyebrow. "Don't you have a few tricks of the trade we haven't used? Things only a pro would know how to do?"

Kelly sighed loudly.

"I'm going to take that as a yes," Cassidy said.

Chapter Fifty-Five

The drive back to St. Louis was a blur of asphalt, off-ramps, and signs with arrows suggesting new destinations. Ian was gripped by an urge to turn and get lost, but as he pulled into the garage and entered the house, he knew there was only one way to go.

Andi gave him a perfunctory kiss in the kitchen. The dinner dishes had been cleared away, but she'd left him a plate covered in aluminum foil.

"Where are the twins?" he asked.

"Upstairs, doing homework."

"Sharon Lysander told me acceptance letters are en route."

"We got them today," she said, pointing at two matching envelopes stamped with the Glenlake logo, on the counter in the butler's pantry. "I thought we could open them together. We could do with a reason to celebrate."

"Why celebrate a foregone conclusion?" he snapped.

He saw how his tone made her wince. "What's going on, Ian?"

"Why don't you tell me?" he asked, walking down the hall into his office, knowing she'd follow. When she did, he closed the door behind them. "And while you're at it, how's your stomach?"

"My stomach?" She seemed genuinely puzzled.

"You know, the chronic condition that required you to request your medical records when you picked Cassidy up for Thanksgiving?"

As recognition dawned on her face, he didn't quite know how to interpret Andi's crestfallen expression.

"If you've been having digestive issues since high school, it seems like you would have mentioned that by now."

"I made that up," she admitted cautiously, avoiding his gaze.

He folded his arms across his chest, daring her to fill the silence.

"I was worried about the investigation. About Cassidy finding out . . . well, she found out anyway. I didn't think you knew about Dallas, and I wanted to make sure there was nothing that could lead anyone to the truth."

"What can your old medical records possibly have to do with this?" he asked with a growing sense of unease.

"Well, anyway, they don't exist anymore."

"That's not an answer." Anger surged within him. "What the fuck aren't you telling me?"

"I could ask you the same question," she said.

"Don't put this on me."

"I've been keeping an eye on things all along," she said defiantly. "What I haven't told you is that I've been logging on to Cassidy's computer for months to read the evidence the journalism class has been compiling."

"And why is that?" he asked.

"When I first saw that photo of Dallas's car on parents' weekend, I knew I had to protect our family." She paused. "Us. You."

Andi's text alert buzzed.

"You're not going to respond, are you?" Ian said, watching in disbelief as she pulled the phone from her back pocket.

"Of course not," she said curtly. Then: "Oh my god. It's Sylvie."

It took him a moment to process the name. "Montgomery? Why would she be texting you?"

Andi looked at him. "She says she's going to call and hopes I'm available to talk."

The phone rang.

"Put her on speaker," he said, annoyed by the interruption, but wanting to hear more than Andi's carefully measured responses to whatever Sylvie had called to talk about.

Andi did as he asked.

Sylvie's voice was still startlingly familiar, as was the guilty feeling he'd always had whenever she turned up.

Whenever they'd hooked up back then.

"Months and months after I sent Tommy a friend request, he finally accepted. Then, within the next twenty-four hours, I'm not only friended by half our class, but I get a message from Georgina suggesting I contact you, followed by a voice mail from your daughter Cassidy."

Ian had been imagining Andi formulating a response along the lines of *And hello to you, too* when their daughter's name caught them both up short.

"Cassidy called you?" Andi asked.

"What's going on, Andi?" pleaded Sylvie in her halting voice.

"She's taking an investigative journalism class, and they're looking into what happened to Dallas Walker," said Andi matter-of-factly.

"I read that some townie had been charged with his murder."

"Our daughter thinks he may have been unfairly accused."

"But . . . why would she call me?" The breathless wonderment in Sylvie's voice made her sound like an ethereal being. Ian wondered whether she'd finally conquered her eating disorder, or if she was still just as delicate physically.

"They're talking to everyone even remotely connected to the case," Andi reassured her. "Me, Georgina, Tommy, Ian—I think you were just the last one they found."

There was a moment's silence, a crackle of static. Tired of standing, Ian eased into his chair as quietly as he could, but the wheeled base knocked against the desk.

"Is someone there?" asked Sylvie as Andi glared at him.

"It's just me," said Andi.

He wished she lied less convincingly.

There was another brief silence. Then Sylvie said, "You were always so kind to me, even when I was chasing Ian. And you covered for me that one day in the bathroom with Mrs. Henry, so I covered for you. I just want you to know I never said anything to anyone about . . ."

"I never realized you knew," whispered Andi.

Ian, stunned, just sat there.

"I want you to know I struggled for years with bulimia, but I'm okay now. We aren't doomed to spend our lives being the people we were in high school."

"I'm so happy to hear you say that," said Andi, some of the color returning to her cheeks.

"And I'm so happy to know that you and Ian are together and have such a wonderful family," Sylvie went on, her voice now strangely calm. "I won't tell Cassidy anything more than she needs to know."

"Thank you," Andi said in a choked voice.

"You don't think anyone really believes I had anything to do with Dallas Walker's death, do you?"

"No, I don't," Andi said.

"Honestly, when I heard they'd found his body, I had to wonder if Ian did it," Sylvie said. "I mean, given what was going on."

And there it was. Ian flinched as if he'd been hit. Andi staggered and caught her balance, steadying herself on the desk with both hands. As their eyes met, Andi's were wide with raw emotion—disbelief, exhaustion, *fear*—and he wondered how much of what he saw was a reflection of what she saw in his own.

"He was so in love with you," Sylvie continued, oblivious to the fact that she had two listeners. "Even when he was with me, I could tell he really wasn't, if you know what I mean. He burned for you, Andi. It was kind of like the rest of us didn't even exist. He would have done anything for you."

"Sylvie, I have to go," Andi said abruptly. "I'm sorry."

She ended the call.

"Did you kill Dallas Walker, Ian?" she asked.

He remembered the red-hot rage. Remembered feeling the power in his strong, growing body.

"We both had reasons." He heard the trembling in his own voice. "The same reason."

"I was going to read your journal the other day," she confessed.

"Then you know where it is."

Her eyes strayed to his hiding place, confirmation enough. He had no idea where she'd kept her own journal since Glenlake.

"Why didn't you?"

"Old taboos die hard, I guess," she said. "That, and I couldn't pick the lock."

"I guess you should read it, then," he told her, kneeling and reaching under the credenza.

"You need to read mine. It'll answer all your questions."

"I have a lot of them."

"I'll get it now." She turned to go.

Chapter Fifty-Six

"This is weird," said Felicia. "There used to be a hundred and seventy-one photos in this folder."

She was talking to herself, a habit she had, but Cassidy happened to be in earshot. Mr. Kelly had momentarily left the room.

"What folder?" she asked, even though she had a sinking feeling she knew exactly which one.

"The crime-scene photos Mr. Kelly got from the local photographer. Now there are only a hundred and seventy."

Cassidy opened Google Drive on her own laptop and quickly navigated to the folder to verify for herself. "How did you even notice that?"

"What are you fine ladies talking about?" asked Noah, sidling up between them.

"Ugh, Noah," said Felicia. "Mr. Kelly told me that keeping track of all our research is really important. Once a week, I compare the master list of everything we have to the files on the drive to make sure I've included it all. My list entry said *folder with one hundred seventy-one photos*, and I just noticed there were only one hundred seventy photos on the drive."

"I thought there were supposed to be one hundred seventy-two," Noah said.

"Don't be an idiot, Noah," Cassidy said to shut him up.

Noah shrugged, used to the abuse and fortunately immune to it.

While Felicia frowned and applied another coat of lip gloss, Cassidy saw she was right. Given her mom's frequent questions about the class's progress, she was the most logical culprit. There must have been another photo she found *incriminating*. Why hadn't she told Cassidy, though?

Cassidy's mind raced while she tried to think of a way to cover the problem. "I'm sure someone just deleted a file by accident," she told Felicia. "All we have to do is ask Mr. Kelly to reupload the photos from the original flash drive. I have to talk to him about something as soon as he gets back, so I can do it."

"Okay, great," Felicia said to Cassidy, while Noah continued to invade her personal space. "And back up, buddy, or I'm getting a restraining order!"

Cassidy took a quiet, deep breath and pondered her next step. Restore the photo or adjust the count on Felicia's list? A week from now, the class "librarian" would never know the difference.

Even better, Cassidy could create a duplicate photo to simply get the file count back up to 171. She distracted Felicia and Noah with a suggestion about presentation boards while she did just that.

Mom, what are you doing?

Chapter Fifty-Seven

Andi shifted her legs to stretch out a cramp and realized the one she'd folded under herself had fallen sound asleep. She was sitting in the bay window in the living room, with a glass of wine within reach. The wine so far untouched in her hurry to read. The moment she'd opened Ian's journal—after rushing the twins to bed—she'd been transfixed. The early journal entries had been as wry, taciturn, and unsentimental as the Ian she remembered. But as the school years went by, and, in particular, once she'd seen herself through his eyes, breaking up with him in a diner because *I need some time to be me*, he'd gradually opened up on the page. He became more expressive and vulnerable in direct proportion to the wound she'd inflicted upon him. She ached as he wrestled with himself over her.

Easing herself into a more comfortable position, she finally took a deep drink of wine, then another, draining half the glass before turning the page to continue. She touched her cheek as if probing for a phantom bruise of that long-ago day in March, anxious to have read his thoughts, and more anxious about what Ian had written next.

What if Ian had been plotting to get rid of Dallas all along? A boy knight in shining armor defending her honor against the *man* who'd done her wrong?

Andi now knew Ian far too well to dismiss the possibility entirely.

Ian Copeland's Glenlake Journal

Thursday, March 20, 1997

What a fucked-up twenty-four hours. How fucked-up we all are. They should change Glenlake's motto to something like "Give us your best and brightest and we'll fuck them up for life," only in Latin. I should get Greg what's-his-name, the Latin valedictorian, to translate that.

My leg feels like a robot leg whose wiring's shot. I mean, it's a leg, and it moves, but I'm carrying it more than it's carrying me. I ran the first hundred yards back to Glenlake after I saw Andi and DFW because I was so messed up with adrenaline, but after that it was barely faster than walking.

I thought about going to Nurse Ratched, but she's not exactly up on the latest sports medicine. Anyway, I don't need her to tell me Rest, Ice, Compress, Elevate given that we already learned that from a poster in the locker room. So I went to the union to buy some Tylenol, an ACE bandage, and a Gatorade.

Sylvie was the only other person in the store, and she looked worse than I did.

"Are you OK?" I asked her.

I thought she might say something like, "Are you?" but she was so shaky she didn't even notice that I was cold, sweaty, limping, and that I had been bawling.

She just looked at me, and Jesus, I don't know if I've ever seen anyone look so . . . lost. Then she put down the bottle of Kaopectate in her hand, staggered, and kind of fell back into the little drugstore display, knocking some toothpaste boxes onto the floor.

I helped her to a bench at the front of the store and told her to wait there. Then I bought both of our stuff and took her back to her dorm. Nobody saw us go in. Her roommate, Kate, was on one of her occasional family vacations that never seem to coincide with the actual Glenlake calendar, so Sylvie was all alone.

I honestly didn't know what to do, but she begged me not to tell anyone. She said she's got an eating problem, and she let it get out of control, but she's going to get better and she just can't deal with adults right now. I guess I can relate.

People whisper about Sylvie and make jokes like "Why does Sylvie love KFC? Because it comes with a bucket." I've even laughed a few times, but I never really knew how bad it was. She was so skinny looking, skinnier than I thought, but then again, when we did it, we were under the covers with the lights off because she wouldn't let me look at her, and most girls are like that anyway.

I didn't feel like I should leave her alone, so I stayed there all night. I made her take sips of water and Gatorade and fed her saltine crackers and little slices of apple like she had the flu. She kept it all down, which was a relief. I wasn't sure if I was ready to hold her hair while she hurled into the toilet.

After a while I remembered to take my Tylenol and wrapped a cold Coke can on either side of my knee. I lay down next to her on the bed and propped my leg up on two pillows. She reached out and put her arm across my chest, but there wasn't anything sexual between us. I don't think there will be again. She's not a bad person, and I definitely don't feel better than her or anyone else. I guess I kind of used to.

She fell asleep a long time before I did. At one point I kind of almost started laughing, because I was thinking about how, for so long, I always thought I was going to have this perfect fucking life, you know? That I would just go on and on, and everything would be OK. Now I just feel like some kind of cripple.

My leg will get better eventually, and people who see me will think I walk normally. But I'm always going to be limping, you know? Because I don't have Andi to lean on.

You can't fix or change people, I guess. I'll be here for Sylvie, but I can't use her as a substitute for Andi. And I guess Andi has to deal with her decisions on her own. Even if I had limped over, tried to kill DFW, and gotten my ass kicked instead, what would that have accomplished? I hate that I left her there, but now that they're broken up, I'll just have to wait and see if she comes back to me.

I'll wait probably forever, so it's time to pull myself back together.

~

Ian sat at his desk. He'd poured three fingers of bourbon from his favorite bottle, a Blanton's Gold Edition. It was an effective anesthetic. And it seemed a moment worth marking somehow, no matter what he read.

Andi had returned from upstairs, the journal already unlocked, and handed it to him without a further word. As he turned page after page, he felt a full-body catharsis, as if he'd been sobbing—only he hadn't shed a tear.

He suspected, though, that it was only a matter of time.

Her distance these past months was clearly born out of fear of being discovered. She now knew that he'd always known about Dallas—but there was something she was still holding back. Was their life and marriage about to be upended when he learned that she'd never loved him, only settled for him because of the security and unconditional love he offered?

Or was it something worse?

He'd seen Dallas slap Andi. Were there bruises he hadn't seen, physical or mental? Given the short time between what he had witnessed and Dallas's disappearance, plus the fact that Andi had maintained her secret for all these years, Ian couldn't help but wonder whether she was somehow responsible in a way she had hoped would remain submerged at the bottom of Lake Loomis.

After learning Dallas's body had been found in his car in the water below the bluffs, Ian had allowed himself to fantasize, almost as if he were watching a true-crime show on TV, about a scenario in which the killer got Dallas wasted enough for an off-road joyride, plied him with even more drinks at the top of the cliff, and thumped him on the back of the head. Ian relished the image of this shadowy figure starting the car, putting it into drive, and then getting the hell out. Even without a foot on the gas, the six-cylinder engine would have taken the car over the cliff at a fast walk.

Had Andi, sick of Dallas's ego-driven bullshit, conjured up a scenario of her own? What if she had brought them back together by making sure the man who preyed on her was permanently out of the picture?

Full of fear and a reckless surge of love for this girl who suddenly felt like a stranger, he forced himself to read.

Andi Bloom's Glenlake Journal

Monday, March 24, 1997

I keep thinking there's going to be a note in the tree, or I'm going to walk into class and he's going to be there, but there isn't and he isn't. I'd like to say that I miss him terribly, but, really, I just feel blank and alone.

The thing is, I need him to come back, because I need him to give me a ride to an appointment that he obviously isn't up for dealing with. But I'll find a way to get there. I'm making the call anyway.

Tomorrow.

~

Tuesday, March 25, 1997

Fuck Dallas for taking off. Fuck him for not being man enough to be there for me. Fuck him for flirting with other people. And fuck him for making me think it ever made sense for us to be together.

I really fucked up by breaking up with Ian. Every time I see him, and it seems like I see him constantly, it takes everything I have not to cry. I've made a horrible mistake. I would give anything to erase what's happened and go back to the way things were. I miss Ian. I miss his friendship. I miss having a cute, smart, normal, stable boyfriend my own age.

I made an appointment for Monday.

I thought about asking Mrs. Henry for a ride to Northbrook and lying to her about why, but she keeps asking me if I'm feeling better, like she's worried I have an eating disorder now, too.

I'll just walk into town and then take a cab.

Fuck.

~

Friday, March 28, 1997

The definition of True Eternal Fucking Boundless Joy: *I. AM. BLEEDING.*

The definition of irony: *IN. POETRY. CLASS.*

I should be mortified by the bloodstain I left on my chair and the fact that I'm all crampy and it's so heavy it has to be a miscarriage and not a late period, but somehow it feels like the fitting end to a really bad poem.

> Literary It Girl
> Falls
> For the smooth lines of her predatory poetry
>   master
> Into the depths of disaster
> Très
> Cliché.

~

Friday, April 4, 1997

"Come on," Georgina said, grabbing my arm and leading me up the stairs.

"Where are we going?"

"Spying mission. You won't believe who's here."

"Who?" I asked, my veins turning to ice as thoughts of Dallas began to loop in my head. How dare he come back and show his face?

I had just decided I wouldn't even give him the courtesy of eye contact when Georgina said:

"Susan Walker. Dallas's wife."

My legs felt frozen. "Ex-wife."

"Whatever," Georgina said dismissively. "She's here to get his stuff."

"How do you know this?"

"I overheard a little birdie, also known as Administrative Aide Darlene O'Leary," she said, tugging on my arm again. "Aren't you curious to see what she looks like?"

"A little," I admitted.

"Pretend you're not looking," Georgina whispered as the door to Dallas's office suddenly opened in front of us.

Georgina flat out stared as I glanced discreetly at a woman who looked nothing like I'd pictured Susan, or Tracy, his "friend with the very comfortable guest room," or whoever it was he'd surely run off with. I was starting to think of Dallas as the kind of man who was forever running toward something new and less complicated.

With gray curly hair, mom jeans, sensible shoes, and no makeup whatsoever, Susan looked ten years older than Dallas.

"Total granola," Georgina muttered as soon as she couldn't hear us. "Not what I expected at all."

"Me either," I said. "I figured she'd be—"

"Younger and prettier?"

Was it as simple as that? "Less like an English professor from a liberal arts college, anyway."

"Good thing he didn't have kids with her," she said as we headed back downstairs.

Thank god there weren't going to be any others in the near future.

∾

Tuesday, April 15, 1997

Today is my eighteenth birthday.

Georgina gave me lottery tickets, a copy of Playgirl, *and a pack of cigarettes.*

In other words, I'm legal. Of age. Jailbait no more.

Dallas once told me he was going to take me to the city for my eighteenth birthday, even though he'd be strapped for cash on tax day.

Even if he shows up today to make good on his promise, it's too late. I won't bother telling him that I didn't stay pregnant for long. He wasn't there to share the relief I felt when I canceled the dreaded appointment.

But I digress. It's a beautiful, sunny spring day, and I feel better than I have in months. Not only did I wake up to my contraband birthday presents from Georgina, but everyone in my dorm had something for me—candy, lotion, candles, and a scarf from Crystal, all of which I opened after I blew out the candles on the cake Mrs. Henry made from scratch.

It was red velvet and the glorious color of blood.

"It's good to see you back to your old self again," she said as Georgina and I fed each other like newlyweds and toasted with sparkling cider.

And I did almost feel like my old self again. Mainly because I got a Bit-O-Honey in my mailbox.

From Ian.

~

Ian poured another finger of bourbon and swallowed it, grateful for the burn in his throat, trying to make sense of all the answers he'd just learned. Some of them to questions he hadn't known.

Andi had been pregnant.

She and Dallas had never broken up—he'd only assumed it, and Andi had let him believe it.

When he saw them, they'd been fighting because she'd asked Dallas for help.

Both of them had failed her.

Her records request at Glenlake had obviously been an attempt to find out whether there was any record of her pregnancy. Any evidence that could tie her to Dallas Walker.

It didn't absolve her of murder. In fact, it gave her a motive. But Jesus . . .

He heard footsteps, and Andi opened the door to his study, her eyes sparkling with the things she had learned about him. He stood up. As soon as they started speaking, tears began to roll down her cheeks.

"You were pregnant," he said, still hardly believing it.

"It . . . didn't progress."

"And Dallas was upset."

"He asked me if I did it on purpose."

"That fucker."

Andi nodded.

"So you hated him at the end. Maybe almost as much as I did."

"I was devastated by the way he treated me. Then he disappeared. All this time I thought it was because of me and my . . . situation."

Ian wanted to take her in his arms, to crush their bodies together, but he couldn't. Yet.

"But you let me believe you broke up."

"I was over him even before it happened."

"I thought it was possible you killed him because he broke up with you. Or because he'd been abusive."

"It never occurred to me you might think that," Andi said, sounding startled. "I was worried you'd find out what Dallas and I were really talking about that day."

"And you were trying to get rid of your medical records so no one would see them and make the connection."

Andi nodded and then looked into his eyes. "Ian, I didn't kill Dallas Walker. I didn't care about him that much. All I did that night was go back to my dorm. I tried to keep my mind off everything by playing a game of Monopoly with Georgina. The next day he was gone."

"Are you saying your fucking alibi was Georgina?"

"Of all people."

They both laughed for the first time in what felt like forever.

"Georgina told me she walked in on you and Sylvie doing it."

"Of course she told you."

"But not until yesterday, if you can believe that."

"It doesn't matter. Andi . . ." He reached for her and let his hand fall. "I need you to know I hated Dallas Walker—Dallas *Fucking* Walker—but for the wrong reasons. I hated him like I've always been seventeen years old. I hated him for breaking us up. But . . . what he did to you . . . you were just a *kid*."

Andi smiled ruefully. "I was a kid, but I thought I was a woman already. I'd read about all these free-spirit artists who lived these amazing lives, who loved hard and broke hearts. Dallas really was one of those. I didn't realize the emptiness that goes along with all of that. All the damage. He only hit me that one time, but he beat me up pretty badly emotionally. More than I allowed myself to see at the time. Once you and I got back together, I put the whole thing in a box and screwed the lid down tight."

"I'll never forgive myself for not protecting you then. I dreamed about that for years." He felt hot, wet tears on his own face. "And I'm just so sorry. So, so sorry you ever had to go through that."

"It wasn't your responsibility. I'm to blame for putting you through hell. For allowing hate into your heart. And for what?"

"I think we both need to forgive each other, and ourselves," Ian said, finally moving forward and taking her in his arms.

She hugged him back fiercely. "Yes."

"We need to protect each other and our family," he said into her shoulder, the familiar smell of her so utterly reassuring.

"But working together this time."

"I still haven't even had a chance to look at those records I picked up at Glenlake."

Andi was silent for a moment. He wanted to push back and look at her, but she continued to hold him closely, maybe so he couldn't.

"Do you ever wish . . . that you actually had killed Dallas?" she asked.

The answer came to him easily. "He's taken up enough room in my life without that. What about you?"

She lifted her head and kissed him. "I feel exactly the same way."

Chapter Fifty-Eight

The morning after, Ian tagged along as she dropped the kids off for school, and then both of them went to a nearby coffee shop to look over the packet he'd picked up from Glenlake. Neither of them had spoken much while getting ready, but there was a comfort between them Andi couldn't remember having for years, if ever. Revisiting the worst year of her life in such vivid detail had been hard, and it would continue to be hard until the memories subsided again, but now she imagined gaining something she'd never believed could happen: closure.

At the coffee shop, she stood in line for drinks while Ian found a secluded table.

By the time she sat down, he had already organized the paperwork and was starting to go through it.

"So this is everything they had on the infamous Roy," she said.

"It's not much, given that he worked there for almost twenty years," he confirmed.

"Why 'Roy'?" she mused. "What was wrong with 'Curt'?"

"People don't always choose their own nicknames," he said. "Could have been a friend, a gym teacher, anybody, and it just stuck."

Leaving unsaid the fact that David Dallas Walker had deliberately left his own first name behind.

"So what's in the piles?" she asked, moving on.

"Original job application, medical and insurance records, salary, W-2s, performance evaluations, and a few other things."

"Let's get started."

They divvied up the work and went through every page, comparing notes as they did, looking for anything out of the ordinary. It seemed like a long shot—what could these impersonal files possibly tell them about what Roy did outside of work?—but at least it was something. Though she still didn't understand what had compelled Roy to suddenly seek gainful employment, at Glenlake no less, even these dry bureaucratic records helped make him seem more real and less like a phantom of her memory.

"Look at this," said Ian suddenly. "He started in June 1997. Just a few months after everything happened."

"That's definitely curious."

She went through the performance evaluations, all of them perfunctory and mostly blank. The necessary boxes were checked, the required lines were signed, but the boxes for additional comments were uniformly empty.

"And check this out," said Ian. "He was hired at a flat thirty thousand per year, which honestly seems a little high for an assistant groundskeeper in 1997. And it's a weirdly round number, too. This sheet that lists other salaries shows someone else receiving twenty-seven thousand eight hundred forty dollars."

"So he was hired at a higher rate than someone else?"

"Higher than the two other assistants." Ian flipped through W-2s, checking something. "But it *never changed*. The other salaries went up, even surpassed his, but his didn't. It's always been a flat thirty grand."

Andi sipped her coffee, which was cooling off faster than she liked, thinking how strange it was that so much suspicion had centered on Roy. Yes, he had a propensity for violence, and she'd been there the night he turned on Dallas, but for the most part the two had seemed like friends. "Who hired him?"

He found the paperwork stapled to Roy's original application. "The head groundskeeper, Ted Orzibal."

"Is he still working there?"

"We need to find that out."

They kept digging, scanning pages. When Andi reached the end of the performance evaluations, she found a few handwritten letters, all from the 1997–1998 school year, in which Orzibal had complained to *his* supervisor, the head of operations, that Roy was an unreliable employee. When he did show up, he arrived late, left early, and performed his tasks erratically. Worse, he was insubordinate, giving sarcastic replies or refusing to answer at all.

The letters were paper-clipped together with a handwritten note that simply read, *Thank you for keeping me apprised of the situation. I understand your concern and will have a conversation with Mr. Royal.*

She showed Ian. "Can you make out this signature?"

He could, instantly. "It's Gerald Matheson."

"The conversation must have done the trick, because Roy continued working there."

"Not without more complaints," he said, handing her a sheaf of memos that thinned over the years, as though his coworkers had come to accept the status quo.

"Should we call Matheson and ask him about it?"

"Let's track down Orzibal first."

Chapter Fifty-Nine

Two weeks had passed since receiving the letters declaring that Whitney and Owen had officially been accepted to Glenlake, and the family had finally gotten the traditional Copeland celebratory dinner at the country club on the schedule. Cope and Biz were dignifying the occasion with a school tie and pearls, respectively. Andi was wearing a cocktail dress, and even the twins had dressed more nicely than usual. Ian wondered at times whether one or both of them might rebel and ask to attend school near home, but neither had. Whitney reverentially attached their acceptance letters to the fridge with magnets on all four corners. Where Cassidy went, they would, too—their parents probably didn't factor too much into the decision.

Judging by her drink orders, Andi was very much in the spirit of things. She chatted happily with the people who stopped by their table. Over the years she'd become better known—and, he suspected, better liked—than he was. Privately, she still joked about dyeing her hair blonde and wearing a Lilly Pulitzer sundress, bemoaning her fate as the "token Jew in WASP-ville," but that was more out of habit than actual aggravation. She'd featured the stately homes of enough club members in her books that they surely saw her as part of their overall PR plan, but that wasn't all of it. She was genuinely liked.

Ian himself was enjoying the smiles and chatter at the table but couldn't quite enter the flow of the conversation. There were just too many loose ends—one in particular he needed to tie up tonight.

"And how is our cub reporter, Cassidy?" asked Biz, interrupting his flow of thought. "Are there any national newspapers threatening to hire her and derail our college plans?"

"Are there any national newspapers left?" cracked Cope, the mainstream media being one of his favorite targets.

"She's still crusading on behalf of Curtis Royal," Ian told them, pretending not to notice as Owen showed Whitney something on the phone in his lap.

"Teenage years are the perfect time to champion lost causes," said Cope sagely.

"He certainly seems guilty," Andi said, quietly so she wouldn't attract the attention of the twins, who found the case fascinating. "But the whole thing is weird. Why would he kill Walker and then take a job on campus?"

Cope sipped his watery bourbon on the rocks. "You know what they say about criminals returning to the scene of the crime. And—"

"Glenlake is the perfect cover, when you think about it," interrupted Biz, earning a glare from Cope. "Nobody would expect the killer to stick around like that."

"Killer to stick around like what?" piped up Owen, noticing as he did the baked caprese appetizer in front of him and forking a bite.

"They're talking about the *Prep School Poet Murder*, dummy," said Whitney. "That's what they called it on the news," she explained in response to Owen's look.

Ian addressed his parents, wishing the whole thing hadn't come up but realizing it was too late to stop now. "The circumstances struck us as funny, so I got in touch with Ted Orzibal, who was Walker's supervisor at the time. He told me Royal was the worst employee they ever had.

The running joke was that he must have had pictures of the headmaster sleeping with somebody," said Ian.

"Ian, the kids," cautioned Andi as Biz coughed, then washed the bite down with a deep drink of water.

"If it was blackmail pictures, they could have turned him loose after Darrow kicked the bucket!" chortled Cope.

"Cope," groaned Biz.

"I am so gonna be a journalist, too," said Owen delightedly. "Dead bodies and people sleeping together!"

"First, you have to cover city council meetings," warned Cope. "You'll want to put your own eyes out."

"The journalism class is presenting their project just before spring break," said Andi, trying to steer the conversation gently back to neutral ground. "It will be interesting to see what they've learned before they wrap up."

"Are you still going to Mexico?" asked Biz, and Andi was all too happy to jump on the gambit, telling her mother-in-law all about their plans to spend six days in Playa del Carmen.

"I know you'll be glad when Cassidy is out of that journalist's clutches," Cope told Ian confidentially. "Not that my heart bleeds for the poet or the groundskeeper, but really, it's time to move on."

～

Ian's innocuous suggestion that his parents might want to take their grandkids for dessert paid immediate dividends, with Cope and Biz driving Whitney and Owen away in their Lexus and promising to drop them home after Ian and Andi had enjoyed a nightcap. Wink, wink.

As he got behind the wheel of his Audi, Ian felt heavy with what he was about to tell Andi, replaying last night's voice mail from Preston in his mind.

What the fuck are you doing, Ian? You want out of our business arrangement, just like that? Well, let me tell you something, buddy—one word from me and we go down together. So I want you to consider your position carefully. I'm going to send this inventory back, and you're going to sell it, only the terms won't be quite as kind as last time.

"You seem distracted tonight, Ian. What's wrong?" asked Andi. Then, as he headed into Clayton, she added, "And why are you going home this way?"

He drove for a few minutes in silence before deciding there was no appropriate transition.

"I have something to tell you," he said.

Andi listened mutely as he explained how he'd surprised Preston in Chicago before digging through his trash. By the time he'd finished, they'd pulled up outside the now-closed Grape and Barley.

"You need to end the partnership, and now," she told him.

"Come with me," he said.

Walking her inside, he showed her the barren shelves in the empty display case, the sign informing customers OUR CUSTOMERS' RESPONSE TO THIS UNIQUE AND IRREPLACEABLE PRODUCT HAS BEEN SUCH THAT WE ARE SIMPLY UNABLE TO KEEP UP WITH DEMAND. PLEASE BE PATIENT WHILE WE SOURCE ADDITIONAL SUPPLIERS FOR VINTAGE SPIRITS.

"So you leave it up until people forget, and then stock something else here?" she asked, relief visible on her face.

Without answering, he led her off the sales floor into his office, closing the door behind them to ensure they weren't overheard by any of the cleaning staff working throughout the store.

"Preston's demanding that I take the stock back. He knows my reputation is at risk if anything gets out, and he's counting on me being afraid to stand up to him. And—"

"And?"

"And if I end the partnership, I'm losing my best chance to pay back the loan I took from Simon."

"As in my father Simon?"

Ian nodded.

"Why would you need to borrow from him?"

"The business was in a pinch with new building costs exceeding estimates, and I'd fronted all I had for store number three. I'd have hit up Cope, but he doesn't have the reserves he used to. Not liquid."

"But we have money."

"Not three hundred fifty thousand dollars."

"Oh," she said, as if the wind had been knocked out of her.

He forced himself to look her in the eye. "The loan was supposed to be short-term, just to bridge the gap. But now I won't be able to pay Simon back in time to avoid the penalty he negotiated."

"And what is the penalty?"

"If I don't make full repayment within one year, he gains a twenty percent ownership stake in Grape and Barley, Incorporated," Ian said.

Ian waited for his wife to explode with righteous anger, berating him for being as stupid as he felt.

"I fucking hate it when Simon pulls this kind of shit," she finally said, her mouth a thin line.

"I've never borrowed money from him before," he said, genuinely surprised.

"This is exactly why you shouldn't," she said, reaching for her phone.

Before he could beg her not to, she'd already dialed.

Ian was both mortified and relieved as his wife began to banter with her father, whose booming basso came through loud and clear.

"Twenty percent of the business if he doesn't pay you back in a year?" she asked, without even saying hello.

"I wondered how long it would take him to tell you," Simon said with a laugh. "He's got six months left, per my calendar."

"You're kidding me, right?" Andi said. "You'd have written me a check without batting an eye."

"It's different when it's man-to-man."

"That's not the most sexist thing you've ever said, but it's close."

"You know what I mean."

As much as he hated having his wife deal with the mess he'd created, Ian had always felt a grudging admiration for the ease with which Andi and Simon communicated, even when they argued. Despite the tension, there was genuine warmth.

"You mean Ian wouldn't feel like a man if he didn't have to work for your generosity."

"Something like that."

"You couldn't have charged him a garden-variety usurious interest rate?"

"I wasn't trying to screw him. He's my son-in-law."

"The road to hell—"

"Put him on the phone," Simon said.

"He's not—"

"Don't bullshit me, Andi. I know he's there."

Ian reached for her phone. She sighed and handed it to him.

"Simon," he said.

"What's going on?"

Simon listened while Ian detailed the Preston situation, interrupting only once to say, "Damn it, I was looking forward to all the authentic *Mad Men*–era Cutty Sark I could drink, not to mention the amazing bottles I was going to give out for Hanukkah."

"It's still all-you-can-drink counterfeit Cutty," Ian said. "At least until I'm found out."

"I know you're good for the money," Simon reassured him. "And if you need more time, that's fine. As for this douchebag in Chicago, I think I know someone who knows someone who can convince him it's in his best interests to pipe down and leave you alone."

Ian quailed, thinking he was about to graduate from unknowing accessory to fraud to something much worse.

"He's not going to get—"

"Hurt? Not if he's got half a brain."

Did he believe Simon? Simon couldn't even know that himself. But without direct knowledge of what was going to happen, Ian was well insulated—with any luck he could stay that way. Giving himself over to the blithe confidence of Simon Bloom seemed the best option all around.

Simon took his silence for the assent it was. "Don't worry about it. Consider the problem handled."

"Thank you, Simon."

"I've had my eye on you for a long time, Ian, and I know you'll always do the right thing by Andi. Keep taking care of my girl," he said, and hung up.

Ian and Andi looked at each other and said, simultaneously, "I think Simon may really be a gangster." And then: "Jinx."

"Can you think of a better place to have our nightcap?" Ian asked.

Andi answered by locking the office door.

Chapter Sixty

Cassidy had never seen Mr. Kelly look so tired. He had bags under his eyes, his hair was sticking up in back as if he'd missed it while combing, and he was wearing a wrinkled blue shirt, untucked, without either of the two blazers he normally alternated. He knew they all noticed, obviously.

"Pretend it's career day," he began, "and I'm dressed not in the uniform of a visiting teacher but of a working journalist. This is what you look like when you've spent the last sixty hours or so chasing leads."

As heads turned quizzically, Cassidy felt a tingle of excitement at where she thought he was going.

"Curtis 'Roy' Royal, he of the unimaginative nickname, is incarcerated pending trial, and most of us believed that, when justice was eventually served, he would be proved guilty. One of your classmates, however"—and here he looked right at her, so briefly she wasn't sure anyone noticed—"didn't feel we'd done enough to eliminate reasonable doubt. And though I cursed her name repeatedly over my lost weekend, she was probably right. Can anyone guess what I was doing?"

No one could guess. Cassidy knew but didn't want to raise her hand. So Tate, whom she'd told, bailed her out by raising his. She wanted to kiss him.

"Checking out the snitch?"

"Well done, Tate," said Mr. Kelly, looking at Cassidy longer this time. "And listen to your hardened slang. You could be a court reporter, a public defender, or even a detective with delivery like that. But because I have been specifically instructed not to let tender young souls such as yourselves anywhere near the machinery of our judicial system, I took it upon myself to learn the identity of the man who fingered Roy in exchange for leniency in an upcoming trial. I then learned that the night in question, when Roy was alleged to have threatened Dallas Walker's life over a drug deal gone bad, was Saturday, February 8, 1997. What was the next logical step?"

"Write the guy a thank-you note?" said Noah to a mix of laughs and groans.

"Any intelligent ideas?" asked Mr. Kelly without smiling.

Hannah raised her hand. "Try to find out who else was there. To see if anyone else could confirm the story."

"Exactly," he said with a nod. "Which, given the nature of the party and how much time had passed, wasn't easy. I did locate three party guests, however. I was able to interview one over email, one by phone, and one I had to track down in person, forty miles away, at a men's shelter in Elgin."

Cassidy knew Mr. Kelly was telling them all this so they'd know how he did it, which was part of the lesson. But he was also drawing it out so much the suspense was killing her. Trying to read his expression, all she could decide was that he didn't look happy. But maybe he was just really, really tired.

"What did you find out?" she blurted, unable to resist.

He sighed and took his usual seat on the corner of his desk. "All of them confirmed that Roy was at the party and that he was known to deal drugs. One of them confirmed that Dallas Walker was there, too, with a young girl nobody recognized. Another one remembered a fight but couldn't remember who was involved."

"So nothing contradicts the snitch's story," said Tate. "Even though nothing adds to it."

"Correct," said Mr. Kelly. "However, there was one more thing they all agreed upon: the snitch himself was never there."

Nobody knew what to make of that, although Cassidy herself was so excited to hear it she let out a weird yelp that made Felicia totally roll her eyes. If the snitch himself was going on secondhand information, and the sheriff's department didn't have anything more detailed to go on, how could they prove Roy was guilty? The case was thin enough to start with.

"Are you going to tell Detective Gavras?" asked Cassidy eagerly.

"I met with him earlier this morning, another reason I look like shit and I'm tired. He received the news with his usual good grace, which is to say he's sick of our meddling in his case. But I guarantee you he'll look at it."

"And charges against Roy will get dropped?" Tate asked.

"I've been in this business too long to predict what will happen, but if charges against Roy are dropped, there's one person besides me you can thank: Cassidy Copeland."

From the looks everyone was giving her, Cassidy wasn't sure she wanted the acknowledgment. Most of them seemed to want Roy found guilty, not innocent. But she knew they'd come around.

Now it was a matter of seeing what the Lake County Sheriff's Office made of this news.

Chapter Sixty-One

As they made their way across campus, past the new writing center, which from the outside looked ready to host events but apparently still lacked carpet and tile, Andi couldn't help but laugh at the twins' different reactions to their first visit since learning they were officially coming to Glenlake. Whitney, perhaps predictably, stayed by their side, bubbly and effusive but displaying the poise she deemed necessary for a freshman-to-be. Owen, meanwhile, ranged ahead like a dog on point, scampering and climbing, casting wistful looks at his sister, who refused to join in.

They still hadn't seen Cassidy, but she had been a presence since morning on the family group text.

BIG NEWS, she'd announced.

College news??? Whitney had texted back.

Owen, ever the supportive little brother, offered his condolences in advance: Sorry they all rejected you.

Yes college, wrote Cassidy. I got into Amherst.

She'd already been accepted to Syracuse, Northeastern, and Colby but, given Copeland tradition, seemed to be leaning toward her father's alma mater.

Terras irradient, texted Ian.

That means "Earth is radioactive," translated Owen helpfully.

Congratulations, Cassidy, Andi had added.

A short while later, Cassidy had texted again: But that's not the really big news.

What??? wondered Whitney.

YOU'LL FIND OUT TONIGHT, answered Cassidy, going radio silent after that.

"Tonight" being the journalism seminar's presentation. Just as Andi had been a key organizer of the poetry slam (in hindsight, horribly named), Cassidy was on the committee for her class's event. And while such presentations usually drew modest audiences, it was the evening before spring break, so families like theirs who were headed off to vacation from O'Hare provided more warm bodies. More to the point, the interest in a case that had made national news guaranteed this one would be standing room only.

As they approached the auditorium, Andi was surprised to see two Lake County Sheriff's Office deputies, in full uniform and with guns on their hips, flanking the steps.

"What's up with the cops?" asked Owen, flushed and panting as he rejoined them.

She arched an eyebrow at Ian.

"To keep reporters out," he deduced instantly. "They don't want news crews crashing an academic event. This is, after all, a private institution."

"Still, it's kind of ironic, don't you think?" asked Whitney. "Keeping reporters from reporting what someone else reported?"

She's a sharp one, in some ways even keener than Cassidy, thought Andi with a hollow feeling in her stomach. Hopefully, she'd make it through Glenlake without any writing-seminar drama.

"This is for students and their families," she said simply.

They were early, so they waited on the steps while Owen burned off some more energy, doing thirteen-year-old parkour between railings, pillars, and stone benches. It was a crisp evening, but spring was definitely on its way.

Katharine Henry, Andi's former dorm mother, made her way toward them, walking alongside Sharon Lysander. Mrs. Lysander had parlayed an administrative assistant job, and plenty of continuing-education credits, into assistant headmastership. Ian was probably right, though, when he said that was as far as she was likely to rise. Partly because she was a loyal grinder, not a rock star.

And because she was a woman in her fifties?

Mrs. Henry beelined for Whitney. "Congratulations, young woman! Your mother told me the good news, and I couldn't be more excited to have another Copeland coming here next year."

Whitney beamed.

"Will you be following in your mother's footsteps?" she asked, glancing at Andi, who kept a smile frozen in place even as she recoiled inwardly at the thought.

"She's more of a STEM girl," parried Ian. "But she's a big reader, and I know she'll do well in her English classes."

"That's wonderful to hear," Mrs. Henry said, waving at Owen, who waved back but may or may not have known who he was waving to.

"Congratulations from me, too," added Sharon. "And welcome to Glenlake."

"Thank you!" chirped Whitney.

"And congratulations on Cassidy, too," Sharon told Ian and Andi. "Her stock will only go up after tonight."

The remark was puzzling, but not wanting to seem as though she wasn't in the loop, Andi let it slide. She'd find out soon enough.

They chatted for a few minutes as faculty and students continued to arrive, then went inside when Whitney insisted all the good seats would be taken.

"Quite a crowd," murmured Ian as the hall continued to fill until the main level and balcony were full and late-arriving students and their parents were forced to stand at the back. Wayne Kelly and his class were seated to one side of the stage, chattering excitedly, and Andi had to wave for a couple of minutes straight before Cassidy picked them out in the crowd and waved back.

Finally, it was time to begin. Headmaster Scanlon spoke first, briefly thanking everyone for coming and citing the long history of the writer-in-residence program at Glenlake—without any acknowledgment of the irony involved. He then introduced Mrs. Henry, who introduced Wayne Kelly by reading seemingly his entire curriculum vitae, as if to reassure the audience that the man they were about to hear from was in fact an esteemed member of his profession.

"You've read a lot about this story in national news," she summed up, "and this hasn't always been an easy story for Glenlakers to take in. But there's still more news to be made—and you'll hear it first!"

Murmurs rippled around the auditorium as Wayne Kelly took the stage and briefly summarized the class project. He called roll, and the students took turns standing up, grinning sheepishly and waving to their parents. The team leaders—Hannah, Tate, Rowan, Felicia, and Cassidy—then stood in a semicircle behind the podium and launched into a PowerPoint, each of them taking turns reading from a script that summarized the known facts, the journalistic methods they'd employed, and what they had been able to deduce. Andi was grateful Georgina didn't have a student in the class, as she wouldn't have wanted to watch her squirm when Tate recited a couple of the choicest quotes from her interview, including the "hottie" one.

Or maybe she *would* have wanted to watch that.

The thought that Dallas had tried to kiss Georgina overshadowed Andi's thoughts of what a cute, smart boy Tate seemed to be, and how much he reminded her of a young Ian.

The twins were surprisingly rapt, given the auditorium setting, especially when their big sister was talking. Owen leaned so far forward during the crime-scene photos he was practically breathing down the neck of the woman in front of him.

But so far, so familiar. Nothing they'd reported deviated in any way from what she and Ian already knew—and it most definitely did *not* include what they'd learned about Curtis Royal's checkered employment history or any mention of the bracelet that had dredged up so many secrets that would otherwise have remained at the bottom of Lake Loomis. Even as Cassidy summed up the most recent developments, ruling out one suspect after another, Andi couldn't for the life of her see where *BIG NEWS* was going to show up.

Until Cassidy paused nervously, cleared her throat, and then took a drink of water from a bottle under the podium. With a glance at Wayne Kelly for reassurance—Andi reading both of their expressions carefully but not finding anything to worry about, she *thought*—Cassidy turned the page.

"We had prepared this presentation believing our summary would refer to the imminent trial of Curtis Royal, and the fact that the true end to this story would not be known until he was found guilty or innocent in a court of law. However, late yesterday, we learned of a new twist to the tale. Based in part on the work of this class, and especially on the reporting of award-winning journalist Wayne Kelly, the Lake County Sheriff's Office reviewed new evidence and reopened their investigation. They, in turn, found new evidence of their own, which they then presented to the Lake County prosecutor. He then"—Cassidy looked up from the podium and, despite the distance, made eye contact with Andi—"withdrew the murder charge. Curtis Royal was released from the Lake County Jail this morning."

The noise in the auditorium didn't quite qualify as an uproar, but there was a collective gasp, followed by excited conversation.

Andi grasped Ian's arm tightly. "What is going on?"

He didn't answer, grimly waiting for the other shoe to drop.

The twins, of course, were loving it.

Wayne Kelly had to rise from his seat and take the mic to quiet everyone down. Then, with what seemed like deference to Cassidy, he took over.

"New evidence received by the sheriff's department convinced them that Dallas Walker, for reasons unknown to us, took his own life or died accidentally. What was thought to be a blow to the back of the head was in fact an injury sustained when his car went over the cliff into Lake Loomis."

All her initial distress over Dallas's death came rushing back like a wave of nauseating heat.

Kelly had to raise his voice to continue. "While this is not quite the exoneration of an innocently convicted criminal, I do believe this is a significant achievement for the students of Glenlake, as this could not have happened without them. You should all be very proud of your sons and daughters, but one student in particular deserves special mention, because it was her encouragement that led me to dig deeper, as I always tell my students to do. That student is Cassidy Copeland."

Cassidy turned beet red but smiled as applause erupted. Mrs. Henry and Sharon Lysander stood up, prompting several other knots of audience members to do likewise. Andi felt rooted to her chair but followed suit when she felt Ian's gentle tug on her arm.

She stood and applauded, numb with shock.

"Cassidy, please introduce our next speaker," said Wayne Kelly, stepping aside again.

Their daughter grinned from ear to ear as she approached the mic. "I think it's only fitting that we hear from Curtis Royal himself!"

Andi collapsed into her seat as Roy shambled out of the wings in an ill-fitting suit and tie he'd no doubt purchased for his court appearances, the snake tattoo just visible above the bright white collar of his shirt. He was stooped and half the size she remembered, but just as ugly and intimidating.

He dabbed his forehead with a handkerchief, pulled a piece of paper from his pocket, and stared down at the podium, trying not to look at the crowd.

Andi felt a momentary pang of sympathy for Roy, who was probably more comfortable in a jail cell than facing a full auditorium.

"I had faith in higher powers," he began in a monotone, leaning too close to the microphone. "I trusted that I wouldn't be made to rot and die in prison. But sometimes I started to question whether anyone was listening. And then an angel appeared before me. She listened to my story. She believed in me. God moved in her, and now I am free."

Roy turned toward Cassidy, who stood beside Mr. Kelly, Mrs. Henry, and Sharon Lysander near the curtains at the edge of the stage. His voice cracked as he finally raised his eyes, squinting at the lights. "Thank you, Cassidy. Thank you, Mr. Kelly. Thank you, Glenlake Academy. And thank you all."

As the crowd cheered, Cassidy and the staff walked toward the podium. Andi recoiled as Roy reached out and enveloped their daughter in a hug.

"We should be proud," Ian whispered, clapping. "Right?"

Andi had too many questions to give him an answer.

At the lobby reception afterward, Cassidy was quickly surrounded by parents whose compliments and questions seemed like thinly veiled attempts to determine why she had outperformed their own children, inquiring which colleges agreed with that assessment. Rather than fight her way through and claim ownership, Andi decided to make her way to Mr. Kelly first.

Ian was in lockstep with her.

"Your daughter is really something," Kelly said, also watching the crowd swell around her. "I'm so proud of her."

Faintly, Andi heard Cassidy repeat the word *hunch* and rattle off her list of schools.

"So are we," Ian said.

"So it was suicide all along?" Andi asked.

Ian put a welcome arm around her.

"Or an accident," Kelly said. "There's no ruling out drugs or alcohol. I'm told Dallas definitely abused both."

"And the injury to the back of his skull was from impact?"

"Apparently, the seat belt wasn't buckled, and it's impossible to tell which position his body was in when the car hit the water. His head could have struck the roof of the car, the steering wheel, or even the top of the seat."

"No headrests on those old cars," Ian said, "and a lot of hard surfaces."

"Exactly," Kelly said.

As the conversation veered into car talk, Andi scanned the room and spotted Roy, alone at the dessert table, munching on a cookie.

Staring directly at her.

"Excuse me for a moment," she said.

Fighting the inclination to turn away, she walked right over to him.

"You look almost the same," he said. "Maybe even better."

Her skin crawled, just as it had the first time she'd met him at Kyle's Kabin, celebrating Dallas's birthday. A night she wished she could forget. She thought about his decrepit home and decided she'd feel just as nervous there now as she had that night.

"I'll admit, I never thought I'd see you again," she said.

"Then again, I never had much of an eye for the young ones," he said, almost as if she hadn't spoken.

"I'd say that's a good thing, since you work at a school."

"They certainly don't look kindly at that kind of thing around here."

She watched as a group of kids swooped in and took all the brownies from a nearby tray.

"I never dreamed your kid would be the one to champion my cause," Roy went on. "Isn't that something? I mean, considering . . ."

Andi lowered her voice. "My husband, and now Cassidy, are aware of my connection to Dallas. But no else knows anything about it."

"Well, that's interesting." Roy laughed.

"And I'd really like to keep it that way."

"Never said a word," he said. "And Lord knows, your secret is safe with me now."

"Thank you."

"No, thank you," he said, grabbing a handful of cookies, wrapping them in a napkin, and stuffing them into his jacket pocket. "I believe I'm out of here."

"Roy," she said, "how do you think Dallas actually died?"

His gaze lingered on hers. "Paying for his sins," he said, and started for the door.

By the time Andi made her way back to Ian and Wayne Kelly, he'd already disappeared.

Chapter Sixty-Two

"If he did commit suicide . . . ," Andi kept repeating, unable to finish the sentence in a way that made sense to either of them. When she wasn't saying it, Ian could tell she was thinking it, unable to complete the thought.

"It just doesn't add up," he told her, more than once.

Which, despite repeated efforts, he couldn't convince Andi to believe. No matter what he said, the guilt she felt over the possibility that Dallas had died by his own hand, whether intentionally or inadvertently, was once again eating away at her.

They both put their best faces forward on their six-day visit to Playa del Carmen, slathering on sunscreen and trooping down to the beach or out to one of the resort's enormous pools. But his own enjoyment, and Andi's, too, was merely a display for the kids.

"It all comes down to Roy's employment at Glenlake," said Ian. "The timing was no accident. Someone was protecting him."

To prove to her he was onto something, he called Gerald Matheson, heedless of the charges to his international roaming plan.

"I was wondering when I'd hear from you," said the former assistant headmaster, answering on the second ring. Apparently, this time Ian had not interrupted him during a workout—his voice sounded calm.

"Because?"

"Because it's all anyone can talk about! Don't get me wrong, we'll all be glad to put this year behind us. But isn't it amazing? Your daughter and her teacher have lifted the school's reputation back up where it belongs."

"I suppose," Ian said.

"You don't sound happy," said Matheson.

"It's taking me a while to get used to the idea of Roy's innocence," said Ian, pacing down a deserted corridor between the hotel's courtyard and the service entrance.

"I don't blame you for that. Between you and me, he looks like the poster boy for *America's Most Wanted*."

"I mean, it's a mystery to me why Glenlake would hire a person like that in the first place."

Now it was Matheson's turn to be silent.

"I spoke to Ted Orzibal, the grounds supervisor," Ian said. "He told me Roy was the worst employee they'd ever had. I saw his file, and there was complaint after complaint about Roy's behavior, but those complaints never went anywhere. I saw a note you wrote saying you were going to deal with him, but nothing ever happened."

"You're making me nervous, Ian."

"Why is that?" he asked, moving out of the way as a deep rumble heralded the passage of a cart piled high with garbage bags. He nodded at the man pushing it.

Matheson sighed so hard that Ian's earpiece crackled with static. "It was Darrow. Darrow told me to hire him and keep him on the payroll. To this day, I have no idea why."

Ian didn't believe that. But he didn't challenge it, thinking Matheson might be more helpful if he thought he was successful in passing the buck.

"But then why wasn't Roy fired after Darrow died?"

"I don't know. Maybe by then Roy had become a more reliable employee. Anyway, I'd forgotten all about it."

He didn't believe that, either.

"And Roy will be going back to work?" Ian asked, knowing Scanlon had told him otherwise.

"No one wants him to, but the man's been exonerated. He could sue us if we let him go. After a year like this, maybe we'll get lucky and he'll retire."

"In the meantime, he stays on the payroll, like always?"

"I don't see how we have a choice."

~

When they dropped Cassidy off after spring break, Andi initially objected to Ian's plan to spend an extra day at Glenlake before heading home. A day in which Whitney and Owen could shadow current freshmen and get a sense of what it would be like when they made their big transition in the fall. A day in which he and Andi could do some digging.

Sleeping dogs, she'd said, mostly because she didn't want to dig anymore. Dallas was dead. And even though it wasn't her fault he'd killed himself or drunk so much he decided to drive his car over the cliff because of her, his pregnant seventeen-year-old student, she just wanted to stop thinking about all of it.

And then Cassidy overheard them discussing a shadow day for her siblings and jumped on the bandwagon.

The next thing Andi knew, it was four against one, and they were back on campus at Glenlake.

Cassidy hugged everyone goodbye and disappeared into a group of friends, all of them acting like they'd been kept apart for months. Ian split off to *get to the bottom of things*, arranging to meet Andi later in the morning. Despite feeling skeptical of his investigative zeal, as she signed Whitney and Owen in, it was impossible to deny their excitement, or the value of having them spend a day with ninth-grade chaperones who would show them around their new home away from home.

Glenlake, which had once felt that way to her.

When Katharine Henry materialized beside her outside the student union and hugged her warmly like the surrogate mother she'd been, Andi almost relaxed.

"A little quieter than the last time I saw you," Katharine said. "The line was so long to congratulate you on your brilliant daughter I didn't have a chance."

"We're very proud of her," Andi said, for what felt like the thousandth time.

"I wouldn't have expected any less," Katharine said kindly. "You know, I've never put too much stock in the various storied couples over the years, but I truly thought you and Ian were a perfect pair."

"We're fortunate to still have such a solid relationship after meeting so young."

"That foundation makes it a lot easier at times like these."

Andi swallowed hard. *Times like these?*

"This whole Dallas situation had to be hard, knowing him as you did," Katharine said, without changing her airy tone.

Andi had barely managed to keep it together all week. Fearful that the floodgates were about to open, she didn't say anything.

Katharine knew.

"My dear," Katharine went on, turning to look her in the eye. "Dallas Walker was responsible for his actions. All of them. Not you."

After Andi lost her mother, she'd spent years trying to hold on to every expression of joy, pain, and grief along with an image of her mom's beautiful face. It was only when Katharine Henry became her dorm mom that she allowed anyone to fill a sliver of that void. And all these years later, Katharine's face told her everything.

She knew.

She had known all along.

"How did you . . . ?"

Katharine sighed. "At first, I chose not to believe the rumors among the faculty, even though I saw the way he looked at you."

Andi thought about Miranda Darrow, who'd also known, even though she didn't remember Andi's name. *I feel like it ended in a vowel sound.*

"That morning, after I stumbled upon you and Sylvie Montgomery getting sick in the bathroom, I went to the nurse, thinking there was something going around I needed to be aware of."

"Sylvie was bulimic," Andi heard herself say.

"Yes. But you weren't," Katharine said. "After I spoke to the nurse, I went back to the girls' bathroom and checked the sanitary receptacle, where I prayed I'd find a tampon wrapper. I found your pregnancy test."

"It didn't . . . *progress*," Andi said blankly.

"No matter what happened, I wasn't sorry to see Dallas Walker disappear."

"What happened to him?" Andi asked, her voice sounding plaintive to her own ears.

"Teacher-student relationships have always been a problem at boarding schools," Katharine said, in an oddly instructional monotone. "Until recently, when a teacher engaged in sexual misconduct with a student, they were quietly asked to resign. In some places they were even sent away with good recommendations, which they used to get jobs at other prep schools."

"Tell me," Andi insisted.

Katharine wouldn't meet her gaze. "I felt I had a duty to report what I saw in the trash. I was just trying to protect you."

"And then Dallas, confronted by the administration . . . ?"

"Never in a million years could I have imagined he'd end up dead." Tears streamed down the furrows in her suddenly aged face. "I had nothing to do with that."

"But you know who did."

"Glenlake has always been renowned for its writer-in-residence program," Katharine recited as though she'd been telling herself those very words for years. "They just couldn't let one man's actions destroy what so many have built."

~

When Ian had told Andi he was going to *get to the bottom of things*, it was just as well she didn't ask what, exactly, he planned to do to make that happen. As he approached the address he'd found on Roy's employment records, he wondered the same thing himself.

After leaving US 41 for a suburban four-lane, then following turns until he found himself on a winding country road, he finally found the street number marked on a mailbox that held on to its post with a single remaining nail. As he rolled slowly up the potholed dirt driveway, he saw a muddy white farmhouse slumped among a grove of neglected trees. Off to one side was a new-looking, corrugated-metal three-car garage, and in the yard behind that was a battered mobile home that still looked more habitable than the house.

He killed the car engine and jerked back as a slobbering rottweiler put its paws on the door and woofed at him through the glass.

All the clichés check out, thought Ian, shaking.

He didn't even think of getting out of the car until the front door opened and Roy appeared, calling the dog as he stepped out on the sloped porch.

"Come on in, Gunner," he shouted.

Reluctantly, Gunner heeded his master's command.

Ian got out of the car, leaving the door open in case he needed to dive back in. The dog had retreated only partway and watched him alertly.

"I'm Ian Copeland," he said.

Roy came down the steps and squinted at him. "I know who you are."

Ian wasn't exactly sure how to ask his questions without having Roy slam the door in his face or, worse, set the dog on him. *How have you held down a job at Glenlake for so many years, given your spotty attendance, shitty attitude, and all-around lack of a work ethic?*

"I knew your wife back then, and now I know your daughter, too," Roy said.

Having watched the once formidable Roy cream Dallas at pool, Ian knew he needed to play to win.

"We both know things about each other," he said.

Roy raised an eyebrow, as if daring him to go on.

"Glenlake's been paying you to work when you feel like it since just after Dallas disappeared," Ian continued. "And they're going to keep paying you whether you show up for work or not."

"You don't think they'll fire me?" Roy asked, taking the bait.

"I know they won't."

"Because it wouldn't look good to pink-slip a guy who couldn't show up for work because he was in jail. Not after the charges were dropped and he was found innocent."

This was the moment. Ian delivered his educated guess as confidently and casually as he could.

"But I know you're not innocent."

Roy folded his arms and looked down at the dog.

Ian stepped forward. "I want to know how Dallas died."

"It was an accident," Roy said, eyes averted.

"You seriously expect me to buy that?" Ian said, hoping his bravado wasn't going to result in his own inadvertent death.

Roy looked up and shrugged, as if it made no difference to him. Ian thought he looked tired.

"We both know each other's secrets," he pressed. "Which is insurance neither of us will tell. I just want to know *how*."

Roy considered that. Apparently, it was enough.

"Can you believe they had a private detective following that little girl? I guess he saw us all together, and someone told him I bitched out the poet pretty good one time. No secret I used to like to fight. So the detective wanted me to rough him up a little, scare the crap out of him so he'd stop messing with the fine young merchandise there at the school."

"Jesus. You were paid to beat him up?"

"I figured I'd pop him once or twice, and he'd be so scared he'd take his pool cue and his poetry books and fuck off," said Roy. "But he must have thought he was tough. Next thing I knew, he came flying at me like he knew MMA. I clocked him, and he fell down and hit the back of his head."

Roy was silent for a beat, then thumbed toward the trailer behind his house. "Happened right back there. Steps to my trailer are made out of cinder blocks. He caught the corner. He twitched for a few minutes, and that was all she wrote."

"An accident," Ian said.

"Didn't mean to kill him."

"Then you got rid of his body and his car in Lake Loomis?"

"Waited until after midnight, then drove up there and sent him over. Long fucking walk home. Pretty good solution, actually."

"Until his body and the car were found."

"Which shouldn't have been my problem at all."

"Why is that?" Ian asked.

"I went to that headmaster guy."

"Darrow?"

"Yeah. I told him I didn't mean to do it, but his boy attacked me, and things went bad. I told him if he wanted to keep me quiet, he needed to make it worth my while."

"So they gave you a job on campus for life."

"And I kept up my end of the bargain. Sometimes I even showed up so no one would ask why I was on the payroll."

"Until you ended up in jail."

"I used my one phone call just right. I knew there was too much riding on me keeping quiet for them bigwigs over at the school to let me sit there for long," he said. "And then your daughter shows up to get me sprung. I still don't know how they worked that, but they're the brainy ones, not me."

When he left, Ian wondered if he could make it far enough down the road so Roy wouldn't see him when he pulled over and threw up.

~

An eternity passed before Andi spotted Ian pulling into the guest parking lot.

She ran over to him as he got out of the car.

"Dallas definitely didn't commit suicide."

"I know," he said, as wild-eyed as she'd ever seen him. "I just met with Roy."

"That was dangerous," she said. "Roy killed Dallas."

"Darrow hired him," Ian said.

"And they've been protecting him all these years."

"But he was only supposed to scare Dallas into leaving you alone," said Ian grimly. "He said it was an accident, and I believe him about that at least."

"My god," Andi said. "What are we going to—"

"I called ahead, and Scanlon is expecting us."

Ian grabbed her hand and led her into the building, past reception, and up the scrolled wood staircase toward the headmaster's office.

Sharon Lysander stopped them at the top of the stairs.

"I'm afraid Headmaster Scanlon's not going to be able to give you any of the answers you're looking for," she said.

"And why is that?" Ian demanded. If he was surprised, he wasn't showing it.

Lysander motioned for them to follow her down the hall and into the conference room across from her office. "Because he doesn't know anything. Neither he nor I were here at the time."

"Go ahead, Gerald," she said as she closed the door behind them.

Gerald Matheson's voice was amplified by a black receiver in the center of the conference table. "It was a complicated situation."

"Is it Glenlake policy to address statutory rape by hiring thugs to deliver beatings?" said Ian, approaching the phone.

"That was Darrow's decision," said Matheson hastily, the volume too loud but no one taking the initiative to turn it down. "Just as Dallas made his own decision. Instead of receiving the message, he decided to . . . escalate."

Andi put her head in her hands, the awful pieces of the puzzle falling quickly into place. "Roy covered up the murder, and Glenlake covered for Roy."

"Obviously, nobody intended for Dallas to die," interrupted Lysander, weirdly dispassionate. "The powers that be erred in pursuing an extrajudicial solution to the problem, but nobody wanted to expose the school or, certainly, the student and her family."

"The 'problem' was a human being," said Andi. "His bad judgment and actions notwithstanding."

Ian's hands were flat on the polished tabletop, his knuckles white. "And everything was just fine until Tate found the car."

"After Curtis Royal was taken into custody, difficult choices had to be made," said Matheson.

"You could have let a guilty man stand trial for the crime he committed," said Ian pointedly.

"And destroy Glenlake Academy in the process?"

"So you used the power and prestige of the institution to pressure the Lake County Sheriff's Office to accept a suicide verdict and release Roy before he talked *out of school*," said Ian bitterly.

"Fortunately, we had your remarkable daughter," said Lysander. "The kids look like heroes and have not only reclaimed Glenlake's reputation but put us on the map for our commitment to social justice."

"And that's it?" Andi heard herself say. "We just go on as if nothing ever happened?"

"Either that or one of our country's preeminent educational institutions, one that has prepared countless bright minds for roles of leadership in society, is engulfed in a disgrace whose repercussions will echo for years."

"The illustrious Copeland legacy, forever tarnished by a tawdry scandal in which your and your daughter's names will figure prominently," Matheson said. "Do you want that, Ian? I know no one else at the school, past or present, would ever want such a thing."

"It would be a shame to see the school implode just as your twins begin their Glenlake careers," Lysander said. "I hear they're having a magnificent day."

Chapter Sixty-Three

Ian scanned the crowd of graduates, parents, and assorted family members, looking for his equally ill-at-ease wife. He'd momentarily lost Andi in the swirl of girls in white dresses and the boys in blazer-and-khaki combos. The storm had blown so hard the night before, rain battering the windows of their room at the Old Road Inn, that Ian had wondered whether the commencement ceremony could take place at all. Finally, by midmorning, the rain had stopped, and by noon, hot sun had replaced the dark-gray clouds. The grounds crew had rushed into action, squeegeeing sidewalks, putting plywood under chairs, and relocating as much seating as possible to the bricked landscaping fronting the peristyle. By the time things got underway in the afternoon, it was a steamy spring day, even if the branches of the newly leafed trees were still drooped and dripping.

He left the twins amid a group of incoming siblings in the refreshment tent. Neither he nor Andi had figured out a way to stop their inevitable matriculation at Glenlake without telling all three kids more about the institution than they ever needed to know.

Watching his footing, Ian weaved through the swirl of giddy graduates and proud parents. Andi was still nowhere in sight. Had he forgotten where they were standing, or had she been pulled into a new conversation?

Picturing Cassidy's flushed face as she stepped off the stage, diploma in hand, he remembered the exuberance of their own graduation as though it had taken place last week. He had been so grateful to be back together with Andi—even though he had sensed a distance at the time, he hadn't wanted to examine it more closely. All he'd been able to think about was that, despite a cruel interruption, their future together was back on track.

That morning at brunch, Cassidy had surprised them by announcing that she would not be attending Amherst as widely assumed. Instead, she wanted to go to NYU.

"Nothing against the family alma mater, Dad," she assured him. "I just need some time to figure out who I am, to be me."

Somehow, he'd managed not to wince at her nearly exact quote, obviously unintentional, of her mother at seventeen. And he couldn't question her logic. Because she really was doing it for herself.

Seeing Sharon Lysander and Katharine Henry standing apart, he confirmed that Andi wasn't in the area before giving them a wide berth. Not that he expected she'd be anywhere near either of them.

Despite the sunny faces, the future didn't feel as fresh and full of possibility as it should have. The dark secrets at the heart of Glenlake Academy had touched only a few of these students, but he couldn't shake the image of the school's corruption as a spore that latched on to each and every person in attendance. Corruption propagated until someone put a stop to it, and those who'd told him the secret had judged him correctly. Rightly or wrongly, he would not be the person to take down the institution his family had done so much to build.

He wondered if he'd ever be able to forgive himself for that.

Finally, he saw Andi, standing with Cope and Biz. Cope had on a jaunty, open-weave summer fedora, and Biz was wearing enormous black sunglasses that obscured not only her eyes but half her face. He hadn't been able to bring himself to share a word of what he knew with his parents. They loved Glenlake so much he imagined it would crush them. Andi, his lifelong love, had exposed her shoulders to the sun and was shading her eyes with one hand as she waved him over.

"We're going to go read Cassidy's senior page," Andi told him when he arrived.

They strolled across campus together to Holmes Library and located Cassidy's page on the newly renovated third floor, a long way from where his and Andi's pages were hung. As to where Cassidy herself was at present, who knew?

They all crowded around to read.

Feeling suddenly wistful, Cassidy just wanted a moment alone. After separating herself from the crowd, she stood under a tree and looked back at campus, taking a mental picture and thinking that leafy, bucolic Glenlake was just about as far as you could get from NYU. Which was good: she was both nervous and excited about the concrete, the crowds, and the chaos.

She had wrestled with the decision to be so far away from Tate, who had never wavered from Duke, his first choice. But even though it looked like her parents would survive their secrets and continue to be the It Couple in everyone's eyes, Cassidy knew that, like penning her senior page, she also had to write her own story. And high school relationships almost never worked out, anyway.

But there was no need to rush the ending. She and Tate had plans to meet up over the summer, and if he really did come to visit her in New York like he promised, they would see where things went from there.

Mr. Kelly saw her and walked over. "Taking a last look?"

"I'll be back," she said. "My little brother and sister are starting next fall."

"It's going to look a lot smaller the next time you see it," he said with a grin.

"How's your book going?" she asked suddenly.

He laughed ruefully. "Not well. Teaching investigative journalism to high school students was a lot more demanding than I expected."

"You're not going to write about all this, are you?"

"Nope," he said with a shake of his head. "I'm too far into the other project. With luck I can find another teaching gig to help me finish—only it better be someplace boring."

"I think this was one in a million," said Cassidy.

"Listen, Cassidy," said Mr. Kelly. "It's been a pleasure having you in class. You're a smart kid and a hard worker. I know you're going to go far."

She surprised herself by giving him a hug. It was quick, and he only half returned it, but the brief contact brought back all the weirdness with Mom, and she regretted it before she even let go.

Mr. Kelly seemed embarrassed.

"Good luck!" he said as he sauntered off.

Then Cassidy saw Tate staring and realized he'd been watching. He looked kind of pissed.

She just gave him a big smile and started moving toward him, taking her time.

He'd get over it.

~

Cassidy Copeland: Class of 2019

Monday, March 25, 2019

I'm guessing most people go through their lives without ever having their teacher (that would be Mr. Kelly) call them aside before class (that would be the journalism seminar) and inform them (i.e., ME) that they played a role in getting an innocent man out of jail where he might have been railroaded into prison for MURDER.

It's not like my life is complete or anything, because I have a long way to go and a lot more to accomplish. But even if this is it, my Big Moment, that's pretty cool.

I'll be honest: I didn't write in this journal much. When I did, I kind of had to make myself do it. And like a lot of people, I spent a lot of time over four years wondering what would possibly be worth recording on my senior page.

I guess I kind of hit that ball over the fence, huh?

Now that I'm ready to leave Glenlake and find out what else is out there, I'm so glad I was able to make my mark on the school. Glenlake should be about more than getting good grades, maintaining traditions, and preparing to become the next generation of leaders. If we're going to be great, we also need to care about the world outside our little bubble. And that, more than anything, is what I'm proud of: that, through Glenlake, I got to change the life of a human being.

Hopefully, social justice will be my legacy and part of the new Glenlake tradition.

~

"To the seventh Copeland generation to survive and thrive at Glenlake," said Cope breezily, holding up an imaginary glass after they finished reading Cassidy's senior page.

For the moment, they were alone in their corner of the library—nonfiction, noted Ian.

"The 'seventh generation,'" said Biz. "That's very poetic."

"It's from some Bible verse," said Cope.

"No, it isn't," Ian contradicted him bluntly. "It's from an Iroquois saying about considering the impact of everything you do on future generations."

Cassidy's deserved feelings of pride over what had been rigged, manipulated, and wholly corrupt machinations filled him with unspeakable sadness. That his brilliant, credulous daughter had been used in this way . . .

"Well, isn't that why we do everything?" asked Cope. "For the next generations?"

"It's a nice sentiment," Biz said matter-of-factly, "but sometimes we do things because we need to protect the present-day generation, too."

Ian didn't like the expression on his mother's face or the tone of her voice. There was something hard there, something he hadn't seen or heard since . . . senior year.

"What are you suggesting, Biz?" asked Andi as if she were having the same sickening realization he was.

They knew, too?

"Things happen, Andi. Affairs of the heart and so on. But we can't let them destroy the institutions we rely upon."

"You were a part of it," stated Andi, going pale.

"We didn't give the order, of course," said Cope, "though we paid for the private investigator. We needed to know who you left Ian for, to help him get back on track. And then we gave a big donation to hide the ongoing payments to Roy. We weren't going to stand by and let it go on, especially once we found out that he took you to a drug house. Not when our son's one true love was involved."

Andi looked stricken, and Ian knew just how much weight she'd been carrying since learning Dallas hadn't abandoned her by choice.

"The snitch was you?" Andi speculated.

"No," Cope said. "Roy's poor choice of companions was all on him."

"We love our son more than anything, and he loved you, and we did want to help free you from the situation you'd gotten yourself into," said Biz, insufferably smug. "Just like Cope and all the trustees helped other students over the years, by getting the wrong men to move along."

"With beatings, or threats of beatings?" demanded Andi.

"The others took the hint," said Cope gruffly.

Ian wondered why it was so hard for him to say anything. Why he felt like a bystander. Thinking about how he'd been duped, too. How his parents had known what was going on all along.

"He was preying on you, Andi, and we couldn't let it go on," said Biz, as another group of parents, recalcitrant son in tow, appeared at the far end of the wall and scanned for his senior page. "He wouldn't leave, and he was bragging about that stupid book of poems he was going to publish, how it was going to make him famous and open everyone's eyes about places like Glenlake."

"*Glenlake Girl,*" said Ian softly, remembering the title from Andi's journal. "Was his death even an accident?"

"Roy told Linc Darrow it was," said Cope with a shrug. "I'll be damned if we were going to let that bastard bring down our school."

The other family, still looking for their son's page, was getting closer. They had to leave or risk being overheard.

"We saw it as our job to make sure the two of you were kept out of harm's way," said Biz. "Helicopter parenting. I think that's what you call it these days. Right?"

Chapter Sixty-Four

Over the years, Andi had done keyword searches on *Dallas Walker*, *David Dallas Walker*, titles of his poems, and even phrases like *bad-boy poets*. For whatever reason, using an actual line of his work never occurred to her until she came across a faded piece of notebook paper at the bottom of an old jewelry box filled with partnerless earrings and other forgotten trinkets.

She entered the first line of the poem Dallas had tucked into the knothole of the tree where they'd exchanged messages.

When every damn thing reminds me of you

On the first page of results was a link to a PDF of the fall 1997 issue of an obscure poetry journal called *Less Traveled*.

Containing Dallas Walker's poem "And I Love."

The poem he'd so obviously written for her.

Remarkably, the journal still existed as an online publication. From the FAQ, she learned that it had also functioned as a publishing house for decades, producing one or two poetry books per year. Most were anthologies, but some were collections of work from single poets. She used the web form to inquire whether any additional work by Dallas Walker had been submitted or published, and an intern replied with a noncommittal note saying she'd look into it.

Andi was surprised when her phone rang two weeks later.

"I received a manuscript from Dallas Walker right after I agreed to publish that first piece in the fall issue," the publisher told her in a soft southern accent, sounding like the aged eccentric he probably was. "I wrote him back and said I liked the poems and wanted to do a book, but he never answered. When I found out he'd disappeared, I tried talking to his ex-wife, but she had zero interest in working with me. So I let it go."

"You wouldn't by any chance still have the manuscript, would you?" Andi asked.

"You're dealing with the last of the original pack rats, sugar," he said. "I've got every scrap of paper that ever passed through my hands. Unfortunately, all the old stuff is in my storage unit, and I don't get around as well as I used to."

But when Andi hinted she might be willing to pay to acquire the manuscript, the publisher said he *could probably put one of my interns on it*. Knowing as she did that almost all poetry was published at a loss, a cash infusion proved to be a powerful incentive.

And a month later, she had in her possession the only known copy of *Glenlake Girl*.

As expected, the manuscript contained thinly obscured but no less fucked-up declarations of his love for a teenager:

Love's half life, the Age of Innocence
Triggering the chain of decay

There were far too keen, even prescient observations about the downsides and potential dangers of boarding school existence:

The old teach the young the ways of the old
Wanting only to be young once again

But, other than a few telling references to the cliffs over Lake Loomis, there was no mention of the bust of Augustus Copeland, no description of Headmaster Darrow's distinctive mansion, not even Dallas's view from the writer in residence's cottage.

He could have been writing about life, love, and the stark beauty of a crisp fall day anywhere.

> The scouring wind stings our cheeks
> Dead leaves burst brightly into bloom
> Lowering sun, we hurry home
> And fall into our room

The word *bloom* recurred in fully one-third of the poems.

Dallas Walker had been a charming, talented sociopath who'd left behind a legacy of pain and secrets. But did he deserve to pay the ultimate price for his devil-may-care approach to art and life?

Did she, for succumbing to his charms?

In some ways, Ian, who'd been in his study reading the manuscript since midafternoon, had suffered the most.

Andi didn't know what to expect when she told Ian she'd not only found the manuscript but now owned the rights. She read every poem dozens of times before sharing her idea to publish the book herself. Living with what they now knew, she explained, was in many ways harder than the secret she'd planned to take to her grave. She accepted the reality that Dallas had preyed on her, but like Cassidy, she couldn't accept the injustice of his sentence. Putting the book out into the world was her gesture against complicity.

Besides, the poems were good.

She expected Ian to argue that she was putting herself at risk of exposure, not to mention his parents, their children, and ultimately Glenlake itself. And wasn't that why they'd had no choice but to remain silent in the first place?

Emerging just before dinner, he went straight to the liquor cabinet and poured himself a bourbon.

"Obviously, the book can't be titled *Glenlake Girl*," he said.

"No," she said. "But you're okay with the idea of publishing it?"

"You realize someone will connect this to Glenlake."

"I know. But it's the only way I can live with the truths we've been forced to bury."

Ian was quiet for a moment. "Then again, how many people are actually going to read a book of poetry?"

"Hopefully enough to break even," she said.

"You're the publisher," he finally said.

She took the drink out of his hand, put it down, and wrapped him in a hug.

"I did see a line that would make an interesting title," he added.

"What was it?" she asked.

"Drowning with others."

ACKNOWLEDGMENTS

This book would not have been possible without Alison Dasho, Alicia Clancy, Caitlin Alexander, and the wonderful Lake Union team, especially Shasti O'Leary Soudant, Gabe Dumpit, and Paul Zablocki. Special thanks to agent extraordinaire Josh Getzler and the talented crew at HSG. Piper Stevens provided helpful insight into boarding school life.

DISCUSSION QUESTIONS

1. In *Drowning with Others*, Andi and Ian both suspect each other of having killed Dallas. Were you surprised by their fierce need to protect each other from the consequences? Are there circumstances in which a spouse should be willing to overlook his or her partner having committed a crime? Why or why not?

2. Legacy is an important theme throughout this novel: at Glenlake, within the Copeland family, and regarding Dallas Walker's poetry. Do you agree that legacy is worth protecting? To what extent?

3. Both Andi and Ian keep secrets from each other: Andi hides her relationship with Dallas, and Ian hides his business partnership with Preston. Why were they unable to be honest with each other? Would the novel have ended differently if they'd been up-front from the beginning? If you found yourself in a similar situation, do you think you would be able to come clean to your significant other?

4. Cassidy finds herself in a difficult position in the novel—hiding evidence to protect her parents. What would you

have done in her place? Is there anything Ian and Andi could have done differently to keep her from having to make that choice?

5.   What is the role of poetry in the novel? Why do you think the authors chose poetry as a creative medium within the novel? How do you express yourself creatively?

6.   *Drowning with Others* unfolds over two timelines and two generations. Were the journal entries an effective way to convey what Glenlake was like twenty years before? Why or why not? Have you ever kept a journal? If so, do you think it offers an accurate reflection of the time period?

7.   The role of parents is very important in the novel. Can you understand why Cope and Biz helped cover up the murder? Would you have done the same, or would you have done something differently? Is there anything you wouldn't do to protect the people you love?

8.   The story centers on an illicit romance between a student and her teacher at boarding school. What are the unique circumstances that can foster such relationships at boarding schools? How do you think these relationships should be handled?

9.   Andi and Ian come from very different families and go to boarding school for very different reasons. What are these reasons, and how do you think they affect the characters' self-esteem? Does Andi's relationship with Dallas stem, at least in part, from insecurity?

10. How is Cassidy influenced by her family name and the pressure to keep up with the legacy of being a Copeland in general and Andi and Ian's daughter in particular?

11. Andi and Ian have built a loving, long-term marriage despite the lie buried in its foundation. Do you believe the secrets of the past always come back to haunt the present? Could the couple have lived in happy denial forever had Dallas's body not been discovered?

12. Boarding school is a tradition in many upper-class families. While a boarding school education is synonymous with academic excellence and future success, what are the emotional drawbacks of being separated from one's family as a minor?